THE GHOST
BRIGADES

John Scalzi

D0037137

TOR

A TOM DOHERTY ASSOCIATES BOOK
NEW YORK

This is a work of fiction. All of the characters, organizations, and events portrayed in this novel are either products of the author's imagination or are used fictitiously.

THE GHOST BRIGADES

Copyright © 2006 by John Scalzi

Edited by Patrick Nielsen Hayden

A Tor Book
Published by Tom Doherty Associates, LLC
175 Fifth Avenue
New York, NY 10010

www.tor.com

Tor® is a registered trademark of Tom Doherty Associates, LLC.

ISBN-13: 978-0-7653-5406-8
ISBN-10: 0-7653-5406-3

First Edition: March 2006
First Mass Market Edition: May 2007

Printed in the United States of America

0 9 8 7 6 5 4 3

To Shara Zoll, for friendship and everything else.
To Kristine and Athena, for their patience and love.

THE GHOST BRIGADES

PART I

ONE No one noticed the rock.

And for a very good reason. The rock was nondescript, one of millions of chunks of rock and ice floating in the orbit of a long-dead short-period comet, looking just like any chunk of that deceased comet might. The rock was smaller than some, larger than others, but on a distribution scale there was nothing to distinguish it one way or another. On the almost unfathomably small chance that the rock was spotted by a planetary defense grid, a cursory examination would show the rock to be composed of silicates and some ores. Which is to say: a rock, not nearly large enough to cause any real damage.

This was an academic matter for the planet currently intersecting the path of the rock and several thousand of its brethren; it had no planetary defense grid. It did, however, have a gravity well, into which the rock fell, along with those many brethren. Together they would form a meteor shower, as so many chunks of ice and rock did each time the planet intersected the comet's orbit, once per planetary revolution. No intelligent creature stood on the surface of this bitterly cold planet, but if one had it could have looked up and seen the pretty streaks and smears of these little chunks of matter as they burned in the atmosphere, super-heated by the friction of air against rock.

The vast majority of these newly minted meteors would vaporize in the atmosphere, their matter transmuted during their incandescent fall from a discrete and solid clump to a long smudge of microscopic particles. These would remain in the atmosphere indefinitely, until they became the nuclei of water droplets, and the sheer mass of the water dragged them to the ground as rain (or, more likely given the nature of the planet, snow).

This rock, however, had mass on its side. Chunks flew as the atmospheric pressure tore open hairline cracks in the rock's structure, the stress of plummeting through the thickening mat of gases exposing structural flaws and weaknesses and exploiting them violently. Fragments sheared off, sparkled brilliantly and momentarily and were consumed by the sky. And yet at the end of its journey through the atmosphere, enough remained to impact the planet surface, the flaming bolus smacking hard and fast onto a plain of rock that had been blown clean of ice and snow by high winds.

The impact vaporized the rock and a modest amount of the plain, excavating an equally modest crater. The rock plain, which extended for a significant distance on and below the planet surface, rang with the impact like a bell, harmonics pealing several octaves below the hearing range of most known intelligent species.

The ground trembled.

And in the distance, beneath the planet surface, someone finally noticed the rock.

"Quake," said Sharan. She didn't look up from her monitor.

Several moments later, another tremor followed.

"Quake," said Sharan.

Cainen looked over to his assistant from his own monitor. "Are you planning to do this every time?" he asked.

"I want to keep you informed of events as they happen," Sharan said.

"I appreciate the sentiment," Cainen said, "but you really don't have to mention it every single time. I *am* a scientist. I understand that when the ground moves we're experiencing a quake. Your *first* declaration was useful. By the fifth or sixth time, it gets monotonous."

Another rumble. "Quake," said Sharan. "That's number seven. Anyway, you're not a tectonicist. This is outside your many fields of expertise." Despite Sharan's typical deadpan delivery, the sarcasm was hard to miss.

If Cainen hadn't been sleeping with his assistant, he might have been irritated. As it was, he allowed himself to be tolerantly amused. "I don't recall *you* being a master tectonicist," he said.

"It's a hobby," said Sharan.

Cainen opened his mouth to respond and then the ground suddenly and violently launched itself up to meet him. It took a moment for Cainen to realize it wasn't the floor that jerked up to meet him, he'd been suddenly driven to the floor. He was now haphazardly sprawled on the tiles, along with about half the objects formerly positioned on his workstation. Cainen's work stool lay capsized a body length to the right, still teetering from the upheaval.

He looked over to Sharan, who was no longer looking at her monitor, in part because it lay shattered on the ground, near where Sharan herself was toppled.

"What was that?" Cainen asked.

"Quake?" Sharan suggested, somewhat hopefully, and

then screamed as the lab bounced energetically around them again. Lighting and acoustic panels fell from the ceiling; both Cainen and Sharan struggled to crawl under workbenches. The world imploded around them for a while as they cowered under their tables.

Presently the shaking stopped. Cainen looked around in what flickering light still remained and saw the majority of his lab on the floor, including much of the ceiling and part of the walls. Usually the lab was filled with workers and Cainen's other assistants, but he and Sharan had come in late to finish up some sequencing. Most of his staff had been in the base barracks, probably asleep. Well, they were awake now.

A high, keening noise echoed down the hall leading to the lab.

"Do you hear that?" Sharan asked.

Cainen gave an affirmative head dip. "It's the siren for battle stations."

"We're under attack?" Sharan asked. "I thought this base was shielded."

"It is," Cainen said. "Or was. Supposed to be, anyway."

"Well, a fine job, I must say," Sharan said.

Now Cainen was irritated. "Nothing is perfect, Sharan," he said.

"Sorry," Sharan said, keying in on her boss's sudden irritation. Cainen grunted and then slid out from underneath his workbench and picked his way to a toppled-over storage locker. "Come help me with this," he said to Sharan. Between them they maneuvered the locker to where Cainen could shove open the locker door. Inside was a small projectile gun and a cartridge of projectiles.

"Where did you get this?" Sharan asked.

"This *is* a military base, Sharan," Cainen said. "They have weapons. I have two of these. One is here and one is back in the barracks. I thought they might be useful if something like this happened."

"We're not military," Sharan said.

"And I'm sure that will make a huge difference to whoever is attacking the base," Cainen said, and offered the gun to Sharan. "Take this."

"Don't give that to me," Sharan said. "I've never used one. You take it."

"Are you sure?" Cainen asked.

"I'm sure," Sharan said. "I'd just end up shooting myself in the leg."

"All right," Cainen said. He mounted the ammunition cartridge into the gun and slipped the gun into a coat pocket. "We should head to our barracks. Our people are there. If anything happens, we should be with them." Sharan mutely gave her assent. Her usual sarcastic persona was now entirely stripped away; she looked drained and frightened. Cainen gave her a quick squeeze.

"Come on, Sharan," he said. "We'll be all right. Let's just try to get to the barracks."

The two had begun to weave through the rubble in the hall when they heard the sublevel stairwell door slide open. Cainen peered through the dust and low light to make out two large forms coming through the door. Cainen began to backtrack toward the lab; Sharan, who had the same thought rather faster than her boss, had already made it to the lab doorway. The only other way off the floor was the elevator, which lay past the stairwell. They were trapped. Cainen patted his coat pocket as he retreated; he didn't have all that much more experience with a gun than Sharan and was not at all confident that he'd be able to hit even one target at a distance, much less two, each presumably a trained soldier.

"Administrator Cainen," said one of the forms.

"What?" Cainen said, in spite of himself, and immediately regretted giving himself away.

"Administrator Cainen," said the form again. "We've come to retrieve you. You're not safe here." The form walked forward into a splay of light and resolved itself into Aten Randt, one of the base commandants. Cainen finally recognized him by the clan design on his carapace and his insignia. Aten Randt was an Eneshan, and Cainen was vaguely ashamed to admit that even after all this time at the base, they all still looked alike to him.

"Who is attacking us?" Cainen asked. "How did they find the base?"

"We're not sure who is attacking us or why," Aten Randt said. The clicking of his mouthpieces was translated into recognizable speech by a small device that hung from his neck. Aten Randt could understand Cainen without the device, but needed it to speak with him. "The bombardment came from orbit and we've only now targeted their landing craft." Aten Randt advanced on Cainen; Cainen tried not to flinch. Despite their time here and their relatively good working relationship, he was still nervous around the massive insectoid race. "Administrator Cainen, you cannot be found here. We need to get you away from here before the base is invaded."

"All right," Cainen said. He motioned Sharan forward to come with him.

"Not her," Aten Randt said. "Only you."

Cainen stopped. "She's my aide. I need her," he said.

The base shook from another bombardment. Cainen felt himself slam into a wall and collapsed to the ground. As he fell he noted that neither Aten Randt nor the other Eneshan soldier had moved so much as a fraction from their position.

"This is not an appropriate time to debate the issue, Administrator," Aten Randt said. The flat affect of the translation device gave the comment an unintentionally sardonic quality.

Cainen began to protest again, but Sharan gently took hold of his arm. "Cainen. He's right," she said. "You need to get out of here. It's bad enough any of us are here. But you being found here would be a very bad thing."

"I won't leave you here," Cainen said.

"*Cainen,*" Sharan said, and pointed at Aten Randt, who was standing by, impassive. "He's one of the highest-ranking military officers here. We're under attack. They're not going to send someone like him on a trivial errand. And now is not the time to argue anyway. So go. I'll find my way back to the barracks. We've been here a while, you know. I remember how to get there."

Cainen stared at Sharan for a minute and then pointed past Aten Randt to the other Eneshan soldier. "You," he said. "Escort her back to her barracks."

"I need him with me, Administrator," Aten Randt said.

"You can handle me by yourself," Cainen said. "And if she doesn't get the escort from him, she'll get the escort from me."

Aten Randt covered his translation device and motioned the soldier over. They leaned in close and clacked at each other quietly—not that it mattered, as Cainen didn't understand Eneshan language. Then the two separated and the soldier went to stand by Sharan.

"He will take her to her barracks," Aten Randt said. "But there is to be no more argument from you. We have wasted too much time already. Come with me now, Administrator." He reached out, grabbed Cainen by the arm and pulled him toward the stairwell door. Cainen glanced back to see Sharan staring up fearfully at the immense Eneshan soldier. This final image of his assistant and lover disappeared as Aten Randt shoved him through the doorway.

"That hurt," Cainen said.

"Quiet," Aten Randt said, and pushed Cainen forward on the stairs. They began to climb, the Eneshan's surprisingly short and delicate lower appendages matching Cainen's own stride up the steps. "It took far too long to find you and too long to get you moving. Why were you not in your barracks?"

"We were finishing up some work," Cainen said. "It's not as if we have much else to do around here. Where are we going now?"

"Up," Aten Randt said. "There is an underground service railroad we need to get to."

Cainen stopped for a moment and looked back at Aten Randt, who despite being several steps below him was nearly at the same height. "That goes to hydroponics," Cainen said. Cainen, Sharan and other members of his staff would go to the base's immense underground hydroponics bay on occasion for the greenery; the planet's surface was not exactly inviting unless hypothermia was something you enjoyed. Hydroponics was the closest you could get to being outside.

"Hydroponics is in a natural cave," Aten Randt said, prodding Cainen back into motion. "An underground river lies beyond it, in a sealed area. It flows into an undergound lake. There is a small living module hidden there that will hold you."

"You never told me about this before," Cainen said.

"We did not expect the need to tell you," Aten Randt said.

"Am I swimming there?" Cainen asked.

"There is a small submersible," Aten Randt said. "It will be cramped, even for you. But it has already been programmed with the location of the module."

"And how long will I be staying there?"

"Let us hope no time at all," Aten Randt said. "Because the alternative will be a very long time indeed. Two more flights, Administrator."

The two stopped at the door two flights up, as Cainen attempted to catch his breath and Aten Randt clicked his mouthpieces into his communicator. The noise of battle several stories above them filtered down through the stone of the ground and the concrete of the walls. "They've reached the base but we're holding them on the surface for now," Aten Randt said to Cainen, lowering his communicator. "They haven't reached this level. We may still get you to safety. Follow close behind me, Administrator. Don't fall behind. Do you understand me?"

"I understand," said Cainen.

"Then let's go," Aten Randt said. He hoisted his rather impressive weapon, opened the door, and strode out into the hall. As Aten Randt began moving, Cainen saw the Eneshan's lower appendages extend as an additional leg articulation emerged from inside his carapace. It was a sprinting mechanism that gave Eneshans terrifying speed and agility in battle situations and reminded Cainen of any number of creepy-crawlies from his childhood. He repressed a shiver of revulsion and raced to keep up, stumbling more than once in the debris-strewn hallway, heading all too slowly for the small rail station on the other side of the level.

Cainen panted up as Aten Randt was examining the controls of the small rail engine, whose passenger compartment was open to the air. He had already disconnected the engine from the railcars behind it. "I told you to keep up," Aten Randt said.

"Some of us are old, and can't double the length of our legs," Cainen said, and pointed to the rail engine. "Do I get on that?"

"We should walk," Aten Randt said, and Cainen's legs began to cramp preemptively. "But I don't think you'll be able to keep pace the entire distance, and we're running out of time. We'll have to risk using this. Get on." Cainen gratefully climbed into the passenger area, which was roomy, built as it was for two Enesha. Aten Randt eased the little engine to its full speed—about twice an Eneshan's sprinting pace, which seemed uncomfortably fast in the cramped tunnel—and then turned around and raised his weapon again, scanning the tunnel behind them for targets.

"What happens to me if the base is overrun?" Cainen asked.

"You'll be safe in the living module," Aten Randt said.

"Yes, but if the base is overrun, who will come to get me?" Cainen asked. "I can't stay in that module forever, and I won't know how to get back out. No matter how well-prepared this module of yours is, it will eventually run out of supplies. Not to mention air."

"The module has the ability to extract dissolved oxygen from the water," Aten Randt said. "You won't suffocate."

"Wonderful. But that still leaves starvation," said Cainen.

"The lake has an outlet—" Aten Randt began, and that was as far as he got before the engine derailed with a sudden jerk. The roar of the collapsing tunnel drowned out all other noise; Cainen and Aten Randt found themselves briefly airborne as they were hurled from the passenger area of the rail engine into the sudden, dusty darkness.

Cainen found himself being prodded awake an indeterminate time later by Aten Randt. "Wake up, Administrator," Aten Randt said.

"I can't see anything," Cainen said. Aten Randt responded by shining a beam from the lamp attached to his weapon. "Thanks," Cainen said.

"Are you all right?" Aten Randt asked.

"I'm fine," Cainen said. "If at all possible I'd like to get through the *rest* of the day without hitting the ground again." Aten Randt clicked in assent and swept his beam away, to look at the rock falls that had them closed in. Cainen started to get up, slipping a bit on the rubble.

Aten Randt swung the light beam back to Cainen. "Stay there, Administrator," Aten Randt said. "You'll be safer." The light beam dipped to the rails. "Those may still have current in them." The light beam trailed off again, back to the caved-in walls of their new holding pen. Whether by accident or design, the bombardment that struck the rail line had securely closed in Cainen and Aten Randt; there were no openings in the wall of rubble. Cainen noted to himself that suffocation had once again become a real consideration. Aten Randt continued his examination of their new perimeter and occasionally tried his communicator, which seemed not to be working. Cainen settled in and tried not to breathe too deeply.

Some time later Aten Randt, who had given up his examination and cast them both into darkness while he rested, flicked his light back on, toward the wall of rubble closest to the base.

"What is it?" Cainen asked.

"Be quiet," Aten Randt said, and moved closer to the wall of rubble, as if trying to hear something. A few moments later, Cainen heard it too: noise that could have been voices, but not of anyone local, or friendly. Shortly thereafter came the blasting noises. Whoever was on the other side of the wall of rubble had decided they were coming in.

Aten Randt moved back from the wall of rubble at speed and came up on Cainen, weapon raised, blinding him with the light beam. "I'm sorry, Administrator," Aten Randt said, and that was when it dawned on Cainen that Aten Randt's orders to get him to safety probably only went so far. On instinct more than thought Cainen twisted away from the light beam; the bullet intended for his center mass instead went into his arm, spinning him around and slamming him into the ground. Cainen struggled to his knees and caught his shadow splayed before him as Aten Randt's light beam fell on his back.

"Wait," Cainen said, to his shadow. "Not in the back. I know what you have to do. Just not in the back. Please."

There was a moment, punctuated by the sounds of rubble blasting. "Turn around, Administrator," Aten Randt said.

Cainen turned, slowly, scraping his knees on the rubble and putting his hands in his coat pockets, as if they were manacles. Aten Randt sighted in; given the luxury of picking his shot he leveled his weapon at Cainen's brain.

"Are you ready, Administrator?" Aten Randt said.

"I am," Cainen said, and shot Aten Randt with the gun in his coat pocket, aiming up into the light beam.

Cainen's shot coincided with a blast from other side of the rubble wall. Aten Randt didn't appear to realize he had been shot until blood began flowing out of the wound in his carapace; the wound was barely visible to Cainen through the light. Cainen saw Aten Randt look down at the wound, stare at it for a moment, and then back at Cainen, confused. By this time Cainen had the gun out of his pocket. He fired at Aten Randt three more times, emptying his projectile cartridge into the Eneshan. Aten Randt leaned forward slightly on his front legs and then fell back an equal amount, the bulk of his large body settling on the ground with each of his legs splayed out at angles.

"Sorry," Cainen said, to the new corpse.

The space filled with dust and then light as the rubble wall was breached, and creatures bearing lights on their weapons flowed through. One of them spotted Cainen and barked; suddenly several light beams were trained on him. Cainen dropped his gun, raised his good arm in surrender and stepped away from Aten Randt's body. Shooting Aten Randt to keep himself alive wouldn't do him much good if these invaders decided to blow holes in him. Through the light beams one of the invaders came forward, jabbering something in its language, and Cainen finally got a look at the species he was dealing with.

His training as a xenobiologist kicked in as he ticked off the particulars of the species phenotype: Bilaterally symmetrical and bipedal, and as a consequence with differentiated limbs for arms and legs; their knees bent the wrong way. Roughly the same size and body plan, which was unsurprising as an inordinately large number of so-called intelligent species were bipedal, bilaterally symmetrical and roughly similarly sized in volume and mass. It was one of the things that made interspecies relationships in this part of the universe as contentious as they were. So many similar intelligent species, so little usable real estate for all their needs.

But now the differences emerge, thought Cainen, as the creature barked at him again: A broader torso and abdominal plain, and a generally awkward skeletal structure and musculature. Stump-like feet; club-like hands. Outwardly obvious sexual differentiation (this one in front of him was female, if he remembered correctly). Compromised sensory input thanks to only two small optical and aural inputs rather than the optical and aural bands that wrapped nearly entirely around Cainen's head. Fine keratinous fibers on the head rather than heat-radiating skin folds.

Not for the first time, Cainen reflected that evolution didn't do this particular species any great favors, physically speaking.

It just made them aggressive, dangerous and damned hard to scrape off a planet surface. A problem, that.

The creature in front of Cainen jabbered at him again and pulled out a short, nasty-looking object. Cainen looked directly into the creature's optical inputs.

"Fucking humans," he said.

The creature swiped him with the object; Cainen felt a jolt, saw a multicolored dance of light and fell to the ground for the last time that day.

"Do you remember who I am?" the human at the table said, as Cainen was led to the room. His captors had provided him with a stool that accommodated his (to them) backwards-facing knees. The human spoke and the translation came out of a speaker on the table. The only other object on the table was a syringe, filled with a clear fluid.

"You are the soldier who knocked me unconscious," Cainen said. The speaker did not give a translation of his words, suggesting that the soldier had another translation device somewhere.

"That's right," the human said. "I am Lieutenant Jane Sagan." She motioned at the stool. "Please sit."

Cainen sat. "It was not necessary to knock me unconscious," he said. "I would have come willingly."

"We had our reasons for wanting you unconscious," Sagan said. She motioned to his injured arm, where Aten Randt's bullet had struck him. "How is your arm?" she asked.

"It feels fine," said Cainen.

"We weren't able to fix it entirely," Sagan said. "Our

medical technology can rapidly heal most of our injuries, but you are Rraey, not human. Our technologies don't map precisely. But we did what we could."

"Thank you," Cainen said.

"I assume you were shot by the Eneshan we found you with," Sagan said. "The one you shot."

"Yes," Cainen said.

"I'm curious as to why you two engaged in a firefight," Sagan said.

"He was going to kill me, and I didn't want to die," said Cainen.

"This begs the question of why this Eneshan wanted you dead," Sagan said.

"I was his prisoner," Cainen said. "I suppose his orders were to kill me rather than to allow me to be taken alive."

"You were his prisoner," Sagan repeated. "And yet you had a weapon."

"I found it," Cainen said.

"Really," Sagan said. "That's poor security on the part of the Enesha. That's not like them."

"We all make mistakes," Cainen said.

"And all the other Rraey we found in the base?" Sagan asked. "They were prisoners as well?"

"They were," Cainen said, and felt a wave of concern for Sharan and the rest of his staff.

"How was it that you all came to be prisoners of the Eneshans?" Sagan asked.

"We were on a Rraey ship that was taking us to one of our colonies for a medical rotation," Cainen said. "The Eneshans attacked our ship. They boarded us and took my crew prisoner and sent us here."

"How long ago was this?" Sagan asked.

"Some time ago," Cainen said. "I'm not exactly sure. We're on Eneshan military time here, and I'm unfamiliar with their units. And then there's the local planetary rotational period, which is fast and makes things more confusing. And I am also unfamiliar with human time divisions, so I can't describe it accurately."

"Our intelligence does not have any record of the Eneshans attacking a Rraey vessel in the last year—that would be about two-thirds of a *hked* for you," Sagan said, using the Rraey term for a full orbit of the home world around its sun.

"Perhaps your intelligence is not as good as you think," Cainen said.

"It's possible," Sagan said. "However, given that the Eneshans and the Rraey are still technically in a state of war, an attacked ship should have been noted. Your two peoples have fought over less."

"I can't tell you any more about it than what I know," Cainen said. "We were taken off the ship and to the base. What happened or didn't happen outside of the base in all this time is not a subject I know much about."

"You were being held prisoner at the base," Sagan said.

"Yes," Cainen said.

"We've been all through the base, and there's only a small detention area," Sagan said. "There's nothing to suggest you were locked up."

Cainen gave the Rraey equivalent of a rueful chuckle. "If you've seen the base you've also no doubt seen the surface of the planet," he said. "If any of us tried to escape we'd freeze before we got very far. Not to mention that there's nowhere to go."

"How do you know that?" Sagan said.

"The Eneshans told us," Cainen said. "And none of my crew planned an excursion to test the proposition."

"So you know nothing else of the planet," Sagan said.

"Sometimes it's cold, other times it is colder," Cainen said. "That is the depth of my knowledge of the planet."

"You're a doctor," Sagan said.

"I'm not familiar with that term," Cainen said, and pointed at the speaker. "Your machine is not smart enough to give an equivalent in my language."

"You're a medical professional. You do medicine," Sagan said.

"I am," Cainen said. "I specialize in genetics. That is why my staff and I were on that ship. One of our colonies was experiencing a plague that was affecting gene sequencing and cell division. We were sent to investigate and hopefully find a cure. I'm sure if you've been through the base you've seen our equipment. Our captors were kind enough to give us space for a lab."

"Why would they do that?" Sagan asked.

"Perhaps they thought if we kept busy with our own projects we would be easier to handle," Cainen said. "If so, it worked, because as a rule we kept to ourselves and tried not to make any trouble."

"Except for when you were stealing weapons, that is," Sagan said.

"I had them for some time, so apparently I didn't arouse their suspicions," Cainen said.

"The weapon you used was designed for a Rraey," Sagan said. "An odd thing for an Eneshan military base."

"They must have taken it from our ship as they boarded," Cainen said. "I'm sure as you search the base you'll find a number of other Rraey-designed items."

"So, to recap," Sagan said. "You and your crew of medical personnel were taken by the Eneshans an indeterminate time ago and brought here, where you've been prisoners and out of communication with any of your peo-

ple. You don't know where you are or what plans the Enesha have for you."

"That's right," Cainen said. "Other than that I suppose
they didn't want anyone to know I was there once the base
was invaded, because one of them tried to kill me."

"That's true," Sagan said. "You fared better than your
crew, I'm afraid."

"I don't know what you mean," Cainen said.

"You're the only Rraey that we found alive," Sagan said.
"The rest had been shot and killed by the Eneshans. Most
of them were in what appeared to be barracks. We found
another near what I imagine was your lab, since it had
quite a bit of Rraey technology in it."

Cainen felt sick. "You're lying," he said.

"I'm afraid not," Sagan said.

"You humans killed them," Cainen said, angrily.

"The Eneshans tried to kill *you*," Sagan said. "Why
wouldn't they kill the other members of your crew?"

"I don't believe you," Cainen said.

"I understand why you wouldn't," Sagan said. "It's still
the truth."

Cainen sat there, grieving. Sagan gave him time.

"All right," Cainen said, eventually. "Tell me what you
want from me."

"For starters, Administrator Cainen," Sagan said, "we'd
like the truth."

It took a moment for Cainen to realize this was the first
time the human had addressed him by his name. And title.
"I've been telling you the truth," he said.

"Bullshit," Sagan said.

Cainen pointed to the speaker again. "I only got a par-
tial translation of that," he said.

"You are Administrator Cainen Suen Su," Sagan said.
"And while it's true enough that you have some medical

training, your two primary areas of study are xenobiology and semi-organic neural net defense systems—two areas of study that I would imagine mesh together well."

Cainen said nothing. Sagan continued. "Now, Administrator Cainen, let me tell you a little of what *we* know. Fifteen months ago the Rraey and the Eneshans were fighting the same off-and-on war they'd been fighting for thirty years, a war that we encouraged since it kept the two of you out of our hair."

"Not entirely," Cainen said. "There was the Battle of Coral."

"Yes, there was," Sagan said. "I was there. I almost died."

"I lost a brother there," Cainen said. "My youngest. Perhaps you met him."

"Perhaps I did," Sagan said. "Fifteen months ago the Rraey and the Enesha were enemies. And then suddenly they were not, for no reason that our intelligence could figure out."

"We've already discussed the shortcomings of your intelligence," Cainen said. "Races stop warring all the time. After Coral, we and you stopped fighting."

"We stopped fighting because we beat you. You retreated and we rebuilt Coral," Sagan said. "Which is the point— there is a reason we stopped fighting, at least for now. You and the Enesha don't have a reason. That worries us.

"Three months ago the spy satellite we parked above *this* planet noticed that for an allegedly uninhabited world, it had suddenly begun to receive a lot of traffic, both Eneshan and Rraey. What makes this especially interesting to us is that this planet is claimed neither by the Enesha or the Rraey, but by the Obin. The Obin don't mix, Administrator, and they are strong enough that neither the Enesha nor the Rraey would think lightly about setting up shop in their territory.

"So we placed a more advanced spy satellite above the planet to look for signs of habitation. We came up with nothing. As a defense specialist, Administrator, would you like to hazard a guess as to why?"

"I would imagine the base was shielded," Cainen said.

"It was," Sagan said. "And as it happens, by the very sort of defense system you specialize in. We didn't know that at the time, of course, but we know it now."

"How did you find the base if it was shielded?" Cainen asked. "I am curious, in a professional sense."

"We dropped rocks," Sagan said.

"Excuse me?" Cainen asked.

"Rocks," Sagan said. "A month ago we salted the planet with several dozen seismic sensors, which were programmed to look for seismic signatures that suggested intelligently designed underground structures. Speaking from experience, secret bases are easier to shield when they're underground. We relied on the planet's natural seismic activity to narrow down areas to investigate. Then we dropped rocks in areas of interest. And then today we dropped several right before our attack, to get an exact sonic image of the base. Rocks are good because they look like naturally occurring meteors. They don't scare anyone. And no one shields against seismic imaging. Most races are too busy shielding against optical and high-energy electromagnetic scans to consider sound waves much of a danger. It's the fallacy of high technology; it ignores the efficiency of lower orders of technology. Like dropping rocks."

"Leave it to humans to bang rocks together," Cainen said.

Sagan shrugged. "We don't mind when the other guy brings a gun to a knife fight," she said. "It just makes it easier for us to cut out his heart. Or whatever it is that he uses to pump blood. Your overconfidence works for us. As you can see because you are here. But what we really want to know, Administrator, is *why* you are here. Eneshans and Rraey working together is puzzling enough, but Eneshans and Rraey *and* Obin? That's not just puzzling. That's *interesting*."

"I don't know anything about who owns this planet," Cainen said.

"And what's even more interesting is you, Administrator Cainen," Sagan said, ignoring Cainen's comment. "While you were sleeping we did a gene scan on you to tell us who you are, then we accessed ship's records to learn a little of your history. We know one of your primary areas of xenobiological interest is humans. You're probably the Rraey's leading authority on human genetics. And we know you've also got a particular interest in how human brains work."

"It's part of my overall interest in neural nets," Cainen said. "I'm not *particularly* interested in human brains, as you say. All brains are interesting in their way."

"If you say so," Sagan said. "But whatever it was you were doing down there, it was important enough that the Eneshans would rather see you and your crew dead than in our hands."

"I told you," Cainen said. "We were their prisoners."

Sagan rolled her eyes. "For a minute, let's pretend we're both not stupid, Administrator Cainen," she said.

Cainen moved forward, leaning closer to Sagan from across the table. "What kind of human are you?" he asked.

"What do you mean?" Sagan said.

"We know there are three kinds of human," Cainen said, and held up his fingers, so much longer and more articulated than human fingers, to count off the variations. "There are the unmodified humans, who are the ones who colonize planets. Those come in varying shapes and sizes and colors—good genetic diversity there. The second group is the largest part of your soldier caste. These also vary in size and shape, but to a far lesser extent, and they're all the same color: green. We know that these soldiers aren't in their original bodies—their consciousness is transferred from bodies of older members of your species to these stronger, healthier bodies. These bodies are extensively genetically altered, so much that they can't breed, either between themselves or with unmodified humans. But they're still recognizably human, particularly the brain matter.

"But the third group," Cainen said, and leaned back. "We hear stories, Lieutenant Sagan."

"What do you hear?" Sagan said.

"That they are created from the dead," Cainen said. "That the human germ plasm of the dead is mixed and remixed with the genetics of other species to see what will arise. That some of them don't even resemble humans, as *they* recognize themselves. That they are born as adults, with skills and ability, but no memory. And not only no memory. No *self*. No morality. No restraint. No—" He paused, as if looking for the right word. "No *humanity*," he said, finally. "As you would put it. Child warriors, in grown bodies. Abominations. Monsters. Tools your Colonial Union uses for the missions they can not or will not offer to soldiers who have life experience and a moral self, or who might fear for their soul in this world or the next."

"A scientist concerned about souls," Sagan said. "That's not very pragmatic."

"I am a scientist, but I am also Rraey," Cainen said. "I know I have a soul, and I tend to it. Do you have a soul, Lieutenant Sagan?"

"Not that I know of, Administrator Cainen," Sagan said. "They are hard to quantify."

"So you *are* the third kind of human," Cainen said.

"I am," Sagan said.

"Built from the flesh of the dead," Cainen said.

"From her genes," Sagan said. "Not her flesh."

"Genes build the flesh, Lieutenant. Genes dream the flesh, wherein the soul resides," Cainen said.

"Now you're a poet," Sagan said.

"I'm quoting," Cainen said. "One of our philosophers. Who was also a scientist. You wouldn't know her. May I ask how old you are?"

"I'm seven, almost eight," Sagan said. "About four and a half of your *hked*."

"So young," Cainen said. "Rraey of your age have barely started their educations. I'm more than ten times your age, Lieutenant."

"And yet, here we both are," Sagan said.

"Here we are," Cainen agreed. "I wish we had met under other circumstances, Lieutenant. I would very much like to study you."

"I don't know how to respond to that," Sagan said. "'Thank you' doesn't seem appropriate, considering what being studied by you would probably mean."

"You could be kept alive," Cainen said.

"Oh, joy," Sagan said. "But you might get your wish, after a fashion. You must know by now that you are a prisoner—for real this time, and you will be for the rest of your life."

"I figured that out when you started telling me things I could report back to my government," Cainen said. "Like the rock trick. Although I assumed you were going to kill me."

"We humans are a pragmatic people, Administrator Cainen," Sagan said. "You have knowledge we can use, and if you were willing to be cooperative, there's no reason you couldn't continue your study of human genetics and brains. Just for us instead of for the Rraey."

"All I would have to do is betray my people," Cainen said.

"There is that," Sagan allowed.

"I think I would rather die first," Cainen said.

"With all due respect, Administrator, if you truly believed that, you probably wouldn't have shot that Eneshan who was trying to kill you earlier today," Sagan said. "I think you want to live."

"You may be right," Cainen said. "But whether you are right or not, *child*, I am done talking to you now. I've told you everything I'm going to tell you of my own free will."

Sagan smiled at Cainen. "Administrator, do you know what humans and Rraey have in common?"

"We have a number of things in common," Cainen said. "Pick one."

"Genetics," Sagan said. "I don't need to tell you that human genetic sequencing and Rraey genetic sequencing are substantially different in the details. But on the macro level we share certain similarities, including the fact that we receive one set of genes from one parent and the other from the other. Two-parent sexual reproduction."

"Standard sexual reproduction among sexually reproducing species," Cainen said. "Some species need three or even four parents, but not many. It's too inefficient."

"No doubt," Sagan said. "Administrator, have you heard of Fronig's Syndrome?"

"It's a rare genetic disease among the Rraey," Cainen said. "Very rare."

"From what I understand of it, the disease is caused because of deficiencies in two unrelated gene sets," Sagan said. "One gene set regulates the development of nerve cells, and specifically of an electrically-insulating sheath around them. The second gene set regulates the organ that produces the Rraey analog for what humans call lymph. It does some of the same things, and does other things differently. In humans lymph is somewhat electrically conductive, but in the Rraey this liquid is electrically insulating. From what we know of Rraey physiology this electrically insulating quality of your lymph usually serves no particular benefit or detriment, just as the electrically conductive nature of human lymph is neither a plus or minus—it's just there."

"Yes," Cainen said.

"But for Rraey who are unlucky enough to have two broken nerve development genes, this electrical insulation *is* beneficial," Sagan said. "This fluid bathes the interstitial area surrounding Rraey cells, including nerve cells. This keeps the nerve's electrical signals from going astray. What's interesting about Rraey lymph is that its composition is controlled hormonally, and that a slight change in the hormonal signal will change it from electrically insulating to electrically conductive. Again, for most Rraey, this is neither here nor there. But for those who code for exposed nerve cells—"

"—it causes seizures and convulsions and then death as their nerve signals leak out into their bodies," Cainen said. "Its fatality is why it's so rare. Individuals who code for electrically-conductive lymph and exposed nerves die during gestation, usually after the cells first begin to differentiate and the syndrome manifests."

"But there's also adult onset Fronig's," Sagan said. "The genes code to change the hormonal signal later, in early adulthood. Which is late enough for reproduction to happen and the gene to be passed on. But it also takes two faulty genes to be expressed."

"Yes, of course," Cainen said. "That's another reason why Fronig's is so rare; it's not often that an individual will receive two sets of faulty nerve genes *and* two sets of genes that cause later-life hormonal changes in their lymph organ. Tell me where this is going."

"Administrator, the genetic sample from you when you came on board shows that you code for faulty nerves," Sagan said.

"But I don't code for hormonal changes," Cainen said. "Otherwise I'd be dead already. Fronig's expresses in early adulthood."

"This is true," Sagan said. "But one can also induce hormonal changes by killing off certain cell bundles within the Rraey lymph organ. Kill off enough of the bundles that generate the correct hormone, and you can still produce lymph. It will simply have different properties. Fatal properties, in your case. One can do it chemically."

Cainen's attention was drawn to the syringe that had been lying on the table through the entire conversation. "And that's the chemical that can do it, I suppose," Cainen said.

"That's the antidote," Sagan said.

Jane Sagan found Administrator Cainen Suen Su admirable in his way; he didn't crack easily. He suffered through several hours as his lymphatic organ gradually replaced the lymph in his body with the new, altered fluid, twitching and seizing as concentrations of the electrically-conductive lymph triggered nerve misfires randomly through his body, and the overall conductivity of his entire system heightened with each passing minute. If he hadn't cracked when he did, it was very likely that he wouldn't have been able to tell them that he wanted to talk.

But crack he did, and begged for the antidote. In the end, he wanted to live. Sagan administered the antidote herself (not really an antidote, as those dead cell bundles were dead forever; he'd have to receive daily shots of the stuff for the rest of his life). As the antidote coursed through Cainen's body, Sagan learned of a brewing war against humanity, and a blueprint for the subjugation and eradication of her entire species. A genocide planned in great detail, based on the heretofore unheard of cooperation of three races.

And one human.

TWO Colonel James Robbins gazed down at the rotted, exhumed body on the morgue slab for a minute, taking in the decay of the body from more than one year under the dirt. He noted the ruined skull, fatally misshaped by the shotgun blast that carried away its top third, along with the life of its owner, the man who might have betrayed humanity to three alien races. Then he looked up at Captain Winters, Phoenix Station's medical examiner.

"Tell me this is Dr. Boutin's body, " Colonel Robbins said.

"Well, it is," said Winters. "And yet it's *not*."

"You know, Ted, that's exactly the sort of qualified statement that's going to get my ass reamed when I report to General Mattson," Colonel Robbins said. "I don't suppose you'd like to be more forthcoming."

"Sorry, Jim," Captain Winters said, and pointed to the corpse on the table. "Genetically speaking, that's your man," Winters said. "Dr. Boutin was a colonist, which meant he's never been swapped into a military body. This means that his body has all his original DNA. I did the standard genetics testing. This body has Boutin's DNA—and just for fun I did a mitochondrial RNA test as well. That matched too."

"So what's the problem?" Robbins asked.

"The problem is with bone growth," Winters said. "In the real universe, human bone growth fluctuates based on environmental factors, like nutrition or exercise. If you spend time on a high-gravity world and then move to one with lower gravity, that's going to influence how your bones grow. If you break a bone, that's going to show up too. Your entire life history shows up in bone development."

Winters reached over and picked up part of the corpse's left leg, which had been sheared from the rest of the body, and pointed to the cross-section of the femur visible there. "This body's bone development is *exceptionally* regular. There's no record of environmental or accidental events on its development, just a pattern of bone growth consistent with excellent nutrition and low stress."

"Boutin was from Phoenix," Robbins said. "It's been colonized for two hundred years. It's not like he grew up on a backwater colony where they're struggling to feed and protect themselves."

"Maybe not, but it still doesn't match up," Winters said. "You can live in the most civilized place in human space and still fall down a flight of stairs or break a bone playing sports. It's possible that you can get through life without even a greenstick fracture, but do you know anyone who's done it?" Robbins shook his head. "This guy did. But actually he didn't, since his medical records show he broke his leg, *this* leg"—Winters shook the chunk of leg—"when he was sixteen. Skiing accident. Collided with a boulder and broke his femur and his tibia. The record of that isn't here."

"I hear medical technology is good these days," Robbins said.

"It is excellent, thank you very much," Winters said. "But it's not magic. You don't snap a femur and not leave a mark. And even getting through life without breaking a bone doesn't explain the consistently regular bone development. The only way you're going to get this sort of bone development is if it develops without environmental stress of any kind. Boutin would have had to live his life in a box."

"Or a cloning crèche," Robbins said.

"Or a cloning crèche," Winters agreed. "The other possible explanation is that your friend here had his leg amputated at some point and had a new one grown, but I checked his records; that didn't happen. But just to be sure I took bone samples from his ribs, his pelvis, his arm and his skull—the undamaged portion, anyway. All these samples showed unnaturally consistent, regular bone growth. You've got yourself a cloned body here, Jim."

"Then Charles Boutin is still alive," Robbins said.

"That I don't know," Winters said. "But this isn't him. The only good news here is that by all physical indications, this clone was vatted right up until just before it died. It's extremely unlikely it was ever awake, or even if it was that it was conscious and aware. Imagine waking up and finding your first and last view of the world was a shotgun barrel. That'd be a hell of a life."

"So if Boutin's still alive, he's also a murderer," Robbins said.

Winters shrugged and set down the leg. "You tell me, Jim," he said. "The Colonial Defense Forces make bodies all time—we create modified superbodies to give to our new recruits, and then when their service is through we give them new normal bodies cloned from their original DNA. Do those bodies really have rights before we put consciousness into them? Each time we transfer their consciousness, we leave a body behind—a body that used to have a mind. Do *those* bodies have rights? If they do, we're all in trouble, because we dispose of them pretty damn quick. Do you know what we do with all those used bodies, Jim?"

"I don't," Robbins admitted.

"We mulch them," Winters said. "There are too many to bury. So we grind them up, sterilize the remains and turn them into plant fertilizer. Then we send the fertilizer to new colonies. Helps to acclimate the soil to the crops humans plant. You could say our new colonies live off the bodies of the dead. Only they're not *really* the bodies of the dead. They're just the cast-off bodies of the living. The only time we actually bury a body is when a mind dies inside of it."

"Think about taking some time off, Ted," Robbins said. "Your job is making you morbid."

"It's not the job that makes me morbid," Winters said, and pointed to the remains of not–Charles Boutin. "What do you want me to do with this?"

"I want you to have it reinterred," Robbins said.

"But it's not Charles Boutin," Winters said.

"No, it's not," Robbins agreed. "But if Charles Boutin is still alive, I don't want him to know *we* know that." He looked back at the body on the slab. "And whether this body knew what was happening to it or not, it deserved better than what it got. A burial is the least we can do."

"Goddamn Charles Boutin," General Greg Mattson said, and kicked up his feet on his desk.

Colonel Robbins stood at the other side of the desk and

said nothing. General Mattson disconcerted him, as he always had. Mattson had been the head of the Colonial Defense Forces Military Research arm for almost thirty years, but like all CDF military personnel had a military issued body that resisted aging; he looked—as did all CDF personnel—no more than twenty-five years old. Colonel Robbins was of the opinion that as people advanced in rank through the CDF they should be made to appear to age slightly; a general who looked twenty-five years old lacked a certain gravitas.

Robbins briefly imagined Mattson appearing to be his true age, which had to be somewhere in the vicinity of 125 years old; his mind's eye saw something like a scrotal wrinkle in a uniform. This would be amusing to Robbins, save for the fact that at ninety years of age himself, he wouldn't look all that much better.

Then there was the matter of the other general in the room, who if his body showed his real age would almost certainly look younger than he already did. Special Forces disconcerted Robbins even more than regular CDF. There was something not quite right about people being three years old, fully grown and totally lethal.

Not that this general was three. He was probably a teenager.

"So our Rraey friend told us the truth," General Szilard said, from his own seat in front of the desk. "Your former head of consciousness research is still alive."

"Blowing the head off his own clone, now, that was a *nice* touch," General Mattson said, sarcasm dripping out his voice. "Those poor bastards were picking brains out of the lab equipment for a week afterward." He glanced up at Robbins. "Do we know how he did that? Grow a clone? That's something you shouldn't be able to do without someone noticing. He couldn't have just whipped one up in the closet."

"As near as we can tell, he introduced code into the clone vat monitoring software," Robbins said. "Made it look like one of the clone vats was out of service to the monitors. It was taken out to be serviced; Boutin had it decommissioned, and then put it in his private lab storage area and ran it off its own server and power supply. The server wasn't hooked into the system and the vat was decommissioned, and only Boutin had access to the storage area."

"So he *did* whip one up in the closet," Mattson said. "That little fucker."

"You must have had access to the storage area after he was presumed dead," Szilard said. "Are you saying that no one thought it odd he had a clone vat in storage?"

Robbins opened his mouth but Mattson answered. "If he was a good research head—and he was—he'd have a lot of decommissioned and surplus equipment in storage, in order to tinker and optimize it without interfering with equipment that we were actually using. And I would assume that when we got to the vat it was drained and sterilized and disconnected from the server and the power supply."

"That's right," Robbins said. "It wasn't until we got your report that we put two and two together, General Szilard."

"I'm glad the information was useful," Szilard said. "I wish you had put two and two together earlier. I find the idea that Military Research had a traitor in its ranks—and as the head of an extremely sensitive division—appalling. You should have known."

Robbins said nothing to this; to the extent that Special Forces had any reputation at all beyond its military prowess, it was that its members were profoundly lacking in tact and patience. Being three-year-old killing machines didn't leave much time for social graces.

"What was to know?" Mattson said. "Boutin never gave any indication he was turning traitor. One day he's doing his work, the next we find him a suicide in his lab, or so we thought. No note. No anything that suggests he had anything on his mind but his work."

"You told me earlier that Boutin hated you," Szilard said to Mattson.

"Boutin *did* hate me, and for good reason," Mattson said. "And the feeling was mutual. But just because a man thinks his superior officer is a son of a bitch doesn't mean he's a traitor to his species." Mattson pointed to Robbins. "The colonel here doesn't particularly like me, either, and he's my adjutant. But he's not going to go running to the Rraey or the Enesha with top-secret information."

Szilard looked over at Robbins. "Is it true?" he said.

"Which part, sir?" Robbins said.

"That you don't like General Mattson," Szilard said.

"He can take some getting used to, sir," Robbins said.

"By which he means I'm an asshole," Mattson said, with a chuckle. "And that's fine. I'm not here to win popularity contests. I'm here to deliver weapons and technology. But whatever was going through Boutin's head, I don't think I had much to do with it."

"So what was it then?" Szilard said.

"You'd know better than we would, Szi," Mattson said. "You're the one with the pet Rraey scientist that you've taught to squeal."

"Administrator Cainen never met Boutin personally, or so he says," Szilard said. "He doesn't know anything about his motivations, just that Boutin gave the Rraey information on the most recent BrainPal hardware. That's part of what Administrator Cainen's group was working on—trying to integrate BrainPal technology with Rraey brains."

"Just what we need," Mattson said. "Rraey with super-computers in their heads."

"He didn't seem to be very successful with the integration," Robbins said, and looked over to Szilard. "At least not from the data your people recovered from his lab. Rraey brain structure is too different."

"Small favors," Mattson said. "Szi, you have to have gotten something else out of your guy."

"Outside of his specific work and situation, Administrator Cainen hasn't been terribly useful," Szilard said. "And the few Eneshans we captured alive were resistant to conversation, to use a euphemism. We know the Rraey, the Enesha and the Obin are allied to attack us. But we don't know why, how or when, or what Boutin brings into the equation. We need your people to figure that one out, Mattson."

Mattson nodded to Robbins. "Where are we with that?" he asked.

"Boutin was in charge of a lot of sensitive information," Robbins said, pitching his answer to Szilard. "His groups han-dled consciousness transfer, BrainPal development and body-generation techniques. Any of that could be useful to an enemy, either to help it develop its own technology or to find weaknesses in ours. Boutin himself was probably the leading expert on getting minds out of one body and into another. But there's a limit to how much of that information he could carry. Boutin was a civilian scientist. He didn't have a BrainPal. His clone had all his registered brain prostheses on him, and he's not likely to have gotten a spare. Prostheses are tightly monitored and he'd have to spend several weeks training it. We don't have any network record of Boutin using anything but his registered prosthesis."

"We're talking about a man who got a cloning vat past you," Szilard said.

"It's not impossible that he walked out of the lab with a store of information," Robbins said. "But it's very unlikely. It's more likely he left only with the knowledge in his head."

"And his motivations," Szilard said. "Not knowing those is the most dangerous thing for us."

"I'm more worried about what he knows," Mattson said. "Even with just what's naturally in his head, that's still too much. I have teams pulled off their own projects to work on updating BrainPal security. Whatever Boutin does know we're going to make obsolete. And Robbins here is in charge of combing through the data Boutin left behind. If there's anything in there, we'll find it."

"I'll be meeting with Boutin's former tech after we're done here," Robbins said. "Lieutenant Harry Wilson. He says he has something I might find interesting."

"Don't let us hold you up," Mattson said. "You're dismissed."

"Thank you, sir," Robbins said. "Before I go, I'd like to know what sort of time constraint we're working under here. We found out about Boutin by attacking that base. No doubt the Eneshans know we know about their plans. I'd like to know how much time we think we have before a retaliation."

"You have some time, Colonel," Szilard said. "Nobody knows we attacked that base."

"How can they not know?" Robbins said. "With all due respect to Special Forces, General, it's difficult to hide that sort of assault. "

"The Eneshans know they've lost contact with the base," Szilard said. "When they investigate, what they're going to find is that a rocky chunk of comet the size of a football field hit the planet about ten klicks from the base, obliterating it and everything else in the immediate area. They can run all the tests they want; nothing will show anything but evidence of a natural catastrophe. Because that's what it was. It just had a little help."

"This is very pretty," Colonel Robbins said, gesturing at what looked like a miniature light show on Lieutenant Harry Wilson's holographic display. "But I don't know what you're showing me here."

"It's Charlie Boutin's soul," Wilson said.

Robbins pulled himself away from the display and looked up at Wilson. "I beg your pardon," he said.

Wilson nodded toward the display. "It's Charlie's soul," he repeated. "Or more accurately, it's a holographic representation of the dynamic electrical system that embodies the consciousness of Charles Boutin. Or a copy of it, anyway. I suppose if you want to be philosophical about it, you could argue whether this is Charlie's mind or his soul. But if what you say about Charlie is true, he's probably still got his wits about him, but I'd say he's lost his soul. And here it is."

"I was told this sort of thing is impossible," Robbins said. "Without the brain the pattern collapses. It's why we transfer consciousness the way we do, live body to live body."

"Well, I don't know that it's *why* we transfer consciousness the way we do," Wilson said, "since I think people would be a lot more resistant to letting a CDF technician suck their mind out of their skull if they knew it was just going to sit in computerized storage. Would *you* do it?"

"Christ, no," Robbins said. "I nearly wet myself as it was when they transferred me over."

"My point exactly," Wilson said. "Nevertheless, you're right. Up until this"—he motioned at the hologram—"we couldn't do it even if we wanted to."

"So how did Boutin do it?" Robbins asked.

"He cheated, of course," Wilson said. "Before a year and a half ago, Charlie and everyone else had to work with human-derived technology, or whatever technology we could borrow or steal from other races. And most other races in our part of space have more or less the same level of technology as we do, because weaker races get kicked off their land and die off or get killed. But there's one species who is light-years ahead of everyone else in the neighborhood."

"The Consu," Robbins said, and pictured one in his mind: large, crab-like and almost unknowably advanced.

"Right," said Wilson. "The Consu gave the Rraey some of their technology when the Rraey attacked our colony on Coral a couple years back, and we stole it from them when we counterattacked. I was part of the team assigned to reverse-engineer the Consu tech, and I can assure you that most of it we still don't understand. But one of the bits we *could* get our brains around we gave to Charlie to work with, to improve the consciousness transfer process. That's how I came to work with him; I taught him how to use this stuff. And as you can see, he's a quick study. Of course, it's easy to get things done when your tools improve. With this we went from banging rocks together to using a blowtorch."

"You didn't know anything about this," Robbins said.

"No," Wilson said. "I've seen something *like* this— Charlie used the Consu technology to refine the consciousness transfer process we have. We can create a buffer now that we couldn't before, which makes the transfer a lot less susceptible to failure on either end of the transfer. But he kept *this* trick to himself. I only found it after you told me to go looking through his personal work. Which was a lucky thing, since the machine I found this on was slated to be wiped and transferred to the CDF observatory. They want to see how well Consu tech models the inside of a star."

Robbins motioned to the hologram. "I think this is a little more important."

Wilson shrugged. "It's actually not very useful in a general sense."

"You're joking," Robbins said. "We can store consciousness."

"Sure, and maybe that *is* useful. But you can't *do* much with it," Wilson said. "How much do you know about the details of consciousness transfer?"

"Some," Robbins said. "I'm not an expert. I was made the general's adjutant for my organizational skills, not for any science background."

"Okay, look," Wilson said. "You noted it yourself—without the brain, the pattern of consciousness usually collapses. That's because the consciousness is wholly dependent on the physical structure of the brain. And not just *any* brain; it's dependent on the brain in which it arose. Every pattern of consciousness is like a fingerprint. It's specific to that person and it's specific right down to the genes."

Wilson pointed to Robbins. "Look at your body, Colonel. It's been deeply modified on a genetic level—you've got green skin and improved musculature and artificial blood that has several times the oxygen capacity of actual blood. You're a hybrid of your own personal genetics and genes engineered to extend your capabilities. So on a genetic level, you're not really you anymore—*except* for your brain. Your brain is entirely human, and entirely based on your genes. Because if it wasn't, your consciousness couldn't transfer."

"Why?" Robbins asked.

Wilson grinned. "I wish I could tell you. I'm passing along what Charlie and his lab crew told me. I'm just the electron pusher here. But I do know that it means that *this*"—Wilson pointed to the hologram—"does you no good as it is because it needs a brain, and it needs *Charlie's* brain, in order to tell you what it knows. And Charlie's brain has gone missing along with the rest of him."

"If this is no damn use to us," Robbins said, "then I'd like to know why you had me come down here."

"I said it's not very useful in a *general* sense," Wilson said. "But in a very specific sense, it could be quite useful."

"Lieutenant Wilson," Robbins said. "Please get to the point."

"Consciousness isn't just a sense of identity. It's also knowledge and emotion and mental state," Wilson said, and motioned back to the hologram. "This thing has the capacity to know and feel everything Charlie knew and felt right up to the moment he made this copy. I figure if you want to know what Charlie's up to and why, this is where you want to start."

"You just said we needed Boutin's brain to access the consciousness," Robbins said. "It's not available to us."

"But his *genes* are," Wilson said. "Charlie created a clone to serve his purposes, Colonel. I suggest you create one to serve yours."

"Clone Charles Boutin," General Mattson said, and snorted. "As if one wasn't bad enough."

Mattson, Robbins and Szilard sat in the general's mess of Phoenix Station. Mattson and Szilard were having a meal; Robbins was not. Technically speaking the general's mess was open to all officers; as a practical matter no one under the rank of general ever ate there, and lesser officers entered the mess only on the invitation of a general and rarely took more than a glass of water. Robbins wondered how this ridiculous protocol ever got started. He was hungry.

The general's mess sat at the terminal of Phoenix Station's rotational axis and was surrounded by a single shaped, transparent crystal that comprised its walls and ceiling. It gave an astounding view of the planet Phoenix, which circled lazily overhead, taking up nearly the entire sky, a perfect blue-and-white jewel whose resemblance to Earth never failed to give Robbins a sharp jab in the homesickness centers of the brain. Leaving Earth was easy when one was seventy-five and the option was death of old age within a few increasingly short years. But once you left you could never go back; the longer Robbins lived in the hostile universe the human colonies found themselves in, the more fondly he remembered the flabby but relatively carefree days of his fifties, sixties and early seventies. Ignorance was bliss, or at the very least was more restful.

Too late now, Robbins thought, and directed his attention back to Mattson and Szilard. "Lieutenant Wilson seems to think it's the best chance we have of understanding what was going on in Boutin's head. In any event, it's better than what we have now, which is nothing."

"How does Lieutenant Wilson know that it's Boutin's brainwave he's got in his machine? That's what I want to know," Mattson said. "Boutin could have sampled someone else's consciousness. Shit, it could be his cat, for all we know."

"The pattern is consistent with human consciousness," Robbins said. "We can tell that much because we transfer hundreds of consciousnesses every day. It's not a cat."

"It was a joke, Robbins," Mattson said. "But it still might not be Boutin."

"It's possible it could be someone else, but it doesn't seem likely," Robbins said. "No one else in Boutin's lab knew he was working on this. There was no opportunity to sample anyone else's consciousness. It's not something you could take from someone without them noticing."

"Do we even know how to transfer it?" General Szilard asked. "Your Lieutenant Wilson said it was on a machine adapted from Consu technology. Even if we want to use it, do we know how to do it?"

"No," Robbins said. "Not yet. Wilson seems confident he can figure it out, but he's not an expert in consciousness transference."

"I am," Mattson said. "Or at least I've been in charge of the people who *are* long enough to know about it. The process involves physical brains as well as the consciousness that's carried over. For this we're down one brain. Not to mention there are ethical issues."

"Ethical issues?" Robbins said. He failed to keep the surprise out of his voice.

"Yes, Colonel, ethical issues," Mattson said, irritably. "Believe it or not."

"I didn't mean to question your ethics, General," Robbins said.

Mattson waved it away. "Forget it. The point stands. The Colonial Union has a long-standing law against cloning non-CDF personnel, alive or dead, but *especially* alive. The only time we clone humans is to stuff people back into unmodified bodies after their term of service is done. Boutin is a civilian, and a colonist. Even if we wanted to, we can't legally clone him."

"Boutin made a clone," Robbins said.

"If it's all the same we won't let the morals of a traitor guide us in this, Colonel," Mattson said, irritated again.

"You could get a research dispensation from Colonial law," Robbins said. "It's been done before. *You've* done it before."

"Not for something like this," Mattson said. "We get dispensations when we test weapons systems on uninhabited planets. Start messing with clones and some of the more reactionary types get a twitch in their skulls. Something like this wouldn't even get out of committee."

"Boutin's a key to whatever the Rraey and their allies have planned," Robbins said. "This might be a time to take a page from the U.S. Marines and beg forgiveness rather than ask permission."

"I'd admire your willingness to hoist the Jolly Roger, Colonel," Mattson said. "But you're not the one they'll shoot. Or not the only one."

Szilard, who had been chewing a steak, swallowed and set down his utensils. "We'll do it," he said.

"Pardon?" Mattson said.

"Give the consciousness pattern to Special Forces, General," Szilard said. "And give us Boutin's genes. We'll use them to craft a Special Forces soldier. We use more than one set of genes to make every soldier; technically, it won't be a clone. And if the consciousness doesn't take, it will make no difference. It will just be another Special Forces soldier. There's nothing to lose."

"Except that if the consciousness *does* take, we'll have a Special Forces soldier with treason on his mind," Mattson said. "That doesn't sound appealing."

"We can prepare for that," Szilard said, and picked up his utensils again.

"You'll be using genes from a live person, and a colonist," Robbins said. "My understanding was that Special Forces only took the genes from CDF volunteers who die before they can serve. That's why they're called 'the Ghost Brigades.'"

Szilard looked up sharply at Robbins. "I don't much like that name," Szilard said. "The genes of dead CDF volunteers are one component. And typically we use the volunteer genes as the template. But Special Forces has a wider latitude in the genetic material we're able to use to build our soldiers. Given our mission for the CDF, it's almost a requirement. Anyway, Boutin *is* legally dead—we've got a dead body with his genes in them. And we don't know that he is alive. Does he have any survivors?"

"No," Mattson said. "He had a wife and kid, but they died before he did. No other family."

"Then there's no problem," Szilard said. "After you're dead, your genes aren't yours anymore. We've used expired colonist genes before. I don't see why we can't do it again."

"I don't remember hearing this about how you build your people, Szi," Mattson said.

"We're quiet about what we do, General," Szilard said. "You know that." He cut a piece of steak and speared it into his mouth. Robbins's stomach grumbled. Mattson grunted, leaned back in his chair, and looked up at Phoenix, imperceptibly turning in the sky. Robbins followed his gaze and felt another pang of homesickness.

Presently Mattson turned his attention back to Szilard. "Boutin is one of my people," he said. "For better or worse. I can't pass the responsibility for this to you, Szi."

"Fine," Szilard said, and nodded to Robbins. "Then let me borrow Robbins. He can act as your liaison, so Military Research will still have a hand in. We'll share information. We'll borrow the technician too. Wilson. He can work with our technicians to integrate the Consu technology. If it works, we have Charles Boutin's memories and motivations and a way to prepare for this war. If it doesn't work, I have another Special Forces solider. Waste not. Want not."

Mattson looked over to Szilard, considering. "You seem eager to do this, Szi," Mattson said.

"Humans are moving toward war with three species who have allied together," Szilard said. "That's never happened before. We could take on any one of them, but not all three at once. Special Forces have been told to stop this war before it starts. If this helps us to do that, we should do it. Try it, at the very least."

"Robbins," Mattson said. "Your thoughts."

"If General Szilard is correct, then doing this would get around the legal and ethical issues," Robbins said. "That makes it worth a shot. And we'll still be in the loop." Robbins had his own personal set of worries about working with Special Forces technicians and soldiers, but it didn't seem the right time to air them.

Mattson, however, did not need to be so circumspect. "Your boys and girls don't play well with normal types, General," Mattson said. "That's one reason why Military Research and Special Forces research don't work together much."

"Special Forces are soldiers, first and last," Szilard said. "They'll follow orders. We'll make it work. We've done it before. We had a regular CDF solider take part in Special Forces missions at the Battle of Coral. If we can make that work, we can get technicians to work together without undue bloodshed."

Mattson tapped the table in front of him, pensively. "How long will this take?" he asked.

"We'll have to build a new template for this body, not just adapt previous genetics," Szilard said. "I'd need to double-check with my techs, but they usually take a month to build from scratch. After that it takes sixteen weeks minimum to grow a body. And then whatever time we need to develop the process to transfer the consciousness. We can do that and grow the body at the same time."

"You can't make that go any faster?" Mattson said.

"We could make it go faster," Szilard said. "But then you'd have a dead body. Or worse. You know you can't rush body manufacture. Your own soldiers' bodies are grown on the same schedule, and I think you remember what happens when you rush that."

Mattson grimaced; Robbins, who had been Mattson's liaison for only eighteen months, was reminded that Mattson had been at this job for a very long time. No matter their working relationship, there were still gaps in Robbins's knowledge of his boss.

"Fine," Mattson said. "Take it. See if you can get anything out of it. But you *watch* him. I had my problems with Boutin, but I never saw him as a traitor. He fooled me. He fooled everyone. You'll have Charles Boutin's mind in one of your Special Forces bodies. God only knows what he could do with one of those."

"Agreed," Szilard said. "If the transfer is a success, we'll know it sooner than later. If it's not, I know where I can put him. Just to be sure."

"Good," Mattson said, and looked up again at Phoenix, circling in sky. "Phoenix," he said, watching the world twirl above him. "A reborn creature. Well, *that's* appropriate. A phoenix is supposed to rise up from the flames, you know. Let's just hope *this* reborn creature doesn't bring everything down in them."

They all stared at the planet above them.

THREE "This is it," Colonel Robbins said to Lieutenant Wilson, as the body, encased in its crèche, was wheeled into the decanting lab.

"This is it," agreed Wilson, who moved over to a monitor that would momentarily display the body's vital signs. "Were you ever a father, Colonel?"

"No," Robbins said. "My personal inclinations didn't run that way."

"Well, then," Wilson said. "This is as close as you'll probably get."

Normally the birthing lab would be filled with up to sixteen Special Forces soldiers being decanted at once— soldiers who would be activated and trained together to build unit cohesion during training, and to ease the soldiers' disorientation at being activated fully conscious but without any memory to speak of. This time, there was just one soldier: The one who would house Charles Boutin's consciousness.

* * *

It had been more than two centuries since the nascent Colonial Union, faced with its spectacular failure to defend the earliest of its colonies (the planet Phoenix was called so for a reason), realized that unmodified human soldiers were unable to get the job done. The spirit was willing—human history recorded some of its greatest doomed battles in those years, with the Battle for Armstrong in particular studied as a masterful example of how to turn an imminent rout by alien forces into a shocking and painful Pyrrhic victory for one's enemy—but the flesh was all too weak. The enemy, *all* of the enemies, were too fast, too vicious, too pitiless and too many. Human technology was good, and weapon to weapon humans were as well-equipped as the vast majority of their adversaries. But the weapon that ultimately matters is the one behind the trigger.

The earliest modifications were relatively simple: increased speed, muscle mass and strength, endurance. Early genetic engineers, however, were hampered by the practical and ethical problems of engineering humans in vitro, and then waiting for them to grow sufficiently large and smart enough to fight, a process that took roughly eighteen years. The Colonial Defense Forces discovered to its intense chagrin that many of its (relatively) lightly genetically-modified humans were not particularly pleased to discover they were raised as a crop of cannon fodder and refused to fight, despite the best indoctrination and propaganda efforts to persuade them otherwise. Unmodified humans were equally scandalized, as the effort smacked of yet another eugenics effort on the part of a human government, and the track record of eugenics-loving governments in the human experience was not exactly stellar.

The Colonial Union survived the wracking waves of political crises that followed in the wake of its earliest attempts to genetically engineer its soldiers, but just barely.

Had the Battle for Armstrong not emphatically shown the colonies what sort of universe they were up against, the Union would likely have collapsed and the human colonies would have been left in the position of competing against each other as well as against every other intelligent species they had encountered to date.

The Union was also saved by the near-simultaneous arrival of dual, critical technological discoveries: the ability to force-grow a human body to adult size in months, and the emergence of the consciousness transfer protocol that allowed the personality and memories of one individual to be transported into another brain, provided that brain had the same genetics, and had been adequately prepared with a series of pre-transfer procedures that developed some of the necessary bioelectrical pathways in the brain. These new technologies allowed the Colonial Union to develop a large, alternate pool of potential recruits: The elderly, many of whom would readily accept a life in the military rather than die of old age, and whose deaths, in any event, would not create the multi-generational demographic damage that ensued when large numbers of healthy young adults were blown out of the gene pool at the end of an alien's weapon.

Presented with this bountiful new pool of potential recruits, the Colonial Defense Forces found it had the luxury of making certain staffing choices. The CDF would no longer ask colonists to serve in the CDF; this had the salutary effect of allowing colonists to focus on developing their new worlds and making as many second-generation colonists as their planets could handle. It also eliminated a key source of political tension between the colonists and their government. Now that the young adults of the colonies were no longer extracted from their homes and families to die on battlefields trillions of miles away, the colonists were largely unconcerned with the ethical issues surrounding genetically modified soldiers, particularly ones who had, after all, volunteered to fight.

In the stead of colonists, the CDF chose to select its recruits from the inhabitants of humanity's ancestral home, Earth. The Earth held billions of people: More people on that single globe, in fact, than existed on all the human colonies combined. The pool of potential recruits was enormous—so large that the CDF further limited its pool, choosing to take its recruits from comfortable and industrialized nations whose economic circumstances allowed their citizens to survive well into their later years, and whose social blueprints created both an overemphasis on the desirability of youth and a parallel and profound national psychic discomfort with aging and death. These senior citizens were patterned by their societies to be excellent and eager recruits for the CDF; the CDF quickly discovered that these senior citizens would join up for a military tour even in the absence of detailed information about what such a tour entailed—and indeed, recruitment yields were higher the less the recruits knew. Recruits assumed military service in the CDF was like military service on Earth. The CDF was content to let the assumption stand.

Recruiting seniors from industrialized nations proved so successful that the Colonial Union protected its recruiting pool by banning colonists from those nations, selecting its colonist pool from nations whose economic and social problems encouraged the more ambitious of its young people to get the hell out as soon as humanly possible. This division of military and colonist recruitment paid rich dividends for the Colonial Union in both areas.

The military recruitment of senior citizens presented the CDF with one unexpected problem: A fair number of recruits died before they could join the service, victims of heart attacks, strokes, and too many cheeseburgers, cheesecakes and cheese curds. The CDF, who took genetic samples from its recruits, eventually found itself stocked with a library of human genomes it wasn't doing anything with. The CDF also found itself with a desire and also a need to continue experimenting with the body models of the Colonial Defense Forces to improve their design, without cutting into the effectiveness of the fighting force it already had.

Then came a breakthrough: an immensely powerful, compact, semi-organic computer, thoroughly integrated with the human brain, which in a moment of profoundly inappropriate branding was lightly dubbed the BrainPal. For a brain already filled with a life's worth of knowledge and experience, the BrainPal offered a critical assist in mental ability, memory storage and communication.

But for a brain that was literally *tabula rasa*, the BrainPal offered even more.

Robbins peered into the crèche, where the body lay, held into place by a suspension field. "He doesn't look much like Charles Boutin," he said to Wilson.

Wilson, who was now making last-minute adjustments on the hardware that contained Boutin's recorded consciousness, didn't look up from his work. "Boutin was an unmodified human," he said. "He was well into middle age when we knew him. He probably looked something like this guy when he was twenty. Minus the green skin, cat's eyes and other modifications. And he probably wasn't as fit as this body is. I know *I* wasn't as fit in real life at age twenty as I am now. And I don't even have to exercise."

"You have a body engineered to take care of itself," Robbins reminded Wilson.

"And thank God. I'm a doughnut fiend," Wilson said.

"All you have to do to get it is get shot at by every other intelligent species in the universe," Robbins said.

"That is the catch," Wilson noted.

Robbins turned back to the body in the crèche. "All those changes won't mess with the transfer of consciousness?"

"Shouldn't," Wilson said. "The genes relating to brain development are unaltered in this guy's new genome. That's Boutin's brain in there. Genetically, at least."

"And how does his brain look?" Robbins asked.

"It looks good," Wilson said, tapping the monitor of the crèche controller. "Healthy. Prepared."

"Think this will work?" Robbins asked.

"Got me," Wilson said.

"Good to see we're brimming with confidence," Robbins said.

Wilson opened his mouth to respond but was interrupted as the door opened and Generals Mattson and Szilard stepped through, accompanied by three Special Forces decanting technicians. The techs went straight to the crèche; Mattson went to Robbins, who saluted along with Wilson.

"Tell me this is going to work," Mattson said, returning the salute.

"Lieutenant Wilson and I were just talking about that," Robbins said, after a nearly imperceptible pause.

Mattson turned to Wilson. "And, Lieutenant?"

Wilson pointed to the body in the crèche, being fussed over by the technicians. "The body is healthy, and so is the brain. The BrainPal is functioning perfectly, which is no surprise. We've been able to integrate Boutin's consciousness pattern into the transfer machinery with surprisingly few problems, and the test runs we've done suggest there won't be a problem with transmission. In theory, we should be able to transfer the consciousness like we do with any consciousness."

"Your words sound confident, Lieutenant, but your voice doesn't," Mattson said.

"There are a lot of uncertainties, General," Wilson said. "Usually the subject is conscious when he transfers over. That helps with the process. We don't have that here. We won't know whether the transfer is successful until we wake up the body. This is the first time we've tried a transfer without two brains involved. If it's not actually Boutin's consciousness in there, the pattern won't take. Even if it *is* Boutin's consciousness in there, there's no guarantee it will imprint. We've done everything we can to assure a smooth transfer. You've read the reports. But there's still so much involved that we don't know about. We know all the ways it could go right, but not all the ways it could go wrong."

"Do you think it will work or don't you?" Mattson said.

"I think it will work," Wilson said. "But we need to have a healthy respect for all the things we don't know about what we're doing. There's a lot of room for error. Sir."

"Robbins?" Mattson said.

"Lieutenant Wilson's assessment seems right to me, General," Robbins said.

The technicians finished their assessment and reported to General Szilard, who nodded and walked over to Mattson. "The techs say we're ready," Szilard said.

Mattson glanced at Robbins, then Wilson. "Fine," he said. "Let's get this over with."

* * *

The Colonial Defense Special Forces build soldiers using a simple recipe: First, start with a human genome. Then *subtract*.

The human genome comprises roughly twenty thousand genes made from three billion base pairs, spread out over twenty-three chromosomes. Most of the genome is "junk"—portions of the sequence that do not code for anything in the final product of the DNA: a human being. Once nature puts a sequence into DNA it appears reluctant to remove it even if it does nothing at all.

Special Forces scientists are not nearly so precious. With each new body model they build, their first step is to strip out the redundant and switched-off genetic matter. What is left is a lean, mean, streamlined DNA sequence that is completely useless; editing the human genome destroys its chromosomal structure, leaving it unable to reproduce. But this is just a first step. Reassembling and replicating the new genome is several steps away.

The new, small DNA sequence features every gene that makes a human what he or she is, and this simply is not good enough. The human genotype does not allow the human phenotype the plasticity the Special Forces require, which is to say: Our genes can't make the superhumans Special Forces soldiers need to be. What is left of the human genome is now rent apart, redesigned and reassembled to build the genes that will code for substantially enhanced abilities. This process can require the introduction of additional genes or genetic material. The genes that come from other humans usually present little problem with their incorporation, since the human genome is fundamentally designed to accommodate genetic information from other human genomes (the process by which this is usually, naturally and enthusiastically accomplished is called "sex"). Genetic material from other terrestrial species is also relatively easy to incorporate, seeing as all life on Earth features the same genetic building blocks and are related to each other genetically.

Incorporating genetic material from non-terrestrial species is substantially more difficult. Some planets evolved genetic structures roughly similar to Earth's, incorporating some if not all the nucleotides involved in terrestrial genetics (perhaps not coincidentally, the intelligent species of these planets have been known to consume humans from time to time; the Rraey, for example, found humans quite tasty). But most alien species have genetic structures and components wildly different from terrestrial creatures. Using their genes is not a simple matter of cutting and pasting.

Special Forces solved this problem by reading the DNA equivalent of the alien species into a compiler that then spat out a genetic "translation" in terrestrial DNA format—the resulting DNA, if allowed to develop, would create an entity as close to the original alien creature in appearance and function as it was possible to get. Genes from the transliterated creatures were then wrought into the Special Forces DNA.

The end result of this genetic designing was DNA that described a creature based on a human, but not a human at all—inhuman enough that the creature, if allowed to develop from this step, would be an unholy agglomeration of parts, a monstrous creature that would have sent its spiritual godmother Mary Wollstonecraft Shelley far around the bend. Having pulled the DNA so far from humanity, Special Forces scientists now sculpted the genetic message to jam the creature they were forming back into a recognizably human shape. Among themselves the scientists brooded that this was the most difficult step; some (quietly) questioned its utility. None of them, it should be noted, looked any less than human themselves.

The DNA, sculpted to offer its owner superhuman abilities in human shape, is now finally assembled. Even with the addition of non-native genes, it is substantially leaner than the original human DNA; supplemental coding causes the DNA to organize into five chromosomal pairs, down substantially from an unaltered human's twenty-three and only one more than a fruit fly. While Special Forces soldiers are provided the sex of their donor and genes related to sexual development are preserved in the final genetic reduction, there is no Y-chromosome, a fact that made the earliest Special Forces–assigned scientists (the male ones) vaguely uncomfortable.

The DNA, now assembled, is deposited into a vacant zygote shell, which is itself placed into a developmental crèche, and the zygote gently prodded into mitotic division. The transformation from zygote to full-fledged embryo proceeds at a profoundly accelerated rate, producing metabolic heat levels that come close to denaturing the DNA. The developmental crèche fills with heat-transferring fluid packed with nanobots, which saturate the developing cells and act as heat sinks for the rapidly growing embryo.

And still Special Forces scientists are not done lowering the percentage of humanity in their soldiers. After the biological overhaul come the technological upgrades. Specialized nanobots injected into the rapidly developing Special Forces embryo head to two destinations. Most head to marrow-rich bone cores, where the nanobots digest the marrow and mechanically breed in its place to create SmartBlood, with better oxygen-carrying capacity than true blood, more efficient clotting and near-immunity to disease. The rest migrate to the fast-expanding brain and lay the groundwork for the BrainPal computer, which when fully constructed will be the size of an aggie marble. This marble, nestled deep in the brain, is surrounded by a dense network of antennae that sample the electric field of the brain, interpreting its wishes and responding through outputs integrated into the soldiers' eyes and ears.

There are other modifications as well, many experimental, tested within a small birthing group to see if they offer any advantages. If they do, these modifications are made more widely available among the Special Forces and hit the list for potential upgrades for the next generation of the Colonial Defense Forces' general infantry. If they don't, the modifications die with their test subjects.

The Special Forces soldier matures to the size of a newborn human in just over twenty-nine days; in sixteen weeks, provided the crèche's adequate metabolic management, it has grown to adult size. CDF attempts to shorten the developmental cycle resulted in bodies that fried in their own metabolic heat. Those embryos and bodies that didn't simply abort and die suffered DNA transcription errors, giving rise to developmental cancers and fatal mutations. Sixteen weeks was pushing the edge of DNA chemical stability as it was. At the end of sixteen weeks, the developmental crèche sends a synthetic hormone washing through the body, resetting the metabolic levels to normal tolerances.

During development the crèche exercises the body to strengthen it and allow its owner to use it from the moment he or she becomes conscious; in the brain, the BrainPal helps develop general neural pathways, stimulate the organs' processing centers, and prepare for the moment its owner was brought to consciousness, to help ease the transition from nothing to something.

For most Special Forces soldiers, all that was left at this

point was "birth"—the decanting process followed by the quick and (usually) smooth transition into military life. For one Special Forces soldier, however, there was still one more step to take.

Szilard signaled to his techs, who began their tasks. Wilson focused again on his hardware, and waited for the signal to begin the transfer. The techs gave the all clear; Wilson sent the consciousness on its way. Machinery hummed quietly. The body in the crèche remained still. After a few minutes Wilson conferred with the techs, then with Robbins, who came over to Mattson. "It's done," he said.

"That's it?" Mattson said, and glanced over the body in the crèche. "*He* doesn't look any different. He still looks like he's in a coma."

"They haven't woken him up yet," Robbins said. "They want to know how you want to do it. Normally with Special Forces soldiers they wake them up with their Brain-Pals switched to conscious integration. It gives the soldier a temporary sense of self until he can create one of his own. But since there may already be a consciousness in there, they didn't want to turn that on. It might confuse the person in there."

Mattson snorted; he found the idea amusing. "Wake him up without switching on the BrainPal," he said. "If that's Boutin in there, I don't want him confused. I want him talking."

"Yes, sir," Robbins said.

"If this thing worked, he'll know who he is as soon as he's conscious, right?" Mattson said.

Robbins glanced over to Wilson, who could hear the conversation; Wilson give a half shrug, half nod. "We think so," Robbins said.

"Good," Mattson said. "Then I want to be the first thing he sees." He walked over to the crèche and placed himself in front of the unconscious body. "Tell them to wake up the son of a bitch," he said. Robbins nodded to one of the techs, who jabbed a finger at the control board she had been working from.

The body jolted, precisely the way people do in the twilight between wakefulness and sleep, when they suddenly feel like they are falling. Its eyelids fluttered and twitched, and flew open. Eyes darted momentarily, seemingly confused, and then fixed on Mattson, who leaned in and grinned.

"Hello, Boutin," Mattson said. "Bet you're surprised to see me."

The body strained to move its head closer to Mattson, as if to say something. Mattson leaned in obligingly.

The body screamed.

General Szilard found Mattson in the head down the hall from the decanting lab, relieving himself.

"How's the ear?" Szilard asked.

"What kind of goddamned question is that, Szi?" Mattson said, still facing the wall. "*You* get a screaming earful from a babbling idiot and tell me how it feels."

"He's not a babbling idiot," Szilard said. "You woke up a newborn Special Forces soldier with his BrainPal switched off. He didn't have any sense of himself. He did what any newborn would do. What did you expect?"

"I expected Charles fucking Boutin," Mattson said, and shook. "That's why we bred that little fucker in the crèche, if you'll recall."

"You knew it might not work," Szilard said. "I told you. Your people told you."

"Thanks for the recap, Szi," Mattson said. He zipped and moved over to the sink. "This little adventure has just been one big goddamn waste of time."

"He still might be useful," Szilard said. "Maybe the consciousness needs time to settle."

"Robbins and Wilson said his consciousness would be there as soon as he woke up," Mattson said. He waved his hands under the faucet. "Goddamn automatic faucet," he said, and finally covered the sensor completely with his hand. The water kicked on.

"This is the first time anyone's done something like this," Szilard said. "Maybe Robbins and Wilson were wrong."

Mattson barked out a short laugh. "Those two *were* wrong, Szi, no maybes about it. Just not in the way you suggest. Besides, are *your* people going to babysit a full-grown, man-sized infant while you're waiting for his 'consciousness to settle'? I'd be guessing 'no,' and I'm sure as hell not going to do it. Wasted too much time on this as it is." Mattson finished washing his hands and looked around for the towel dispenser.

Szilard pointed to the far wall. "Dispenser is out," he said.

"Well, of *course* it is," Mattson said. "Humanity can build soldiers from the DNA up but it can't stock a head with fucking paper towels." He shook his hands violently and then wiped the excess moisture on his pants.

"Leaving the issue of paper towels to the side," Szilard said, "does this mean you're relinquishing the soldier to me? If you are, I'm going to have his BrainPal turned on, and get him into a training platoon as soon as possible."

"You in a rush?" Mattson said.

"He's a fully developed Special Forces solider," Szilard said. "While I wouldn't say I am in a rush, you know as well as I do what the turnover rate for Special Forces is. We always need more. And let's just say I have faith that this particular soldier may yet turn out to be useful."

"Such optimism," Mattson said.

Szilard smiled. "Do you know how Special Forces soldiers are named, General?" Szilard asked.

"You're named after scientists and artists," Mattson said.

"Scientists and philosophers," Szilard said. "Last names, anyway. The first names are just random common names. I'm named after Leo Szilard. He was one of the scientists who helped to build the first atomic bomb, a fact that he would later come to regret."

"I know who Leo Szilard was, Szi," Mattson said.

"I didn't mean to imply you didn't, General," Szilard said. "Although you never know with you realborn. You have funny gaps in your knowledge."

"We spend most of our later educational years trying to get laid," Mattson said. "It distracts most of us from stockpiling information about twentieth-century scientists."

"Imagine that," Szilard said, mildly, and then continued on his train of thought. "Aside from his scientific talents, Szilard was also good at predicting things. He predicted both of Earth's world wars in the twentieth century and other major events. It made him jumpy. He made it a point to live in hotels and always have a packed bag ready. Just in case."

"Fascinating," Mattson said. "What's your point?"

"I don't pretend to be related to Leo Szilard in any way," Szilard said. "I was just assigned his name. But I think I share his talent for predicting things, especially when it comes to wars. I think this war we've got coming is going to get very bad indeed. That's not just speculation; we've been gathering intelligence now that my people know what to look for. And you don't have to be in possession of intelligence to know that humanity going up against three different races makes for bad odds for us." Szilard motioned his head in the direction of the lab. "This soldier may not have Boutin's memories, but he's still got Boutin in him—in his genes. I think it'll make a difference, and we're going to need all the help we can get. Call him my packed bag."

"You want him because of a hunch," Mattson said.

"Among other things," Szilard said.

"Sometimes it really shows that you're a teenager, Szi," Mattson said.

"Do you release this soldier to me, General?" Szilard asked.

Mattson waved, dismissively. "He's yours, General," he said. "Enjoy. At least I won't have to worry about this one turning traitor."

"Thank you," Szilard said.

"And what are you going to do with your new toy?" Mattson asked.

"For starters," Szilard said, "I think we'll give him a name."

FOUR He came into the world like most newborns do: screaming.

The world around him was formless chaos. Something was close to him and making noises at him when the world showed up; it frightened him. Suddenly it went away, leaking loud noises as it went.

He cried. He tried to move his body but could not. He cried some more.

Another form approached; based on his only previous experience, he yelled in fear and tried to get away. The form made noise and movement.

Clarity.

It was as if corrective lenses had been placed on his consciousness. The world snapped into place. Everything remained unfamiliar, but everything also seemed to make sense. He knew that even though he couldn't identify or name anything he saw, it all had names and identities; some portion of his mind surged into life, itching to label it all but could not.

The entire universe was on the tip of his tongue.

::Can you perceive this?:: the form—the person—in front of him asked. And he could. He could hear the question, but he knew that no sound had been made; the question had been beamed directly into his brain. He didn't know how he knew this, or how it was done. He also didn't know how to respond. He opened his mouth to reply.

::Don't,:: the person in front of him said. ::Try *sending* me your reply instead. It's faster than speaking. It's what we all do. Here's how.::

Inside his head instructions appeared, and more than instructions, an awareness that suggested that anything he didn't understand would be defined, explained and placed into context; even as he thought this he felt the instructions he'd been sent expand, individual concepts and ideas branching off into pathways, searching for their own meanings in order to give him a framework he could use. Presently it coalesced into one big idea, a gestalt that allowed him to respond. He felt the urge to respond to the person in front of him grow; his mind, sensing this, offered up a series of possible responses. Each unpacked itself as the instructions had, offering up understanding and context as well as a suitable response.

All of this took slightly under five seconds.

::I perceive you,:: he said, finally.

::Excellent,:: the person in front of him said. ::I am Judy Curie.::

::Hello, Judy,:: he said, after his brain unpacked for him the concepts of names and also the protocols for responding to those who offer their names as identification. He tried to give his name, but came up blank. He was suddenly confused.

Curie smiled at him. ::Having a hard time remembering your name?:: she asked.

::Yes,:: he said.

::That's because you don't have one yet,:: Curie said. ::Would you like to know what your name is?::

::Please,:: he said.

::You are Jared Dirac,:: Curie said.

Jared sensed the name unpack in his brain. Jared: A biblical name (the definition of *biblical* unpacked, leading him to the definition of *book* and to the Bible, which he did not read, as he sensed the reading and subsequent unpacking thereof would take more than a few seconds), son of Mahalalel and the father of Enoch. Also the leader of the Jaredites in the Book of Mormon (another book left unpacked). Definition: The descendant. *Dirac* had a number of definitions, most derived from the name of Paul Dirac, a scientist. Jared had previously unpacked the meaning of names and the implications of naming conventions; he turned to Curie.

::I am a descendant of Paul Dirac?:: he asked.

::No,:: Curie said. ::Your name was randomly selected from a pool of names.::

::But my first name means *descendant*,:: Jared said. ::And last names are family names.::

::Even among realborn, first names usually don't mean anything,:: Curie said. ::And among us, last names don't either. Don't read too much into your names, Jared.::

Jared thought about this for a few moments, letting these ideas unpack themselves. One concept, "realborn," refused to unpack itself; Jared noted it for further exploration but left it alone for now. ::I am confused,:: he said, eventually.

Curie smiled. ::You will be confused a lot to begin with,:: she said.

::Help me be less confused,:: Jared said.

::I will,:: Curie said. ::But not for too long. You have been born out of sequence, Jared; your training mates already have a two-day start on you. You must integrate with them as soon as possible, otherwise you may experience a delay from which you may never recover. I will tell you what I can while I take you to your training mates. They will fill in the rest. Now, let's get you out of that crèche. Let's see if you can walk as well as think.::

The concept of "walk" unpacked itself as the restraints holding Jared in the crèche removed themselves. Jared braced himself and pushed forward, out of the crèche. His foot landed on the floor.

::One small step for man,:: Curie said. Jared was surprised that the unpacking inherent in that phrase was substantial.

::First order of business,:: Curie said, as she and Jared walked through Phoenix Station. ::You think you're thinking, but you're not.::

Jared's first impulse was to say *I don't understand,* but he held back, intuiting for the first time that this was likely to be his response to most things in the near future. ::Please explain,:: he said instead.

::You are newly born,:: Curie said. ::Your brain—your *actual* brain—is entirely empty of knowledge and experience. In its place, a computer inside your head known as a BrainPal is feeding you knowledge and information. Everything you think you understand is being processed by your BrainPal and fed back to you in a way you can grasp. It is also the thing that is offering you suggestions on how to respond to things. Mind the crowd.:: Curie weaved to avoid a clot of CDF soldiers in the middle of the walkway.

Jared weaved with her. ::But I feel like I *almost* know so much,:: Jared said. ::Like I knew it once but now I don't.::

::Before you are born, the BrainPal conditions your brain,:: Curie said. ::It helps set down neural pathways common in all humans, and prepares your brain for rapid learning and processing of information. That's why it feel likes you know things already, because your brain has been *prepared* to learn it. For the first month of your life, everything feels like *déjà vu*. Then you learn it, it gets stored in your actual brain, and you stop using your Brain-Pal like a crutch. Because of the way we are, we can gather information and process it—and learn it—several times faster than Realborn.::

Jared stopped, partly to let his mind unpack everything Curie had just said to him, but partly because of something else. Curie, sensing he had stopped, stopped as well. ::What?:: she said.

::That's the second time you've used that word. "Realborn." I can't find out what that means.::

::It's not something they put in your BrainPal,:: Curie said. She began walking again and motioned at the other soldiers on the walkway. ::"Realborn" is *them*. They're people who are born as babies and have to develop over a very long period of time—years. One of them who is sixteen years old might not know as much as you do now, and you've been alive for about sixteen minutes. It's really an inefficient way to do things, but it's the way it's done naturally and they think that means it's a good thing.::

::You don't?:: Jared asked.

::I don't think it's good or bad, aside from being inefficient,:: Curie said. ::I'm just as alive as they are. "Realborn" is a misnomer—we're really born too. Born, live, die. It's the same.::

::So we're just like them,:: Jared said.

Curie glanced back. ::No,:: she said. ::*Not* just like them. We're designed to be better physically and mentally. We move faster. We think faster. We even talk faster than they do. The first time you talk to a realborn it will seem like they're moving at half speed. See, watch.:: Curie stopped, appeared to look confused, and then tapped the shoulder of a soldier who was walking by.

"Excuse me," she said, and she used her mouth to say it. "I was told there was a commissary on this level where I could get a really excellent hamburger, but I can't seem to find it. Can you help me?" Curie was speaking in a voice that mirrored to a close degree the voice Jared heard in his head . . . but slower, slow enough that for the briefest of seconds Jared had a hard time understanding what she was saying.

"Sure," the soldier said. "The place you're thinking of is a couple hundred yards from here. Just keep going the direction you're going and you'll hit it. It's the first commissary you come to."

"Great, thanks," Curie said, and started walking again. ::See what I mean?:: she said to Jared. ::It's like they're retarded or something.::

Jared nodded absently. His brain had unpacked the concept of "hamburger," which lead to an unpacking of "food," which caused him to realize something else entirely. ::I think I'm hungry,:: he said to Curie.

::Later,:: Curie said. ::You should eat with your training mates. It's part of the bonding experience. You'll be doing most things with your training mates.::

::Where are your training mates?:: Jared asked.

::What a funny question,:: Curie said. ::I haven't seen them for years. You rarely see your training mates once you're *out* of training. After that you're assigned to wherever they need you, and then you integrate with your squad and platoon. Right now I'm integrated with one of the Special Forces platoons that decants soldiers as they're born.::

Jared unpacked the concept of "integration" in his brain, but found he was having a problem understanding it. He tried working through it again but was interrupted by Curie, who kept talking. ::You're going to be at a disadvantage to the rest of your training mates, I'm afraid,:: she said to him. ::They woke up integrated and are already used to each other. It might take them a couple of days to get used to you. You should have been decanted and integrated at the same time as they were.::

::Why wasn't I?:: Jared asked.

::Here we are,:: Curie said, and stopped at a door.

::What's in here?:: Jared asked.

::Shuttle pilot ready room,:: Curie said. ::Time to get you a ride. Come on.:: She opened the door for him, then followed him inside.

Inside the room were three pilots, playing poker. "I'm looking for Lieutenant Cloud," Curie said.

"He's the one who's currently getting his ass kicked," said one of the pilots, who tossed a chip into the pot. "Raise ten."

"*Badly* kicked," said one of the others, and threw in his own chip. "See your ten."

"Your words of scorn would hurt so much more if we were actually playing for money," said the third, who by process of elimination would be Lieutenant Cloud. He dropped in three chips. "I see your ten, and raise you twenty."

"This is one of the drawbacks of having an all-expenses-paid tour of hell," said the first pilot. "When everything's paid for, they don't have a reason to give you money. Call."

"If I knew I was going to be working for socialists, I never would have signed up," said the second. "Call."

"Well, then, in addition to being dumb, you'd also be dead, wouldn't you?" Cloud said. "Talk about being alienated from your labor. You'd be alienated from *everything*. Also, you'd be out a couple hundred dollars on this hand." He spread out his cards. "Snake eyes and a trio of snowmen. Read 'em and weep."

"Aw, crap," said the first pilot.

"Thank God for Karl Marx," intoned the second.

"That's the first time in history *that* has been said at a poker table," said Cloud. "You should be proud."

"Oh, I am," said the other pilot. "But please don't tell my momma. It would break her Texan heart."

"Your secret is safe with me," Cloud said.

"Lieutenant Cloud," Curie said. "Sometime this century would be good."

"My apologies, Lieutenant," Cloud said. "I just had to finish up some ritual humiliation. I'm sure you understand."

"Not really," Curie said, and nodded to Jared. "Here is the recruit you need to take to Camp Carson. You should already have the orders and clearance."

"Probably," Cloud said, and paused for a minute as he accessed his BrainPal. "Yeah, it's here. It looks like my shuttle has been prepped and fueled too. Let me file a flight plan and we'll be good to go." He looked at Jared. "Taking anything with you but you?"

Jared glanced over to Curie, who shook her head. "No," he said. "It's just me." He was mildly startled to hear the sound of his own voice speaking for the first time, and how slowly the words formed. He became acutely aware of his tongue and its movement in his mouth; it made him vaguely queasy.

Cloud took in the exchange between Jared and Curie wordlessly and then motioned to a chair. "Okay, then. Have a seat, pal. I'll be with you in a just a minute."

Jared sat and looked up at Curie. ::What do I do now?:: he asked.

::Lieutenant Cloud here will shuttle you down to Phoenix, to Camp Carson, where you'll join your training mates,:: Curie said. ::They're a couple days ahead in their training but the first few days are mostly just for integrating and stabilizing personalities. You probably haven't missed any real training.::

::Where will you be?:: Jared asked.

::I'll be here,:: Curie said. ::Where did you think I would be?::

::I don't know,:: Jared said. ::I'm scared. I don't know anyone but you.::

::Be calm,:: Curie said, and Jared felt an emotional sense come from her to him. His BrainPal processed the wash of feeling and unpacked the concept of "empathy" for him. ::In a couple of hours you'll be integrated with your training mates and you'll be fine. It'll make more sense then.::

::Okay,:: Jared said, but felt doubtful.

::Good-bye, Jared Dirac,:: Curie said, and with a small smile turned and left. Jared felt her presence in his mind for a few moments longer until finally, as if Curie suddenly remembered she left the connection open, it shut off. Jared found himself revisiting their brief time together; his BrianPal unpacked the concept of "memory" for him. The concept of memory provoked an emotion; his BrainPal unpacked the concept of "intriguing."

"Hey, can I ask you a question?" Cloud asked Jared, after they had begun their descent to Phoenix.

Jared considered the question, and the ambiguity of its structure that allowed for multiple interpretations. In one sense, Cloud had answered his question by asking it; he was clearly capable of asking Jared a question. Jared's BrainPal suggested, and Jared agreed, this was not likely the correct interpretation of the question. Presumably Cloud knew he was procedurally capable of asking questions, and if he previously was not, he would be now. As Jared's BrainPal unpacked and sorted additional intepretations, Jared found himself hoping that one day he'd be able to hit upon the correct interpretation of sentences without having to do endless unpacking. He'd been alive and aware just over an hour and already it was tiresome.

Jared considered his options and after a period of time that seemed long to him but seemed to be imperceptible to the pilot, ventured forth with the answer that seemed most appropriate in the context.

"Yes," Jared said.

"You're Special Forces, right?" Cloud asked.

"Yes," Jared said.

"How old are you?" Cloud asked.

"Right now?" Jared asked.

"Sure," Cloud said.

Jared's BrainPal informed him he had an internal chronometer; he accessed it. "Seventy-one," Jared said.

Cloud looked over. "Seventy-one years old? That makes you pretty old for Special Forces, from what they tell me."

"No. Not seventy-one years," Jared said. "Seventy-one minutes."

"No shit," Cloud said.

This required another quick moment of interpretational choices. "No shit," Jared said, finally.

"Damn, that's just weird," Cloud said.

"Why?" Jared asked.

Cloud opened his mouth, closed it, and shot a look at Jared. "Well, not that *you* would know this," Cloud said. "But for most of humanity it'd be a little odd to be having a conversation with someone who is only slightly more than an hour old. Hell, you weren't even alive when I started that poker game back there. At your age most humans have barely got the hang of breathing and taking a dump."

Jared consulted his BrainPal. "I'm doing one of those right now," he said.

This got an amused noise out of Cloud. "That's the first time I've ever heard one of you guys tell a joke," he said.

Jared considered this. "It's not a joke," he said. "I really *am* doing one of those right now."

"I sincerely hope it's the breathing," Cloud said.

"It is," Jared said.

"That's fine, then," Cloud said, and chuckled again. "For a minute there, I thought I'd discovered a Special Forces soldier with a sense of humor."

"I'm sorry," Jared said.

"Don't be sorry, for God's sake," Cloud said. "You're barely an hour old. People can live to a hundred without developing a sense of humor. I've got at least one ex-wife who went through most of our marriage without cracking a smile. At least you have the excuse of just being born. She had no excuse."

Jared considered this. "Maybe you weren't funny."

"See," Cloud said, "now you *are* telling jokes. So you are really seventy-one minutes old."

"Seventy-three now," Jared said.

"How is it so far?" asked Cloud.

"How is what so far?"

"This," Cloud said, and motioned around him. "Life. The universe. Everything."

"It's lonely," Jared said.

"Huh," Cloud said. "Didn't take you long to figure that one out."

"Why do you think Special Forces soldiers have no sense of humor?" Jared asked.

"Well, I don't want to suggest it's *impossible*," Cloud said. "I've just never seen it. Take your friend back on Phoenix Station. The fair Miss Curie. I've been trying to get a laugh out of her for a year now. I see her every time I transport a gaggle of you Special Forces down to Camp Carson. So far, no luck. And maybe it's just her, but then from time to time I try to get a laugh out of the Special Forces soldiers I'm transporting down to the surface or bringing back up. So far, nothing."

"Maybe you really aren't funny," Jared suggested again.

"There you go again with the jokes," Cloud said. "No, I thought it might be that. But I don't have any problems making ordinary soldiers laugh, or at least some of them. Ordinary soldiers don't really have a lot of contact with you Special Forces types, but those of us that have all agree that you have no sense of humor. The best we can figure it's because you're born grown-up, and developing a sense of humor takes time and practice."

"Tell me a joke," Jared said.

"Are you serious?" Cloud said.

"Yes," Jared said. "Please. I'd like to hear a joke."

"Now I have to think of a joke," Cloud said, and thought for a moment. "Okay, I thought of one. I don't suppose you have any idea who Sherlock Holmes is."

"I do now," Jared said, after a couple of seconds.

"That's a very scary thing you just did," Cloud said. "All

right. Here's the joke. Sherlock Holmes and his sidekick Watson decide to go camping one night, right? So they make a campfire, have a bottle of wine, roast some marshmallows. The usual. Then they bed down for the night. Later that night, Holmes wakes up and wakes up Watson. 'Watson,' he says, 'look up at the sky and tell me what you see.' And Watson says, 'I can see the stars.' 'And what does that tell you?' Holmes asks. And Watson starts listing things, like that there are millions of stars, and how a clear sky means good weather for the next day, and how the majesty of the cosmos is proof of a powerful God. When he's done, he turns to Holmes and says 'What does the night sky tell you, Holmes?' And Holmes says, 'That some bastard has stolen our tent!' "

Cloud looked over at Jared, expectantly, and then frowned after Jared stared back blankly. "You don't get it," Cloud said.

"I get it," Jared said. "But it's not funny. Someone *did* steal their tent."

Cloud stared at Jared for a moment, and then laughed. "I may not be funny, but you sure the hell are," he said.

"I'm not trying to be," Jared said.

"Well, that's part of your charm," Cloud said. "All right, we're entering the atmosphere. Let's put the joke-swapping on hold while I focus on getting us down in one piece."

Cloud left Jared on the tarmac of Camp Carson's skyport. "They know you're here," he said to Jared. "Someone is on the way to get you. Just stay put until they arrive."

"I will," Jared said. "Thank you for the trip and the jokes."

"You're welcome for both," Cloud said, "although I

think one was probably more useful to you than the other." Cloud stuck out his hand; Jared's BrainPal unpacked the protocol and Jared stuck his hand into Cloud's. They shook.

"And now you know how to shake hands," Cloud said. "That's a skill to have. Good luck, Dirac. If I fly you back after your training maybe we'll swap a few more jokes."

"I'd like that," Jared said.

"Then you better learn a few between now and then," Cloud said. "Don't expect me to do all the heavy lifting. Look, someone's heading your way. I think he's for you. Bye, Jared. Stay clear of the lifters, now." Cloud disappeared back in his shuttle to prepare for his departure. Jared stepped away from the shuttle.

::Jared Dirac,:: said the rapidly approaching person.

::Yes,:: Jared responded.

::I am Gabriel Brahe,:: the other man said. ::I am the instructor assigned to your training squad. Come with me. It's time to meet the others you'll be training with.:: As quickly as he reached Jared, Brahe turned around and started walking toward camp. Jared hustled to follow.

::You were speaking to that pilot,:: Brahe said as they walked. ::What were you discussing?::

::He was telling me jokes,:: Jared said. ::He said that most soldiers don't think Special Forces have a sense of humor.::

::Most soldiers don't know anything about the Special Forces,:: Brahe said. ::Listen, Dirac, don't do that again. You're just adding fuel to their prejudices. When realborn soldiers say Special Forces don't have a sense of humor, it's their way of insulting us. Suggesting we're less human than they are. If we don't have a sense of humor we're like every other subhuman automaton humanity has made up to amuse itself. Just another emotionless robot for them to feel superior to. Don't give them a chance to do that.::

After Brahe's rant was unpacked by his BrainPal, Jared thought back to his talk with Cloud; he didn't sense that Cloud was suggesting he was superior to Jared. But Jared also had to admit he was only a couple of hours old. There were a lot of things he could be missing. Still, Jared felt a dissonance between what Brahe was saying and his own experience, small though it might be. He ventured a question.

::*Do* Special Forces have a sense of humor?:: he asked.

::Of course we do, Dirac,:: said Brahe, glancing back briefly. ::Every human has a sense of humor. We just don't have *their* sense of humor. Tell me one of your pilot's jokes.::

::All right,:: Jared said, and repeated the Sherlock Holmes joke.

::See, now, that's just stupid,:: Dirac said. ::As if Watson wouldn't know that the tent was missing. This is the problem with realborn humor. It's predicated on the notion that someone's an idiot. There's no shame in not having *that* sense of humor.:: Brahe radiated a sense of irritation; Jared decided not to carry the topic of conversation further.

Instead, Jared asked, ::Is everyone here Special Forces?::

::They are,:: Brahe said. ::Camp Carson is one of only two training sites for Special Forces, and the only training base of any kind on Phoenix. See how the camp is ringed by forest?:: Brahe motioned with his head to the edge of the camp, where earth-derived trees and native Phoenix megaflora competed for supremacy. ::We're more than six hundred klicks from civilization in any direction.::

::Why?:: Jared asked, remembering Brahe's earlier comment about the realborn. ::Are they trying to keep us away from everybody else?::

::They're trying to keep everybody else away from *us*,:: Brahe said. ::Special Forces training isn't like training for realborn. We don't need the distraction of regular CDF or civilians, and they might misinterpret what they see here. It's best if we're left alone to do what we do, and to do our training in peace.::

::I understand I am behind in my training,:: Jared said.

::Not in your training,:: Brahe said. ::In your integration. We begin training tomorrow. But your integration is as important. You can't train if you're not integrated.::

::How do I integrate?:: Jared asked.

::First, you meet your training mates,:: Brahe said, and stopped at the door of a small barracks. ::Here we are. I've told them you're here; they're waiting for you.:: Brahe opened the door to let Jared in.

The barracks were sparsely furnished and like every barracks for the last few centuries. Two rows of eight beds lined the sides of the barracks. In and among them fifteen men and women sat and stood, eyes focused on Jared. He felt overwhelmed by the sudden attention; his BrainPal unpacked the concept of "shy." He felt the urge to say hello to his training mates, and was suddenly aware that he wasn't sure how to speak to more than one person through his BrainPal; near simultaneously he realized that he could just open his mouth and speak. The complexities of communication confounded him.

"Hello," he said, finally. Some of his future training mates smiled at his primitive form of communication. None of them returned the salutation.

::I don't think I'm off to a good start,:: Jared sent to Brahe.

::They're waiting to say their introductions after you've integrated,:: Brahe said.

::When do I do that?:: Jared asked.

::Now,:: Brahe said, and integrated Jared with his training mates.

Jared had about a tenth of a second of mild surprise as his BrainPal informed him that as his superior officer, Brahe had limited access to his BrainPal, and then that datum was superseded by the fact that suddenly there were fifteen other people in Jared's head, and he was in the heads of fifteen other people. An uncontrolled bolt of information seared through Jared's consciousness as fifteen life stories poured into him and his own meager store of experiences branched into fifteen pipelines. Salutations and introductions were unnecessary and superfluous; in an instant Jared knew and felt everything he would need to know about these fifteen strangers who were now as intimately part of him as any human could be with another human. It was a mercy that each of these lives was unnaturally short.

Jared collapsed.

::That was interesting,:: Jared heard someone say. Almost instantaneously he recognized the comment as coming from Brian Michaelson, even though he'd never communicated with him before.

::I hope he's not planning to make a habit out of *that*,:: another voice said. Steve Seaborg.

::Give him a break,:: said a third voice. ::He was born without being integrated. It's a lot to handle all of a sudden. Come on, let's get him up off the floor.::

Sarah Pauling.

Jared opened his eyes. Pauling was kneeling down next to him; Brahe and his other training mates formed a curious semicircle above him.

::I'm fine,:: Jared sent to all of them, keying his response to the squad-wide communication channel, which included Brahe. The choice to do this came naturally, part of the info dump of the integration. ::I didn't know what to expect. I didn't know how to handle it. But I'm fine now.::

From his training mates radiated emotions like auras, each different: concern, confusion, irritation, indifference, amusement. Jared followed the amused emotion back to its source. Pauling's amusement was visible not only as an emotional aura but from the quirky smile on her face.

::Well, you don't seem all that much worse for wear,:: Pauling said. She stood up and then extended her hand. ::Up you go,:: she said. Jared reached up, took her hand, and pulled himself up.

::Sarah's got a pet,:: Seaborg said, and there was a ripple of amusement among some of the squad, and a strange emotional ping that Jared suddenly recognized as a form of laughter.

::Shut up, Steve,:: Pauling said. ::You hardly know what a pet is.::

::Doesn't make him less of one,:: Seaborg said.

::Doesn't make you less of a jerk,:: Pauling said.

::I'm not a pet,:: Jared said, and suddenly all eyes turned to him. He found it less intimidating than the first time, now that he had all of them in his head. He focused his attention on Seaborg ::Sarah was simply being kind to me. It doesn't make me a pet, it doesn't make her my master. It just means she was nice enough to help me off the floor.::

Seaborg audibly snorted and then removed himself from the semicircle, intently finding something else to be interested in. A few others broke off to join him. Sarah turned to Brahe. ::Does this happen with every training squad?:: she asked.

Brahe smiled. ::Did you think being inside each other's heads would make it *easier* for you to get along? There's no place to hide. What's *really* surprising is that one of you hasn't taken a punch at someone else yet. Usually by this time I have to pry a couple of trainees apart with a crowbar.:: Brahe turned to Jared. ::You going to be all right?::

::I think so,:: Jared said. ::I need a little time to sort everything out. I have a lot in my head, and I'm trying to figure out where it all goes.::

Brahe looked back over to Pauling. ::You think you can help him sort it out?::

Pauling smiled. ::Sure,:: she said.

::You've got Dirac-watch, then,:: Brahe said. ::We start training tomorrow. See if you can get him up to speed with everything before then.:: Brahe walked off.

::I guess I really am your pet,:: Jared said.

A wash of amusement flowed off Pauling toward Jared ::You're a funny man,:: she said.

::You're the second person to tell me that today,:: Jared said.

::Yeah?:: Pauling said. ::Know any good jokes?::

Jared told Pauling the one about Sherlock Holmes. She laughed out loud.

FIVE Training for Special Forces soldiers takes two weeks. Gabriel Brahe began the training of Jared's squad— formally the 8th Training Squad—by asking its members a question.

::What makes you different than other human beings?:: he asked. ::Raise your hand when you have the answer.::

The squad, arrayed in a ragged semicircle in front of Brahe, was silent. Finally Jared raised his hand. ::We're smarter, stronger and faster than other humans,:: he said, remembering the words of Judy Curie.

::Good guess,:: Brahe said. ::But wrong. We are designed to be stronger, faster and smarter than other humans. But we're that way as a *consequence* of what makes us different. What makes us different is that alone among humans, we were born with a purpose. And that purpose is simple: to keep humans alive in this universe.::

The members of the squad looked around at each other. Sarah Pauling raised her hand. ::Other people help to keep humans alive. We saw them on Phoenix Station, on our way here.::

::But they weren't *born* for it,:: Brahe said. ::Those people you saw—the realborn—are born without a plan. They're born because biology tells humans to make more humans; but it doesn't consider what to *do* with them after that. Realborn go for years without the slightest clue what they're going to do with themselves. From what I understand, some of them never actually figure it out. They just walk through life in a daze and then fall into their graves at the end of it. Sad. And inefficient.

::You may do many things in your life, but walk though it in a daze will not be one of them,:: Brahe continued. ::You are born to protect humanity. And you are *designed* for it. Everything in you down to your genes reflects that purpose. It's why you are stronger, and faster, and smarter than other humans::—Brahe nodded toward Jared—::and why you are born as adults, ready to fight quickly, effectively and efficiently. It takes the Colonial Defense Forces three months to train realborn soldiers. We do the same training—and more—in two weeks.::

Steve Seaborg raised his hand. ::Why does it take the realborn so long to train?:: he asked.

::Let me show you,:: Brahe said. ::Today is the first day of training. Do you know how to stand at attention, or other basic drill maneuvers?:: The members of the training squad looked at Brahe blankly. ::Right,:: Brahe said. ::Here come your instructions.::

Jared sensed his brain flooding with new information. The perception of this knowledge sat thickly upon his consciousness, unorganized; Jared sensed his BrainPal funneling the information into the right places, the now-familiar unpacking process launching branching paths of information that connected with things that Jared, now a full day old, already knew.

Now Jared knew the military protocols of parade drilling. But more than that came an unexpected emotion that arose natively in his own brain, and was amplified and augmented by the integrated thoughts of his training squad: Their informal array in front of Brahe, with some standing, some sitting and some leaning back on the steps of their barracks, felt *wrong*. Disrespectful. Shameful. Thirty seconds later they were in four orderly rows of four, standing at attention.

Brahe smiled. ::You got it on the first try,:: he said. ::Parade rest.:: The squad shifted into parade rest position, feet apart, hand behind backs. ::Excellent,:: Brahe said. ::At ease.:: The squad visibly relaxed.

::If I told you how long it takes to train Realborn to do just that much just as well as you did, you wouldn't believe me,:: Brahe said. ::Realborn need to drill, to repeat, to practice again and again to get things right, to learn to do the things you that you will learn and absorb in one or two sessions.::

::Why don't the realborn train this way?:: asked Alan Millikan.

::They can't,:: Brahe said. ::They have old minds, set in their ways. They have a hard enough time just learning to use a BrainPal. If I tried sending them the drill protocols like I just sent to you, their brains simply couldn't handle it. And they can't integrate—they can't share information between themselves automatically like you do, and like all Special Forces do. They're not designed for it. They're not born to it.::

::We're superior, but there are realborn soldiers,:: Steven Seaborg said.

::Yes,:: Brahe said. ::Special Forces are less than one percent of the entire CDF fighting force.::

::If we're so good, why are there so few of us?:: asked Seaborg.

::Because the realborn are scared of us,:: Brahe said.

::What?:: asked Seaborg.

::They doubt us,:: Brahe said. ::They've bred us for the purpose of defending humanity, but they're not sure we're human enough. They've designed us to be superior soldiers but they worry our design is flawed. So they see us as less than human and assign us the jobs they fear might make *them* less than human. They make just enough of us for those jobs but no more than that. They don't trust us because they don't trust themselves.::

::That's stupid,:: Seaborg said.

::That's ironic,:: Sarah Pauling said.

::It's both,:: Brahe said. ::Rationality is not one of humanity's strong points.::

::It's hard to understand why they think that way,:: Jared said.

::You're right,:: Brahe said, looking at Jared. ::And you've unintentionally hit on the racial flaw of the Special Forces. Realborn have a hard time trusting the Special Forces—but Special Forces have a hard time *understanding* the realborn. And it doesn't go away. I'm eleven years old::—a sharp pinging of amazement ricocheted through the squad; none of them could conceive of being that ancient—::and I swear to you I still don't *get* the realborn most of the time. Their sense of humor, which you and I have discussed, Dirac, is only the most obvious example of this. This is why in addition to physical and mental conditioning, Special Forces training also includes specialized training into the history and culture of the realborn soldiers you will meet, so you can understand them, and how they see *us*.::

::Seems like a waste of time,:: Seaborg said. ::If the realborn don't trust us, why should we protect them?::

::It's what we were born to do—:: Brahe said.

::I didn't *ask* to be born,:: Seaborg said.

::—and you're thinking like a realborn,:: Brahe said. ::*We* are human too. When we fight for humans, we fight for ourselves. No one asks to be born, but we *are* born, and we *are* human. We fight for ourselves, as much as for any other human. If we don't defend humanity, we'll be just as dead as the rest of them. This universe is implacable.::

Seaborg lapsed into silence, but his irritation broadcast itself.

::Is this all we do?:: Jared asked.

::What do you mean?:: Brahe said.

::We are born for this purpose,:: Jared said. ::But can we do something else too?::

::What do you suggest?:: Brahe asked.

::I don't know,:: Jared said. ::But I'm only a day old. I don't know much.:: This got pings of amusement, and a smile from Brahe.

::We are born to this, but we're not slaves,:: Brahe said. ::We serve a term of service. Ten years. After that, we can choose to retire. Become like the realborn and colonize. There's even a colony set aside for us. Some of us go there; some of us choose to blend in with the realborn in the other colonies. But most of us stay with the Special Forces. I did.::

::Why?:: Jared asked.

::It's what I was born for,:: Brahe repeated. ::And I'm good at it. You're all good at it. Or will be, soon enough. Let's get started.::

::We do a lot of things faster than realborn,:: Sarah Pauling said, dipping into her soup. ::But I'm guessing that eating isn't one of them. If you ate too fast you'd choke. That'd be funny, but it would also be bad.::

Jared sat across from her at one of the two mess tables

assigned to the 8th Training Squad. Alan Millikan, curious about the differences between realborn and Special Forces training, discovered that realborn trained in platoons, not squads, and that Special Forces training squads were not the same size as squads in the CDF. Everything that Millikan learned on the subject was sent to the other members of the 8th and added to their store of information. Thus another benefit of integration made itself known: Only one member of the 8th had to learn something in order for all the other members to know it.

Jared slurped at his own soup. ::I think we eat faster than realborn,:: he said.

::Why is that?:: Pauling said.

Jared took a big spoonful of soup. "Because if they talk and eat soup at the same time, *this* happens," he said, drooling soup out of his mouth as he spoke.

Pauling put her hand to her mouth to stifle a laugh. ::Uh-oh,:: she said, after a second.

::What?:: Jared said.

Pauling glanced left, then right. Jared looked around, and saw the entire mess hall looking at him. Jared belatedly realized that everyone could, in fact, hear him speak when he used his mouth. Nobody else in the mess hall had spoken with their mouth during the entire meal. Jared suddenly realized that the last time he'd heard anyone else speak was when Lieutenant Cloud offered his farewells. Speaking out loud was weird.

::Sorry,:: he said, on a general band. Everyone returned to their food.

::You're making a fool of yourself,:: Steven Seaborg, down the table, said to Jared.

::It was just a joke,:: Jared said.

::"It was just a *joke*,":: Seaborg said, mockingly. ::Idiot.::

::You're not very nice,:: Jared said.

::"You're not very *nice*,":: Seaborg said.

::Jared may be an idiot, but at least he can think up his own words,:: Pauling said.

::Hey, shut up, Pauling,:: Seaborg said. ::No one asked *you* to butt in.::

Jared began to respond when an image popped up in his visual field. Squat, misshapen humans were arguing about something in high-pitched voices. One of them began to mock the other by repeating his words, like Seaborg had been doing to Jared.

::Who are these people?:: Seaborg asked. Pauling too looked mystified.

Gabriel Brahe's voice popped into their heads. ::They're children,:: he said. ::Immature humans. And they're having an argument. I'll have you note they are arguing just like you were.::

::He started it,:: Seaborg said, looking for Brahe in the mess hall. He was at a far table, eating with other officers. He didn't turn to look at the trio.

::One of the reasons the realborn don't trust us is because they're convinced we're children,:: Brahe said. ::Emotionally stunted children in adult-sized bodies. And the thing about that is, they're *right*. We have to learn to control ourselves like adults do, just like all humans do. And we have far less time to learn how to do it.::

::But—:: Seaborg began.

::Quiet,:: Brahe said. ::Seaborg, after our afternoon drill you have an assignment. From your BrainPal you can access Phoenix's data net. You get to research etiquette and interpersonal conflict resolution. Find out as much as you can, and share it with the rest of the 8th by the end of the evening. Do you understand me?::

::Yes,:: Seaborg said. He glanced over at Jared accusingly and then lapsed silently into his food.

::Dirac, you get an assignment too. Read *Frankenstein*. See where it takes you.::

::Yes, sir,:: Jared said.

::And don't drool any more soup,:: Brahe said. ::You look like an ass.:: Brahe dropped his connection.

Jared looked over to Pauling. ::How come you didn't get in trouble?:: he asked her.

Pauling dipped the spoon into her soup. ::My food stays where it's supposed to,:: she said, and swallowed. ::And I don't act like a child.:: And then she stuck out her tongue.

The afternoon drill introduced the 8th to their weapon, the MP-35A "Empee" assault rifle. The rifle was bonded to its owner by use of BrainPal authentication; from that point forward only its owner or another human with a BrainPal could fire the rifle. This cut down on the chance of a CDF soldier having his own weapon used against him. The MP-35A was additionally modified for Special Forces soldiers to take advantage of their integration abilities; among other things, the MP-35A could be fired remotely. Special Forces had used this ability to fatally surprise any number of curious aliens over the years.

The MP-35A was more than a simple rifle. It could, at the discretion of the soldier using it, fire rifled bullets, shot, grenades, or small guided missiles. It also featured flamethrower and particle beam settings. Any of this panoply of ammunition was constructed on the fly by the MP-35A out of a heavy metallic block of nanobots. Jared wondered idly how the rifle managed the trick; his Brain-Pal obligingly unpacked the physics behind the weapon, leading to a massive and terribly inconvenient unpacking of general physical principles while the 8th was on the shooting range. Naturally all of this unpacked information was forwarded onto the rest of the squad, all of whom looked over at Jared with varying levels of irritation.

::Sorry,:: Jared said.

By the end of the long afternoon, Jared had mastered the MP-35A and its myriad of options. Jared and another recruit named Joshua Lederman focused on the options the Empee allowed for its rifled bullets, experimenting with different designs of the bullets and assessing the advantages and disadvantages of each, duly noting each to the other members of the squad.

When they were ready to move on to the other ammunition options available to them, Jared and Lederman took ample advantage of the information about those weapons fed in by other members of the 8th to master those options as well. Jared had to admit that whatever personal problems he might have with Steven Seaborg, if he ever needed someone to wield a flamethrower for him, Seaborg was going to be his first choice. Jared told him so as they hiked back to the barracks; Seaborg ignored him and pointedly started a private conversation with Andrea Gell-Mann.

After dinner, Jared staked out a spot on the steps of the barracks. After a brief tutorial from his BrainPal (and taking care to cache his explorations so as not to repeat his embarrassing data spill from earlier in the day), he signed on the Phoenix's public data net and secured a copy of Mary Wollstonecraft Shelley's *Frankenstein, or the Modern Prometheus*, revised third edition, 1831.

Eight minutes later he finished it and was in something of a state of shock, intuiting (correctly) why Brahe had him read it: He and all the members of the 8th—all of the Special Forces soldiers—were the spiritual descendants of the pathetic creature Victor Frankenstein had assembled from the bodies of the dead and then jolted into life. Jared saw how Frankenstein felt pride in creating life, but how he feared and rejected the creature once that life had been given; how the creature lashed out, killing the doctor's family and friends, and how creator and created were finally consumed in a pyre, their fates interlocked. The allusions between the monster and the Special Forces were all too obvious.

And yet. As Jared considered whether it was the fate of the Special Forces to be as misunderstood and reviled by the realborn as the monster was by his creator, he thought back on his brief encounter with Lieutenant Cloud. Cloud certainly didn't seem terrified or repulsed by Jared; he'd offered his hand to him, a gesture that Victor Frankenstein, pointedly, refused from the monster he created. Jared also considered the fact that while Victor Frankenstein was the creator of the monster, *his* creator—Mary Shelley—implicitly offered pity and empathy to the monster. The real human in this story was a rather more complex person than the fictional one, and more inclined toward the creature than its fictional creator.

He thought about *that* for a good, solid minute.

Jared greedily sought out links to the text, quickly alighting on the famous 1931 motion picture version of the story and devouring it at ten times speed, only to find himself greatly disappointed; the eloquence of Shelley's monster was replaced by a sad shambling grunter. Jared quickly sampled other filmed versions but was continually disappointed. The monster he identified with was almost nowhere to be seen in any of these, even in the versions that paid lip service to the original text. Frankenstein's monster was a joke; Jared gave up on filmed versions before he reached the end of the twenty-first century.

Jared tried another tack and sought out stories of other created beings, and was soon acquainted with Friday, R. Deneel Olivaw, Data, HAL, Der Machinen-Mensch, Astro Boy, the various Terminators, Channa Fortuna, Joe the Robot Bastard and all manner of other droids, robots, computers, replicants, clones and genetically-engineered whatsits that were as much the spiritual descendants of Frankenstein's monster as he was. Curious, Jared moved backward in time from Shelley to find Pygmalion, golems, homunculi and clockwork automatons.

He read and watched the sad and often dangerous humorlessness of many of these creatures, and how it was used to make them objects of pity and comic relief. He now understood why Brahe was touchy about the whole sense of humor issue. Implicit in that touchiness was the idea that Special Forces were misrepresented in their depictions by the realborn, or so Jared thought until he went searching for literature or recorded entertainments featuring the Special Forces as main characters.

There were none. The Colonial era was rife with entertainments about the Colonial Defense Forces and its military battles and events—the Battle for Armstrong seemed a particularly revisited topic—but in none of them were the Special Forces even hinted at; the closest thing was a series of pulpy novels published on Rama colony featuring the adventures of a secret force of erotic superhuman soldiers, who mostly overcame fictional alien species by having energetic sex with them until they surrendered. Jared, who at this time understood sex largely in the reproductive sense, wondered why anyone would think this was a viable way to conquer one's enemies. He decided that he was probably missing something important about this sex thing and filed it away to ask Brahe about later.

In the meantime there was the mystery of why, from the point of view of the fiction output of the colonies, the Special Forces didn't exist.

But that was for another night, perhaps. Jared was eager to share his current explorations with his squad mates. He uncached his findings and released them to the others. As he did he became aware that he wasn't the only one sharing discoveries; Brahe had assigned homework to the majority of the 8th, and these explorations came flooding into his perception. Among them, etiquette and the psychology of conflict resolution from Seaborg (whom Jared could sense rolling his eyes at almost all of the material he was passing along); major battles of the Colonial Defense Forces from Brian Michaelson; animated cartoons from a recruit named Jerry Yukawa; human physiology from Sarah Pauling. Jared made a note to make fun of her later for giving him grief about his own assignment earlier in the day. His BrainPal merrily began to unpack everything Jared's mates had learned. Jared leaned back into the stairs and watched the sunset as the information branched and expanded.

Phoenix's sun had well and truly set by the time Jared had unpacked all his new learning; he sat inside the small pool of light illuminating the barracks and watched Phoenix's analogue to insects zip around the light. One of the more ambitious of these small creatures landed on Jared's arm and plunged a needle-like proboscis into his flesh to suck out his fluids. A few seconds later it was dead. The nanobots in Jared's SmartBlood, alerted to their situation by his BrainPal, self-immolated inside the tiny animal, using the oxygen they carried as a combustible agent. The poor creature crisped from the inside; miniscule and almost invisible wisps of smoke vented out of its spicules. Jared wondered who it was who programmed that sort of defensive response into his BrainPal and SmartBlood; it seemed hateful of life in its intent.

Maybe the realborn are right to fear us, Jared thought.

From inside the barracks Jared could perceive his squad mates arguing about what they'd learned that night; Seaborg just declared Frankenstein's monster a bore. Jared launched himself inside to defend the monster's honor.

During the morning and afternoons of the first week, the 8th learned to fight, to defend, and to kill. In the evenings they learned everything else, including some things Jared suspected were of questionable value.

In the early evening of the second day, Andrea Gell-Mann introduced the 8th to the concept of profanity, which she picked up at lunch and shared just before dinner. At dinner members of the 8th enthusiastically told each other to pass the fucking salt, you fucking sack of shit, until Brahe told them to quit that goddamn shit, cock-suckers, because it got old pretty goddamn quick. There was general agreement that Brahe was correct, until Gell-Man taught the squad to swear in Arabic.

On the third day, members of the 8th asked for, and received, permission to enter the mess hall kitchens and use the ovens and certain ingredients. The next morning the other training squads at Camp Carson were presented with enough sugar cookies for every recruit (and their superior officers).

On the fourth day the members of the 8th tried to tell each other jokes they'd found on the Phoenix data net, and mostly failed to make them work; by the time their Brain-Pals unpacked the context of the joke, it was no longer funny. Only Sarah Pauling seemed to be laughing most of the time, and it was eventually determined she was laughing because she thought it was funny that none of the rest of them could tell a joke. No else thought that was funny, to which Pauling laughed hard enough to fall off her cot.

They all agreed *that* was funny.

Also, puns were all right.

On the fifth day, during which the afternoon was spent in an informational session about the disposition of the human colonies and their relationship with other intelligent species (which was to say, bad all the time), the 8th critically evaluated pre–Colonial era speculative fiction and entertainments about interstellar wars with aliens. The verdicts were reasonably consistent. *The War of the Worlds* met with approval until the ending, which struck the 8th as a cheap trick. *Starship Troopers* had some good action scenes but required too much unpacking of philosophical ideas; they liked the movie better, even though they recognized it was dumber. *The Forever War* made most of the 8th unaccountably sad; the idea that a war could go on that long was almost unfathomable to a group of people who were a week old. After watching *Star Wars* everyone wanted a lightsaber and was irritated that the technology for them didn't really exist. Everyone also agreed the Ewoks should all die.

Two classics stuck with them. *Ender's Game* delighted them all; here were soldiers who were just like them, except smaller. The main character was even bred to fight alien species like they were. The next day the members of the 8th greeted each other with the salutation ::Ho, Ender,:: until Brahe told them to knock it off and pay attention.

The other was *Charlie's Homecoming*, one of the last books before the Colonial era began, and one of the last books, therefore, to be able to imagine a universe other than what it was—one where the alien species humanity would meet greeted them with a welcome instead of a weapon. The book was eventually adapted into a film; by that time it was clear it wasn't science fiction, but fantasy, and a bitter one at that. It was a flop. The members of the 8th were transfixed by both the book and film, captivated by a universe they could never have, and one which would never have had them, because they wouldn't be needed.

On the sixth day, Jared and the rest of the 8th finally figured out what that sex thing was all about.

On the seventh day, and as a direct consequence of the sixth day, they rested.

::They're not of questionable value,:: Pauling said to Jared about the things they had learned, as they lay together in her cot late on the seventh day, intimate but not sexual. ::Maybe all of these things don't have any use in themselves, but they bring all of us closer together.::

::We *are* closer together,:: Jared agreed.

::Not just like this.:: Pauling pressed herself into Jared briefly, and then released. ::Closer as people. As a group. All of those things you mentioned are silly. But they're training us how to be human.::

It was Jared's turn to press himself into Pauling, snuggling into her chest. ::I like being human,:: he said.

::I like you being human too,:: Pauling said, and then audibly giggled.

::For fuck's sake, you two,:: Seaborg said. ::I'm trying to sleep over here.::

::Grump,:: Pauling said. She looked down at Jared to see if he would add anything, but he had fallen asleep. She kissed him lightly on the top of his head and then joined him.

* * *

::In your first week, you physically trained to do all the things realborn soldiers can do,:: Brahe said. ::Now it's time to train you to do things only you can do.::

The 8th stood at the beginning of a long obstacle course.

::We've already run this course,:: said Luke Gullstrand.

::Good of you to notice, Gullstrand,:: Brahe said. ::For your observational skills, you get to be the first one to run it today. Stay here. The rest of you spread out over the length of the course, please, as equally as possible.::

Presently members of the 8th were strung along the course. Brahe turned to Gullstrand. ::You see the course?:: he asked.

::Yes,:: Gullstrand said.

::Do you think you could run it with your eyes closed?::

::No,:: Gullstrand said. ::I don't remember where everything is. I'd trip over something and kill myself.::

::Do you all agree?:: Brahe asked. There were pings of affirmation. ::And yet, all of you will run this course with your eyes closed before we leave here today. Because you have an ability that will allow you to do this: your integration with your squad members.::

From around the squad came varying levels of skepticism. ::We use our integration to talk and to share data,:: said Brian Michaelson. ::This is something entirely different.::

::No. Not different at all,:: Brahe said. ::The nighttime assignments of the last week were not just punishments and frivolity. You already knew that through your BrainPal and your pre-birth conditioning you could learn quickly *by yourself*. In the last week—without realizing it—you've learned to share and absorb immense amounts of information *between yourselves*. There is no difference between that information and *this*. Pay attention.::

Jared gasped audibly, as did other members of the 8th.

In his head was not only the presence of Gabriel Brahe but an intimate sensation of his physical presence and personal situation, overlaid on Jared's own consciousness.

::Look through my eyes,:: Brahe said. Jared focused on the command and then had a sickening sense of vertigo as his perspective wheeled from his own vantage point to Brahe's. Brahe panned left and right and Jared saw himself, looking toward Brahe. Brahe snapped off the view.

::It gets easier the more you do it,:: Brahe said. ::And from now on, in every combat practice you *will* do it. Your integration gives you situational awareness that is unique in this universe. All intelligent species share information in combat however they can—even realborn soldiers keep a communication channel open through their BrainPals during battle. But only Special Forces have this level of sharing, this level of tactical awareness. It's at the heart of how we work and how we fight.

::As I said, last week you covered the basics of fighting like the realborn—you learned how to go into combat as an individual. Now it's time to learn to fight like Special Forces, to *integrate* your combat skills with your squad. You will learn to share and you will learn to trust what is shared with you. It will save your life and it will save the life of your squad mates. This will be the hardest and most important thing you learn. So pay attention.::

Brahe turned back to Gullstrand. ::Now, close your eyes.::

Gullstrand hesitated. ::I don't know if I can keep my eyes closed,:: he said.

::You're going to have to trust your squad,:: Brahe said.

::I trust the squad,:: Gullstrand said. ::I just don't trust *myself*.:: This got a sympathetic round of pings.

::That's part of the exercise as well,:: Brahe said. ::Off you go.::

Gullstrand closed his eyes and took a step. From his vantage point halfway down the course, Jared could see Jerry Yukawa, in the first position, lean in slightly, as if physically attempting to close the distance between his mind and Gullstrand's. Gullstrand's passage through the obstacle course was slow but became progressively steadier; just before reaching Jared, and just after balancing on a wood beam suspended over mud, Gullstrand began to a smile. He had become a believer.

Jared felt Gullstrand reach for his point of view. Jared give him full access to his senses and passed along a feeling of encouragement and assurance. He sensed Gullstrand receiving it and briefly passing along his thanks; then Gullstrand focused on scaling the rope wall Jared stood to the side of. At the top, he felt Gullstrand move on to the next squad member in the line, fully confident. By the end of the course, Gullstrand was moving nearly at full speed.

::Excellent,:: Brahe said. ::Gullstrand, take over that last position. Everybody else move down one position. Yukawa, you're up.::

Two run-throughs later, not only were members of the squad sharing their perspective with the squad mate running the course; the squad mate on the course was sharing his shared perspective with them, giving everyone who hadn't run through the course a preview of what was coming up next. The next run-through after that had the squad mates on the side sharing vantage points with the person one station up from them, so they could better help the person on the course when they shifted into the position. By the time Jared was himself on the court, the entire squad had fully integrated their perspectives and were getting the hang of quickly sampling another perspective and picking out the relevant information without breaking from their own point of view. It was like being in two places at once.

When Jared was on the course himself, he exulted in the strange intelligence of it all, at least until the beams over the mud, when his borrowed visual vantage point suddenly wheeled away from where his feet were. Jared missed his footing and fell flat into the mud.

::Sorry about that,:: said Steven Seaborg a few seconds later, as Jared pulled himself out, eyes open. ::Got bit by something. Distracted me.::

::*Bullshit*,:: Alan Millikan sent to Jared, privately. ::*I was one station down and looking right at him. He didn't get bit.*::

Brahe cut in. ::Seaborg, when you're in combat, letting a squad mate get killed because of a bug bite is the sort of thing that gets you on the unfortunate side of an airlock,:: he said. ::Keep it in mind. Dirac, keep moving.::

Jared closed his eyes and put one foot in front of the other.

::What does Seaborg have against me, anyway?:: Jared asked Pauling. The two of them were practicing fighting with their combat knives. The squad members practiced for five minutes with each other member of the squad, with their integration sense on full. Fighting someone who was intimately aware of your internal state of mind made it an interesting extra challenge.

::You really don't know?:: Pauling said, circling with her knife held casually in her left hand. ::It's two things. One, he's just a jerk. Two, he likes me.::

Jared stopped circling. ::What?:: he said, and Pauling attacked viciously, feinting right and then slashing upward toward Jared's neck with her left hand. Jared stumbled backward and right to avoid the slashing; Pauling's knife switched hands and stabbed downward, missing Jared's leg by about a centimeter. Jared righted himself and settled into a defensive position.

::You distracted me,:: he said, circling again.

::You distracted yourself,:: Pauling said. ::I just took advantage of it when it happened.::

::You won't be happy until you cut open an artery,:: Jared said.

::I won't be happy until you shut up and focus on trying to kill me with that knife,:: Pauling said.

::You know,:: Jared began, and suddenly leaned back; he felt Pauling's intent to slash a fraction of a second before she made her lunge. Before she could pull back Jared leaned back in, inside the reach of her extended arm, and brought up the blade in his right hand to touch it lightly to her rib cage. Before it got there Pauling brought her head up and jammed it into the bottom of Jared's jaw. There was an audible *clack* as Jared's teeth slammed together; Jared's field of vision whited out. Pauling took advantage of Jared's stunned pause to step back and sweep his legs out from under him, spilling him flat on his back. When Jared came to, Pauling had pinned his arms with her legs and held her knife directly on top of a carotid artery.

::*You know,*:: Pauling said, mocking Jared's last words, ::if this were real combat I'd have sliced four of your arteries by now and moved on to whoever was next.:: Pauling sheathed her knife, and took her knees off his arms.

::Good thing we're not in real combat,:: Jared said, and propped himself up. ::About Seaborg—::

Pauling punched Jared square in the nose; his head snapped back. Pauling's knife was back at his throat, and her legs pinning his arms, a fraction of a second later.

::What the hell?:: Jared said.

::Our five minutes aren't up,:: Pauling said. ::We're still supposed to be fighting.::

::But you—:: Jared began. Pauling jabbed him in the neck and drew SmartBlood. Jared exclaimed aloud.

::There's no "but you—":: Pauling said. ::Jared, I like you, but I've noticed that you don't *focus*. We're friends, and I know you think that means that we can have a nice conversation while we're doing this. But I swear to you that the next time you give me an opening like you did just now, I'm going to cut your throat. Your SmartBlood will *probably* keep you from dying. And it'll keep you from thinking that just because we're *friends* doesn't mean I won't seriously hurt you. I like you too much. And I don't want you to die in real combat because you're thinking about something else. The things we'll be fighting in real combat aren't going to pause for conversation.::

::You'd watch out for me in combat,:: Jared said.

::You know I would,:: Pauling said. ::But this integration thing only goes so far, Jared. You have to watch out for yourself.::

Brahe told them their five minutes were up. Pauling let Jared off the floor. ::I'm serious, Jared,:: Pauling said, after she hauled him up. ::Pay attention next time, or I'll cut you bad.::

::I know,:: Jared said, and touched his nose. ::Or punch me.::

::True,:: Pauling said, and smiled. ::I'm not picky.::

::So all that about Seaborg liking you was just to distract me,:: Jared said.

::Oh, no,:: Pauling said. ::It's completely true.::

::Oh,:: Jared said.

Pauling laughed aloud. ::There you go, getting distracted again,:: she said.

* * *

Sarah Pauling was one of the first to get shot; she and Andrea Gell-Mann were ambushed as they were scouting a small valley. Pauling went down immediately, shot in the head and the neck; Gell-Mann managed to identify the locations of the shooters before a trio of shots in the chest and abdomen brought her down. In both cases their integration with the rest of the squad collapsed; it felt as if they were ripped out bodily from the squad's pooled consciousness. Others fell in short order, gutting the squad and sending its remaining members into disarray.

It was a bad war game for the 8th.

Jerry Yukawa compounded the problem by getting shot in the leg. The training suit he was wearing registered the "hit" and froze the mobility to the limb; Yukawa fell midstride and barely kicked his way behind the boulder Katherine Berkeley had gotten behind a few seconds before.

::You were supposed to lay down suppressing fire,:: Yukawa said, accusingly.

::I *did*,:: Berkeley said. ::I *am*. There is one of me and five of them. *You* do better::

The five members of the 13th Training Squad who had trapped Yukawa and Berkeley behind the boulder sent another volley their way. The members of the 13th felt the simulated mechanical kick of their training rifles while their BrainPals visually and aurally simulated the bullets tearing down the tiny cul-de-sac of a valley; Yukawa and Berkeley's BrainPals correspondingly simulated some of these bullets smacking the bulk of the boulder and others whining as they shot past. The bullets weren't real but they were as real as fake could get.

::We could use a little help here,:: Yukawa said to Steven Seaborg, who was the commander for the exercise.

::We hear you,:: Seaborg said, and then turned to look at Jared, his only other surviving soldier, who was standing mutely looking at him. Four members of the 8th were still standing (only figuratively speaking in the case of Yukawa), while seven members of the 13th were roaming the forest. The odds weren't good.

::Stop looking at me like that,:: Seaborg said. ::This isn't my fault.::

::I didn't say anything,:: Jared said.

::You were thinking it,:: Seaborg said.

::I wasn't thinking it, either,:: Jared said. ::I was reviewing data.::

::Of what?:: Seaborg asked.

::Of how the 13th moves and thinks,:: Jared said. ::From the other members of the 8th before they died. I'm trying to see if there's something we can use.::

::Can you do it a little quicker?:: Yukawa said. ::Things are looking mighty bleak on this end.::

Jared looked over to Seaborg. Seaborg sighed. ::Fine,:: he said. ::I'm open to suggestion. What have you got.::

::You're going to think I'm crazy,:: Jared said. ::But there's something I've noticed. So far, neither us or them look up very much.::

Seaborg looked up into the forest canopy, looking at the sunlight peek through the canopy of native Terran trees and their Phoenix equivalent, thick, bamboo-like stalks that threw off impressive branches. The two types of flora did not compete genetically—they were naturally incompatible because they developed on different worlds—but they competed for sunlight, reaching as far into the sky as possible and branching thickly to offer scaffolding for leaves and leaf-equivalents to do their photosynthetic work.

::We don't look up because there's nothing up there but trees,:: Seaborg said.

Jared started counting off seconds in his head. He got as far as seven before Seaborg said, ::Oh.::

::Oh,:: Jared agreed. He popped up a map. ::We're here. Yukawa and Berkeley are here. There's forest all the way between here and there.::

::And you think we can get from here to there in the trees,:: Seaborg said.

::That's not the question,:: Jared said. ::The question is whether we can do it fast enough to keep Yukawa and Berkeley alive, and quietly enough not to get ourselves killed.::

Jared quickly discovered that walking through the trees was an idea better in theory than in execution. He and Seaborg almost fell twice within the first two minutes; moving from branch to branch required rather more coordination then either expected. The Phoenix trees' branches were not nearly as load bearing as they assumed and the Terran trees featured a surprising number of dead branches. Their progress was slower and louder than they would have liked.

A rustling came from the east; in separate trees Jared and Seaborg hugged trunks and froze. Two members of the 13th walked out of the brush thirty meters away and six meters below Jared's position. The two were alert and wary, looking and listening for their quarry. They didn't look up.

Out of the corner of his eye, Jared saw Seaborg slowly reach toward his Empee. ::Wait,:: Jared said. ::We're still in their peripheral vision. Wait until we're behind them.:: The two soldiers edged forward, putting Jared and Seaborg behind them; Seaborg nodded to Jared. They silently unslung their Empees, stabilized as best they could, and sighted in on the backs of the soldiers. Seaborg gave the order; bullets flew in a short burst. The soldiers stiffened and fell.

::The rest have Yukawa and Berkeley pinned down,:: Seaborg said. ::Let's get cracking.:: He set off. Jared was amused at how Seaborg's take-charge spirit, so recently dampened, had suddenly returned.

Ten minutes later, Yukawa and Berkeley were down to the last of their ammunition, and Jared and Seaborg caught sight of the remaining members of the 13th. To the left of them, eight meters below, two soldiers were camped behind a large fallen tree; to the right and about thirty me-ters forward, another pair were behind a collection of boulders. These soldiers were keeping Yukawa and Berke-ley busy while the fifth soldier quietly flanked their posi-tion. All of them had their backs to Jared and Seaborg.

::I'll take the ones by the log; you take the ones at the boulders,:: Seaborg said. ::I'll tell Berkeley about the flanker but tell her not to get him until we get our guys. No point giving ourselves away.:: Jared nodded; now that Seaborg was feeling confident, his planning was getting better. Jared filed that datum away to consider later, and moved to steady himself in their tree, putting his back against the trunk and hooking his left foot under a lower branch for additional support.

Seaborg moved one branch lower on the tree to get around a branch that was impeding his sight line. The branch he stepped on, dead, cracked loudly under his weight and collapsed, falling out of the tree in what seemed the loudest possible way. Seaborg lost his footing and grabbed wildly at the branch below where he had stepped, dropping his Empee; four soldiers on the ground turned, looked up and saw him dangling there helplessly. They raised their weapons.

::Shit,:: Seaborg said, and looked up at Jared.

Jared fired in automatic-burst mode at the two soldiers at the boulders. One seized up and fell; the other dove around the boulders. Jared swiveled and fired on the soldiers at the log; he didn't hit anything but unnerved them long enough to switch his Empee to guided-missile mode and fire at the space between the two soldiers. The simulated rocket peppered both with virtual bits of shrapnel. They fell. Jared turned just in time to see the remaining soldier at the boulder lining up her shot. He launched a guided missile at her as she pulled her trigger. Jared felt his ribs go stiff and painful as his training suit constricted, and fumbled his Empee. He'd been shot, but the fact he didn't drop out of the tree told him he was still alive.

Training exercise! Jared was so pumped full of adrenaline that he thought he might pee himself.

::A little help here,:: Seaborg said, and reached over with his left hand for Jared to pull him up just as the fifth soldier, who had circled back, shot him in the right shoulder. Seaborg's entire arm stiffened in its suit; he let go of the branch he was dangling from. Jared grabbed at his left hand and caught him before his fall had gained momentum. Jared's left leg, still hooked under its branch by the foot, strained painfully from the additional load put on it.

On the ground, the soldier lined up his shot; virtual bullets or not, Jared knew if he were shot the stiffening of his suit would make him drop Seaborg and probably fall himself. Jared reached over with his right hand, grabbed his combat knife and threw hard. The knife buried itself in the meat of the soldier's left thigh; the soldier collapsed, screaming and pawing gingerly at the knife until Berkeley came up behind him and shot him into immobility.

::The 8th wins the war game,:: Jared heard Brahe say. ::I'm relaxing the training suits now for everyone who is still frozen. Next war game matchups in thirty minutes.:: The pressure on Jared's right side was suddenly and considerably relieved, as was the stiffness of Seaborg's suit. Jared hauled him up and then they both carefully picked their way to the forest floor to retrieve their weapons.

The unfrozen members of the 13th were waiting for them, breaking off from their squad mate, who was still moaning on the ground. ::You fuck,:: one of them said, getting directly into Jared's face. ::You threw a knife into Charlie. You're not supposed to try to *kill* anyone. That's why it's called a war *game*.::

Seaborg jammed in between Jared and the soldier. ::Tell that to your friend, asshole,:: he said. ::If your friend had shot us, I would have dropped eight meters without any way to control my fall. He didn't seem particularly worried about *me* dying as he was lining up his shot. Jared knifing your friend saved my life. And your friend will *survive*. So fuck him, and fuck you.::

Seaborg and the soldier sized each other up for another few seconds before the other soldier turned his head, spat on the ground, and walked back to his squad mate.

::Thanks,:: Jared said to Seaborg.

Seaborg glanced over to Jared, and then to Yukawa and Berkeley. ::Let's get out of here,:: he said. ::We've got another war game.:: He stomped off. The three of them followed.

On the way back, Seaborg dropped back to pace Jared. ::It was a good idea to use the trees,:: he said. ::And I'm glad you caught me before I dropped. Thank you.::

::You're welcome,:: Jared said.

::I still don't like you much,:: Seaborg said. ::But I'm not going to have a problem with you anymore.::

::I'll take that,:: Jared said. ::It's a start, anyway.::

Seaborg nodded and picked up his pace again. He was silent the rest of the way in.

"Well, look who we have here," Lieutenant Cloud said, as Jared entered the shuttle with the other former members of the 8th. They were on their way back to Phoenix Station for their first assignments. "It's my pal Jared."

"Hello, Lieutenant Cloud," Jared said. "It's good to see you again."

"It's Dave," Cloud said. "Done with your training, I see. Damn, I wish my training had just been two weeks."

"We still cover a lot," Jared said.

"I don't doubt that in the least," Cloud said. "So what's your assignment, Private Dirac? Where will you be headed?"

"I've been assigned to the *Kite*," Jared said. "Me and two of my friends, Sarah Pauling and Steven Seaborg." Jared pointed at Pauling, who had already sat down; Seaborg had yet to get on the shuttle.

"I've seen the *Kite*," Cloud said. "Newer ship. Nice lines. Never been on it, of course. You Special Forces types keep to yourselves."

"That's what they tell me," Jared said. Andrea Gell-Mann came on board, bumping Jared slightly. She pinged an apology to him; Jared looked over and smiled.

"Looks like it's going to be a full-up flight," Cloud said. "You can sit up in the copilot's seat again if you like."

"Thanks," Jared said, and glanced over to Pauling. "I think I'll sit with my other friends this time."

Cloud looked over at Pauling. "That's entirely under-standable," Cloud said. "Although remember you owe me some new jokes. I hope in all that training you did they gave you some time to work on your sense of humor."

Jared paused for a minute, recalling his first conversa-tion with Gabriel Brahe. "Lieutenant Cloud, did you ever read *Frankenstein?*" he asked.

"Never did," Cloud said. "I know the story. Saw the most recent movie version not too long ago. The monster talked, which I'm told means it's closer to the actual book than not."

"What did you think of it?" Jared said.

"It was all right," Cloud said. "The acting was a little over-the-top. I felt sorry for the monster. And the Dr. Frankenstein character was something of an asshole. Why do you ask?"

"Just curious," Jared said, and nodded toward the seat-ing compartment, which was now almost completely full. "We all read it. Gave us a lot to think about."

"Ah," said Cloud. "I see. Jared, allow me to share with you my philosophy of human beings. It can be summed up in four words: I like good people. You seem like good people. I can't say that's all that matters to everyone, but it's what matters to me."

"That's good to know," Jared said. "I think my philoso-phy runs the same way."

"Well then, we're going to get along just fine," Cloud said. "Now: Any new jokes?"

"I might have a few," Jared said.

SIX

"We'll talk out loud here, if you don't mind," General Szilard said to Jane Sagan. "It makes the waitstaff nervous to see two people staring intently at each other without actually making any sounds. If they don't see we're talking, they'll come over every other minute to see if there's anything we need. It's distracting."

"As you wish," Sagan said.

The two of them sat in the general's mess, with Phoenix spinning above them. Sagan stared. Szilard followed her gaze.

"It's amazing, isn't it," he said.

"It is," Sagan said.

"You can see the planet out of any portal on the station, at least some of the time. But no one ever looks," Szilard said. "And then you come here, and you just can't stop staring at it. I can't, in any event." He pointed to the crystal dome that encased them. "This dome was a gift, did you know that?" Sagan shook her head. "The Ala gave it to us as we built this station. It's diamond, this whole thing. They said it was a natural diamond that they carved out of an even larger crystal they hauled up from the core of one of their system's gas giants. The Ala were amazing engineers, so I've read. The story might even be true."

"I'm not familiar with the Ala," Sagan said.

"They're extinct," Szilard said. "A hundred fifty years ago they got into a war with the Obin over a colony. They had an army of clones and the means to make those clones quickly, and for a while it looked like they were going to beat the Obin. Then the Obin tailored a virus keyed to the clones' genetics. The virus was initially harmless and transmitted by air, like a flu. Our scientists estimated it spread through the entire Alaite army in about a month, and then a month after that the virus matured and begun to attack the cellular reproduction cycle of every single Ala military clone. The victims literally dissolved."

"All at once?" Sagan asked.

"It took about a month," Szilard said. "Which is why our scientists estimated it took that long to infect the entire army in the first place. With the Alaite army out of the way the Obin wiped out the civilian population in short order. It was a fast and brutal genocide. The Obin are not a compassionate species. Now all the Alaite planets are owned by the Obin, and the Colonial Union learned two things. One, clone armies are a very bad idea. Two, stay out of the way of the Obin. Which we have done, until now."

Sagan nodded. The Special Forces battle cruiser *Kite* and her crew had recently begun recon and stealth raids in Obin territory, to gauge the Obin's strength and response capabilities. It was dangerous work since the Obin were unforgiving of assaults, and technically speaking the Obin and the Colonial Union were not in a state of hostilities. Knowledge of the Obin-Rraey-Eneshan alliance was a closely guarded secret; the majority of the Colonial Union and the CDF were unaware of the alliance and its threat to humans. The Eneshans even maintained a diplomatic presence on Phoenix, in the Colonial capital of Phoenix City. Strictly speaking, they were allies.

"Do you want to talk about the Obin raids?" Sagan said. In addition to being a squad leader on the *Kite*, she was the ship's intelligence officer, charged with force assessment. Most Special Forces officers held more than one post and also led combat squads; it kept the ship rosters lean, and keeping officers in combat positions appealed to the Special Forces' sense of mission. When you are born to protect humanity, no one is above combat.

"Not now," Szilard said. "This isn't the place for it. I wanted to talk to you about one of your new soldiers. The *Kite* has three new recruits, and two of them will be under you."

Sagan bristled. "They will, and that's a problem. I had only one hole in my squad, but I have two replacements. You took one of my veterans to make room." Sagan remembered the helpless look on Will Lister's face when his transfer order to the *Peregrine* came through.

"The *Peregrine* is a new ship and it needs some experienced hands," Szilard said. "I assure you there are other squad leaders on other ships just as irritated as you. The *Kite* had to give up one of its veterans, and as it happens I had a recruit I wanted to place under you. So I had the *Peregrine* take one of yours."

Sagan opened her mouth to complain again, then thought better of it and clammed up, stewing. Szilard watched the play of emotions on her face. Most Special Forces soldiers would have said the first thing that came into their heads, an artifact of not having social niceties banged into their head through a childhood and adolescence. Sagan's self-control was one of the reasons why she had come to Szilard's attention; that and other factors.

"Which recruit are we talking about?" Sagan said finally.

"Jared Dirac," Szilard said.

"What's so special about him?" Sagan asked.

"He's got Charles Boutin's brain in him," Szilard said, and watched again as Sagan fought back an immediate visceral response.

"And you think this is a *good* idea," is what eventually came out of her mouth.

"It gets better," Szilard said, and sent over Dirac's entire classified file, complete with technical material. Sagan sat silently, digesting the material; Szilard sat, watching the junior officer. After a minute one of the mess staff approached their table and asked if there was anything they needed. Szilard ordered tea. Sagan ignored the waiter.

"All right, I'll bite," Sagan said, after she was done examining the file. "Why are you sticking me with a traitor?"

"Boutin's the traitor," Szilard said. "Dirac has just got his brain."

"A brain that you tried to imprint with a traitor's consciousness," Sagan said.

"Yes," Szilard said.

"I submit the question to your attention once more," Sagan said.

"Because you have experience with this sort of thing," Szilard said.

"With traitors?" Sagan asked, confused.

"With unconventional Special Forces members," Szilard said. "You once temporarily had a realborn member of the CDF under your command. John Perry." Sagan stiffened slightly at the name; Szilard noted it but chose not to comment. "He did quite well under you," Szilard said. This last sentence was a bit of an ironic understatement; during the Battle of Coral, Perry carried Sagan's unconscious and injured body over several hundred meters of battlefield to get her medical attention, and then located a key piece of enemy technology as the building it was in collapsed around him.

"The credit for that goes to Perry, not me," Sagan said. Szilard sensed another play of emotion from Sagan at Perry's name, but again left it on the table.

"You are too modest," Szilard said, and paused as the waiter delivered the tea. "My point is, Dirac is something of a hybrid," he continued. "He's Special Forces, but he may also be something else. I want someone who has experience with something else."

"'Something else,'" Sagan repeated. "General, am I hearing that you think Boutin's consciousness is actually somewhere inside Dirac?"

"I didn't say that," Szilard said, in a tone that implied that perhaps he had.

Sagan considered this and addressed the implicit rather than the expressed. "You are aware, of course, that the *Kite*'s next series of missions will have us engaging both the Rraey and the Enesha," she said. "The Eneshan missions in particular are ones of great delicacy." *And ones I needed Will Lister for,* Sagan thought, but did not say.

"I am of course aware," Szilard agreed, and reached for his tea.

"You don't think having someone with a possibly emergent traitorous personality might be a *risk*," Sagan said. "A risk not only to his mission but to others serving with him."

"Obviously it's a risk," Szilard said, "for which I rely on your experience to deal with. But he may also turn out to be a trove of critical information. Which will also need to be dealt with. In addition to everything else, you're an intelligence officer. You're the ideal officer for this soldier."

"What did Crick have to say about this?" Sagan said, referring to Major Crick, the commanding officer of the *Kite*.

"He didn't have anything to say about it because I haven't told him," Szilard said. "This is need-to-know material, and I've decided he doesn't need to know. As far as he knows he simply has three new soldiers."

"I don't like this," Sagan said. "I don't like this at all."

"I didn't ask you to like it," Szilard said. "I'm telling you to deal with it." He sipped his tea.

"I don't want him playing a critical role in any of the missions that deal with the Rraey or the Enesha," Sagan said.

"You'll treat him no differently from any other soldier under your command," Szilard said.

"Then he could get killed like any other soldier," Sagan said.

"Then for your sake you'd better hope it's not by friendly fire," Szilard said, and set down his cup.

Sagan was silent again. The waiter approached; Szilard impatiently waved him off.

"I want to show this file to someone," Sagan said, pointing to her head.

"It's classified, for obvious reasons," Szilard said. "Everyone who needs to know about it already does, and we don't want to spread it around to anyone else. Even *Dirac* doesn't know about his own history. We want to keep it that way."

"You're asking me to take on a soldier who has the capability to be an *immense* security risk," Sagan said. "The least you can do is let me prepare myself. I know a specialist in human brain function and BrainPal integration. I think his insights on this could be useful."

Szilard considered this. "This is someone you trust," he said.

"I can trust him with this," Sagan said.

"Do you know his security clearance?" Szilard asked.

"I do," Sagan said.

"Is it high enough for something like this?"

"Well," Sagan said. "That's where things get interesting."

"Hello, Lieutenant Sagan," Administrator Cainen said, in English. The pronunciation was bad, but that was hardly Cainen's fault; his mouth was not well formed for most human languages.

"Hello, Administrator," Sagan said. "You're learning our language."

"Yes," Cainen said. "I have time to learn, and little to do." Cainen pointed to a book, written in Ckann, the predominant Rraey language, nestled next to a PDA. "Only two books here in Ckann. I had choice of language book or religion book. I chose language. Human religion is . . ."—Cainen searched his small store of English words—". . . harder."

Sagan nodded toward the PDA. "Now that you have a computer, you should have more reading options."

"Yes," Cainen said. "Thank you for getting that to me. It makes me happy."

"You're welcome," Sagan said. "But the computer comes with a price."

"I know," Cainen said. "I have read files you asked me to read."

"And?" Sagan said.

"I must change to Ckann," Cainen said. "My English does not have many words."

"All right," Sagan said.

"I've looked at the files concerning Private Dirac in depth," Cainen said, in the harsh but rapid consonants of the Ckann language. "Charles Boutin was a genius for finding a way to preserve the consciousness wave outside of the brain. And you people are *idiots* for how you tried to stuff that consciousness back in."

"Idiots," Sagan said, and cracked the smallest of smiles, the translation of the word in Ckann coming from a small speaker attached to a lanyard around her neck. "Is that your professional assessment, or just an editorial comment?"

"It's both," Cainen said.

"Tell me why," Sagan said. Cainen moved to send files from his PDA to her, but Sagan held up her hand. "I don't need the technical details," she said. "I just want to know if this Dirac is going to be a danger to my troops and my mission."

"All right," Cainen said, and paused for a moment. "The brain, even a human one, is like a computer. It's not a perfect analogy, but it works for what I'm going to tell you. Computers have three components for their operation: There's the hardware, there's the software, and there's the data file. The software runs on the hardware, and the file runs on the software. The hardware can't open the file without the software. If you place a file on a computer that lacks the necessary software, all it can do is sit there. Do you understand me?"

"So far," Sagan said.

"Good," Cainen said. He reached over and tapped Sagan on the head; she suppressed an urge to snap off his finger. "Follow: The brain is the hardware. The consciousness is the file. But with your friend Dirac, you're missing the software."

"What's the software?" Sagan asked.

"Memory," Cainen said. "Experience. Sensory activity. When you put Boutin's consciousness into his brain, that brain lacked the experience to make any sense of it. If that consciousness is still in Dirac's brain—*if*—it's isolated and there's no way to access it."

"Newborn Special Forces soldiers are conscious from the moment they are woken up," Sagan said. "But we also lack experience and memory."

"That's not *consciousness* they're experiencing," Cainen said, and Sagan could sense the disgust in his voice. "Your damned BrainPal forces open sensory channels artificially and offers the illusion of consciousness, and your brain knows it." Cainen pointed to his PDA again. "Your people gave me a rather wide range of access to brain and Brain-Pal research. Did you know this?"

"I did," Sagan said. "I asked them to let you look at any file you needed to help me."

"Because you knew that I would be a prisoner for the rest of my life, and that even if I could escape I would soon be dead of the disease you gave me. So it couldn't *hurt* to give me access," Cainen said.

Sagan shrugged.

"Hmmmp," Cainen said, and continued. "Do you know that there's no explainable reason why a Special Forces soldier's brain absorbs information so much more quickly than a regular CDF? They're both unaltered human brains; they're both the same BrainPal computer. Special Forces brains are preconditioned in a different way from the regular soldiers' brains, but not in a way that should noticeably speed up the rate at which the brains process information. And yet the Special Forces brain sucks down information and processes it at an incredible rate. Do you know why? *It's defending itself*, Lieutenant. Your average CDF soldier already has a consciousness, and the experience to use it. You Special Forces soldiers have nothing. Your brain senses the artificial consciousness your BrainPal is pressing on it and rushes to build its own as quickly as it can, before that artificial consciousness permanently deforms it. Or kills it."

"No Special Forces soldiers have died because of their BrainPal," Jane said.

"Oh, no, not *now*," Cainen said. "But I wonder what you would find if you went back far enough."

"What do you know?" Sagan asked.

"I know nothing," Cainen said, mildly. "It's merely idle speculation. But the point here is that you can't compare Special Forces waking up with 'consciousness' with what you were trying to do with Private Dirac. It's not the same thing. It's not even close."

Sagan changed the subject. "You said that it's possible Boutin's consciousness might not even be in Dirac's brain anymore," she said.

"It's possible," Cainen said. "The consciousness needs input; without it, it dissipates. That's one reason why it's near impossible to keep a consciousness pattern coherent outside the brain, and why Boutin's a genius for doing it. My suspicion is that if Boutin's consciousness was in there, it's already leaked away, and you've got just another soldier on your hands. But there's no way to tell whether it's in there or not. Its pattern would be subsumed by Private Dirac's consciousness."

"If it *is* in there, what would wake it up?" Sagan asked.

"You're asking me to speculate?" Cainen asked. Sagan nodded. "The reason you couldn't access the Boutin consciousness in the first place is that the brain didn't have memory and experience. Maybe as your Private Dirac accumulates experiences, one will be close enough in its substance to unlock some part of that consciousness."

"And then he'd become Charles Boutin," Sagan said.

"He might," Cainen said. "Or he might not. Private Dirac has his own consciousness now. His own sense of self. If

Boutin's consciousness woke up, it wouldn't be the only consciousness in there. It's up to you to decide whether that's good or bad, Lieutenant Sagan. I can't tell you that, or what would truly happen if Boutin got woken up."

"Those are the things I needed you to tell me," Sagan said.

Cainen gave the Rraey equivalent of a chuckle. "Get me a lab," he said. "Then I might be able to give you some answers."

"I thought you said you would never help us," Sagan said.

Cainen switched back to English. "Much time to think," he said. "Too much time. Language lessons not enough." And then back to Ckann. "And this doesn't help you against my people. But it helps *you*."

"Me?" Sagan said. "I know why you helped me this time; I bribed you with computer access. Why would you help me beyond this? I made you a prisoner."

"And you struck me with a disease that will kill me if I don't get a daily dose of antidote from my enemies," Cainen said. He reached into the shallow desk moulded from the wall of the cell and pulled out a small injector. "My medicine," he said. "They allow me to self-administer. Once I decided not to inject myself, to see if they would let me die. I'm still here, so that's the answer to that. But they let me writhe on the floor for hours first. Just like *you* did, come to think of it."

"None of this explains why you would want to help me," Sagan said.

"Because you *remembered* me," Cainen said. "To everyone else, I am just another one of your many enemies, barely worth providing a book to keep me from going insane with boredom. One day they could simply forget my antidote and let me die, and it would be all the same to them. You at least see me as having value. In the very small universe I live in now, that makes you my best and only friend, enemy though you are."

Sagan stared at Cainen, remembering the *haughtiness* of him the first time they met. He was pitiful and craven now, and that momentarily struck Sagan as the saddest thing she'd ever seen.

"I'm sorry," she said, and was surprised the words came out of her mouth.

Another Rraey chuckle from Cainen. "We were planning to destroy your people, Lieutenant," Cainen said. "And we still might. You needn't feel too apologetic."

Sagan had nothing to say to that. She signaled to the brig officer that she was ready to leave; a guard came and stood with an Empee while the cell door opened.

As the door slid shut behind her, she turned back to Cainen. "Thank you for your help. I will ask about a lab," she said.

"Thank you," Cainen said. "I won't get my hopes up."

"That's probably a good idea," Sagan said.

"And Lieutenant," Cainen said. "A thought. Your Private Dirac will be participating in your military actions."

"Yes," Sagan said.

"Watch him," Cainen said. "In humans and Rraey both, the stress of battle leaves permanent marks on our brains. It's a primal experience. If Boutin is still in there, it might be war that brings him out. Either by itself or through some combination of experiences."

"How do you suggest I watch him in battle?" Sagan asked.

"That's your department," Cainen said. "Except for when you captured me, I've never been to war. I couldn't begin to tell you. But if you're worried about Dirac, that's what I would do if I were you. You humans have an expression: 'Keep your friends close and your enemies closer.' It seems like your Private Dirac could be both. I'd keep him very close indeed."

The *Kite* caught the Rraey cruiser napping.

The Skip Drive was a touchy piece of technology. It made interstellar travel possible not by propelling ships faster than the speed of light, which was impossible, but by punching through space-time and placing spaceships (or anything equipped with a Skip Drive) into any spot within that universe those using the Skip Drive pleased.

(Actually, this wasn't exactly true; on a logarithmic scale Skip Drive travel became less reliable the more space there was between the initiation point and the destination point. The cause of what was called the Skip Drive Horizon Problem was not entirely understood, but its effects were lost ships and crews.

This kept humans and other races that used the Skip Drive in the same interstellar "neighborhood" as their home planets in the short run; if a race wanted to keep control of its colonies, as almost all did, its colonial expansion was ruled by the sphere defined by the Skip Drive horizon. In one sense this point was moot; thanks to the intense competition for real estate in the neighborhood humanity lived in, no intelligent race save one had a reach that came close to its own Skip Drive horizon. The exception was the Consu, whose technology was so advanced relative to the other races in the local space that it was an open question as to whether it used the Skip Drive at all.)

Among the many quirks of the Skip Drive, which had to be tolerated if one were to employ it, were its departure and arrival needs. When departing, the Skip Drive needed relatively "flat" space-time, which meant the Skip Drive could only be activated when the ship using it was well outside the gravity well of close-by planets; this required travel in space using engines. But a ship using the Skip Drive could arrive as close to a planet as it wanted—it could even, theoretically, arrive on a planet surface, if a navigator confident enough of his or her skill could be found to do it. While landing a spacecraft on a planet via Skip Drive navigation was officially and strongly discouraged by the Colonial Union, the Colonial Defense Forces recognized the strategic value of sudden and unexpected arrivals.

When the *Kite* arrived over the planet its human settlers called Gettysburg, it popped into existence within a quarter of a light-second from the Rraey cruiser, and with its dual rail guns warmed up and ready to fire. It took the *Kite*'s prepared weapons crew less than a minute to orient and target the hapless cruiser, which only at the end could be seen trying to respond, and the magnetized rail-gun projectiles needed less than two and a third seconds to travel the distance between the *Kite* and its quarry. The sheer speed of the rail-gun projectiles was more than sufficient to pierce the hide of the Rraey craft and tunnel through its innards like a bullet through soft butter, but the projectile designers hadn't left it at that; the projectiles themselves were designed to expand explosively at the merest contact with matter.

An infinitesimal fraction of a second after the projectiles penetrated the Rraey craft, they fragmented and shards vectored crazily relative to their initial trajectory, turning the projectile into this universe's fastest shotgun blast. The expenditure of energy required to change these trajectories was naturally immense and slowed down the shards considerably. However, the shards had energy to spare, and it simply meant each shard had more time to damage the Rraey vessel before it exited the wounded ship and began a long and frictionless journey through space.

Thanks to the relative positions of the *Kite* and the Rraey cruiser, the first rail-gun projectile struck the Rraey cruiser forward and starboard; the fragments from this projectile tunneled through diagonally and upward, not-so-cleanly chewing through several levels of the ship and turning a number of the Rraey crew into bloody mist. The entrance wound of this projectile was a clean circle seventeen centimeters wide; the exit wound was a ragged hole ten meters wide with a gout of metal, flesh and atmosphere blasting silently into the vacuum.

The second rail-gun projectile entered aft of the first, following a parallel directory, but failed to fragment; its exit wound was only marginally larger than its entrance wound. It made up for this failure by breaching one of the engines of the Rraey craft. The cruiser's automatic damage controls slammed down bulkheads, isolating the damaged engine, and took the other two engines off-line to avoid a cascading failure. The Rraey ship was switched to emergency power, which offered it only a minimum of offensive and defensive options, none of which would be at all effective against the *Kite*.

The *Kite*, its own power partially drained (but recharging) through the use of the rail guns, sealed the deal by launching five conventional tactical nuclear missiles at the Rraey cruiser. It would take them more than a minute to reach the cruiser, but the *Kite* now had the luxury of time. The cruiser was the only Rraey ship in the area. A small flash issued forth from the Rraey ship: The doomed cruiser was launching a Skip drone, designed to quickly get to Skip distance and let the rest of the Rraey military know what happened to it. The *Kite* launched a sixth and final missile toward the drone, which would be overtaken and destroyed less than ten thousand klicks from Skip distance. By the time the Rraey found out about their cruiser, the *Kite* would be light-years away.

Presently the Rraey cruiser was an expanding debris field, and Lieutenant Sagan and her 2nd Platoon received their clearance for their part of the mission.

Jared tried to calm the first-mission nerves, and the mild fear brought by the choppiness of the troop transport's descent into the Gettysburg atmosphere, by trying to close out distractions and focus his energies. Daniel Harvey, sitting next to him, was making that difficult.

::Goddamn wildcat colonists,:: Harvey said, as the troop transport plunged through the atmosphere. ::They go off and build illegal colonies and then come crying to us when some other fucking species is crawling up their holes.::

::Relax, Harvey,:: said Alex Roentgen. ::You're going to give yourself a migraine.::

::What I want to know is how these fuckers even manage to *get* to these places,:: Harvey said. ::The Colonial Union doesn't bring 'em out here. And you can't go anywhere without CU say-so.::

::Sure you can,:: Roentgen said. ::The CU doesn't control *all* interstellar travel, just the travel that humans do.::

::These colonists are human, Einstein,:: Harvey said.

::Hey,:: said Julie Einstein. ::Leave me out of this.::

::It's just an expression, Julie,:: Harvey said.

::The colonists are human, but the people who are transporting them *aren't*, you idiot,:: Roentgen said. ::Wildcat colonists buy transport from aliens the CU trades with, and the aliens take them where they want to go.::

::That's stupid,:: Harvey said, and looked around the

platoon for agreement. Most of the platoon were either resting with their eyes closed or studiously avoiding the discussion; Harvey had a reputation as an argumentative blowhard. ::The CU could stop that if they wanted to. Tell the aliens to stop picking up wildcat passengers. That would save us from having to risk getting *our* asses shot off.::

From the forward seat, Jane Sagan turned her head toward Harvey. ::The CU doesn't want to stop wildcat colonists,:: she said, in a bored tone.

::Why the hell not?:: Harvey asked.

::They're troublemakers,:: Sagan said. ::The sort of person who will defy the CU and start a wildcat colony is the sort of person who could cause trouble at home if he wasn't allowed to go. The CU figures it's not worth the trouble. So they let them go, and look the other way. Then they're on their own.::

- ::Until they get in trouble,:: Harvey sneered.

::Usually even then,:: Sagan said. ::Wildcatters know what they're getting into.::

::Then what *are* we doing here?:: Roentgen said. ::Not to take Harvey's side, but these *are* wildcat colonists.::

::Orders,:: Sagan said, and closed her eyes, ending the discussion. Harvey snorted and was about to reply when the turbulence suddenly became especially bad.

::Looks like the Rraey on the ground just figured out we're up here,:: Chad Assisi said from the pilot's seat. ::-We've got three more missiles on their way. Hang on, I'm going to try to burn them before they get too close.:: Several seconds later came a low, solid hum; the transport's defensive maser fired up to deal with the missiles.

::Why don't we just plaster these guys from orbit?:: Harvey said. ::We've done that before.::

::There are humans down there, aren't there?:: Jared

said, venturing a comment. ::I'd guess we'd want to avoid using tactics that would injure or kill them.::

Harvey gave Jared the briefest of glances and then changed the subject.

Jared glanced over to Sarah Pauling, who gave him a shrug. In the week they had been attached to the 2nd Platoon, the best adjective to describe relations was *frosty*. Other members of the platoon were diffidently polite when forced to be but otherwise ignored the two of them whenever possible. Jane Sagan, the platoon's superior officer, let them know briefly that this was par for the course for new recruits until their first combat mission. ::Just deal with it,:: she said, and returned to work of her own.

It made both Jared and Pauling uneasy. Being casually ignored was one thing, but the two of them were also denied full integration with the platoon. They were lightly connected and shared a common band for discussion and sharing information concerning the upcoming mission, but the intimate sharing offered by their training squad was not in evidence here. Jared looked back at Harvey and not for the first time wondered if integration was simply a training tool. If it was, it seemed cruel to offer it to people only to take it away later. But he'd seen evidence of integration among his platoon mates: the subtle movements and actions that suggested an unspoken common dialogue and a sensory awareness beyond one's own senses. Jared and Pauling yearned for it but also knew the lack of it was a test to see how they would respond.

To combat the lack of integration with their platoon, Jared and Pauling's integration was defensively intimate; they spent so much time in each other's heads that by the end of the week, despite their affection together, they were very nearly sick of each other. There was, they discovered, such a thing as too much integration. The two of them diluted their sharing slightly by inviting Steven Seaborg to integrate with them informally. Seaborg, who had been receiving the same cold shoulder from the 1st Platoon but who had no training mates in the platoon to keep him company, was almost pathetically grateful for the offer.

Jared glanced down at Jane Sagan and wondered if the platoon leader would tolerate having him and Sarah unintegrated during the mission; it seemed dangerous. For him and Pauling, at the very least.

As if responding to his thoughts, Sagan glanced up at him and then spoke. ::Assignments,:: she said, and sent a map of the tiny Gettysburg colony to the platoon with their assignments overlaid. ::Remember this is a sweep and clean. There's been no Skip drone activity, so either they're all dead or they're all herded somewhere where they can't get a message out. The idea is to clean out the Rraey with a minimum of structural damage to the colony. That's *minimal*, Harvey,:: staring pointedly at the soldier, who squirmed uncomfortably. ::I don't mind blowing things up when necessary but anything we destroy is something these settlers have less of.::

::What?:: Roentgen said. ::Are you seriously suggesting we're going to let these people stay? If they're still alive?::

::They're wildcatters,:: Sagan said. ::We can't force them to act intelligently.::

::Well, we *could* force them,:: Harvey said.

::We *won't* force them,:: Sagan said. ::We have new people to take under our wings. Roentgen, you're responsible for Pauling. I'll take Dirac. The rest of you, two by two to your assignments. We land here::—a small landing zone illuminated—::and I'll let you use your own creativity to get to where you need to be. Remember to note your surroundings and the enemy; you're looking for all of us.::

::Or at least *some* of us,:: Pauling said privately to Jared.

Then the both of them felt the sensuous rush of integration, the hyperawareness of having so many points of view overlaid on one's own. Jared struggled to control a gasp.

::Don't cream yourself,:: Harvey said, and there were a few pings of amusement in the platoon. Jared ignored this and drank in the emotional and informational gestalt offered by his platoon mates: the confidence in their abilities to confront the Rraey; a substrata of early planning for their paths to their mission destinations; a tense and subtle anticipatory excitement that seemed to have little to do with the combat to come; and shared communal feeling that taking care to keep structures intact was pointless, since the colonists were almost certainly dead already.

::Behind you,:: Jared heard Sarah Pauling say, and he and Jane Sagan turned and fired even as they received the image and data, from Pauling's distant point of view, of three Rraey soldiers moving silently but not invisibly around a small general-purpose building to ambush the pair. The trio stepped out into a hail of bullets from Jared and Sagan; one dropped dead while the other two broke and ran in separate directions.

Jared and Sagan quickly polled the viewpoints of the other members of the platoon to see who might pick up one or both of the fleeing soldiers. Everyone else was engaged, including Pauling, who had returned to her primary task of flushing out a Rraey sniper on the edge of the Gettysburg settlement. Sagan audibly sighed.

::Get that one,:: she said, taking off after the second. ::Try not to get killed.::

Jared followed the Rraey soldier, who used its powerful, bird-like legs to build a considerable lead on him. As Jared raced to catch up, the Rraey spun and shot wildly at him with a one-handed grip on its weapon; the kick knocked the gun up and out of the Rraey's hand. The bullets spat up dirt directly in front of Jared, who veered for cover as the weapon clattered to the ground. The Rraey ran on without retrieving its weapon and disappeared into the colony's motor pool garage.

::I could use some help,:: Jared said, at the bay of the garage.

::Join the club,:: Harvey said, from somewhere. ::These fuckers outnumber us at least two to one.::

Jared entered the garage through the bay. The quick glance showed that the only other way out was a door on the same wall as the bay and one of a series of windows designed to ventilate the garage. The windows were both high and small; it seemed unlikely the Rraey had gone through those. It was still somewhere inside the garage. Jared moved to one side and started a methodical search of the shop.

A knife shot out from a tarp on a low shelf and slashed Jared in his calf. The nanobotic fabric of Jared's military unitard stiffened where the knife blade made contact. Jared didn't receive a scratch. But his own shocked movement tripped him up; he went sprawling on the floor, ankle twisted, his Empee clattering out of his hand. The Rraey scrambled out of its hiding place before Jared could get to it, clambered over Jared and pushed the Empee with the fist that still held the knife. The Empee danced out of reach and the Rraey stabbed Jared's face, cutting him savagely in the cheek and drawing SmartBlood. Jared yelled; the Rraey scrambled off him and toward the Empee.

When Jared spun around the Rraey had the Empee trained on him, its elongated fingers awkwardly but solidly on the stock and trigger. Jared froze. The Rraey squawked something and pulled the trigger.

Nothing. Jared remembered that the Empee was trained to his BrainPal; it wouldn't fire for a nonhuman. He cracked a smile in relief; the Rraey squawked again and jammed the Empee hard into Jared's face, tearing into the cheek it had already slashed. Jared screamed and scrambled back in pain. The Rraey threw the Empee onto a high shelf, out of the reach of both of them. It reached onto a counter to grab a tire rod and advanced on Jared, swinging viciously.

Jared blocked the swing with his arm; his unitard stiffened again but the hit made his arm ache in pain. On the next swing he reached to grab the rod but misjudged the speed of the approach; the rod came down hard on his fingers, breaking bones in the ring and middle fingers of his right hand and driving down his arm. The Rraey moved the iron sideways and clocked Jared in the head with it; he went down to his knees, dazed, retwisting the ankle he'd fallen on earlier. Jared groggily went for his combat knife with his left hand; the Rraey kicked the hand, hard, sending the knife spinning out of his grip. A second rapid kick tapped Jared on the chin, driving his teeth into his tongue, causing SmartBlood to spurt into his mouth and over his teeth. The Rraey pushed him over, pulled out its knife, and bent down to cut Jared's throat. Jared's mind suddenly ricocheted back to a training session with Sarah Pauling, when she straddled him with her knife on his throat and told him he lacked focus.

He focused now.

Jared sucked in suddenly and spat a gobbet of Smart-Blood at the Rraey's face and eye band. The creature recoiled, revulsed, giving Jared the time he needed to instruct his BrainPal to do with the SmartBlood on the Rraey's face what it did when it was ingested by the blood-sucking bug on Phoenix: combust.

The Rraey screamed as the SmartBlood began to burn into its face and eye band, dropping its knife as it clawed at its face. Jared grabbed the knife and drove it into the side of the Rraey's head. The Rraey issued an abrupt, surprised cluck and then went boneless, slumping backwards on the floor. Jared followed its example, lying silently, doing nothing but resting his eyes and becoming more and more aware of the heavy, acrid smell of smoldering Rraey.

::Get up,:: someone said to him some time later, and prodded him with a boot toe. Jared winced and looked up. It was Sagan. ::Come on, Dirac. We got them all. You can come out now.::

::I hurt,:: Jared said.

::Hell, Dirac,:: Sagan said. ::I hurt just looking at you.:: She motioned over to the Rraey. ::Next time, just shoot the damn thing.::

::I'll keep that in mind,:: Jared said.

::Speaking of which,:: Sagan said, ::where's your Empee?::

Jared looked up at the high shelf the Rraey had flung it onto. ::I think I need a ladder,:: Jared said.

::You need stitches,:: Sagan said. ::Your cheek is about to come off.::

::Lieutenant,:: Julie Einstein said. ::You're going to want to come over here. We found the settlers.::

::Any of them alive?:: Sagan said.

::God, no,:: Einstein said, and through the integration both Sagan and Jared felt her shudder.

::Where are you?:: Sagan asked.

::Um,:: Einstein said. ::Maybe you should come and see.::

A minute later Sagan and Jared were at the colony slaughterhouse.

::Fucking Rraey,:: Sagan said as they walked up. She

turned to Einstein, who was waiting outside for her. ::They're in here?::

::They're here,:: Einstein said. ::In the cold room in the back.::

::All of them?:: Sagan asked.

::I think so. It's hard to tell,:: Einstein said. ::They're mostly in parts.::

The cold room was crammed with meat.

Special Forces soldiers gaped up at the skinned torsos on hooks. Barrels below the hooks were filled with offal. Limbs in various states of processing lay stacked on tables. On a separate table lay a collection of heads, skulls sawed open to extract the brains. Discarded heads rested in another barrel next to the table.

A small pile of unprocessed bodies was heaped under a tarp. Jared went to uncover it. Children lay underneath.

::Christ,:: Sagan said. She turned to Einstein. ::Get someone over to the colony administration offices,:: she said. ::Pull up any medical and genetic records you can find, and pictures of the colonists. We're going to need them to identify people. Then get a couple of people to dig through trash cans.::

::What are we looking for?:: Einstein asked.

:: Scraps,:: Sagan said. ::Whoever the Rraey already ate.::

Jared heard Sagan give her orders as a buzz in his head. He crouched and stared, transfixed, at the pile of small bodies. At the top lay the body of a small girl, elfin features silent, relaxed and beautiful. He reached over and gently touched the girl's cheek. It was ice-cold.

Unaccountably Jared felt a hard stab of grief. He turned away with a retching sob.

Daniel Harvey, who had found the cold room with Einstein, stood over Jared. ::First time,:: he said.

Jared looked up. ::What?:: he said.

Harvey motioned to the bodies with his head. ::This is the first time you've seen children. Am I right?::

::Yes,:: Jared said.

::This is how it happens with us,:: Harvey said. ::The first time we see colonists, they're dead. The first time we see children, they're dead. The first time we see an intelligent creature who isn't human, it's dead or trying to kill us, so we have to kill it. Then *it's* dead. It took me months before I saw a live colonist. I've never seen a live child.::

Jared turned back to the pile. ::How old is this one?:: he asked.

::Shit, I don't know,:: Harvey said, but looked anyway. ::I'd guess three or four years old. Five, tops. And you know what's funny? She was older than both of us put together. She was older than both of us put together *twice*. It's a fucked-up universe, my friend.::

Harvey wandered away. Jared stared at the little girl for another minute, then covered her and the pile with the tarp. He went looking for Sagan, who he found outside the colony's administration building.

::Dirac,:: Sagan said as he approached. ::What do you think of your first mission?::

::I think it's pretty awful,:: Jared said.

::That it is,:: Sagan said. "Do you know why we're here? Why we're out here at a wildcat settlement?" she asked him.

It took Jared a second to realize she had spoken the words out loud. "No," he said, responding in kind.

"Because the leader of this settlement is the son of the Secretary of State for the Colonial Union," Sagan said. "The dumb bastard wanted to prove to his mother that the Colonial Union regulations against wildcat settlements were an affront to civil rights."

"Are they?" Jared asked.

Sagan looked over at Jared. "Why do you ask?"

"I'm just curious," Jared said.

"Maybe they are, and maybe they aren't," Sagan said. "But either way, the last place to prove that point would have been *this* planet. It's been claimed by the Rraey for years, even if they didn't have a settlement on it. I guess the asshole thought that because the CU beat the Rraey in the last war maybe they'd look the other way for fear of retaliation. Then ten days ago the spy satellite we put in over the planet got shot out of the sky by that cruiser we took out. It got a picture of the cruiser first. And here *we* are."

"It's a mess," Jared said.

Sagan laughed mirthlessly. "Now I've got to go back into that fucking cold room and test corpses until I find the secretary's son," she said. "Then I'll have the pleasure of telling her that the Rraey chopped up her son and his family for food."

"His family?" Jared asked.

"Wife," Sagan said, "and a daughter. Four years old."

Jared shuddered violently, thinking of the girl on the pile. Sagan watched him intently. "Are you okay?" she asked.

"I'm fine," Jared said. "It just seems a waste."

"The wife and kid are a waste," Sagan said. "The dumb bastard who brought them here got what he deserved."

Jared shuddered again. "If you say so," he said.

"I do say so," Sagan said. "Now, come on. Time to identify the colonists, or what's left of them."

::Well,:: Sarah Pauling said to Jared, as he came out of the *Kite*'s infirmary. ::You sure don't do things the easy way.:: She reached out to his cheek, to the welt that remained there despite the nano-stitching. ::You can still see where you got cut.::

::It doesn't hurt,:: Jared said. ::Which is more than I can say about my ankle and my hand. The ankle wasn't broken, but the fingers will take a couple of days to fully heal.::

::Better that than being dead,:: Pauling said.

::This is true,:: Jared admitted.

::And you taught everybody a new trick,:: Pauling said. ::Things you didn't know you could do with SmartBlood. They're calling you Red-Hot Jared now.::

::Everybody knows you can get SmartBlood to heat up,:: Jared said. ::I saw people using it to fry up bugs on Phoenix all the time.::

::Yes, everyone uses it to smoke the little bugs,:: Pauling said, ::But it takes a certain kind of mind to think of using it to smoke the big bugs.::

::I wasn't really thinking about it,:: Jared said. ::I just didn't want to die.::

::Funny how that will make a person creative,:: Pauling said.

::Funny how it makes you focus,:: Jared said. ::I remembered you telling me I needed to work on that. I think you may have saved my life.::

::Good,:: Pauling said. ::Try to return the favor sometime.::

Jared stopped walking for a moment. ::What?:: Pauling asked.

::Do you feel that?:: Jared asked.

::Feel what?:: Pauling asked.

::I'm feeling like I really want to have sex,:: Jared said.

::Well, Jared,:: Pauling said. ::You stopping abruptly in a hallway is not usually how I know you really want to have sex.::

::Pauling, Dirac,:: Alex Roentgen said. ::Rec room. Now. Time for a little after-battle celebration.::

::Oooh,:: Pauling said. ::A celebration. Maybe there will be cake and ice cream.::

There was no cake or ice cream. There was an orgy. All the members of the 2nd Platoon were there, save one, in various stages of undress. Couples and trios lay on couches and cushions, kissing and pressing into each other.

::This is an after-battle celebration?:: Pauling asked.

::*The* after-battle celebration,:: Alex Roentgen said. ::Every battle we do this.::

::Why?:: Jared asked.

Alex Roentgen stared at Jared, mildly incredulous. ::You actually need a *reason* to have an orgy?:: Jared began to respond, but Roentgen held up his hand. ::One, because we've been through the valley of the shadow of death and come through the other side. And there's no better way to feel alive than this. And after the shit we've seen today, we need to get our minds off it right quick. Two, because as great as sex is, it's even better when everyone you're integrated with is doing it at the same time.::

::So this means you're not going to pull the plug on our integration?:: Pauling asked. She said it teasingly, but Jared sensed the smallest thread of anxiety in the question.

::No,:: Roentgen said, gently. ::You're one of us now. And it's not just sex. It's a deeper expression of communion and trust. Another level of integration.::

::That sounds suspiciously like bullshit to me,:: Pauling said, smiling.

Roentgen sent a ping of high amusement. ::Well, you know. I won't deny that we're in it for the sex too. But you'll see.:: He held out a hand to Pauling. ::Shall we?::

Pauling looked over at Jared, winked, and took Roentgen's hand. ::By all means,:: she said. Jared watched them walk off, and then felt a poke on his shoulder. He turned. Julie Einstein, nude and perky, stood there.

::I've come to test the theory that you are red-hot, Jared,:: she said.

Some indefinite time later Pauling found her way to Jared and lay next to him.

::This has been an interesting evening,:: she said.

::That's one way to put it,:: Jared said. Roentgen's comment that sex was different when everyone with whom you're integrated is involved turned out to be a rather dramatic understatement. Everyone but one, Jared corrected. ::I wonder why Sagan wasn't here,:: Jared said.

::Alex said she used to participate but now she doesn't,:: Pauling said. ::She stopped after a battle where she nearly died. That was a couple of years ago. Alex said participation is strictly optional; no one gives her grief for it.::

At the name "Alex," Jared felt a sharp pang; he'd glimpsed Roentgen and Pauling together earlier while Einstein was on him. ::That would explain it,:: Jared said, awkwardly.

Pauling sat up on an arm. ::Did you have a good time? With this?:: she asked.

::You know I did,:: Jared said.

::I know,:: Pauling said. ::I could feel you in my head.::

::Yes,:: Jared said.

::And yet, you don't seem entirely happy,:: Pauling said. Jared shrugged. ::I couldn't tell you why,:: he said.

Pauling reached over, kissed Jared lightly. ::You're cute when you're jealous,:: she said.

::I don't mean to be jealous,:: Jared said.

::No one means to be jealous, I think,:: Pauling said.

::I'm sorry,:: Jared said.

::Don't be,:: Pauling said. ::I'm happy we've been integrated. I'm pleased to be a part of this platoon. And *this* is a lot of fun. But you are special to me, Jared, and you always have been. You are my best beloved.::

::Best beloved,:: Jared agreed. ::Always.::

Pauling smiled widely. ::Glad to get that settled,:: she said, and reached down. ::Now,:: she said. ::Time for me to get the benefit of my best beloved privileges.::

SEVEN

::Thirty klicks,:: Jane Sagan said. ::Everyone off the bus.::

The soldiers of the 2nd Platoon removed themselves from the troop transport and fell into the night sky over Dirluew, the capital city of the Eneshan nation. Below them, explosions pocked the sky; not the violent, potentially transport-shattering eruptions that would mark anti-craft defenses, but the pretty multicolored flashes that signaled fireworks. It was the final evening of Chafalan, the Eneshan celebration of rebirth and renewal. Eneshans worldwide were out in their streets, partying and carrying on in a manner appropriate for the time of day where they were, most the Eneshan equivalent of slightly drunk and horny.

Dirluew was especially raucous this Chafalan. In addition to the usual festivities the celebration this year had also included the Consecration of the Heir, in which Fhileb Ser, the Eneshan Heirarch, officially pronounced her daughter Vyut Ser as the future ruler of Enesha. To commemorate the consecration, Fhileb Ser had provided a sample of the royal jelly she fed to Vyut Ser and allowed a mass-produced synthetic version to be produced, in diluted form, placed in tiny jars and offered as gifts to the citizens of Dirluew for the final night of Chafalan.

In its natural form, and fed to a pre-metamorphic Eneshan, the royal jelly caused profound developmental changes that resulted in clear physical and mental advantages once the Eneshan developed into adult form. In its diluted and synthesized version, the royal jelly gave adult Eneshans a truly excellent hallucinogenic buzz. Most of the citizens of Dirluew had consumed their jelly prior to the city's fireworks display and light show and were now sitting in their private gardens and public parks, clacking their mouthpieces together in the Eneshan equivalent of *ooooh* and *aaaaah* as the naturally brilliant and explosive nature of the fireworks was pharmaceutically extended across the entire Eneshan sensory spectrum.

Thirty klicks up (and descending rapidly), Jared could not see or hear the dazzled Eneshans, and the fireworks below were brilliant but distant, the sound of their explosions lost in the distance and the thin Eneshan stratosphere. Jared's perception was occupied with other things: the location of his squad mates, the rate of his descent and the maneuvering required to ensure he was both where he needed to be at landing and yet well out of the way when certain events transpired not too far in the future.

Locating his squad mates was the easiest task. Every member of the 2nd Platoon was blanked out visually and through most of the electromagnetic spectrum by their blackbody nanobiotic unitards and equipment covers, save for a small tightbeam transmitter/receiver each platoon member wore. These polled the position of the other platoon members before the jump and continued doing so at microsecond intervals since. Jared knew that Sarah Pauling was forty meters fore and starboard, Daniel Harvey sixty meters below and Jane Sagan two hundred meters above, the last out of their transport. The first time Jared participated in a nighttime high-altitude jump, not long after Gettysburg, he managed to lose the tightbeam signal and landed several klicks away from his squad, disoriented and alone. He received no end of shit for that.

Jared's final destination lay now less than twenty-five klicks below him, highlighted by his BrainPal, which also offered up a descent pathway computed to get him where he needed to be. The pathway was updated on the fly as the BrainPal took into consideration wind gusts and other atmospheric phenomena; it also tracked carefully around three closely grouped virtual columns, superimposed on Jared's vision. These columns stretched down from the heavens to terminate in three areas of a single building: the Heirarch's Palace, which served as both the residence of Fhileb Ser and her court, and the official seat of the government.

What these three columns represented became apparent when Jared and the 2nd Platoon had descended to less than four kilometers and three particle beams appeared in the sky, lancing downward from the satellites the Special Forces had positioned in low orbit above Enesha. One beam was dim, one furiously bright and the third was dimmest of all and with a curious flicker. The citizenry of Dirluew cooed over the sight and the resonant thunderclap wall of sound that accompanied their appearance. In their simultaneously heightened and diminished state of awareness, they thought the beams were part of the city's light show. Only the invaders and the actual coordinators of Dirluew's light show initially knew any different.

Particle beam–producing satellites are not something the Enesha planetary defense grid would have failed to notice; noticing enemy weapons is what planetary defense grids are *for*. In this particular case, however, the satellites were well-disguised as a trio of repair tugs. The tugs had been planted months earlier—not long after the incident at Gettysburg—as part of the routine service fleet for the Colonial Union's diplomatic berths at one of Enesha's three major space stations. They did, in fact, work perfectly fine as tugs. Their rather unusually modified engines were not apparent externally or by internal systems checks, the latter due to clever software modifications that hid the engines' capabilities to all but the most determined of investigators.

The three tugs had been assigned to haul in the *Kite* after the ship appeared in Eneshan space and asked for permission to repair damage done to its hull and systems after a recent battle with a Rraey cruiser. The *Kite* had won the exchange but had to retreat before its damage could be totally repaired (the *Kite* had picked a fight at one of the Rraey's more moderately defended colonies, where the military strength was strong enough to repel a single Special Forces craft but not strong enough to blast it wholly out of the sky). A routine courtesy tour of the *Kite* for the Eneshan military was offered by its commander but declined as a matter of course by the Eneshan military, who had already confirmed the *Kite*'s story through its informal intelligence channels with the Rraey. The *Kite* also asked for and received permission for members of its crew to have shore leave at Tresh, a resort that had been set aside for Colonial Union diplomats and staff stationed on Enesha. Tresh lay to the southeast of Dirluew, which was just north of the flight path the troop transport carrying two squads' worth of "vacationing" members of the 2nd Platoon had filed.

As the troop transport passed near Dirluew, it reported an atmospheric disturbance and changed course north-ward to avoid chop, edging briefly into the no-fly zone over the Dirluew airspace. Eneshan transport command noted the correction but required the transport to return to its previous flight plan as soon as it edged past the turbu-lence. The transport did, its load two squads lighter, a few minutes later.

It was interesting what you could do, when your enemy was officially your ally. And unaware you knew it was your enemy.

The particle beams seared forth from the tugs assigned to the *Kite* and struck the Hierarch's Palace. The first, the strongest of the beams by a significant margin, tore through six levels of palace, into the guts of the place, to vaporize the palace's backup generator and, twenty me-ters below that, the main power line. Severing the main power line switched the palace's electrical systems to the backup, which had been destroyed milliseconds earlier. In the absence of centralized backup power, various local backups sprang to life and locked down the palace through a system of security doors. The designers of the palace's electrical and security systems reasoned that if both the main power and the backup power were taken down, the entire palace itself would probably be under at-tack. This was correct as far as it went; what the designers did not expect or intend was for the decentralized system of local backups to play an integral part in the attacker's plans.

This beam caused relatively little secondary damage; its energies were tuned specifically to stay contained within its circumference and to bore deep into the Eneshan ground. The resulting hole was more than eighty yards deep before some of the debris thrown up from the beam's work (and some of the debris from the six levels of palace) filled the bottom of the hole to a depth of several meters.

The second beam pierced the palace's administrative wing. Unlike the first beam, this beam was tuned wide and designed to throw off a massive amount of waste heat. The administrative wing of the palace buckled and sweated where the beam struck. Superheated air tore through the offices, blasting wide doors and windows and igniting everything inside with a combustion point below 932 degrees centigrade. More than three dozen Eneshan night-shift government workers, military guards and janitors immolated, broiling instantly within their carapaces. The hierarch's private office and everything in it, directly in the focused center of the beam, turned to ash only fractions of a second before the firestorm the beam's heat and energy created blew those ashes to all corners of the rapidly deconstructing wing.

The second beam was by far the most destructive but the least critical of the three beams. The Special Forces certainly didn't intend or expect to assassinate the heirarch in her private office; she was rarely in it on any evening and would absolutely not have been in it on this night, when she was attending to public functions as part of the Chafalan celebrations. She was on the other side of Dirluew entirely. It would have been a clumsy attempt at best. But the Special Forces wanted it to *look* like a clumsy attempt on the heirarch's life, so the heirarch—and her immense and formidable personal security detail—would be kept far from the palace while the 2nd Platoon accomplished its actual goal.

The third beam had the lowest power of any of them

and flickered as it surgically battered away at the roof of the palace, like a surgeon cauterizing and removing skin one layer at a time. The goal of this beam was not terror or wholesale destruction but to cut a direct pathway to a palace chamber, in which resided the 2nd Platoon's goal, and the lever that, it was hoped, would serve to pry the Eneshans out of their tripartite plan to attack humanity.

::We're going to kidnap what now?:: asked Daniel Harvey.

::We're going to kidnap Vyut Ser,:: Jane Sagan said. ::Heir to the Eneshan throne.::

Daniel Harvey gave a look of sheer incredulousness, and Jared was reminded why Special Forces soldiers, despite their integration, actually bothered to meet physically for briefings: In the end, nothing could really top body language.

Sagan forwarded the intelligence report on the mission and the mission specs, but Harvey piped up again before the information could unpack completely. ::Since when have we gotten into the kidnapping business?:: Harvey asked. ::That's a new wrinkle.::

::We've done abductions before,:: Sagan said. ::This is nothing new.::

::We've abducted *adults*,:: Harvey said. ::And generally speaking they've been people who mean us harm. This kidnapping actually involves a kid.::

::It's more like a grub,:: said Alex Roentgen, who by now had unpacked the mission briefing and had begun to go through it.

::Whatever,:: Harvey said. ::Grub, kid, child. The point is, we're going to use a young innocent as a bargaining chip. Am I right? And that's the first time we've done *that*. It's scummy.::

::This from the guy who usually has to be told not to blow shit up,:: Roentgen said.

Harvey glanced over to Roentgen. ::That's right,:: he said. ::I usually am the guy you have to tell not to blow shit up. And I'm telling you that this mission stinks. What the fuck is wrong with the rest of you?::

::Our enemies don't have the same high standards as you, Harvey,:: Julie Einstein said, and forwarded a picture of the pile of children's corpses at Gettysburg. Jared shivered again.

::Does that mean we have to have the same low standards as they do?:: Harvey said.

::Look,:: Sagan said. ::This isn't up to a vote. Our intelligence people tell me the Rraey, the Eneshans and the Obin are getting close to a big push into our space. We've been harassing the Rraey and the Obin on the margins but we haven't been able to move against the Eneshans because we're still working under the polite fiction that they're our allies. This has given them the time to prepare, and despite all the disinformation we've been feeding them they still know too much about where our weak points are. We've got solid intelligence that says the Eneshans are right up front on any plan of attack. If we move against the Eneshans openly, all three of them will be at our necks, and we don't have the resources to fight them all. Harvey's right: This mission takes us into new territory. But none of our alternative plans have the same impact this one does. We can't break the Eneshans militarily. But we can break them psychologically.::

By this time Jared had absorbed the entire report. ::-We're not stopping with kidnapping,:: he said to Sagan.

::No,:: Sagan said. ::Kidnapping alone won't be enough to make the hierarch agree to our terms.::

::Christ,:: Harvey said. He'd finally absorbed the entire briefing. ::This shit stinks.::

::It beats the alternative,:: Sagan said. ::Unless you really think the Colonial Union can take on three enemies at once.::

::Can I just ask one question?:: said Harvey. ::Why do we get stuck with this crap?::

::We're Special Forces,:: Sagan said. ::This is the sort of thing we do.::

::Bullshit,:: Harvey said. ::You said it yourself. We *don't* do this. *Nobody* does this. We're being made to do this because no one else wants to do this.::

Harvey looked around in the briefing room. ::Come on, we can admit this, to ourselves at least,:: he said. ::Some realborn asshole in military intelligence thought up this plan and then a bunch of realborn generals signed off on it, and then the Colonial Defense Forces' realborn commanders didn't want to have anything to do with it. So *we* get it, and everyone thinks we won't mind because we're a bunch of two-year-old amoral killers. Well, I have morals, and I know everyone in this room does too. I won't back away from a stand-up fight. All of you know that about me. But this isn't a stand-up fight. This is bullshit. First-class bullshit.::

::All right, it's bullshit,:: Sagan said. ::But this is also our mission.::

::Don't ask me to be the one who snatches the thing,:: Harvey said. ::I'll have the back of whoever does it, but that's one cup I'll ask to have passed from me.::

::I won't ask you,:: Sagan said. ::I'll find something else for you to do.::

::Who are you going to get to do the deed?:: Alex Roentgen said.

::I'll do it myself,:: Sagan said. ::I'll want two volunteers to go with me.::

::I already said I'd have your back,:: Harvey said.

::I need someone who will make the snatch if I get a bullet in the head, Harvey,:: Sagan said.

::I'll do it,:: Sarah Pauling said. ::Harvey's right that this shit stinks, though::

::Thank you, Pauling,:: Harvey said.

::You're welcome,:: Pauling said. ::Don't get cocky.::

::That's one,:: Sagan said. ::Anyone else?::

Everyone in the briefing room turned to look at Jared.

::What?:: Jared said, suddenly defensive.

::Nothing,:: said Julie Einstein. ::It's just that you and Pauling are usually a matched pair.::

::That's not true at all,:: Jared said. ::We've been with the platoon for seven months now and I've had all your backs at one time or another.::

::Don't get worked up about it,:: Einstein said. ::No one said you were *married*. And you have had all our backs. But everyone tends to pair off on missions with one person more than others. I get paired with Roentgen. Sagan gets stuck with Harvey because no one else wants to deal with him. You pair up with Pauling. That's all.::

::Stop teasing Jared,:: Pauling said, smiling. ::He's a nice guy, unlike the rest of you degenerates.::

::We're *nice* degenerates,:: Roentgen said.

::Or nicely degenerate, anyway,:: said Einstein.

::If we're all done with our fun,:: Sagan said, ::I still need another volunteer.::

::Dirac,:: Harvey prompted.

::Stop already,:: Sagan said.

::No,:: Jared said. ::I'll do it.::

Sagan seemed about to object, but stopped herself. ::Fine,:: she said, and then continued on with her briefing.

::She did it again,:: Jared sent to Pauling, on a private channel, as the briefing continued. ::You saw it, didn't you? How she was about to say "no."::

::I saw it,:: Pauling said. ::But she didn't. And when it comes down to it she's always treated you just like she treats anyone.::

::I know,:: Jared said. ::I just wish I knew why she doesn't seem to like me.::

::She doesn't really seem to like anyone all *that* much,:: Pauling said. ::Stop being paranoid. Anyway, I like you. Except when you're paranoid.::

::I'll work on that,:: Jared said.

::Do,:: Pauling said. ::And thank you for volunteering.::

::Well, you know,:: Jared said. ::Give the crowd what they want.::

Pauling giggled audibly. Sagan shot her a look. ::Sorry,:: Pauling said, on a common channel.

After a few minutes Jared hailed Pauling on a private channel. ::Do you really think this mission is a bad one?::

::It fucking stinks,:: Pauling said.

The beams ceased, and Jared and the rest of the 2nd popped their parafoils. Charged nanobots extended in tendrils from backpacks and formed individual gliders. Jared, no longer free-falling, tilted himself toward the palace and the smoking hole left by the third beam—a hole that led to the heir's nursery.

At roughly the size of St. Peter's Basilica, the Hierarch's Palace was no small edifice, and outside the main hall where the hierarch held formal court and the now-shattered administrative wing, no non-Eneshans were allowed to enter. There were no architectural plans of the palace in the public record, and the palace itself, constructed in the fluid and chaotically natural Eneshan architectural style that resembled nothing so much as a series of termite mounds, did not lend itself to easy discovery of significant areas or rooms. Before the plan to kidnap the Eneshan heir could be put into action, it had to be discovered where the heir's private chambers lay. Military Research considered it a pretty puzzle, but one without a lot of time to be solved.

Their solution was to think small; indeed, to think single-celled—to think of *C. xavierii*, an Eneshan prokaryotic organism evolutionarily parallel to bacteria. Just as strains of bacteria live in happily symbiotic relationships with humans, so did *C. xavierii* with Eneshans, primarily internally but also externally. Like many humans, not all Eneshans were fastidious about their bathroom habits.

Colonial Union Military Research cracked *C. xavierii* open and resequenced it to create the subspecies *C. xavierii movere*, which coded to construct mitochondrion-sized radio transmitters and receivers. These tiny organic machines recorded the movements of their hosts by polling their positions relative to *C. xavierii movere* housed by other Eneshans within their transmitting range. The recording capacity of these microscopic devices was small—they had the capacity to store less than an hour's worth of movement—but each cellular division created a new recording machine, tracking movement anew.

Military Research introduced the genetically-modified bug into the Hierarch's Palace by way of a hand lotion, provided to an unsuspecting Colonial Union diplomat who had regular physical contact with her Eneshan counterparts. These Eneshans then transmitted the germ to other members of the palace staff simply through everyday contact. The diplomat's personal brain prostheses (and those of her entire staff) were also surreptitiously modified to record the tiny transmissions that would soon emanate from the palace staff and all its inhabitants, including the hierarch and her heir. In less than a month

Military Research had a complete map of the internal structure of the Hierarch's Palace, based on the movement of its staff.

Military Research never told the Colonial Union diplomatic staff of its unintentional espionage. Not only was it safer for the diplomats, but they would have been appalled at how they had been used.

Jared reached the roof of the palace and dissolved his glider, landing away from the hole in case it collapsed. Other members of the 2nd were landing or had landed and were preparing for their descent by securing rappelling lines. Jared spotted Sarah Pauling, who had walked up the hole and was now peering down through the smoke and debris cloud.

::Don't look down,:: Jared said to her.

::Too late for that,:: she replied, and sent him a vertiginous image from her point of view. Through their integration Jared could sense her anxiety and anticipation; he felt that way himself.

The rappelling lines were secure. ::Pauling, Dirac,:: said Jane Sagan. ::Time to move.:: It had been less than five minutes since the beams had torn down from the sky, and each additional second brought the increased chance that their quarry had been moved. They were also working against the eventual arrival of troops and emergency responders. Blowing up the executive wing would distract and delay attention to the 2nd Platoon, but not for long.

The three clipped in and dropped down four levels, straight into the heirarch's residential apartments. The nursery was directly beyond; they had decided not to send the beam down directly on top of the nursery to avoid an accidental collapse. As Jared dropped he sensed the wisdom of that decision; "surgical" or not, the beam had made a mess of the three floors above the heirarch's apartments, and much of the damage had fallen straight down.

::Activate your infrared,:: Sagan said, as they rappelled. ::The lights are down and there's a lot of dust down there.:: Jared and Pauling did as they were told. A glow suffused the air, heated by the exertions of the beam and the smoldering remains below.

Residential guards assigned to the heirarch's apartments flowed into the chamber as the three rappelled down, battering through doors to get at the invaders. Jared, Sagan and Pauling unclipped and dropped heavily into the debris pile below them, hastened by Enesha's heavier gravity. Jared could feel the debris attempting to impale him as he struck it; his unitard stiffened to avoid that. The three swept the room visually and with infrared to locate the guards, and sent the information upward. A few seconds later there were several sharp cracks from the roof. The residential guards dropped.

::You're clear,:: said Alex Roentgen. ::The wing is sealed off and we're not seeing any more guards. More of us are coming down.:: As he said this Julie Einstein and two other members of the 2nd began their descent on the lines.

The nursery adjoined the heirarch's private chamber, and for security purposes the rooms were a single sealable unit, impenetrable to most violent attempts at entry (save massively powerful particle beams shot down from space). Because the two rooms were assumed to be externally secure, the internal security between the rooms was light. A gorgeously carved but single-bolted door was the nursery's only security from the heirarch's chamber. Jared shot the lock and entered the room as Pauling and Sagan covered him.

Something hurtled toward Jared as he checked his corners; he ducked and rolled, and looked up to find an Eneshan attempting to bring an improvised club crashing down on his head. Jared blocked the hit with his arm and kicked upward, connecting with the Eneshan between its forward lower limbs. The Eneshan roared as the kick cracked its carapace. In his peripheral vision Jared registered a second Eneshan in the room, huddled in the corner and holding something that was screaming.

The first Eneshan lunged again, bellowing, and then stopped bellowing but kept lunging, collapsing in a pile on top of Jared. After the Eneshan lay on top of him Jared realized that somewhere in there he'd heard a burst of gunfire. He looked around the body of the Eneshan and saw Sarah Pauling behind it, reaching over to grab the Eneshan's mantle, to pull the corpse off Jared.

::You could have tried killing it when it wasn't moving toward me,:: Jared said.

::Complain again and I'll leave you underneath the damn thing,:: Pauling said. ::Also, if you wouldn't mind pushing, we'll get it off you quicker.:: Pauling pulled and Jared pushed, and the Eneshan rolled to the side. Jared crawled out and got a good look at his attacker.

::Is it him?:: Pauling asked.

::I can't tell,:: Jared said. ::They kind of all look alike.::

::Move,:: Pauling said, and came in close to get a look at the Eneshan. She accessed her mission briefing. ::It's him,:: she said. ::It's the father. It's the heirarch's consort.::

Jared nodded. Jahn Hio, the heirarch's consort, chosen for political reasons to sire the heir. The matriarchal traditions of the Eneshan royalty dictated that the father of the heir was directly responsible for the heir's pre-metamorphic care. Tradition also dictated the father would stay awake at the side of the heir after her consecration ceremony for three Eneshan days, to symbolize the acceptance of his paternal duties. This—among other reasons related to the consecration ceremony—was why the kidnapping was planned when it was. Jahn Hio's assassination was a secondary but critical part of the mission.

::He died for protecting his child,:: Jared said.

::It's *how* he died,:: Pauling said. ::It's not *why* he died.::

::I don't think the distinction matters much to him,:: Jared said.

::This mission stinks,:: Pauling agreed.

A burp of gunfire erupted from the corner of the room. The screaming that had been constant in the room since their entrance stopped briefly and then started up again even more urgently. Sagan came out of the corner, Empee in one hand, a wriggling white mass secured in the other against the crook of her arm. The second Eneshan slumped where Sagan shot it.

::The nanny,:: Sagan said. ::She wouldn't give me the heir.::

::You asked?:: Pauling said.

::I did,:: Sagan said, pointing to the small translation speaker she had clipped on to her belt. It would have use later in the mission. ::I tried, anyway.::

::Our killing the consort probably didn't help,:: Jared said.

The screaming thing in Sagan's arm twisted mightily and nearly got out of her grip. Sagan dropped her Empee to get a better grip on it. It screamed ever louder as she squeezed it securely between her arm and body. Jared peered intently to look at it.

::So that's the heir,:: Jared said.

::This is it,:: Sagan said. ::She, actually. Pre-metamorphic Eneshan. Like a big, screaming maggot.::

::Can we sedate her?:: Pauling asked. ::She's pretty loud.::

::No,:: Sagan said. ::We need the heirarch to see that

she's still alive.:: The heir wriggled again; Sagan began to stroke it with her free hand in an attempt to soothe it. ::Get my Empee for me, Dirac,:: she said. Jared bent down to retrieve the rifle.

The lights went on.

::Oh, shit,:: Sagan said. ::Power's back.::

::I thought we blasted the backup generator,:: Jared said.

::We did,:: Sagan said. ::Looks like there was more than one. Time to go.:: The three backed out of the nursery, Sagan with the heir, Jared with his Empee and Sagan's up and ready.

In the main apartment, two members of the platoon were shimmying up the ropes. Julie Einstein had positioned herself to cover the two doors into the apartment.

::They're going to cover the two levels above us,:: Einstein said. ::The hole goes through rooms on those levels with only one entrance to them. At least that's what the floor plan says. Top level is wide open, though.::

::Transport on its way,:: Alex Roentgen said. ::We've been spotted up here and we're starting to take fire.::

::We need people to cover us coming up,:: Sagan said. ::And to lay down suppressing fire on the first level. It's open; that's where they're going to come through.::

::On it,:: Roentgen said.

Sagan handed the heir to Pauling, unslung her equipment pack and pulled out a shoulder sling with a pouch sized to accommodate the heir. She stuffed the squalling heir into the pouch with some difficulty, secured it and placed the sling across her body with the strap over her right shoulder.

::I'm center line,:: Sagan said. ::Dirac, you're left; Pauling, right. Einstein will cover us as we climb, and then you two cover her and the other two from the top as they get out. Clear?::

::Clear,:: Jared and Pauling said.

::Reload my Empee and give it to Einstein,:: Sagan said to Jared. ::She won't have time to reload.:: Jared cleared the magazine from Sagan's Empee, reloaded it with one of his spares, and handed it to Einstein. She took it and nodded.

::We're ready for you,:: Roentgen said from above. ::You better hurry.::

As they went to their lines they heard the sound of heavy Eneshan footfalls. Einstein began firing as they started to climb. At each of the next two levels Jared's platoon mates were calmly waiting, sighted in on their sole entrances. Jared's integration told him they were both scared shitless and waiting for the shoe to drop.

From above Jared new firing began. The Eneshans had come through on the top level.

Sagan was weighed down by the heir but lacking her Empee or her equipment pack; on balace she was traveling light, and flew up her line, ahead of Jared and Pauling. The pair of bullets that stitched across her shoulder hit her as she was within reach of the top, and grasping for the hand of Julian Lowell to pull her up. A third bullet slipped past Sagan's shoulder and struck Lowell directly above his right eye, passing through his brain before ricocheting off the inside of his skull and burying itself in his neck, severing his carotid in the process. Lowell's head snapped back and then forward, his body slumping and falling forward into the hole. He collided with Sagan as he fell, tearing the final scrap of fabric that kept intact the sling holding the heir. Sagan felt the tear and the sling falling away but was too occupied trying to keep herself from falling to do anything about it.

::Catch it,:: she said, and was grabbed by Alex Roentgen and pulled to safety.

Jared grabbed and missed; it was too far away. The sling

rippled past Pauling, who snatched it as it fell and then swung as it described an arc around her.

From below, Jared sensed a surprised shock of pain from Julie Einstein. Her Empee went silent. The rustling sound that followed was the sound of Eneshans climbing into the heirarch's chambers.

Pauling looked up at Jared. ::Climb,:: she said.

Jared climbed without looking down. As he passed the upper level of the palace he glimpsed the bodies of a score of dead Eneshans, and more live Eneshans behind them firing at Jared as he climbed, while Jared's platoon mates fired back with bullets and grenades. Then he was beyond them, pulled up by an unseen platoon mate onto the roof of the palace. He turned back to see Sarah Pauling on her line, sling in hand, Eneshans below her aiming upward at her. Holding the sling, she could not climb.

Pauling looked at Jared, and smiled. ::Beloved,:: she said, and flung the sling to him as the first of the bullets struck her body. Jared reached as she danced on her line, moved by the force of the projectiles that overwhelmed the defenses of her unitard and tore into her legs, torso, back and skull. He caught the sling as she fell, and pulled it from the hole as she found its bottom. He felt the last second of her life and then it was gone.

He was screaming as they pulled him into the transport.

The Eneshan culture is both matriarchal and tribal, as befits a race whose far distant ancestors were hive-dwelling, insect-like creatures. The hierarch comes to power through the vote of the matriarchs of the major Eneshan tribes; this makes the process sound rather more civilized than it is, since the vote-gathering process can involve years of unspeakably violent civil war, as the tribes battle to make their own matriarch ascendant. To avoid massive unrest at the end of every hierarch's reign, once a hierarch is chosen the position becomes hereditary, and aggressively so: A hierarch must produce *and* consecrate a viable heir within two Eneshan years of assuming the mantle—thus assuring an orderly transfer of power for the future—or have the hierarchical rule of her tribe end with her reign.

Eneshan matriarchs, fed hormonally-dense royal jellies that produce sweeping changes in their bodies (another artifact of their ancestry), are fertile lifelong. The ability to produce an heir was rarely an issue. What would become an issue was from which tribe to choose the father. Matriarchs do not marry for love (strictly speaking, Eneshans don't marry at all), so political considerations would now come into play. The tribes unable to achieve hierarchy now competed (on a much subtler and usually less violent level) to produce a consort, with the reward being social advantages for the tribe directly, and the ability to influence hierarchical policies as part of the "dowry" provided the consortial tribe. Hierarchs from newly-ascendent tribes traditionally took their consort either from their tribe's greatest ally, as a reward for service, or from the tribe of their greatest enemy, if the hierarchical "vote" had been particularly messy and there was a perception that the entire Eneshan nation needed to be cobbled back together. Hierarchs from established lines, on the other hand, had far greater leeway in choosing their consorts.

Fhileb Ser was the sixth hierarch in the current Ser line (the tribe had held the hierarchy three times previous over the last several hundred Eneshan years). Upon ascending she chose her consort from the Hio tribe, a tribe whose expansionist colonial ambitions eventually led to the decision to ally in secret with the Rraey and the Obin, in order to attack human space. For its primary role in the war,

Enesha would come away with some of the Colonial Union's prime real estate, including the Colonial Union home planet of Phoenix. The Rraey would come away with somewhat fewer planets but would get Coral, the planet that was the site of their recent humiliation by the Colonial Union.

The Obin, cryptic to the last, offered to contribute forces only slightly less expansive than the Eneshans but asked only for a single planet: the overpopulated and resource-stripped Earth, which was in such apparent poor repair that the Colonial Union had it under quarantine. Both the Eneshans and the Rraey were happy to cede the planet.

Hierarchical policy, prompted by the Hio, inclined the Enesha to plan a war with the humans. But although united by hierarchical rule, each Eneshan tribe kept its own counsel. At least one tribe, the Geln, strongly opposed attacking the Colonial Union, since humans were reasonably strong, distressingly tenacious and not especially principled when they felt threatened. The Geln felt that the Rraey would have been a far better target, given that race's long-standing enmity with the Eneshans and its weak military state after being crushed by the humans at Coral.

Hierarch Fhileb Ser chose to ignore the Gelns' counsel in this matter, but, noting the tribe's apparent fondness for humanity, selected one of the Gelns' tribal counselors, Hu Geln, as Enesha's ambassador to the Colonial Union. Hu Geln, recently recalled to Enesha to witness the Consecration of the Heir and to celebrate Chafalan with the hierarch. Hu Geln, who was with the hierarch when the 2nd Platoon attacked, and who was with her now, in hiding, as she was hailed by the humans who had murdered her consort and stolen her heir.

* * *

::They've stopped firing at us,:: Alex Roentgen said. ::Looks like they've figured out we have the heir.::

::Good,:: Sagan said. Pauling and Einstein were dead but she had other soldiers stuck in the palace and she wanted to get them out. She signaled them to make their way to the transport. She winced as Daniel Harvey tended to her shoulder; her unitard blocked the first hit completely but the second managed to get through and did some real damage. For now, her right arm was entirely useless. She motioned with her left hand to the small gurney in the middle of the transport, where the wriggling form of Vyut Ser, heir to the hierarch, lay securely strapped in. The heir no longer screamed but mewled, her fear tempered by exhaustion.

::Someone needs to give her the shot,:: Sagan said.

::I'll do it,:: Jared said, stood before anyone else could volunteer, and retrieved the long needle stored in a medical kit below Sagan's transport seat. He turned and stood over Vyut Ser, hating the thing. An overlay popped into his vision, via his BrainPal, showing him where to insert the needle and how far to push into the heir's guts to deliver what was inside the syringe.

Jared jabbed the needle savagely into Vyut Ser, who screamed horribly at the invasion of the cold metal. Jared pressed the button on the syringe that shot half the contents into one of the heir's two immature reproductive sacs. Jared extracted the needle and plunged it into Vyut Ser's second reproductive sac, emptying the syringe. Inside the sacs nanobots coated the interior walls and then burned, searing the tissues dead, rendering their owner irreversibly sterile.

Vyut Ser wailed in confusion and pain.

::I've got the hierarch on the line,:: Roentgen said. ::Audio and video.::

::Pipe her into the general feed,:: Sagan said. ::And Alex, stand by the gurney. You get to be the camera.::

Roentgen nodded and stood in front the gurney, fixing on Sagan and allowing the audio and visual feeds to his BrainPal from his ears and eyes to serve as microphone and camera.

::Piping in now,:: Roentgen said. In Jared's field of vision—and in the field of vision of everyone in the transport—the Hierarch of Enesha appeared. Even without knowing the map of Eneshan expressions, it was clear the hierarch was incandescent with rage.

"You fucking piece of human shit," the hierarch said (or the translation said, eschewing a literal translation for something that expressed the intent behind the words). "You have thirty seconds to give me my daughter or I will declare war on every last one of your worlds. I swear to you I will reduce them to rubble."

"Shut up," Sagan said, the translation coming from her belt speaker.

From the other end of the line came multiple loud clacks, indicating absolute shock from the hierarch's court. It was simply inconceivable someone would speak to her that way.

"I beg your pardon," the hierarch said, eventually, shocked herself.

"I said, 'shut up,' " Sagan said. "If you are smart you will listen to what I have to say to you and spare both our peoples needless suffering. Hierarch, you won't declare war on the Colonial Union here because you've already declared war on us. You, the Rraey and the Obin."

"I don't have the slightest—" the heirarch began.

"Lie to me again and I'll cut off your daughter's head," Sagan said.

More clacks. The hierarch shut up.

"Now," Sagan said. "Are you at war with the Colonial Union?"

"Yes," the hierarch said, after a long moment. "Or will be, presently."

"I think not," Sagan said.

"Who *are* you?" the hierarch said. "Where is Ambassador Hartling? Why I am negotiating with someone who is threatening to kill my child?"

"I imagine Ambassador Hartling is in her office right now, trying to figure out what's going on," Sagan said. "As you did not feel the need to enlighten her concerning your military plans, neither did we. You are negotiating with the person who has threatened to kill your child because you have threatened to kill *our* children, Hierarch. And you are negotiating with me because at the moment I am the negotiator you deserve. And you can be assured on this matter you will not be able to negotiate with the Colonial Union again."

The hierarch fell silent again. "Show me my daughter," she said, when she spoke again.

Sagan nodded to Roentgen, who turned and showed Vyut Ser, who had once again downshifted into whimpering. Jared saw the reaction of the hierarch, who was reduced from the leader of a world to merely a mother, feeling the pain and fear of her own child.

"What are your demands?" the hierarch said, simply.

"Call off your war," Sagan said.

"There are two other parties," the hierarch said. "If we back out they will want to know why."

"Then continue preparing for war," Sagan said. "And then attack one of your allies instead. I would suggest the

Rraey. They are weak, and you could take them by surprise."

"And what of the Obin?" the hierarch said.

"We'll deal with the Obin," Sagan said.

"Will you, now," the hierarch said, clearly skeptical.

"Yes," Sagan said.

"Are you suggesting we can simply hide what happened here tonight?" the hierarch said. "The beams you used to destroy my palace could be seen for a hundred miles."

"Don't hide it, investigate it," Sagan said. "The Colonial Union will gladly help our Eneshan friends in their investigation. And when it's discovered the Rraey are behind it, you'll have your rationale for war."

"Your other demands," the hierarch said.

"There is a human, named Charles Boutin," Sagan said. "We know he's helping you. We want him."

"We don't have him," the hierarch said. "The Obin do. You can ask them for him, for all I care. Your other demands."

"We want assurances that you will call off your war," Sagan said.

"You want a treaty?" the hierarch asked.

"No," Sagan said. "We want a new consort. One of our choosing."

This generated the loudest clack of all from the court.

"You *murder* my consort, and then you *demand* to pick the next one?" the hierarch said.

"Yes," Sagan said.

"To what end?" the hierarch implored. "My Vyut has been consecrated! She is the legal heir. If I meet your demands and you let my daughter go, she is still of the Hio clan and by our traditions they will still have political influence. You would have to kill my daughter to break their influence"—the hierarch paused brokenly, then continued—"and if you do that, why would I fulfill any of your demands?"

"Hierarch," Sagan said, "your daughter is sterile."

Silence.

"You didn't," the hierarch said, pleading.

"We did," Sagan said.

The hierarch rubbed her mouthpieces together, creating an unworldly keening noise. She was crying. She got up from her seat, out of frame, keening, and then suddenly reappeared, too close to the camera. "You are monsters!" the hierarch screamed. Sagan said nothing.

The Consecration of the Heir cannot be undone. A sterile heir means the death of a hierarchical line. The death of a hierarchical line means years of unyielding and bloody civil war as tribes compete to found a new line. If the tribes knew an heir was sterile, they would not wait for the natural span of the heir's life to begin their internecine warfare. First the sitting hierarch would be assassinated, to bring the sterile heir to power. Then she would be a constant assassination target as well. When power is within reach, few will wait patiently for it.

By making Vyut Ser sterile, the Colonial Union had sentenced the Ser hierarchical line to oblivion and the Enesha to anarchy. Unless the hierarch gave in to their demands and consented to something unspeakable. And the hierarch knew it.

She fought it anyway. "I will not allow you to choose my consort," the hierarch said.

"We will inform the matriarchs your daughter is sterile," Sagan said.

"I will destroy your transport where it sits, and my daughter with you," the hierarch screamed.

"Do it," Sagan said. "And all the matriarchs will know that your incompetence as hierarch led us to attack you and caused the death of your consort and your heir. And then you may find that while you may *choose* a tribe to provide you with a consort, the tribe itself may not agree to provide one. No consort, no heir. No heir, no peace. We know Eneshan history, Hierarch. We know the tribes have withheld consorts for less, and that those boycotted hierarchs didn't last long after that."

"It won't happen," the hierarch said.

Sagan shrugged. "Kill us, then," she said. "Or refuse our demands, and we'll give you back your sterile daughter. Or do it our way and have our cooperation in extending your hierarchical line and keeping your nation from civil war. These are your choices. And your time is almost up."

Jared watched emotions play the hierarch's face and body, strange because of their alien nature but no less powerful for that. It was a quiet and heartrending struggle. Jared was reminded that at the briefing for the mission Sagan said that humans couldn't break the Eneshans militarily; they had to break them psychologically. Jared watched as the hierarch bent and bent and bent and then broke.

"Tell me who I am to seize upon," the hierarch said.

"Hu Geln," Sagan said.

The hierarch turned to look at Hu Glen, standing quietly in the background, and gave the Eneshan equivalent of a bitter laugh. "I am not surprised," she said.

"He is a good man," Sagan said. "And he will counsel you well."

"Try to console me again, human," the hierarch said, "and I will send us all into war."

"My apologies, Hierarch," Sagan said. "Do we have agreement?"

"Yes," the hierarch said, and began her keening again. "Oh, God," she cried. "Oh, Vyut. Oh, God."

"You know what you have to do," Sagan said.

"I can't. I can't," the hierarch cried. At the sound of the cries, Vyut Ser, who had been silent, stirred and cried for her mother. The hierarch broke anew.

"You have to," Sagan said.

"Please," the most powerful creature on the planet begged. "I can't. Please. Please, human. Please help me."

::Dirac,:: Sagan said. ::Do it.::

Jared unsheathed his combat knife and approached the thing that Sarah Pauling had died for. She was strapped to a gurney and she wriggled and cried for her mother, and she would die alone and frightened, and far away from anyone that ever loved her.

Jared broke too. He did not know why.

Jane Sagan walked over to Jared and took his knife and raised it. Jared turned away.

The crying stopped.

PART II

EIGHT

It was the black jellybeans that did it.

Jared saw them as he was browsing at a Phoenix Station commissary candy stand, and passed them over, more interested in the chocolates. But his eye kept going back to them, a small container segregated out from the rest of the jellybeans, which were in a mixed assortment.

"Why do you do that?" Jared asked the vendor, after his eyes tracked back to the black jellybeans for the fifth time. "What makes the black jellybeans so special?"

"People either love 'em or hate 'em," the vendor said. "The people who hate 'em—that's most people—don't like having to pick them out of the rest of the jellybeans. The people who love 'em like to have their own little bag of 'em. So I keep some on hand but in their own space."

"Which sort are you?" Jared asked.

"I can't stand them," the vendor said. "But my husband can't get enough. And he'll breathe on me while he's eating them, just to annoy me. I kicked him right off the bed, once, for doing that. You've never had a black jellybean?"

"No," Jared said. His mouth was watering slightly. "But I think I'll try some."

"Brave man," the vendor said, and filled a small clear plastic bag with the candies to hand to Jared. Jared took it and fished out two jellybeans while the vendor rang up the order; being in the CDF, Jared didn't pay for the jellybeans (they, like everything else, were gratis on what CDF soldiers lovingly referred to as their all-inclusive package tour of hell), but vendors kept track of what they sold to soldiers and billed the CDF accordingly. Capitalism had made it to space and was doing reasonably well.

Jared took the pair of jellybeans and popped them into his mouth, crushed them with his molars and then held them there as his saliva suffused the licorice flavor over his tongue, vapors of its scent moving beyond his palate and expanding in his sinus cavity. His eyes closed, and he realized that they were just as he remembered. He took a handful and crammed them into his mouth.

"How are they?" the vendor said, watching the enthusiastic consumption.

"They're good," Jared said, between jellybeans. "Really good."

"I'll tell my husband there's another on his team," the vendor said.

Jared nodded. "Two," he said. "My little girl loves them too."

"Even better," the vendor said, but by this time Jared had stepped away, lost in thought, heading back toward his office. Jared took ten steps, completely swallowed the mass of jellybeans in his mouth, reached to get more and stopped.

My little girl, he thought, and was hit with a thick knot of grief and memory that made him convulse, gag and vomit his jellybeans on the level walkway. As he coughed the last fragment of the candies from his throat, a name formed in his head.

Zoë, Jared thought. *My daughter. My daughter who is dead*.

A hand touched his shoulder. Jared recoiled, almost slipping on the vomit as he twisted away, bag of jellybeans flying from his hand. He looked at the woman who had touched him, a CDF soldier of some sort. She looked at him strangely and then there was a short, sharp buzz in his head like a human voice accelerated to ten times speed. It happened again and once more, like two slaps on the inside of his head.

"What?" Jared yelled at the woman.

"Dirac," she said. "Calm down. Tell me what's wrong."

Jared felt disoriented fear and quickly stepped away from the solider, clipping other pedestrians as he heaved away.

Jane Sagan watched Dirac stumble away and then looked down at the dark splash of vomit and the splay of jellybeans on the floor. She looked back toward the candy stand and stalked over.

"You," she said, pointing to the vendor. "Tell me what happened."

"The guy came over and bought some black jellybeans," the vendor said. "Said he loved them and shoved a bunch into his mouth. Then he takes a couple of steps and throws up."

"That's it," Sagan said.

"That's it," the vendor said. "I made small talk about how my husband likes black jellybeans, he said his kid likes them too, he took the jellybeans and he walked off."

"He talked about his kid," Sagan said.

"Yeah," the vendor said. "He said he had a little girl."

Sagan looked down the walkway. There was no sign of Dirac. She starting running in the direction she last saw him going and tried to open a channel to General Szilard.

Jared reached a station lift as others were exiting, jabbed the button for his lab's level and suddenly realized his arm was green. He retracted it with such violence that it smacked hard against the lift wall, bringing into sharp, painful focus that it was, in fact, his arm, and that he wasn't going to get away from it. The other people in the lift looked at him strangely, and in one case with actual venom; he'd almost hit a woman when he drew back his arm.

"Sorry," he said. The woman snorted and performed the forward-looking elevator stare. Jared did the same and saw a smeary reflection of his green self in the brushed metal walls of the lift. Jared's confused anxiety by this point was peaking toward terror, but one thing he did know was that he didn't want to lose his shit in an elevator filled with strangers. Social conditioning was, for the moment, stronger than panic over confused identity.

If Jared were to have taken a moment to question who he was, standing there silently in the lift and waiting for his level, he would have come to the startled realization that he wasn't exactly sure. But he hadn't; on a day-to-day basis people don't question their identity. Jared knew that being green wasn't right, his lab was three levels down from where he was, and that his daughter Zoë was dead.

The lift reached Jared's level; he stepped out to a wide hallway. This level of Phoenix Station had no candy stands or commissaries; it was one of the two levels of the station given over primarily to military research. CDF soldiers stood every hundred feet or so, monitoring hallways that led deeper into the level. Each hallway was fronted by biometric and BrainPal/brain prosthesis scanners that scanned every individual who approached. If that person was not allowed down the hallway, the CDF guard would intercept them before they made it to the hallway itself.

Jared knew that he was supposed to have access to most of these hallways, but doubted that this strange body would have clearance for any of them. He set down the hall, walking as if he had a purpose, toward the hallway he knew held his lab and his office. Maybe by the time he got there he'd figure out what to do next. He was almost there when he saw every CDF guard in front of him in the hallway turn and look at him.

Crap, Jared thought. His hallway was less than fifty feet away. On impulse he sprinted toward it and was surprised at how fast his body took off toward his goal. So was the soldier guarding it; he whipped up his Empee but by the time it was up Jared was on him. Jared shoved the soldier, hard. The soldier bounced off the hallway wall and fell. Jared sprinted past him without breaking his stride and ran to his lab door, two hundred feet down the corridor. As Jared ran, sirens blared and emergency doors slammed shut; Jared barely passed the threshold of the one that would have separated him from his goal when it shot out from the corridor sides, sealing the section in less than half a second.

Jared reached the door to his lab and thrust it open. Inside were a CDF military research technician and a Rraey. Jared was struck immobile by the cognitive dissonance of having a Rraey in his lab, and through the confusion came a knife-like frisson of fear, not of the Rraey, but from having been caught doing something dangerous and terrible and punishable. Jared's brain surged, looking for a memory or explanation to attach to the fear, but arrived at nothing.

The Rraey wiggled its head and came around the desk at which it had been standing, and moved toward Jared.

"You're him, aren't you?" the Rraey said, in strangely pronounced but recognizable English.

"Who?" Jared asked.

"The soldier they made to trap a traitor," the Rraey said. "But they couldn't do it."

"I don't understand you," Jared said. "This is my lab. Who are you?"

The Rraey wiggled its head again. "Or maybe they did, after all," the Rraey said. It pointed to itself. "Cainen. Scientist and prisoner. Now you know who I am. Do you know who *you* are?"

Jared opened his mouth to answer and realized he did not know who he was. He stood there dumb and open-mouthed until the emergency doors flew open a few seconds later. The woman soldier he had talked to earlier stepped through, raised a pistol, and shot him in the head.

::First question,:: General Szilard said. Jared lay in the Phoenix Station infirmary, recovering from his stun bolt, with two CDF guards stationed at the foot of his bed and Jane Sagan standing by the wall. ::Who are you?::

::I'm Private Jared Dirac,:: Jared said. He did not ask who Szilard was; his BrainPal ID'd him as he entered the room. Szilard's own BrainPal could have as easily ID'd Jared, so the question wasn't a matter of mere identification. ::I'm stationed on the *Kite*. My commanding officer is Lieutenant Sagan, who is over there.::

::Second question,:: General Szilard said. ::Do you know who Charles Boutin is?::

::No, sir,:: Jared said. ::Should I?::

::Possibly,:: Szilard said. ::It was his lab we found you standing in front of. It was his lab that you told that Rraey was yours. Which suggests that you thought you *were* Charles Boutin, at least for a minute. And Lieutenant Sagan tells me that you wouldn't respond to your name when she tried to talk to you.::

::I remember not knowing that I was me,:: Jared said. ::But I don't remember thinking I was anyone else.::

::But you got to Boutin's lab without ever having been there before,:: Szilard said. ::And we know you didn't access your BrainPal for a station map in order to find it.::

::I can't explain it,:: Jared said. ::The memory of it was just in my head.:: Jared saw Szilard glance over at Sagan at that.

The door opened and two men walked through. One of the men stalked over to Jared before his BrainPal could identify him.

"Do you know who I am?" he said.

Jared's punch sent the man to the floor. The guards raised their Empees; Jared, already coming down from his sudden surge of rage and adrenaline, immediately put his hands up.

The man stood up as Jared's BrainPal finally identified him as General Greg Mattson, head of Military Research.

"That answers *that*," Mattson said, holding his hand to his right eye. He stalked off toward the room's lavatory, to check out the damage.

"Don't be so sure," Szilard said. He turned to Jared. "Private, do you know the man you just struck?"

"I know now he's General Mattson," Jared said. "But I didn't know that when I struck him."

"Why did you strike him?" Szilard asked.

"I don't know, sir," Jared said. "It just . . ." He stopped.

"Answer the question, Private," Szilard said.

"It just seemed like the right thing to do at the time," Jared said. "I can't explain why."

"He's definitely remembering some things," Szilard said, turning to Mattson. "But he's not remembering it all. And he doesn't remember who he was."

"Crap," Mattson said, from the lavatory. "He remembered enough to punch me in the head. That son of a bitch has been waiting to do that for years."

"He could be remembering it all and trying to convince you that he doesn't, General," the other man said to Szilard. Jared's BrainPal identified him as Colonel James Robbins.

"It's possible," Szilard said. "But his actions so far don't seem to suggest it. If he really were Boutin, it wouldn't be in his interest to let us know he remembered anything at all. Punching out the general wouldn't have been very smart."

"Not smart," Mattson said, coming out of the lavatory. "Just cathartic." He turned to Jared and pointed to his eye, ringed in gray where the SmartBlood had been smashed out of blood vessels, causing a bruise. "Back on Earth, you'd have hung this shiner on me for a couple of weeks. I should have you shot just on principle."

"General," Szilard began.

"Relax, Szi," Mattson said. "I buy your theory. Boutin wouldn't be stupid enough to punch me, so this isn't Boutin. Bits of him are coming out, though, and I want to see how much we can get."

"The war Boutin tried to start is over, General," Jane Sagan said. "The Enesha are going to turn on the Rraey."

"Well, that's wonderful, Lieutenant," Mattson said. "But in this case two out of three won't do. The Obin may still be planning something, and since it looks like Boutin is with them, perhaps we shouldn't go declaring victory and calling off the search just yet. We still need to know what

Boutin knows, and now that the private here has got two people rattling around in his skull, perhaps we can do a little more to encourage the other one to come out and play." He turned to Jared. "What do you say, Private? They call you guys the Ghost Brigades, but you're the only one with a *real* ghost in your head. Want to get it out?"

"With all due respect, sir, I have no idea what you're talking about," Jared said.

"Of course you don't," Mattson said. "Apparently, other than where his lab is, you don't know a goddamn thing about Charles Boutin at all."

"I know one other thing," Jared said. "I know he had a daughter."

General Mattson touched his hand gingerly to his black eye. "That he did, Private." Mattson dropped his hand and turned to Szilard. "I want you to give him back to me, Szi," he said, and then noticed Lieutenant Sagan shoot Szilard a glance; no doubt she was sending him one of those rat-a-tat mental messages Special Forces used instead of speech. "It's only temporary, Lieutenant," he said. "You can have him back when we're done. And I promise I won't break him. But we're not going to get anything useful out of him if he gets shot dead on a mission."

"You didn't have a problem with him getting shot dead on a mission before," Sagan said. "Sir."

"Ah, the vaunted Special Forces snotty attitude," Mattson said. "I was wondering when it would become obvious you were six."

"I'm nine," Sagan said.

"And I'm one hundred and thirty, so listen to your great-great-grandfather," Mattson said. "I didn't care if he died before because I didn't think he was useful. Now he may be useful, so I'd rather he didn't die. If it turns out he's not useful, then you can have him back and he can die all over again for all I care. Regardless, you don't get a vote. Now shut up, Lieutenant, and let the grown-ups talk." Sagan stewed but shut up.

"What are you going to do with him?" Szilard asked.

"I'm going to put him under the microscope, of course," Mattson said. "Find out why he's leaking memories now and see what it takes to leak a few more." He jerked a thumb back to Robbins. "Officially, he'll be assigned to Robbins as an assistant. Unofficially, I expect he'll be spending a lot of time down at the lab. That Rraey scientist we took off your hands has been coming in useful down there. We'll see what he can do with him."

"You think you can trust a Rraey?" Szilard asked.

"Shit, Szi," Mattson said. "We don't let him turd without a camera up his ass. And he'll die in a day without his medicine. He the only scientist I have that I absolutely know I *can* trust."

"All right," Szilard said. "You gave him to me once when I asked. You can have him now. Just remember he's one of ours, General. And you know how I am about my people."

"Fair enough," Mattson said.

"The transfer order is in your queue," Szilard said. "As soon as you approve it, it's done." Szilard nodded to Robbins and Sagan, glanced over to Jared, and left.

Mattson turned to Sagan. "If you've got any good-byes to make, now's the time to do them."

"Thank you, General," Sagan said. ::What an asshole,:: she said to Jared.

::I still don't know what's going on or who Charles Boutin is,:: Jared said. ::I tried accessing information on him but it's all classified.::

::You're going to find out soon enough,:: Sagan said. ::Whatever you learn, I want to you to remember one thing. At the end of it all, you're Jared Dirac. No one else. No matter how you were made or why or what happens. I sometimes forgot that about you, and I'm sorry for it. But I want you to remember it.::

::I'll remember it,:: Jared said.

::Good,:: Sagan said. ::When you see this Rraey they're talking about, his name is Cainen. Tell him that Lieutenant Sagan asked him to look out for you. Tell him I would consider it a favor.::

::I've met him,:: Jared said. ::I'll tell him.::

::And I'm sorry for shooting you in the head with the stun bolt,:: Sagan said. ::You know how it is.::

::I do,:: Jared said. ::Thank you. Good-bye, Lieutenant.::
Sagan left.

Mattson pointed to the guards. "You two are dismissed." The guards left. "Now," Mattson said, turning to Jared. "I'm going to work under the assumption that your little seizure earlier today is not going to be a frequent occurrence, Private. Just the same, from now on your Brain-Pal is set to record and locate, so we have no surprises from you and we always know how to find you. Change the setting just once and every CDF soldier on Phoenix Station will get the go-ahead to shoot you dead. Until we know exactly who and what's in your head, you don't get any private thoughts. Do you understand me?"

"I understand you," Jared said.

"Excellent," Mattson said. "Then welcome to Military Research, son."

"Thank you, sir," Jared said. "And now, will someone please *finally* tell me what the hell is going on?"

Mattson smiled, and turned to Robbins. "You tell him," Mattson said, and left.

Jared turned his gaze to Robbins.

"Uh," Robbins said. "Hello."

* * *

"That's an interesting bruise you have there," Cainen said, pointing to the side of Jared's head. Cainen was speaking his own language; Jared's BrainPal provided the translation.

"Thanks," Jared said. "I was shot." Jared spoke his own language as well; after several months, Cainen's English proficiency was quite good.

"I remember," Cainen said. "I was there. As it happens, I was once stunned by your Lieutenant Sagan too. We should start a club, you and I." Cainen turned to Harry Wilson, who was standing nearby. "You can join too, Wilson."

"I'll pass," Wilson said. "I'm reminded of a wise man who once said that he would never want to join a club that would have him for a member. Also, I'd rather not get zapped."

"Coward," said Cainen.

Wilson bowed. "At your service."

"And now," Cainen said, bringing his attention back to Jared. "I trust you have some idea of why you're here."

Jared recalled the awkward and not especially forthcoming conversation with Colonel Robbins the day before. "Colonel Robbins told me that I had been born for the purpose of transferring this Charles Boutin's consciousness into my brain, but that it didn't take. He told me that Boutin had been a scientist here but that he'd turned traitor. And he told me that these new memories that I'm sensing are actually Boutin's old memories, and that no one knows why they are coming out now instead of earlier."

"How much detail did he give you about Boutin's life or research?" Wilson asked.

"None, really," Jared said. "He said if I learned too

much from him or from their files, it might interfere with my memory coming back naturally. Will it?"

Wilson shrugged. Cainen said, "Since you're the first human to whom this has happened, there's no history to go on as to what we should do next. The closest thing to this are certain types of amnesia. Yesterday, you were able to find this lab and recall the name of Boutin's daughter, but you don't know how you knew it. That's similar to source amnesia. What makes it entirely different is that the problem isn't your own memory, it's someone else's."

"So *you* don't know how to get any more memories out of me, either," Jared said.

"We have theories," Wilson said.

"Theories," Jared said.

"Hypotheses, more accurately," Cainen said. "I remember many months ago telling Lieutenant Sagan that the reason I thought Boutin's consciousness didn't take in you was that his was a mature consciousness, and when it was put into an immature brain that hadn't had enough experiences, it couldn't find a grip. But now you have those experiences, don't you? Seven months at war will season any mind. And perhaps something you experienced acted as a bridge to Boutin's memories."

Jared thought back. "My last mission," he said. "Someone very important to me died. And Boutin's daughter is dead as well." Jared didn't mention the assassination of Vyut Ser to Cainen, and his breakdown as he held the knife that would kill her, but it was in his mind as well.

Cainen nodded his head, showing his understanding of human language included nonverbal signals. "That could have been the moment, indeed."

"But why didn't the memories come back then?" Jared asked. "It happened when I was back on Phoenix Station, eating black jellybeans."

"*Remembrance of Things Past,*" Wilson said.

Jared looked at Wilson. "What?"

"Actually, *In Search of Lost Time* is a better translation of the original title," Wilson said. "It's a novel by Marcel Proust. The book begins with the main character experiencing a flood of memories from his childhood, brought on by eating some cake he dipped in his tea. Memories and senses are closely tied in humans. Eating those jellybeans could easily have triggered those memories, especially if the jellybeans were significant in some way."

"I remember saying that they were Zoë's favorites," Jared said. "Boutin's daughter. Her name was Zoë."

"That might have been enough," Cainen agreed.

"Maybe you should have some more jellybeans," Wilson joked.

"I did," Jared said, seriously. He had asked Colonel Robbins to get him a new bag; he was too embarrassed from his earlier vomiting to ask for one himself. Jared had sat in his new quarters, bag in hand, slowly eating black jellybeans for an hour.

"And?" Wilson asked. Jared just shook his head.

"Let me show you something, Private," Cainen said, and pressed a button on his keyboard. In the display area of his desk, three small light shows appeared. Cainen pointed to one. "This is a representation of Charles Boutin's consciousness, a copy of which, thanks to his technological industriousness, we have on file. This next one is a representation of your own consciousness, taken from during your training period." Jared looked surprised. "Yes, Private, they've been keeping tabs on you; you've been their science experiment since you were born. But this is just a representation. Unlike Boutin's consciousness, they don't have yours on file.

"This third image is your consciousness right now,"

Cainen said. "You're not trained to read these representations, but even to an uninformed eye it is clearly different than either of the other two representations. This is—we think—the first incident of your brain trying to meld what it's received of Boutin's consciousness with your own. Yesterday's incident changed you, probably permanently. Can you feel it?"

Jared thought about it. "I don't feel any different," he said, finally. "I have new memories, but I don't think I'm acting any differently than I usually do."

"Except for punching out generals," Wilson pointed out.

"It was an accident," Jared said.

"No, it wasn't," Cainen said, suddenly animated. "This is my point to you, Private. You were born to be one person. You became another. And now, you're becoming a third—a combination of the first two. If we continue on, if we're successful, more of who Boutin was will come through. You will change. Your personality could change, perhaps dramatically. Who you will *become* will be something different from what you are *now*. I want to make sure you understand this, because I want you to make a choice about whether you want this to happen."

"A choice?" Jared asked.

"Yes, Private, a *choice*," Cainen said. "Which is something you rarely make." He pointed to Wilson. "Lieutenant Wilson here chose this life: He signed up for the Colonial Defense Forces of his own accord. You, and all your Special Forces kind, were not given that choice. Do you realize, Private, that Special Forces soldiers are slaves? You have no say in whether you fight. You are not allowed to refuse. You're not even allowed to know that refusal is *possible*."

Jared was uncomfortable with this line of reasoning. "We don't see it that way. We're proud to serve."

"Of course you are," Cainen said. "That's how they've conditioned you since you were born, when your brain was turned on and your BrainPal thought for you and chose particular branches on the decision tree instead of others. By the time your brain was able to think on its own, the pathways that turn against choice were already laid down."

"I make choices all the time," Jared countered.

"Not big ones," Cainen said. "Through conditioning and a military life, choices were made for you all your short life, Private. Someone else chose to create you—no different than anyone else, that. But then they chose to imprint someone else's consciousness on your brain. They chose to make you a warrior. They chose the battles you would face. They chose to hand you over to us when it was convenient for them. And they would choose to have you become someone else by cracking your brain like an egg and letting Charles Boutin's consciousness run out all over yours. But *I* am choosing to have you choose."

"Why?" Jared asked.

"Because I can," Cainen said. "And because you should. And because apparently no one else will let you. This is *your* life, Private. If you choose to proceed, we'll suggest to you the ways we think will unlock more of Boutin's memories and personality."

"And if I don't?" Jared said. "What happens then?"

"Then we tell Military Research that we refuse to do anything to you," Wilson said.

"They could find someone else to do it," Jared said.

"They almost certainly *will*," Cainen said. "But you'll have made your choice, and we'll have made ours too."

Jared realized that Cainen had a point: In his life, all of the major choices that affected him had been decided by others. His decision-making had been limited to inconsequential things or to military situations where not choosing something would have meant he was dead. He didn't consider himself a slave, but he was forced to admit that he'd never considered *not* being in Special Forces. Gabriel Brahe had told his training squad that after their ten-year term of service they could colonize, and no one ever questioned why they were made to serve the ten years at all. All the Special Forces training and development subsumed individual choice to the needs of the squad or platoon; even integration—the Special Forces' great military advantage—smeared the sense of self outside of the individual and toward the group.

(At the thought of integration, Jared felt an intense pang of loneliness. When his new orders came through, Jared's integration with the 2nd Platoon was switched off. The constant low-level hum of thought and emotion from his platoon mates was cavernous in its absence. If he had not been able to draw on his first isolated experiences of consciousness, he might have gone a little mad the moment he realized he could not sense his platoon anymore. As it was, Jared had spent most of the intervening day in a solid depression. It was an amputation, bloody and raw, and only the knowledge it was likely only temporary made it bearable.)

Jared realized with a growing sense of unease just how much of his life had been dictated, chosen, ordered and commanded. He realized how ill-prepared he was to make the choice Cainen had offered him. His immediate inclination was to say yes, that he wanted to go on: to learn more about Charles Boutin, the man he was supposed to be, and to become him, in some way. But he didn't know if it was something he really wanted, or merely something that was expected of him. Jared felt resentment, not at the Colonial Union or the Special Forces, but at Cainen—for putting him in a position to question himself and his choices, or lack thereof.

"What would you do?" Jared asked Cainen.

"I'm not you," Cainen said, and refused to speak any more about it. Wilson was likewise notably unhelpful. Both went about their work in the lab while Jared thought, staring into the three representations of consciousness that were all him, in one way or another.

"I've made a choice," Jared said, more than two hours later. "I want to go on."

"Can you tell me why?" Cainen said.

"Because I want to know more about all of this," Jared said. He motioned to the image of the third consciousness. "You tell me that I'm changing. I'm becoming someone else. I believe that. But I still *feel* like me. I think I'll still *be* me, no matter what happens. And *I* want to know."

Jared pointed to Cainen. "You say we Special Forces are slaves. You're right. I can't argue that. But we were also told that we are the only humans born with a purpose: To keep other humans safe. I wasn't given a choice for that purpose before, but I choose it now. I *choose* this."

"You choose to be a slave," Cainen said.

"No," Jared said. "I stopped being a slave when I made this choice."

"But you're choosing the path those who made you a slave would have you follow," Cainen said.

"It's my choice," Jared said. "If Boutin wants to harm us, I want to stop him."

"That means you might become like him," Wilson said.

"I was supposed to *be* him," Jared said. "Being *like* him still leaves room to be me."

"So this is your choice," Cainen said.

"It is," Jared said.

"Well, thank Christ," Wilson said, clearly relieved. Cainen also appeared to relax.

Jared looked at the two of them strangely. "I don't understand," he said to Cainen.

"We were ordered to bring out as much of Charles Boutin in you as possible," Cainen said. "If you had said no, and we refused to follow our orders, it probably would have been a death sentence for me. I'm a prisoner of war, Private. The only reason I'm allowed what little freedom I have is because I've allowed myself to be useful. The moment I stop being useful is the moment the CDF withdraws the medicine that keeps me alive. Or they decide to kill me in some other way. Lieutenant Wilson here is not likely to be shot for disobeying the order, but from what I understand CDF prisons aren't very nice places to be."

"Insubordinates check in, but they don't check out," Wilson said.

"Why didn't you tell me?" Jared said.

"Because then it wouldn't have been a fair choice for you," Wilson said.

"We decided between us that we would offer you this choice and accept the consequences," Cainen said. "Once we made our own choice on the matter, we wanted to be sure you had the same freedom we did in making *your* choice."

"So thank you for choosing to go on," Wilson said. "I nearly crapped myself waiting for you to make up your damn mind."

"Sorry," Jared said.

"Think on it no more," Wilson said, "because now you have another choice to make."

"We've come up with two options we think will spark a

larger cascade of memories from your Boutin consciousness," Cainen said. "The first is a variation of the consciousness transfer protocol used to put Boutin in your brain in the first place. We can cycle the protocol again and embed the consciousness a second time. Now that your brain is more mature, there's an excellent chance more of the consciousness would take—indeed, that it could *all* take. But there are some serious possible consequences."

"Like what?" Jared asked.

"Like that your consciousness would be entirely wiped out as the new one comes in," Wilson said.

"Ah," Jared said.

"You can see how it's problematic," Cainen said.

"I don't think I want to do that one," Jared said.

"We didn't think so," Cainen said. "In which case, we have a rather less invasive plan B."

"Which is?" Jared said.

"A trip down memory lane," Wilson said. "Jellybeans were only the beginning."

NINE Colonel James Robbins looked up at Phoenix, hovering over him in the sky. *Here I am again*, he thought.

General Szilard noticed Robbins's discomfort. "You don't really like the general's mess, do you, Colonel?" he asked, and jammed more steak in his mouth.

"I hate it," Robbins said, before he quite knew what was coming out of his mouth. "Sir," he added, quickly.

"Can't say that I blame you," Szilard said, around the beef. "The whole thing of barring non-generals from eating here is six kinds of stupid. How's your water, by the way?"

Robbins glanced down at the sweating glass in front of him. "Delightfully refreshing, sir," he said.

Szilard motioned with his fork to encompass the entire general's mess. "This is our fault, you know," he said. "The Special Forces, I mean."

"How so?" asked Robbins.

"Special Forces generals would bring anyone in their command structure in here—not just officers, but their enlisted too. Because outside of combat situations, no one in

Special Forces really gives a shit about rank. So you had all these Special Forces troops in here, eating the nice steaks and ogling Phoenix overhead. It got on the other generals' nerves—not just that there were enlisted in here, but that they were *Ghost Brigade* enlisted. This was in the early days, when the idea of soldiers less than a year old gave you realborn the creeps."

"It still does," Robbins said. "Sometimes."

"Yeah, I know," Szilard said. "But you people hide it better now. Anyway, after a while the realborn generals let it be known that this was their own playpen. And now all anyone else gets in here is one of those delightfully refreshing glasses of water you've got there, Colonel. So on behalf of the Special Forces, I apologize to you for the inconvenience."

"Thank you, General," Robbins said. "I'm not hungry anyway."

"Good for you," Szilard said, and ate some more of his steak. Colonel Robbins eyed the general's meal. In fact, he was hungry, but it wouldn't have been politic to note it. Robbins made a mental note for the next time he was summoned to a meeting in the general's mess: Eat something first.

Szilard swallowed his steak and turned his attention back to Robbins. "Colonel, have you heard of the Esto system? Don't look it up, just tell me if you know it."

"I'm not aware of it," Robbins said.

"How about Krana? Mauna Kea? Sheffield?"

"I know the Mauna Kea on Earth," Robbin said. "But I assume that's not the one you're talking about."

"It's not." Szilard motioned again with his fork, waving it to indicate some point past the eastern limb of Phoenix. "Mauna Kea system is that way, just short of Phoenix's Skip Drive horizon. New colony there."

"Hawaiians?" Robbins asked.

"Of course not," Szilard said. "It's mostly Tamils, from what my data tell me. They don't name the system, they just live there."

"What's so interesting about this system?" Robbins said.

"The fact that less than three days ago a Special Forces cruiser disappeared in it," Szilard said.

"It was attacked?" Robbins asked. "Destroyed?"

"No," Szilard said. "It *disappeared*. No contact once it arrived in the system."

"Did it hail the colony?" Robbins asked.

"It wouldn't have done that," Szilard said, in a flat tone that suggested to Robbins that he shouldn't pursue the details.

He didn't. "Maybe something happened to the ship when it reentered real space," he said instead.

"We skipped in a sensor done," Szilard said. "No ship. No black box. No debris along the projected flight path. Nothing. It's gone."

"That's weird," Robbins said.

"No," Szilard said. "What's weird is that it was the fourth Special Forces ship this has happened to this month."

Robbins stared at Szilard blankly. "You've lost four cruisers? How?"

"Well, if we knew *that*, Colonel, we'd be off stomping on someone's neck," Szilard said. "The fact that what I'm actually doing is eating this steak in front of you should be an indication we are as in the dark as anyone."

"But you *do* think someone is behind this," Robbins said. "And it's not just an issue with the ships or their Skip Drives."

"Of course we do," Szilard said. "Having one ship disappear is a random incident. Having four disappear in a month is a fucking trend. This is not a problem with the ships or the drives."

"Who do you think is behind it?" Robbins said.

Szilard set down his utensils, irritable. "Christ, Robbins," he said. "Do you think I'm talking to you because I don't have *friends*?"

Robbins smiled wryly, in spite of himself. "The Obin, then," he said.

"The Obin," Szilard said. "Yes. The ones who have Charles Boutin tucked away somewhere. All the systems our ships disappeared from either are close to Obin space or are planets the Obin contested for at one point or another. That's a slender thread, but it's what we have at the moment. What we don't have is the how or why, and that's where I was hoping you might be able to shed some light."

"You want to know where we are with Private Dirac," Robbins said.

"If you don't mind," Szilard said, and picked up his utensils again.

"It's slow going," Robbins admitted. "We think the memory breach happened because of stress and sensory input. We can't put the same sort of pressure on him that combat did, but we have been introducing him to parts of Boutin's life one piece at a time."

"His records?" Szilard asked.

"No," Robbins said. "At least not the reports and files on Boutin that were written or recorded by other people. Those aren't from Boutin himself, and we don't want to introduce an outside point of view. Cainen and Lieutenant Wilson are working with primary sources—Boutin's recordings and notes—and with Boutin's things."

"You mean things Boutin owned?" Szilard asked.

"Things he owned, things he liked—remember the jellybeans—or things from other people that he knew. We've also taken Dirac to the places where Boutin lived and grew up. He was originally from Phoenix, you know. It's just a quick trip down by shuttle."

"It's nice he gets field trips," Szilard said, only a little dismissively. "But you said it was slow going."

"More of Boutin is coming out," Robbins said. "But much of it seems to be in personality. I've read Private Dirac's psychological profile; up to now he's been something of a passive character. Things happened to him rather than him making them happen. And for the first week or so he was with us he was like that. But over the last three weeks he's been becoming more assertive and more directed. And that's more in line with who Boutin was, psychologically speaking."

"So he's becoming more like Boutin. Fine," Szilard said. "But is he remembering anything?"

"Well, that's just it," Robbins said. "There's very little memory coming back. What's coming back is mostly about his family life, not his work. We'll run him recordings of Boutin making voice notes of his projects and he'll listen to them blankly. Show him a picture of Boutin's little girl, and he gets twitchy for a minute, and then he'll tell you about what was going on in the picture. It's frustrating."

Szilard chewed for a moment, thinking. Robbins took advantage of the pause to enjoy his water. It wasn't quite as refreshing as he'd previously suggested.

"The memories of his little girl don't lead to any tangential memories coming up?" Szilard asked.

"Sometimes," Robbins said. "A picture of Boutin and his daughter at some research base he was stationed at reminded him of some of the work he'd been doing there.

Some early research on consciousness buffering, before he came back to Phoenix Station and started working on it using the technology we'd gotten from the Consu. But he didn't remember anything *useful*, in terms of why Boutin would decide to turn traitor."

"Show him another picture of Boutin's daughter," Szilard said.

"We showed him all we could find," Robbins said. "There aren't that many. And there aren't any of her physical things around—no toys or drawings or anything like that."

"Why not?" Szilard asked.

Robbins shrugged. "She died before Boutin came back to Phoenix Station," he said. "I guess he didn't want to bring her things with him."

"Now that's interesting," Szilard said. His eyes looked like they were focused on something at a distance, a sign he was reading something off his BrainPal.

"What?" Robbins said.

"I pulled Boutin's file while you were talking," Szilard said. "Boutin's a colonial, but his work for the Colonial Union required him to be stationed at Military Research facilities. The last place he worked before coming here was at Covell Research Station. Ever hear of it?"

"It sounds familiar," Robbins said. "But I can't place it."

"Says it was a zero-g-capable research facility," Szilard said. "They did some biomedical work, which is why Boutin was there, but it was mostly weapons and navigation systems. This is interesting: The station was actually positioned directly above a planetary ring system. It was just a klick above the ring plane. Used the ring debris to test their close-quarter navigation systems."

Now Robbins got it. Rocky planets with ring systems

were rare, and ones with human colonies rarer still. Most colonists preferred not to live where stadium-sized chunks of falling rock plunging through the atmosphere were a common occurrence rather than a once-in-a-millennium sort of thing. One with a Military Research station orbiting overhead—that was pretty singular.

"Omagh," Robbins said.

"Omagh," Szilard agreed. "Which we no longer own. We could never prove that the Obin originally attacked the colony or the station. It's possible the Rraey attacked the colony, and then the Obin attacked them when they were weakened from fighting us and before they could be reinforced. Which is one reason we never went to war with them over it. But we know they decided to claim the system for their own pretty damn quickly, before we could mount a force to take it back."

"And Boutin's daughter was on the colony," Robbins said.

"She was on the station, from what the casualty lists say," Szilard said, sending over the list for Robbins to view. "It was a large station. It would have had family quarters."

"Jesus," Robbins said.

"You know," Szilard said, casually, forking the last bite of steak into his mouth, "when Covell Station was attacked, it wasn't entirely destroyed. In fact, we have reliable data that suggest the station is largely intact."

"Okay," Robbins said.

"Including the family quarters."

"Oh, *okay*," Robbins said, the light coming on. "I can already tell you I don't like where this is going."

"You said that Dirac's memory responds most strongly to stress and sensory input," Szilard said. "Taking him to the place where his daughter died—and where all her physical things are likely to be—would qualify as a significant sensory input."

"There is the minor problem that the system is now owned and patrolled by the Obin," Robbins said.

Szilard shrugged. "That's where the stress comes in," he said. He set his utensils into the "done" position on his plate and pushed it away from him.

"The reason General Mattson took over Private Dirac is because he didn't want him to die in combat," Robbins said. "Dropping him into Omagh space seems rather counter to that desire, General."

"Yes, well, the general's desire to keep Dirac out of harm's way has to be tempered by the fact that as of three days ago, four of my ships and more than a thousand of my people have up and disappeared, as if they never even existed," Szilard said. "And at the end of the day, Dirac is still Special Forces. I could force the issue."

"Mattson wouldn't like it," Robbins said.

"Neither would I," Szilard said. "I have a good relationship with the general, despite his patronizing attitude toward Special Forces and me."

"It's not just you," Robbins said. "He's patronizing to everyone."

"Yes, he's an equal opportunity asshole," Szilard said. "And he's aware of it, which he thinks means it's okay. Be that as it may, as much as I don't want to get on his bad side, I will if I have to. But I don't think I will have to."

A waiter came over to take Szilard's plate; Szilard ordered dessert. Robbins waited until the server left. "Why don't you think you'll have to?" he asked.

"What would you say if I told you we already had Special Forces at Omagh, making preparations to take back the system?" Szilard asked.

"I'd be skeptical," Robbins said. "That sort of activity would be noticed sooner or later, and the Obin are ruthless. They wouldn't tolerate their presence if they found out about it."

"You're right about that," Szilard said. "But you'd be wrong to be skeptical. Special Forces have been at Omagh for over a year now. They've even been inside Covell Station. I think we can get Private Dirac in and out without raising too much attention."

"How?" Robbins asked.

"Very carefully," Szilard said. "And by using a few new toys."

The waiter returned with the general's dessert: Two large Toll House cookies. Robbins stared at the plate. He loved Toll House cookies. "You realize that if you're wrong, and you can't sneak Dirac past the Obin, they'll kill him, your secret Omagh reclamation project will be exposed, and any information Dirac has about Boutin will die with him," Robbins said.

Szilard took a cookie. "Risk," he said. "It's always in the equation. If we do this and we botch it, then we are well and truly fucked. But if we don't do it, we risk Dirac never recovering Boutin's memories, and then we're vulnerable to what the Obin have planned next. And then we'll be well and truly fucked *then*. If we're going to be fucked, Colonel, I prefer to get fucked on my feet instead of on my knees."

"You have a way with mental imagery, General," Robbins said.

"Thank you, Colonel," Szilard said. "I try." He reached over, took the second cookie, and offered it to Robbins. "Here," he said. "I saw you coveting it."

Robbins stared at the cookie, then looked around. "I can't take that," he said.

"Sure you can," Szilard said.

"I'm not supposed to eat anything here," Robbins said.

"So what?" Szilard said. "Screw 'em. It's a ridiculous tradition and you know it. So break it. Take the cookie."

Robbins took the cookie and stared at it glumly.

"Oh, good God," Szilard said. "Do I have to order you to eat the damn thing?"

"It might help," Robbins said.

"Fine," Szilard said. "Colonel, I'm giving you a direct order. Eat the fucking cookie."

Robbins ate it. The waiter was scandalized.

"Behold," Harry Wilson said to Jared, as they walked into the cargo hold of the *Shikra*. "Your chariot."

The "chariot" in question consisted of a carbon fiber basket seat, two extremely small ion engines of limited power and maneuverability, one on each side of the basket seat, and an office-refrigerator–sized object positioned directly behind the seat.

"This is an ugly chariot," Jared said.

Wilson chuckled. Jared's sense of humor had improved over the last few weeks, or at the very least it had become more to Wilson's liking—it reminded him of the sarcastic Charles Boutin he knew. Wilson felt both pleasure and wariness about this: pleasure that his and Cainen's work was making a difference; wariness because Boutin was, after all, a traitor to humanity. Wilson liked Jared enough not to wish that fate on him.

"It's ugly but it's state-of-the-art," Wilson said. He walked over and slapped the refrigerator-looking object. "This is the smallest Skip Drive ever created," he said. "Hot off the assembly line. And not only is it small, but it's an example of the first real advance we've had in Skip Drive technology in decades."

"Let me guess," Jared said. "It's based on that Consu technology we stole from the Rraey."

"You make it sound like a bad thing," Wilson said.

"Well, you know," Jared said, tapping his head. "I'm in this predicament *because* of Consu technology. Let's just say I'm not neutral on its uses."

"You make an excellent point," Wilson said. "But *this* is sweet. A friend of mine worked on this; we'd talk about it. Most Skip Drives require you to get out into flat time-space before you can engage them. You have to get far away from a planet. This one is less picky: it can use a Lagrange point. So long as you've got a planet with a reasonably large moon, you've got five nearby spots in space where it's gravitationally flat enough to engage this drive. If they can work out the kinks, it could revolutionize space travel."

" 'Work out the kinks'?" Jared said. "I'm about to use this thing. Kinks are bad."

"The kink is that the drive is touchy about the mass of the object it's attached to," Wilson said. "Too much mass creates too much of a local warp on the time-space. Makes the Skip Drive do weird things."

"Like what?" Jared asked.

"Like explode," Wilson said.

"That's not encouraging," Jared said.

"Well, *explode* is not quite the accurate word," Wilson said. "The physics for what *really* goes on are much weirder, I assure you."

"You can stop now," Jared said.

"But *you* don't have to worry about it," Wilson continued. "It takes about five tons of mass before the drive gets wobbly. That's why this sled looks like a dune buggy. It falls well under the mass threshold, even with you in it. You should be fine."

"*Should* be," Jared said.

"Oh, stop being a baby," Wilson said.

"I'm not even one year old," Jared said. "I can be a baby if I want. Help me get into this thing, would you."

Jared negotiated his way into the sled's basket seat; Wilson strapped him in, and stowed his Empee in a storage box to the side of the seat. "Do a systems check," Wilson said. Jared activated his BrainPal and connected with the sled, checking the integrity of the Skip Drive and the ion engines; everything was nominal. The sled had no physical controls; Jared would control it with his BrainPal. "The sled's fine," Jared said.

"How's the unitard?" Wilson asked.

"It's fine." The sled had an open cockpit; Jared's unitard was formatted for hard vacuum, including a cowl that would slide down completely over his face, sealing him in. The nanobotic fabric of the unitard was photosensitive and passed visual and other electromagnetic information directly to Jared's BrainPal. As a result Jared would be able to "see" better with his eyes covered by the cowl than he could if he were using them. Around Jared's waist was a rebreather system that could, if necessary, provide breathable air for a week.

"Then you're good to go," Wilson said. "Your coordinates are programmed in for this side, and you should also have them to get back from the other side. Just put them in and sit back and let the sled do the rest. Szilard said that the Special Forces recovery team will be ready for you on the other side. You'll be on the lookout for a Captain Martin. He's got a confirmation key for you to verify his identity. Szilard says to follow his orders to the letter. Got it?"

"Got it," Jared said.

"Okay," Wilson said. "I'm out of here. We're going to start cycling out the air. Suit up. As soon as the bay doors open, activate the nav program and it will handle it from there."

"Got it," Jared repeated.

"Good luck, Jared," Wilson said. "Hope you find something useful." He walked out of the bay to the sound of the *Shikra*'s life-support system sucking the air out of the bay. Jared activated his cowl; there was momentary blackness followed by a rather impressive gain in Jared's peripheral awareness as the unitard's visual signal kicked in.

The rushing noise of air thinned into nothingness; Jared was sitting in vacuum. Through the metal of the ship and the carbon fibers of the sled, he could feel the bay doors sliding open. Jared activated the sled's navigation program; the sled lifted from the floor of the bay and slid gently out the door. Jared's vision included the visual track of his flight plan, and its destination more than a thousand klicks away: the L4 position between Phoenix and its moon Benu, currently unoccupied by any other object. The ion engines kicked in; Jared felt his weight under the engines' acceleration.

The Skip Drive activated as the sled intersected the L4 position. Jared noted the sudden and impressively disconcerting appearance of a broad system of rings less than a klick above his point of view, girding the limb of a blue, Earth-like planet to his left. Jared's sled, which had been previously moving forward at an impressive rate of speed, was motionless. The ion engines had stopped firing just before the Skip translation and the inertial energy of the sled did not carry forward after it. Jared was glad about this. He doubted the tiny ion engines would have been able to stop the sled before it would have wandered into the ring system and squashed him into a tumbling rock.

::Private Dirac,:: Jared heard, as a verification key pinged his BrainPal.

::Yes,:: he said.

::This is Captain Martin,:: Jared heard. ::Welcome to Omagh. Please be patient; we're coming to get you.::

::If you send me directions, I could come to you,:: Jared said.

::We'd rather you didn't,:: Martin said. ::The Obin have been scanning the area more than usual recently. We'd prefer not to give them anything to see. Just sit tight.::

A minute or so later, Jared noticed three of the rings' rocks moving slowly his way. ::It looks like I've got some debris headed toward me,:: he sent to Martin. ::I'm going to maneuver out of the way.::

::Don't do that,:: Martin said.

::Why not?:: Jared asked.

::Because we hate chasing after shit,:: Martin said.

Jared directed his unitard to focus on the incoming rocks and magnify. Jared noticed the rocks had limbs, and that one of them was dragging what looked like a tow cable. Jared watched as they approached and finally arrived at the sled. One of them maneuvered itself in front of Jared while the other two attached the two cables. The rock was human-sized and irregularly hemispherical; up close it looked like a turtle shell without an opening for a head. Four limbs of equal length sprouted in quadrilateral symmetry. The limbs had two joints of articulation and terminated in splayed hands with opposable thumbs on either side of the palm. The underside of the rock was flat and mottled, with a line that went down the center, suggesting the underside could open. Across the topside of the rock were flat, glossy patches that Jared suspected were photosensitive.

::Not what you were expecting, Private?:: said the rock, using Martin's voice.

::No, sir,:: Jared said. He accessed his internal database of the few intelligent species that were friendly to (or at least not openly antagonistic toward) humans but was coming up with nothing that was even remotely like this creature. ::I was expecting someone human.::

Jared felt a sharp ping of amusement. ::We *are* human, Private,:: Martin said. ::As much as you are.::

::You don't look human,:: Jared said, and immediately regretted it.

::Of course we don't,:: Martin said. ::But we don't live in typical human environments, either. We've been adapted for where we live.::

::Where do you live?:: Jared asked.

One of Martin's limbs motioned around him. ::Here,:: he said. ::Adapted for life in space. Vacuum-proof bodies. Photosynthetic stripes for energy.:: Martin tapped his underside. ::And in here, an organ that houses modified algae to provide oxygen and the organic compounds we need. We can live out here for weeks at a time, spying on and sabotaging the Obin, and they don't even know we're here. They keep looking for CDF spaceships. It confuses the hell out of them.::

::I'll bet,:: Jared said.

::Okay, Stross tells me we're good to go,:: Martin said. ::We're ready to reel you in. Hang on.:: Jared felt a jolt and then felt a small vibration as the tow cable was reeled in, dragging the sled into the ring. The rocks kept pace, manipulating small jet packs with their hind limbs.

::Were you born this way?:: Jared asked.

::*I* wasn't,:: Martin said. ::They created this body type three years ago. Everything new. They needed volunteers to test it. It was too extreme to drop a consciousness into without testing. We needed to see if people could adapt to it without going insane. This body is almost entirely a closed system. I get oxygen, nutrients and moisture from my algae organ, and my waste gets dumped back into it to feed the algae. You don't eat and drink like people are supposed to. You don't even pee normally. And not doing things you're hardwired to do will make you nuts. You wouldn't think that not peeing could prey on your mind. But trust me, it does. It was one of the things they had to find a way around when they went into full production.::

Martin pointed toward the other two rocks. ::Stross and Pohl, now, *they* were born in these bodies,:: Martin said. ::And they're perfectly at home in them. I tell them about eating a hamburger or taking a dump, they look at me like I'm insane. And trying to describe regular sex to them is just a complete loss.::

::They have sex?:: Jared asked, surprised.

::You don't want to screw with the sex drive, Private,:: Martin said. ::That's bad for the species. Yes, *we* have sex all the time.:: He motioned to his underside. ::We open up here. The edges of our cowl can seal with someone else's. The number of positions we can perform are a bit more limited than the ones you can. Your body is more flexible than ours. On the other hand, we can fuck in total vacuum. Which is a neat trick.::

::I'd say so,:: Jared said. He felt the captain was veering into "too much information" territory.

::But we are a different breed, no doubt about it,:: Martin said. ::We even have a different naming scheme than the rest of Special Forces. We're named after old science fiction writers, instead of scientists. I even took a new name, when I switched over.::

::Are you going to switch back?:: Jared asked. ::To a normal body?::

::No,:: Martin said. ::When I first switched over, I would have. But you get used to it. This is my normal now. And this is the future. The CDF made us to give them an advantage in combat, just like they made the original Special Forces. And it works. We're dark matter. We can sneak up on a ship and the enemy thinks we're debris, right until the pocket nuke we stuck on their hull as we scraped by goes off. And then they don't think about anything anymore.

::But we're more than that,:: Martin continued. ::We're the first people *organically* adapted to living in space. Every body system is organic, even the BrainPal—we've got the first totally organic BrainPals. That's one improvement that's going to be passed down to the general Special Forces population the next time they do a new body edition. Everything we are is expressed in our DNA. If they can find a way to let us breed naturally, we'll have a new species: *Homo astrum,* who can live between the planets. We won't have to fight anyone for real estate then. And that means humans win.::

::Unless you don't want to look like a turtle,:: Jared said.

Martin sent a sharp ping of amusement. ::Fair enough,:: he said. ::There is that. And we know it. We call ourselves the Gamerans, you know.::

Jared fuzzed a moment until the reference came into his head, from back in the evenings at Camp Carson, watching science fiction films at ten times speed. ::Like the Japanese monster?::

::You got it,:: Martin said.

::Do you shoot fire too?:: Jared asked.

::Ask the Obin,:: Martin said.
The sled entered the ring.

Jared saw the dead man almost as soon as they slipped through the hole in the side of Covell Station.

The Gamerans had informed Special Forces that Covell Station was largely intact, but "largely intact" clearly meant something different to troops who thrive in hard vacuum. Covell Station was airless and lifeless and gravityless, although some electrical systems remarkably still had power, thanks to solar panels and hardy engineering. The Gamerans knew the station well; they had been in it before, retrieving files, documents, and objects that had not already been destroyed or looted by the Obin. The one thing they didn't retrieve was the dead; the Obin still came to the station from time to time and might notice if the number of the dead dramatically reduced over time. So the dead remained, floating cold and desiccated through the station.

The dead man was wedged up against a corridor bulkhead. Jared suspected he hadn't been there when the hole in the hull they slipped through was made: The explosive decompression would have sucked him right out into space. Jared turned to confirm this with Martin.

::He's new,:: Martin confirmed. ::To this section, anyway. The dead drift a lot around here, along with everything else. Is that someone you're looking for?::

Jared drifted toward the dead man. The man's body was parched and dried, all the moisture long since boiled away. He would have been unrecognizable even if Boutin had known him. Jared looked at the man's lab coat; the name tag claimed him to be Uptal Chatterjee. His papery skin was green. The name was right for a colonist, but he'd clearly been a citizen of a Western nation at one point.

::I don't know who he is,:: Jared said.

::Come on, then,:: Martin said. He grabbed the railing with both left hands and propelled himself down the corridor. Jared followed, letting go of the railing on occasion to get past a dead body bumping through the corridor. He wondered if he might find Zoë Boutin floating in the corridors or other part of the station.

No, a thought said. *They never found her body. They found hardly any colonist bodies.*

::Stop,:: Jared said to Martin.

::What is it?:: Martin said.

::I'm remembering,:: Jared said, and closed his eyes, even through they were behind his cowl. When he opened them, he felt sharper and more focused. He also knew exactly where he wanted to go.

::Follow me,:: Jared said.

Jared and Martin had entered the station in the weapons wing of the station. Coreward lay navigation and biomedical research; in the center was a large zero-g lab. Jared led Martin coreward and then clockwise through the corridors, pausing occasionally to let Martin pry open deactivated emergency doors with a jack-like piston. Corridor lights, fed by the solar panels, glowed feebly but more than enough for Jared's enhanced vision.

::Here,:: Jared said, eventually. ::This is where I did my work. This is my laboratory.::

The laboratory was filled with detritus and bullet holes. Whoever had come through was not interested in preserving the technical work of the lab; they had just wanted everyone dead. Blackened, dried blood was visible on tabletops and down the side of a desk. At least one person had been shot here, but there was no body.

Jerome Kos, Jared thought. *That was the name of my assistant. He was originally from Guatemala but immigrated to the United States when he was a kid. He was the one to solve the buffer overflow—*

::Crap,:: Jared said. The memory of Jerry Kos floated in his head, looking for context. Jared scanned the room, looking for computers or memory storage devices; there was nothing. ::Did your people take the computers from here?:: he asked Martin.

::Not from this room,:: Martin said. ::Some of the labs were missing computers and other equipment before we ever got a chance to swing through. The Obin or whoever must have taken them.::

Jared pushed himself over to a desk he knew was Boutin's. Whatever had been on the top of the desk had long since floated away. Jared opened the desk drawers to find office supplies, hanger folders and other, not particularly useful things. As Jared was closing the drawer with the hanger folders, he saw the papers in one of them. He stopped and pulled one out; it was a drawing, signed by Zoë Boutin with more enthusiasm than precision.

She drew me one a week, in Wednesday art period, Jared remembered. *I would take the new one and hang it with a pushpin, and take the old one and file it. I never threw any away.* Jared glanced up at the corkboard above the desk; there were pushpins in it, but no picture. The last one was almost certainly floating somewhere in the room. Jared had to fight off the urge to look for it until he found it. Instead he pushed off from the desk toward the door, slipping out into the corridor before Martin could ask him where he was going. Martin raced to keep up.

The work corridors of Covell Station were clinical and sterile; the family quarters worked hard to be the opposite. Carpeting—albeit of the industrial sort—covered the floors. Children in art classes had been encouraged to paint the corridor walls, which featured suns and cats and hills with flowers in pictures that were not art unless you were a parent and could be nothing but if you were. The debris in the corridor and occasional dark smear against the wall worked against the cheer.

As a research head with a child, Boutin received larger quarters than most, which still meant it was almost unbearably compact; space is at a premium in space stations. Boutin's apartment lay at the end of C corridor (C for cat— the walls were painted with anatomically divergent cats of all sorts), apartment 10. Jared pulled himself down the corridor toward apartment 10. The door was closed but unlocked. Jared slid the door open and let himself in.

As everywhere, objects floated silently in the room. Jared recognized some things but not others. A book that was a gift from a college friend. Some picture in a frame. A pen. A rug he and Cheryl bought on their honeymoon.

Cheryl. His wife, dead from a fall while hiking. She died just before he left for this posting. Her funeral was on the second-to-last day before he came here. He remembered holding Zoë's hand at the funeral, listening to Zoë ask why her mother had to leave and making him promise he would never leave her. He promised, of course.

Boutin's bedroom was compact; Zoë's, one room over, would have been uncomfortable for anyone who wasn't five. The tiny child's bed was shoved along one corner, so securely wedged there that it hadn't floated away; even the mattress stayed stuck. Picture books, toys and stuffed animals hovered. One caught Jared's eye, and he reached for it.

Babar the Elephant. Phoenix had been colonized before

the Colonial Union stopped accepting colonists from wealthy countries; there was a large French population, from which Boutin was descended. Babar was a popular children's character on Phoenix, along with Asterix, Tintin and the Silly Man, reminders of childhoods on a planet so distant from Phoenix that no one thought much about it. Zoë had never seen an elephant in real life—very few of them ever made it into space—but she had nonetheless been delighted with the Babar when Cheryl gave it to her on her fourth birthday. After Cheryl died Zoë made Babar a totem; she refused to go anywhere without it.

He remembered Zoë crying for it while he was dropping her off at Helene Greene's apartment, as he prepared to travel to Phoenix for several weeks of late-stage testing work. He was already late for the shuttle; he had no time to get it. He finally settled her down by promising to find her a Celeste for her Babar. Placated, she gave him a kiss and went into Kay Greene's room to play with her friend. He then promptly forgot about Babar and Celeste until the day he was scheduled to return to Omagh and Covell. He was thinking of some reasonable excuse to explain why he was coming home empty-handed when he was pulled aside and told that Omagh and Covell had been attacked, and that everyone on the base and on the colony was dead, and that his daughter, best beloved, died alone and frightened, and far away from anyone that ever loved her.

Jared held Babar while the barrier between his consciousness and Boutin's memories crumbled, feeling Boutin's grief and anger as if it were his own. *This* was it. This was the event that set him on the path to treason, the death of his daughter, his Zoë Jolie, his joy. Jared, helpless to guard against it, felt what Boutin felt: the sick horror of unwillingly picturing his child's death, the hollow, horrible ache standing in that place in his life where his daughter had been, and mad, acidic desire to do something more than mourn.

The torrent of memory wracked Jared, and he gasped as each new *thing* hit his consciousness and dug in. They tumbled in too fast to be complete or to be completely understood, the broad strokes of memory defining the shape of Boutin's path. Jared had no memory of his first contact with the Obin; only a sense of release, as if making the decision freed him from a lingering sense of pain and rage—but he saw himself making a deal with the Obin for a safe haven in exchange for his knowledge of the BrainPal and consciousness research.

The details of Boutin's scientific work eluded him; the training they required to comprehend required pathways of understanding Jared simply didn't have. What he had were the memories of sensual experience: the pleasure in planning to fake his death and make his escape, the pain of separation from Zoë, the desire to leave the human sphere and start his work and create his revenge.

Here and there in this cauldron of sensation and emotion, concrete memories winked like jewels—data repeated across the memory field; things to be remembered from more than one incident. Even then some things still flickered in memory, but just out of reach—knowing Zoë was the key to Boutin's defection but not knowing exactly why the key turned, and feeling the answer sway from his grasp as he reached for it, tantalizing and torturous.

Jared turned away to focus on the nuggets of memory that were hard, solid and within reach. Jared's consciousness circled one of these, a place name, roughly translated from a language spoken by creatures that didn't speak like humans.

And Jared knew where Boutin was.

The front door to the apartment slid open and Martin clambered through. He spotted Jared in Zoë's room and pushed over to him. ::Time to go, Dirac,:: he said. ::Varley tells me Obin are on their way. They must have bugged the place. Stupid of me.::

::Give me a minute,:: Jared said.

::We don't have a minute,:: Martin said.

::All right,:: Jared said. He pushed out of the room, taking Babar with him.

::Now's not the best time for souvenirs,:: Martin said.

::Shut up,:: Jared said. ::Let's go.:: He pushed out of Boutin's apartment without looking back to see if Martin was keeping up.

Uptal Chatterjee was where Jared and Martin had left him. The Obin scout craft hovering outside the hull breach was new.

::There are other ways out of this place,:: Jared said, as he and Martin huddled by Chatterjee's body. The scout was visible at an angle, but it apparently hadn't spotted them yet.

::Sure there are other ways,:: Martin said. ::The question is can we get to any of them before more of these guys show up. We can take one of them if we have to. More, there's going to be a problem.::

::Where is your squad?:: Jared asked.

::They're on their way,:: Martin said. ::We try to keep our movements outside the rings to a bare minimum.::

::A fine idea any other time but this,:: Jared said.

::I don't recognize that ship,:: Martin said. ::It looks like a new type of scout. I can't even tell if it has weapons. If it doesn't, between the two of us we might be able to take it out with our Empees.::

Jared considered this. He grabbed Chatterjee and gently

pushed him in the direction of the hull breach. Chatterjee slowly floated across the breach.

::So far, so good,:: Martin said, when Chatterjee's body was halfway across the breach.

Chatterjee's body shattered as the projectiles from the scout craft blasted through his frozen body. Limbs twirled violently and then were shattered themselves as another volley coursed through the breach. Jared could feel the impact of the projectiles on the far wall of the corridor.

Jared felt a peculiar sensation, like his brain being picked. The scout's position shifted slightly. ::*Duck*,:: Jared tried to say to Martin, but the communication didn't make it through. Jared dug in his heel, grabbed Martin and yanked him down as a fresh volley ripped through the corridor, shredding the hull breach wider and passing dangerously close to Jared and Martin.

Bright orange blazed outside and from his position Jared could see the scout tilt wildly. From below the scout, a missile arced its way up and impacted on the scout's underside, cracking the scout in two. Jared noted to himself that the Gamerans did indeed shoot fire.

::—was sure a lot of fun,:: Martin said. ::Now we'll get to spend a week or two in hiding while the Obin scour around looking for whoever blew up their ship. You've made our lives very interesting, Private. Now, time to go. The boys have shot up the tow rope. Let's get out of here before any more show up.:: Martin scrambled up and over and then launched himself out of the breach, toward the tow cable hovering five meters beyond it. Jared followed, grabbing the cable with one hand and holding on for dear life, while Babar stayed clenched in the other.

It was three days before the Obin stopped hunting for them.

* * *

"Welcome back," Wilson said, as he approached the sled, and then stopped. "Is that *Babar*?"

"It is," Jared said, sitting in the sled with Babar secured in his lap.

"I'm not sure I even want to know what *that's* about," Wilson said.

"You do," Jared said. "Trust me."

"It has something to do with Boutin?" Wilson said.

"It has everything to do with him," Jared said. "I know why he turned traitor, Harry. I know everything."

TEN One day before Jared returned to Phoenix Station, clutching Babar, the Special Forces cruiser *Osprey* skipped into the Nagano system to investigate a distress call sent by Skip courier from a mining operation on Kobe. The *Osprey* was not heard from again.

Jared was supposed to report in to Colonel Robbins. Instead he stomped past Robbins's office and into General Mattson's before Mattson's secretary could stop him. Mattson was inside and looked up as Jared walked in.

"Here," Jared said, thrusting Babar into the hands of a surprised Mattson. "Now I know why I punched you, you son of a bitch."

Mattson looked down on the stuffed animal. "Let me guess," he said. "This is Zoë Boutin's. And now you've got your memory back."

"Enough of it," Jared said. "Enough to know you're responsible for her death."

"Funny," Mattson said, putting Babar down on his desk.

"Seems to me that either the Rraey or the Obin are responsible for her death."

"Don't be obtuse, General," Jared said. Mattson raised an eyebrow. "You ordered Boutin here for a month. He asked to bring his daughter with him. You refused. Boutin left his daughter and she died. He blames you."

"And you do too, apparently," Mattson said.

Jared ignored this. "Why didn't you let him bring her?" he asked.

"I'm not running a day care, Private," Mattson said. "I needed Boutin focused on his work. Boutin's wife was already dead. Who was going to take care of the girl? He had people at Covell who could do it for him; I told him to leave her there. I didn't *expect* that we'd lose the station and the colony and that the girl would die."

"This station houses other civilian scientists and workers," Jared said. "There are families here. He could have found or hired someone to watch Zoë while he worked. It wasn't an unreasonable request, and you know it. So, *really*, why didn't you let him bring her?"

By this time Robbins, alerted by Mattson's secretary, had entered the room. Mattson twisted uncomfortably. "Listen," Mattson said. "Boutin was a top-flight mind, but he was a goddamned flake. Especially after his wife died. Cheryl was a heat sink for the man's eccentricities; she kept him on an even keel. Once she was gone he became erratic, particularly where his daughter was involved."

Jared opened his mouth; Mattson held up a hand. "I'm not blaming him, Private," Mattson said. "His wife was dead, he had a little girl, he was worried about her. I was a parent too. I remember what it's like. But that topped with his own organizational issues created problems. He was behind on his projects as it was. It's one of the reasons I brought him back here for the testing phase. I wanted him to be able to get work done and not be distracted. And it worked; we finished testing ahead of schedule and things went so well that I gave the go-ahead to have him bumped up to the director level, which was something I wouldn't have done before the test phase. He was on his way back to Covell when it was attacked."

"He thought you turned down his request because you're a pissant tyrant," Jared said.

"Well, of course he did," Mattson said. "That's Boutin all over. Look, he and I never got along. Our personalities didn't mesh. He was high maintenance, and if it weren't for the fact he was a fucking genius, he wouldn't have been worth the trouble. He resented the fact that I or one of my people was always looking over his shoulder. He resented having to explain and justify his work. And he resented that I didn't give a shit if he resented it. I'm not surprised he thought it was just me being petty."

"And you're saying it *wasn't*," Jared said.

"It wasn't," Mattson said, and then threw up his hands when Jared gave him a skeptical look. "Okay. Look. *Perhaps* our history of bad blood played a small role. Maybe I was less willing to cut him a break than I would be someone else. Fine. But my main concern was getting work out of him. And I *did* promote the son of a bitch."

"But he never forgave you for what happened to Zoë," Jared said.

"Do you think I wanted his little girl dead, Private?" Mattson said. "Do you think that I wasn't aware that if I had just said yes to his request, she'd be alive now? Christ. I don't *blame* Boutin for hating me after that. I didn't intend for Zoë Boutin to die, but I accept I bear a part of the responsibility for the fact she is dead. I said as much to Boutin himself. See if *that* is in your memories."

It was. Jared saw in his mind Mattson approaching him

in his lab, awkwardly offering his condolences and sympathy. Jared recalled how appalled he felt at the fumbled words, and their implicit suggestion that Mattson should be absolved of the death of his child. He felt some of the cold rage wash over him now, and had to remind himself that the memories he was feeling were from another person, about a child who was not his own.

"He didn't accept your apology," Jared said.

"I'm aware of *that*, Private," Mattson said, and sat there for a moment before he spoke up again. "So, who *are* you now?" he asked. "It's clear you have Boutin's memories. Are you him now? In your gut, I mean."

"I'm still me," Jared said. "I'm still Jared Dirac. But I feel what Charles Boutin felt. I understand what he did."

Robbins spoke up. "You understand what he did," he repeated. "Does that mean you agree with it?"

"His treason?" Jared asked. Robbins nodded. "No. I can feel what he felt. I feel how angry he was. I feel how he missed his daughter. But I don't know how he got from there to turning on all of us."

"You can't feel it, or you don't remember it?" Robbins asked.

"Both," Jared said. More memory was returning after his epiphany at Covell, specific incidents and data from all parts of Boutin's life. Jared could sense that whatever happened there had changed him and made him more fertile ground for Boutin's life. But the gaps were still there. Jared had to keep himself from worrying about them. "Maybe more will come the more I think about it," he said. "But right now I've got nothing on that."

"But you know where he is now," Mattson said, bringing Jared back from his reverie. "Boutin. You know where he is."

"I know where he was," Jared said. "Or at least I know

where he was going when he left." The name was clear in Jared's brain; Boutin had focused on the name like a talisman, burning it indelibly into memory. "He went to Arist."

There was a brief moment while Mattson and Robbins accessed their BrainPals for information on Arist. "Well, crap," Mattson said, eventually.

The Obin home system housed four gas giants, one of which—Cha—orbited in a "Goldilocks zone" for carbon-based life and had three planet-sized moons among several dozen smaller satellites. The smallest of the large moons, Saruf, lay in orbit just outside the planet's Roche limit, and was wracked by immense tidal forces that turned it into an uninhabitable ball of lava. The second, Obinur, was half again the size of Earth but less massive due to a metal-poor composition. This was the Obin home world. The third, of Earth size and mass, was Arist.

Arist was thickly populated with native life-forms but largely uninhabited by the Obin, with only a few outposts of any size on the moon. Nevertheless, its close proximity to Obinur would make it almost impossible to assault. CDF ships wouldn't be able to simply sneak in; Arist was only a few light-seconds from Obinur. Almost as soon as they appeared the Obin would be moving in for the kill. Nothing short of a large assault force would stand a chance of extracting Boutin from Arist. Extracting Boutin would be declaring war, a war the Colonial Union wasn't ready to commit to even with the Obin standing alone.

"We're going to have to talk to General Szilard about this," Robbins said to Mattson.

"No shit," Mattson said. "If there was ever a job for Special Forces, this is it. Speaking of which"—Mattson focused on Jared—"once we drop this in Szilard's lap, you're going back to Special Forces. Dealing with this is going to be his problem, and that means you're going to be his problem too."

"I'm going to miss you too, General," Jared said.

Mattson snorted. "You really are sounding more like Boutin every day. And that's not a good thing. Which reminds me, as my last official order to you, get down to see the bug and Lieutenant Wilson and let them get another look at your brain. I'm giving you back to General Szilard, but I promised I wouldn't break you. Being a little too much like Boutin might qualify as 'broken' by his standard. It does by mine."

"Yes, sir," Jared said.

"Good. You're dismissed." Mattson picked up Babar and tossed it to Jared. "And take this thing with you," he said.

Jared caught it and set it back down on Mattson's desk, facing the general. "Why don't you keep it, General," Jared said. "As a reminder." He left before Mattson could protest, nodding at Robbins as he left.

Mattson stared glumly at the stuffed elephant and then up at Robbins, who appeared about to say something. "Don't say a goddamned thing about the elephant, Colonel," Mattson said.

Robbins changed the topic. "Do you think Szilard will take him back?" he asked. "You said it yourself: He's sounding more like Boutin every day."

"You're telling *me* this," Mattson said, and waved in the direction of where Jared had gone. "You and the general were the ones who wanted to build this little bastard from spare parts, if you'll recall. And now you've got him. Or Szi's got him. Christ."

"So you're worried," Robbins said.

"I've never *stopped* being worried about him," Mattson said. "When he was with us I kept hoping he'd do something stupid so I would have a legitimate excuse to have him shot. I don't *like* that we've bred a second traitor, especially one with a military body and brain. If it were up to me I'd take Private Dirac and put him in a nice big room that features a toilet and a food slot, and keep him there until he rots."

"He's still technically under your command," Robbins said.

"Szi's made it clear he wants him back, for whatever damn fool reason he has," Mattson said. "He commands combat troops. If we go to the mat on it, he'll get the decision." Mattson picked up Babar, examined him. "I just hope to holy fuck he knows what he's doing."

"Well," Robbins said. "Maybe Dirac won't actually be as much like Boutin as you think he will be."

Mattson snorted derisively, and wiggled Babar at Robbins. "See this? This isn't just some goddamned souvenir. It's a message straight from Charles Boutin himself. No, Colonel. Dirac is exactly as much like Boutin as I think he is."

"There's no question about it," Cainen said to Jared. "You've become Charles Boutin."

"The hell I have," Jared said.

"The hell you have," Cainen agreed, and motioned to the display. "Your consciousness pattern is now almost entirely identical to what Boutin left us. There's still some variation, of course, but it's trivial. For all intents and purposes, you have the same mind as Charles Boutin had."

"I don't feel any different," Jared said.

"Don't you?" Harry Wilson said, from the other side of the lab.

Jared opened his mouth to respond, then stopped. Wilson grinned. "You *do* feel different," he said. "I can tell it. So can Cainen. You're more aggressive than you were before. You're sharper with the retort. Jared Dirac was quieter, more subdued. More innocent, although that's probably not the absolute best way to put it. You're not quiet and subdued anymore. And certainly not innocent. I remember Charlie Boutin. You're a lot more like him than like who Jared Dirac used to be."

"But I don't feel like becoming a traitor," Jared said.

"Of course you don't," Cainen said. "You share the same consciousness, and you even share some of the same memories. But you had your own experiences, and that has shaped how you look at things. It's as with identical twins. They share the same genetics, but they don't share the same lives. Charles Boutin is your mind twin. But your experiences are still your own."

"So you don't think I'll go bad," Jared said.

Cainen did a Rraey shrug. Jared looked over to Wilson, who did a human shrug. "You say you know Charlie's motivation for going bad was the death of his daughter," he said. "You have the memory of that daughter and her death in you now, but nothing you've done or that we've seen in your head suggests you're going to crack because of it. We're going to suggest they let you back into active duty. Whether they take our recommendation or not is another thing entirely, since the lead scientist on the project is one who until about a year ago was plotting to overthrow humanity. But I don't think that's your problem."

"It certainly is my problem," Jared said. "Because I want to find Boutin. Not just help with the mission, and absolutely not to sit it out. I want to find him and I want to bring him back."

"Why?" Cainen asked.

"I want to understand him. I want to know what it takes to make someone do this. What makes them a traitor," Jared said.

"You would be surprised at how little it takes," Cainen said. "Something even as simple as kindness from an enemy." Cainen turned away; Jared suddenly remembered Cainen's status and his allegiance. "Lieutenant Wilson," Cainen said, still looking away. "Would you give me and Private Dirac a moment." Wilson arched his eyebrows but said nothing as he left the lab. Cainen turned back to Jared.

"I wanted to apologize to you, Private," Cainen said. "And to warn you."

Jared gave Cainen an uncertain smile. "You don't need to apologize to me for anything, Cainen," he said.

"I disagree," Cainen said. "It was my cowardice that brought you into being. If I had been strong enough to hold out against the torture your Lieutenant Sagan put me through, I would be dead, and you humans would not have known of the war against you or that Charles Boutin was still alive. If I had been stronger, there would have never been a reason for you to have been born, and to be saddled with a consciousness that has taken over your being, for better or for worse. But I was weak, and I wanted to live, even if living was as a prisoner and a traitor. As some of your colonists would say, that is my karma, which I have to grapple with on my own.

"But quite unintentionally I have sinned against you, Private," Cainen said. "As much as anyone, I am your father, because I am the cause of the terrible wrong they have committed against you. It's bad enough that humans bring soldiers to life with artificial minds—with those damned BrainPals of yours. But to have you born only to carry the consciousness of another is an abomination. A violation of your right to be your own person."

"It's not as bad as all that," Jared said.

"Oh, but it *is*," Cainen said. "We Rraey are a spiritual and principled people. Our beliefs are at the core of how we respond to our world. One of our highest values is the sanctity of self—the belief that every person must be allowed to make their own choices. Well"—Cainen did a neck bobble—"every Rraey, in any event. Like most races, we're less concerned about the needs of other races, especially when they are opposed to our own.

"Nevertheless," Cainen continued. "Choice matters. Independence matters. When you first came to Wilson and me, we gave you the choice to continue. You remember?" Jared nodded. "I must confess to you that I did that not only for your sake but for my own. Since I was the one who caused you to be born without choices, it was my moral duty to give one to you. When you took it—when you made a choice, I felt some of my sin lift away. Not all of it. I still have my karma. But some. I thank you for that, Private."

"You're welcome," Jared said.

"Now my warning to you," Cainen said. "Lieutenant Sagan tortured me when we first met, and at the end of it I broke and told her almost everything she wanted to know about our plans to attack you humans. But I told her one lie. I told her I never met Charles Boutin."

"You've met him?" Jared asked.

"I have," Cainen said. "Once, when he came to talk to me and other Rraey scientists about the architecture of the BrainPal, and how we might adapt it for the Rraey. A fascinating human. Very intense. Charismatic in his way, even to the Rraey. He is passionate, and we as a people respond to passion. Very passionate. Very driven. And very angry."

Cainen leaned in close. "Private, I know you think that this is about Boutin's daughter, and to some extent, maybe it is. But there is something else motivating Boutin as well. His daughter's death may simply have been the discrete event that caused an idea to crystallize in Boutin's mind, and it's that idea that fuels him. It's what made him a traitor."

"What is it?" Jared asked. "What's the idea?"

"I don't know," Cainen confessed. "Revenge is the easy guess, of course. But I've met the man. Revenge doesn't explain it all. You would be in a better position to know, Private. You *do* have his mind."

"I have no idea," Jared said.

"Well, perhaps it will come," Cainen said. "My warning is to remember that whatever it is that motivates him, he has given himself to it, entirely and completely. It's too late to convince him otherwise. The danger for you will be that if you meet him, you will empathize with him and with his motivation. You are *designed* to understand him, after all. Boutin will use this if he can."

"What should I do?" Jared asked.

"Remember who you are," Cainen said. "Remember that you're not him. And remember that you always have a choice."

"I'll remember," Jared said.

"I hope you do," Cainen said, and stood. "I wish you luck, Private. You can go now. When you leave, let Wilson know he can come back in." Cainen wandered over to a cabinet, intentionally choosing to put his back to Jared. Jared stepped out the door.

"You can go back in," Jared said to Wilson.

"Okay," Wilson said. "I hope you two had a useful conversation."

"It was," Jared said. "He's an interesting fellow."

"That's one way of putting it," Wilson said. "You know, Dirac, he feels very paternal toward you."

"So I gathered," Jared said. "I like it. Not exactly what I was expecting in a father, though."

Wilson chortled. "Life is full of surprises, Dirac," he said. "Where are you off to now?"

"I think I'll go see Cainen's granddaughter," Jared said.

The *Kestrel* flicked on its Skip Drive six hours before Jared returned to Phoenix Station and translated to the system of a dim orange star that from Earth would be seen in the Circinus constellation, but only if one had a proper telescope. It was there to pick through the remains of the Colonial Union freighter *Handy*; the black box data sent back to Phoenix via emergency Skip drone suggested that someone had sabotaged the engines. No black box data was ever recovered from the *Kestrel*; nothing of the *Kestrel* was ever recovered.

Lieutenant Cloud looked up from his lair in the pilots lounge, a table laid out with enticements to trap the unwary (namely, a deck of cards), and saw Jared in front of him.

"Well, if it isn't the jokester himself," Cloud said, smiling.

"Hello, Lieutenant," Jared said. "Long time, no see."

"Not my fault," Cloud said. "I've been here this whole time. Where have you been?"

"Out saving humanity," Jared said. "You know, the usual."

"It's a dirty job, but someone has to do it," Cloud said. "And I'm glad it's you instead of me." Cloud kicked his leg to push out a chair and picked up the cards. "Have a seat, why don't you. I'm due to the prelaunch formalities of my supply run in about fifteen minutes; that's just enough time to teach you how to lose at Texas hold 'em."

"I already know how to do that," Jared said.

"See? There's one of your jokes again," Cloud said.

"I actually came to see you about your supply run," Jared said. "I was hoping you'd let me deadhead down with you."

"I'll be happy to have you," Cloud said, and began shuffling the cards. "Ping me your leave clearance, and we'll be able to continue this game on board. The supply transport's on autopilot most of the way down anyway. I'm just on board so that if it crashes, they can say someone died."

"I don't have leave clearance," Jared said. "But I need to get down to Phoenix."

"What for?" Cloud asked.

"I need to visit a dead relative," Jared said. "And I'm going to be shipping out soon."

Cloud chuckled and cut the deck of cards. "I'm guessing the dead relative will be there when you get back," he said.

"It's not the dead relative I'm worried about," Jared said. He reached his hand out and pointed to the deck. "May I?" Cloud handed over the deck; Jared sat and began shuffling it. "I can see you're a gambling man, Lieutenant," he said. He finished shuffling and put the deck in front of Cloud.

"Cut it," Jared said. Cloud cut the deck a third of the way down. Jared took the smaller portion and placed it in front of himself. "We'll pick a card from our decks at the same time. I get the high card, you take me to Phoenix, I go see who I need to see, I'm back before you lift."

"And if I get the high card we try for two out of three," Cloud said.

Jared smiled. "That wouldn't be very sporting, now

would it. Are you ready?" Cloud nodded. "Draw," Jared said.

Cloud drew an eight of diamonds; Jared drew a six of clubs. "Damn," Jared said. He pushed his cards over to Cloud.

"Who's the dead relative?" Cloud asked, taking the cards.

"It's complicated," Jared said.

"Try me," Cloud said.

"It's the clone of the man whose consciousness I was created to house," Jared said.

"Okay, so you were absolutely correct about this being complicated," Cloud said. "I haven't the slightest idea what you just said."

"Someone who is like my brother," Jared said. "Someone I didn't know."

"For someone who is just a year old, you lead an interesting life," Cloud said.

"I know," Jared said. "It's not my fault, though." He stood up. "I'll catch you later, Lieutenant."

"Oh, stop it," Cloud said. "Give me a minute to take a leak and we'll go. Just keep quiet when we get to the transport and let me do all the talking. And remember if we get in trouble I'm going to blame it all on you."

"I wouldn't have it any other way," Jared said.

Getting past the transport bay crew was almost ridiculously simple. Jared stuck close to Cloud, who ran through his preflight check and consulted his crew with businesslike efficiency. They ignored Jared or assumed that since he was with Cloud he had every right to be there. Thirty minutes later the transport was easing its way down to Phoenix Station, and Jared was showing Cloud that he wasn't actually very good at losing at Texas hold 'em. This annoyed Cloud greatly.

At the Phoenix Station ground port, Cloud consulted with the ground crew and then came back to Jared. "It's going to take them about three hours to load her up," he said. "Can you get to where you're going and be back before then?"

"The cemetery is just outside Phoenix City," Jared said.

"You should be fine then," Cloud said. "How are you going to get there?"

"I haven't the slightest idea," Jared said.

"What?" Cloud said.

Jared shrugged. "I didn't actually think you'd take me," he confessed. "I didn't plan this far ahead."

Cloud laughed. "God loves a fool," he said, and then motioned to Jared. "Come on, then. Let's go meet your brother."

Metairie Catholic Cemetery lay in the heart of Metairie, one of the oldest neighborhoods in Phoenix City; it was around when Phoenix was still called New Virginia and Phoenix City was still Clinton, before the attacks that leveled the early colony and forced humans to regroup and reconquer the planet. The earliest graves in the cemetery dated back to the early days, when Metairie was a line of plastic and mud buildings, and proud Louisianans had settled there with the pretensions of its being Clinton's first suburb.

The graves Jared visited were on the other side of the cemetery from the first line of the dead. The graves were marked by a single headstone, upon which three names were engraved, each with their separate dates: Charles, Cheryl and Zoë Boutin.

"Jesus," Cloud said. "An entire family."

"No," Jared said, kneeling down at the headstone. "Not

really. Cheryl is here. Zoë died far away, and her body was lost with many others. And Charles isn't dead. This is someone else. A clone he created so it would look like he had killed himself." Jared reached out and touched the headstone. "There's no family here."

Cloud looked at Jared kneeling by the headstone. "I think I'll take a look around," he said, trying to give Jared some time.

"No," Jared said, and looked over. "Please. I'll be done in just a minute and then we can go." Cloud nodded in assent but looked toward the close-by trees. Jared returned his attention to the headstone.

He lied to Cloud about who he had come to see, because who he wanted to see wasn't here. Outside of a bit of pity, Jared found himself at an emotional loss regarding the poor nameless clone Boutin killed to fake his own death. Nothing in the still-emerging bank of memories Jared shared with Boutin featured the clone in anything but the most clinical of settings, emotional or otherwise; the clone wasn't a person to Boutin, but a means to an end—an end that Jared, naturally enough, had no memory of since the recording of his consciousness was done before Boutin pulled the trigger. Jared tried to feel some sympathy for the clone, but there were others here he had come for. Jared hoped the clone indeed had never woken up and left it at that.

Jared focused on the name Cheryl Boutin and felt muted, conflicted emotions echo back from his memory. Jared realized that while Boutin had affection for his wife, labeling that affection as love would have been overstating the case. The two married because they both wanted children and they both understood and liked being around the other well enough, although Jared sensed that even that emotional attachment had been tamped down by the end. Their mutual joy of their daughter kept them from separation; even their cooled relationship was tolerable and preferable to the mess of a divorce and the trouble it would cause their child.

From some crevasse in Jared's mind came an unexpected memory about Cheryl's death, that on her fatal trip she had not been hiking alone; she had been with a friend who Boutin suspected was her lover. There was no jealousy that Jared could detect. Boutin didn't begrudge her a lover; he had one of his own. But Jared felt the anger Boutin felt at the funeral, when the suspected lover had lingered over the grave too long at the end of the funeral ceremony. It took time away from Boutin's final farewell to his wife. And Zoë's to her mother.

Zoë.

Jared traced her name on the gravestone, and said the name in the place she should have rested but did not, and felt again the grief that spilled from Boutin's memories into his own heart. Jared touched the gravestone once more, felt the name engraved into stone, and wept.

A hand rested on Jared's shoulder; he looked up to see Cloud there.

"It's all right," Cloud said. "We all lose the people we love."

Jared nodded. "I know," he said. "I lost someone I loved. Sarah. I felt her die and then I felt the hole she left inside me. But this is different."

"It's different because it's a child," Cloud said.

"It's a child I never knew," Jared said, and looked up at Cloud again. "She died before I was born. I didn't know her. I couldn't know her. But I *do*." He gestured to his temples. "Everything about her is in here. I remember her being born. I remember her first steps and her first words. I remember holding her here at her mother's funeral. I remember the last time I saw her. I remember hearing that she was dead. It's all *here*."

"No one has anyone else's memories," Cloud said. He said it in a way to soothe Jared. "It just doesn't work that way."

Jared laughed, bitterly. "But it *does*," he said. "It does with me. I told you. I was born to hold someone else's mind. They didn't think that it worked, but it did. And now his memories are my memories. His life is my life. His daughter—"

Jared stopped talking, unable to go on. Cloud kneeled down next to Jared and put an arm around his shoulder and let him mourn.

"It's not fair," Cloud said eventually. "It's not fair you have to mourn this child."

Jared gave a small laugh. "We're in the wrong universe for fair," he said, simply.

"That we are," Cloud agreed.

"I *want* to mourn her," Jared said. "I feel her. I can feel the love I had for her. That *he* had for her. I want to remember her, even if that means I have to mourn her. That's not too much to bear for her memory. It's not, is it?"

"No," Cloud said. "I guess it's not."

"Thank you," Jared said. "Thank you for coming with me here. Thank you for helping me."

"That's what friends are for," Cloud said.

::Dirac,:: Jane Sagan said. She was standing behind them. ::You've been reactivated.::

Jared felt the sudden snap of reintegration, and felt Jane Sagan's awareness wash over him, and felt mildly revolted by it even as other parts of him rejoiced at coming back into a larger sense of being. Some part of Jared's brain noted that being integrated wasn't just about sharing information and becoming part of a higher consciousness. It was also about control, a way to keep individuals tied to the group. There was a reason why Special Forces soldiers hardly ever retired—being retired means losing integration. Losing integration means being alone.

Special Forces soldiers were almost never alone. Even when they were by themselves.

::Dirac,:: Sagan said again.

"Speak normally," Jared said, and stood up, still looking away from Sagan. "You're being rude."

There was an infinitesimal pause before Sagan responded. "Very well," she said. "Private Dirac, it's time to go. We're needed back on Phoenix Station."

"Why?" Jared said.

"I'm not going to talk about it in front of him," Sagan said, indicating Cloud. "No offense, Lieutenant."

"None taken," Cloud said.

"Tell me out loud," Jared said. "Or I'm not going."

"I'm giving you an order," Sagan said.

"And I'm telling you to take your orders and shove them up your ass," Jared said. "I'm suddenly very tired of being part of Special Forces. I'm tired of being shoved around from place to place. Unless you tell me where I'm going and why, I think I'm just staying right here."

Sagan audibly sighed. She turned to Cloud. "Believe me when I tell you that if any of this passes your lips, I will shoot you myself. At very close range."

"Lady," Cloud said. "I believe every word you say."

"Three hours ago the *Redhawk* was destroyed by the Obin," Sagan said. "It managed to launch a Skip drone before it was totally destroyed. We've lost two other ships in the last two days; they've entirely disappeared. We think the Obin tried to do the same with the *Redhawk* but weren't able to do it for whatever reason. We got lucky, if you want to call this lucky. Between these three ships and four other Special Forces ships that have disappeared in the last month, it's clear the Obin are targeting Special Forces."

"Why?" Jared said

"We don't know," Sagan said. "But General Szilard has decided we're not going to wait until more of our ships get attacked. We going in to get Boutin, Dirac. We move in twelve hours."

"That's crazy," Jared said. "All we know is that he's on Arist. That's an entire moon to look at. And no matter how many ships we use, we'll be attacking the Obin home system."

"We know where he is on Arist," Sagan said. "And we have a plan to get past the Obin to get him."

"How?"

"*That* I'm not saying out loud," Sagan said. "It's the end of discussion, Dirac. Come with me or don't. We've got twelve hours until the attack begins. You've already caused me to waste time coming down here to get you. Don't let's waste any more time getting back."

ELEVEN

Goddamn it, General, Jane Sagan thought, as she tracked through the *Kite,* heading toward the landing bay control room. *Stop hiding from me, you officious prick.* She took care not to actually send the thought in the conversational mode of the Special Forces. Because of the similarity between thinking and speaking for Special Forces members, nearly every one of them had had a "did I say that out loud" moment or two. But that particular thought spoken aloud would be more trouble than it was worth.

Sagan had been on the hunt for General Szilard since the moment she had gotten the order to retrieve Jared Dirac from his AWOL adventure on Phoenix. The order had come with the notice that Dirac was once again under her command, and with a set of classified memos from Colonel Robbins detailing the latest events in Dirac's life: his trip to Covell, his sudden memory dump and the fact that his consciousness pattern was now definitively that of Charles Boutin. In addition to this material was a note forwarded by Robbins, from General Mattson to Szilard, in which Mattson strongly urged Szilard not to return Dirac to active duty, suggesting he be detained at least until the upcoming round of hostilities featuring the Obin was settled one way or another.

Sagan thought General Mattson was a jackass, but she had to admit he'd hit the nail on the head. Sagan had never been comfortable with Dirac under her command. He'd been a good and competent soldier, but knowing he had a second consciousness in his skull waiting to leak down and contaminate the first made her wary, and aware of the chance that he'd crack on the mission and get someone killed besides himself. Sagan considered it a victory that when he *did* crack, that day on the Phoenix Station promenade, he was on shore leave. And it wasn't until Mattson swooped in to relieve her of further responsibility toward Dirac that she allowed herself to feel pity for him, and to recognize that he had never justified the suspicion she held him in.

That was then, Sagan thought. Now Dirac was back and he was certifiably around the bend. It had taken most of her will not to tear him a new asshole when he had been insubordinate on Phoenix; if she had had the stun pistol she used on him when he originally cracked, she would have shot him in the head a second time just to make the point that his transplanted attitude didn't impress her. As it was she could barely remain civil to him on the ride back, this time by fast courier shuttle, directly to the *Kite*'s bay. Szilard was on board, conferring with *Kite* commander Major Crick. The general had ignored Sagan's earlier hails when she was on the *Kite* and he was on Phoenix Station, but now that the two of them were on the same ship, she was prepared to block his path until she had her say. She marched herself up the stairwell, two steps at a time, and opened the door to the control room.

::I knew you were coming,:: Szilard said to her, as she entered the room. He was sitting in front of the control panel that operated the bay. The officer that operated the bay could do nearly all his tasks via BrainPal, of course, and usually did. The control panel was there as a backup. When it got right down to it, all the ship controls were essentially BrainPal backups.

::Of course you knew I was coming,:: Sagan said. ::You're the commander of the Special Forces. You can locate any of us from our BrainPal signal.::

::It wasn't that,:: Szilard said. ::I just know who you are. The possibility of you *not* coming to find me once I put Dirac back under your command didn't even cross my mind.:: Szilard turned his chair slightly and stretched out his legs. ::I was so confident you were coming that I even cleared out the room so we'd have some privacy. And here we are.::

::Permission to speak freely,:: Sagan asked.

::Of course,:: Szilard said.

::You're out of your goddamned mind, sir,:: Sagan said.

Szilard laughed out loud. ::I didn't expect you to speak *that* freely, Lieutenant,:: he said.

::You've seen the same reports I have,:: Sagan said. ::I know you're aware of how much Dirac is like Boutin now. Even his brain works the same. And yet you want to put him on a mission to find Boutin.::

::Yes,:: Szilard said.

"Christ!" Sagan said, out loud. Special Forces speak was fast and efficient but it wasn't very good for exclamations. Nevertheless, Sagan backed herself up, sending a wave of frustration and irritation toward General Szilard, which he accepted wordlessly. ::I don't want responsibility for him,:: Sagan said, finally.

::I don't remember asking you if you wanted the responsibility,:: Szilard said.

::He's a danger to the other soldiers in my platoon,:: Sagan said. ::And he's a danger to the mission. You know what it means if we don't succeed. We don't need the additional risk.::

::I disagree,:: Szilard said.

::For God's sake,:: Sagan said. ::*Why?*::

::"Keep your friends close and your enemies closer,":: Szilard said.

::What?:: Sagan said. She was suddenly reminded of a conversation with Cainen, months before, when he had said the same thing.

Szilard repeated the saying, then said, ::We have the enemy as close as he can possibly get. He's in our ranks, and he doesn't know he's the enemy. Dirac thinks he's one of us because as far as he knows he *is*. But now he thinks like our enemy thinks and acts like our enemy acts, and we'll know everything he knows. That's incredibly useful and it's worth the risk.::

::Unless he turns,:: Sagan said.

::You'll know it if he does,:: Szilard said. ::He's integrated with your whole platoon. The minute he acts against your interests you'll know about it and so will everyone else on the mission.::

::Integration isn't mind reading,:: Sagan said. ::We'll only know after he starts doing something. That means he could kill one of my soldiers or give away our positions or any number of other things. Even with integration he's still a real danger.::

::You're right about one thing, Lieutenant,: Szilard said.

::Integration isn't mind reading. Unless you have the right firmware.::

Sagan felt a ping in her communication queue: an upgrade to her BrainPal. Before she could give assent it began to unpack. Sagan felt an uncomfortable jolt as the upgrade propagated, causing a momentary flux in her brain's electrical patterns.

::What the hell was that?:: Sagan asked.

::That was the mind-reading upgrade,:: Szilard said. ::Usually only generals and certain very specialized military investigators get this one, but in your case, I think it's warranted. For this mission, anyway. Once you're back we're going to yank it back out, and if you ever speak about it to anyone we'll have to put you somewhere very small and distant.::

::I don't understand how this is possible,:: Sagan said.

Szilard made a face. ::Think about it, Lieutenant,:: he said. ::Think about how we're communicating. We're thinking, and our BrainPal is interpreting that we are choosing to speak to someone else when we do so. Outside of intent, there is no significant difference between our public thoughts and our private ones. What would be remarkable is if we *couldn't* read minds. It's what the BrainPal is supposed to do.::

::But you don't tell people that,:: Sagan said.

Szilard shrugged. ::No one wants to know they have no privacy, even in their own heads.::

::So you can read my private thoughts,:: Sagan said.

::You mean, like the one where you called me an officious prick?:: Szilard asked.

::There was context for that,:: Sagan said.

::There always is,:: Szilard said. ::Relax, Lieutenant. Yes, I can read your thoughts. I can read the thoughts of anyone who is in my command structure. But usually I *don't*. It's not necessary and most of the time it's almost completely useless anyway.::

::But you can read people's thoughts,:: Sagan said.

::Yes, but most people are *boring*,:: Szilard said. ::When I first got the upgrade, after I was put in command of the Special Forces, I spent an entire day listening to people's thoughts. You know what the vast majority of people are thinking the vast majority of the time? They're thinking, I'm hungry. Or, I need to take a dump. Or, I want to fuck that guy. And then it's back to I'm hungry. And then they repeat the sequence until they die. Trust me, Lieutenant. A day with this capability and your opinion of the complexity and wonder of the human mind will suffer an irreversible decline.::

Sagan smiled. ::If you say so,:: she said.

::I do say so,:: Szilard said. ::However, in your case this capability will be of actual use, because you'll be able to hear Dirac's thoughts and feel his private emotions without him knowing he's being observed. If he is thinking of treason, you'll know it almost before he does. You can react to it before Dirac kills one of your soldiers or compromises your mission. I think that's a sufficient check to the risk of bringing him along.::

::And what should I do if he turns?:: Sagan asked. ::If he becomes a traitor?::

::Then you kill him, of course,:: Szilard said. ::Don't hesitate about it. But you be *sure*, Lieutenant. Now you know that I can get inside your head, so I trust you'll refrain from blowing his head off just because you're feeling twitchy.::

::Yes, General,:: Sagan said.

::Good,:: Szilard said. ::Where is Dirac now?::

::He's with the platoon, getting ready, down there in the

bay. I gave him our orders on the way up,:: Sagan said.

::Why don't you check in on him?:: Szilard asked.

::With the upgrade?:: Sagan asked.

::Yes,:: Szilard said. ::Learn to use it before your mission. You're not going to have time to fiddle with it later.::

Sagan accessed her new utility, found Dirac, and listened in.

::This is nuts,:: Jared thought to himself.

::You got that right,:: Steven Seaborg said. He'd joined 2nd Platoon while Jared had been away.

::Did I say that out loud?:: Jared said.

::No, I read minds, you jerk,:: Seaborg said, and sent a ping of amusement Jared's way. Whatever issues Jared and Seaborg had had disappeared after the death of Sarah Pauling; Seaborg's jealousy of Jared, or whatever it was, was outweighed by their mutual feeling of the loss of Sarah. Jared would hesitate to call him a friend, but the bond they had was more amicable than not, now reinforced by their additional bond of integration.

Jared glanced around the bay, at the two dozen Skip Drive sleds in it—the total fleet of Skip Drive sleds that had been produced to that point. He looked over at Seaborg, who was climbing into one to check it out.

::So this is what we're going to use to attack an entire planet,:: Seaborg said. ::A couple dozen Special Forces soldiers, each in their own space-traveling gerbil cage.::

::You've seen a gerbil cage?:: Jared asked.

::Of course not,:: Seaborg said. ::I've never even seen a gerbil. But I've seen pictures, and that's what this looks like to me. What sort of idiot would ride in one of these things.::

::I've ridden in one,:: Jared said.

::That answers that,:: Seaborg said. ::And what was it like?::

::I felt exposed,:: Jared said.

::Wonderful,:: Seaborg said, and rolled his eyes.

Jared knew how he felt, but he also saw the logic behind the assault. Nearly all space-faring creatures used ships to get from one point to another in real space; planetary detection and defense grids, by necessity, had the resolution power to detect the large objects that ships tended to be. The Obin defense grid around Arist was no different. A Special Forces ship would be spotted and attacked in an instant; a tiny, wire-frame object barely larger than a man would not.

Special Forces knew this because it had already sent the sleds on six different occasions, sneaking through the defense grid to spy on the communications coming off the moon. It was on the last of these missions that they heard Charles Boutin on a communication beam, broadcasting in the open, sending a voice note toward Obinur asking about the arrival time of a supply ship. The Special Forces soldier who had caught the signal chased it down to its source, a small science outpost on the shore of one of Arist's many large islands. He'd waited to hear a second transmission from Boutin to confirm his location before he returned.

Upon hearing this fact, Jared had accessed the recorded file to hear the voice of the man he was supposed to have been. He'd heard Boutin's voice before, on voice recordings that Wilson and Cainen had played for him; the voice on those recordings was the same as the one on this one. Older, creakier and more stressed, but there was no mistaking the timbre or cadence. Jared was aware just how much Boutin's sounded like his own, which was to be expected and also more than a little disconcerting.

I've got a strange life, Jared thought, and then glanced up to make sure the thought hadn't leaked. Seaborg was still examining the sled and gave no indication of having heard him.

Jared walked through the collection of sleds toward another object in the room, a spherical object slightly larger than the sleds itself. It was a piece of interesting Special Forces skullduggery called a "capture pod," used when Special Forces had something or someone they wanted to evacuate but couldn't evacuate themselves. Inside the sphere was a hollow designed to hold a single member of most midsized intelligent species; Special Forces soldiers shoved them in, sealed the pod, and then backed off as the pod's lifters blasted the pod toward the sky. Inside the pod a strong antigravity field kicked in when the lifters did, otherwise the occupant would be flattened. The pod would then be retrieved by a Special Forces ship located overhead.

The capture pod was for Boutin. The plan was simple: Attack the science station where they had located Boutin, and disable its communications. Grab Boutin and stuff him into the capture pod, which would head out to Skip Drive distance—the *Kite* would pop in just long enough to grab the pod and then get out before the Obin could give chase. After Boutin's capture, the science station would be destroyed with an old favorite: a meteor just large enough to wipe the station off the planet, which would hit just far enough away from the station that no one would get suspicious. In this case it would be a hit in the ocean several miles off the coast, so the science station would be obliterated in the ensuing tsunami. The Special Forces had been working with falling rocks for decades; they knew how to make it look like an accident. If everything went to plan, the Obin wouldn't even know they had been attacked.

To Jared's eye, there were two major flaws in the plan, both interrelated. The first was that the Skip Drive sleds could not land; they wouldn't survive contact with Arist's atmosphere, and even if they did, they wouldn't be steerable once they were in it. The members of 2nd Platoon on the mission would pop out into real space on the edge of Arist's atmosphere and then perform a near-space skydive down to the surface. Members of 2nd Platoon had done it before—Sagan had done it at the Battle of Coral and was none the worse for wear—but it struck Jared as asking for trouble.

The method of their arrival created the second major flaw in the plan: There was no simple way to extract the 2nd Platoon after the mission was completed. Once Boutin was captured, the 2nd's orders were ominous: Get as far away from the science station as possible, so as not to die in the scheduled tsunami (the mission plan had thoughtfully provided a map to a nearby high point that they figured should—*should*—stay dry during the deluge), and then hike into the uninhabited interior of the island to hide out for several days until Special Forces could send a clutch of capture pods to retrieve them. It would take more than one round of capture pod retrievals to evacuate all twenty-four members of the 2nd that would be on the mission, and Sagan had already informed Jared that he and she would be the last people off the planet.

Jared frowned at the memory of Sagan's pronouncement. Sagan had never been a big fan of his, he knew, and he knew that was because she was aware from the start that he'd been bred out of a traitor. She'd known more about him than he had. Her farewell when he was transferred to Mattson seemed sincere enough, but since he'd seen her at the cemetery, and been returned to her command, she'd seemed genuinely angry with him, as if he actually *was* Boutin. On one level Jared could sympathize—after all, as Cainen noted, he was more like Boutin now than he was like his older self—but on a more immediate level Jared resented being treated like the enemy. Jared wondered darkly if the reason Sagan was having him stay behind with her was so she could take care of him without anyone knowing.

Then he shook the idea out of his head. Sagan was capable of killing him, he was sure. But she wouldn't unless he gave her a reason. *Best not to give her a reason*, Jared thought.

Anyway, it wasn't Sagan he was worried about, it was Boutin himself. The mission anticipated some resistance from the small Obin military presence at the science station, but none from the scientists or from Boutin. This struck Jared as wrong. Jared had Boutin's anger in his head and knew the intelligence of the man, even if the details of all his work remained unclear to him. Jared doubted Boutin would go without a fight. This didn't mean Boutin would take up arms—he emphatically wasn't a warrior—but Boutin's weapon was his brain. It was Boutin's brain formulating a way to betray the Colonial Union that had put them all in this position to begin with. It was a bad assumption that they would simply be able to snatch and stuff Boutin. He almost certainly had a surprise in store.

What that surprise would be, however, eluded Jared.

::You hungry?:: Seaborg asked Jared. ::Because thinking about how insane a mission is going to be always makes me want to eat.::

Jared grinned. ::You must be hungry a lot.::

::One of the benefits of being Special Forces,:: Seaborg said. ::That and skipping the awkward teenage years.::

::Studying up on teenagers?:: Jared asked.

::Sure,:: Seaborg said. ::Because if I'm lucky I'll get to be one one day.::

::You just said we get to skip the awkward teenage years,:: Jared said.

::Well, when I get there they won't be awkward,:: Seaborg said. ::Now come on. It's lasagna tonight.::

They went to get something to eat.

Sagan opened her eyes.

::How did it go?:: asked Szilard, who had been watching her as she listened in to Jared.

::Dirac's worried that we're underestimating Boutin,:: Sagan said. ::That he's planned for being attacked in some way we've missed.::

::Good,:: Szilard said. ::Because I feel the same way. *That's* why I want Dirac on the mission.::

Arist, green and cloudy, filled Jared's vision, surprising him with its immensity. Popping into existence at the bare edge of a planet's atmosphere with nothing but a carbon fiber cage around you was profoundly disturbing; Jared felt like he was going to fall. Which was of course exactly what he was doing.

Enough of this, he thought, and began disconnecting himself from his sled. Planetward, Jared located the five other members of his squad, all of whom translated before him: Sagan, Seaborg, Daniel Harvey, Anita Manley and Vernon Wigner. He also spotted the capture pod, and breathed a sigh of relief. The capture pod's mass was just short of the five-ton mark; there was a small but real concern it would be too massive to use the mini–Skip Drive. All of Jared's squad had pulled themselves from their sleds and were free-floating, slowly drifting from the spidery vehicles that had brought them this far.

The six of them were the forward force; their job was to guide down the capture pod and secure a landing area for the remaining members of 2nd Platoon, who would be following quickly behind. The island Boutin was on was carpeted with a thick tropical forest, which made any landing difficult; Sagan had chosen a small meadowed area about fifteen klicks from the science station to land at.

::Keep dispersed,:: Sagan said to her squad. ::We'll regroup when we get through the worst of the atmosphere. Radio silence until you hear from me.::

Jared maneuvered himself to look at Arist and drank it in until his BrainPal, sensing the first tenuous effects of the atmosphere, wrapped him in a protective sphere of nanobots that flowed from a pack on his back and secured him in the middle, to keep him from making contact with the sphere and crisping himself where they intersected. The inside of the sphere let in no light; Jared was suspended in a small, dark private universe.

Left to his own thoughts, Jared returned to the Obin, the implacable and fascinating race whose company Boutin kept. The Colonial Union's records of the Obin went all the way back to the beginning of the Union, when a discussion over who owned a planet the human settlers had named Casablanca ended with the settlers removed with horrifying efficiency, and the Colonial Forces charged with taking back the planet likewise utterly routed. The Obin wouldn't surrender and would not take prisoners. Once they decided they wanted something they kept coming at it until they had it.

Get in their way enough and they would decide it was in their interest to remove you permanently. The Ala, who had fashioned the diamond dome of the general's mess at

Phoenix, were not the first race the Obin had methodically wiped out, nor the last.

The one saving grace about the Obin was that they were not particularly acquisitive as starfaring races went. The Colonial Union would start ten colonies in the time it took the Obin to start one, and while the Obin were not shy about taking a planet held by another race when it suited them, it didn't suit them all that often. Omagh had been the first planet since Casablanca that the Obin had taken from humans, and even then it appeared that it was more of a case of opportunism (taking it from the Rraey, who presumably had fought to get it from the humans) than genuine expansion. The Obin reluctance to unnecessarily expand the race's holdings was one of the primary reasons the CDF suspected someone else had initiated the attack. If, as was suspected, it had been the Rraey who attacked Omagh and then managed to keep it, the Colonial Union would almost certainly have retaliated and attempted to take back the colony. The Rraey knew when to quit.

The other interesting thing about the Obin—which made their putative alliance with the Rraey and the Enesha so puzzling to Jared—was that in general, unless you were in their way or trying to get into their face, the Obin were utterly uninterested in other intelligent races. They kept no embassies nor had official communication with other races; as far as the Colonial Union was aware never once did the Obin ever formally declare war *or* sign a treaty with any other race. If you were at war with the Obin, you knew it because they were shooting at you. If you weren't at war with them, they had no communication with you at all. The Obin were not xenophobes; that would imply they hated other races. They simply didn't care about them. That the Obin, of all races, would align with not one but two other races was extraordinary; that they would align against the Colonial Union was ominous.

Underneath all of the data about Obin's relations—or lack thereof—with other intelligent races was a rumor about the race that the CDF did not give much credence to, but noted due to its widespread belief among other races: The Obin did not evolve intelligence but were given it by another race. The CDF discounted the rumor because the idea that any of the fiercely competitive races in this part of the galaxy would take the time to uplift some rock-banging underachievers was unlikely to the point of ridiculousness. The CDF knew of races who had exterminated the near-intelligent creatures they had discovered on the real estate they wanted, on the grounds that it was never too early to eliminate a competitor. It had known of none that did the opposite.

If the rumor were true, it would rather strongly imply that the intelligent designers of the Obin were the Consu, the only species in the local neighborhood with the high-end technological means to attempt a species-wide uplift, and also the philosophical motive, given that the Consu's racial mission was to bring all other intelligent species in the area into a state of perfection (i.e., like the Consu). The problem with that theory was that the Consu's method of bringing other races closer to Consu-like perfection usually involved forcing some poor hapless race to fight them, or pitting one lesser race against another, as the Consu did when they matched humans against the Rraey for the Battle of Coral. Even the species most likely to have created another intelligent species was more likely to destroy one instead, directly or indirectly, the race a victim of not meeting the Consu's high and inscrutable standards.

The Consu's high and inscrutable standards were the

primary argument against the Consu creating the Obin, because the Obin, unique among all intelligent races, had almost no culture to speak of. What few xenographical studies of the Obin had been done by humans or other races discovered that aside from a spare and utilitarian language, and a facility for practical technology, the Obin produced nothing of creative note: No significant art across any of their perceivable senses, no literature, no religion or philosophy that xenographers could recognize as such. The Obin barely even had politics, which was unheard of. The Obin society was so bereft of culture that one researcher contributing to the CDF file on the Obin suggested quite seriously that it was an open question whether Obin performed casual conversation—or indeed were even capable of it. Jared was no expert on the Consu, but it seemed unlikely to him that a people so concerned with the ineffable and eschatological would create a people incapable of concerning themselves with either. If the Obin were what happened with intelligent design, it was an affirming argument for the value of evolution.

The sphere of nanobots surrounding Jared flung away and behind. He blinked furiously in the light until his eyes adjusted, and then sensed around for his squad. Tightbeams found him and highlighted the others, their bodies almost invisible thanks to their input-sensitive unitards; even the capture pod was camoed. Jared floated toward the capture pod to check its status but was warned away from it by Sagan, who checked it herself. Jared and the rest of the squad grouped closer together but not so close they would get in each other's way when they deployed their chutes.

The squad deployed chutes at the lowest possible height; even camouflaged, parachutes could be seen by an eye that knew what to look for. The capture pod's parachute was immense and designed to support dramatic air-braking; it made impressive snapping sounds as the nanobot-created canopy formed, filled with air and then violently tore apart, only to form again a second later. Finally the capture pod slowed enough that its parachute held.

Jared turned to the science station, several klicks to the south, and upped the magnification on his cowl to see if there was any movement at the science station that would suggest they had been seen. He saw nothing and had his observation confirmed by Wigner and Harvey. Moments later they were all on the ground, grunting as they moved the capture pod past the edge of the meadow and into the woods, and then moving quickly to augment its camouflage with foliage.

::Everyone remember where we parked,:: Seaborg said.

::Quiet,:: Sagan said, and appeared to be focusing on something internal. ::That was Roentgen,:: she said. ::The others are getting ready to deploy chutes.:: She hoisted her Empee. ::Come on, let's make sure there aren't any surprises.::

Jared felt a peculiar sensation, like his brain being picked.

::Oh, shit,:: Jared said.

Sagan turned to look at him. ::What?:: she said.

::We're i::*n trouble,* Jared said, and halfway through saying it Jared felt his integration with his squad violently cut off. He gasped and clutched his head, overwhelmed by the feeling of having one of his major senses ripped out of his skull. Around him Jared saw and heard the other squad members collapsing, crying out and vomiting from the pain and disorientation. He fell to his knees and tried to breathe. He retched.

Jared struggled back to his feet and stumbled over to Sagan, who was on her knees, wiping her mouth from vomiting. He grabbed her arm and tried to pull her up. "Come on," Jared said. "We have to get up. We have to hide."

"Wha—" Sagan coughed and spat, and looked up at Jared. "What's going on?"

"We're cut off," Jared said. "It's happened to me before, when I was at Covell. The Obin are blocking us from using our BrainPals."

"How?" Sagan yelled the question, too loudly.

"I don't know," Jared said.

Sagan stood up. "It's Boutin," she said, groggily. "He told them how. Must have."

"Maybe," Jared said. Sagan wobbled slightly; Jared steadied her and came around to face her. "We have to move, Lieutenant," he said. "If the Obin are blocking us, that means they know we're here. They're coming for us. We have to get our people up and moving."

"We have more people coming," Sagan said. "Have to . . ." She stopped, and straightened, as if something cold and horrible had just washed over her. "Oh, my God," she said. "Oh, my God." She looked up into the sky.

"What is it?" Jared asked, and looked up, scanning for the telltale subtle ripples of camouflaged parachutes. It took him a second to realize he didn't see any. It took him another second to realize what it meant.

"Oh, my God," Jared said.

Alex Roentgen's first guess was that he managed to lose his tightbeam connection with the rest of the platoon.

Well, shit, he thought, and shifted his position, spread-eagling and spinning a few times to let the tightbeam receiver seek out and locate the other members of the platoon, letting his BrainPal extrapolate their positions based on where they had been on their last transmission. He didn't need to find them all; just one would do nicely and then he would be reconnected, reintegrated.

Nothing.

Roentgen pushed his concerns away. He'd lost tight-beam before—only once, but once was enough to know it happened. He had reconnected when he made it to ground then; he'd do it again this time. He didn't have any more time to waste on it anyway because he was coming up on deployment altitude; they were deploying as low as possible to cover their tracks, so when to deploy was a matter of some precision. Roentgen checked his BrainPal to determine his altitude and it was then he realized that for the last minute he'd had no contact with his BrainPal at all.

Roentgen spent ten seconds processing the thought; it refused to process. Then tried again and this time his brain not only refused to process it but pushed back against it, expelling it violently, knowing the consequences of accepting the thought as truth. He attempted to access his BrainPal once, and then again and then again and then again and then again, each time fighting back a sense of panic that fed on itself exponentially. He called out inside his head. No one answered. No one had heard him. He was alone.

Alex Roentgen lost most of his mind then, and for the rest of his fall twisted and kicked and tore at the sky, screaming with a voice he used so rarely that some small, disassociated part of his brain marveled at the sound of it in his skull. His parachute did not deploy; it, like nearly every physical object and mental process Roentgen used, was controlled and activated by his BrainPal, a piece of equipment that had been so reliable for so long that the Colonial Defense Forces had simply stopped thinking of it as equipment and considered it as a given, like the rest of the brain and the soldier's physical body. Roentgen plummeted past the deployment line unknowing, uncaring, and insensate to the implications of passing through that final barrier.

It wasn't the knowledge that he was going to die that had driven Roentgen insane. It was being alone, separated, unintegrated for the first time and the last time in the six years he had been alive. In that time he'd felt the lives of his platoon mates in every intimate detail, how they fought, how they fucked, every moment that they lived, and the moment when they died. He took comfort in knowing he was there in their final moments and that others would be there for him in his. But they wouldn't be, and he wouldn't be there for them. The terror of his separation was matched by the shame of not being able to comfort his friends who were plunging to the same death as he was.

Alex Roentgen twisted again, faced the ground that would kill him, and screamed the scream of the abandoned.

Jared watched in dread as the pinwheeling gray dot above him appeared to gain speed in the final few seconds and, revealed as a screaming human, ground into the meadow with a sickening, splashy thud, followed by a horrifying bounce. The impact shocked Jared out of immobility. He shoved Sagan, screaming at her to run, and ran toward the others, hauling them up and shoving them toward the tree line, trying to make them get out of the way of the falling bodies.

Seaborg and Harvey had recovered but were staring at the sky, watching their friends die. Jared pushed Harvey and slapped Seaborg, yelling at both of them to move. Wigner refused to move and lay there, seemingly catatonic;

Jared picked him up and handed him to Seaborg and told him to move. He reached down for Manley; she pushed him away and began crawling toward the meadow, screeching. She picked herself up and ran as bodies tore apart on impact around her. Sixty meters out she stopped, turned around rapidly and screamed away the rest of her sanity. Jared turned away and missed seeing the leg of the body that fell next to her clip her on the neck and shoulder, crushing arteries and bones and driving shattered ribs into her lungs and heart. Manley's scream clipped off with a grunt.

From the first hit, it took only two minutes for the rest of 2nd Platoon to hit the ground. Jared and the rest of his squad watched from the tree line as they fell.

When it was over, Jared turned to the four remaining members of the squad and took stock. All of them seemed to be in varying stages of shock, with Sagan being the most responsive and Wigner the least, although he finally seemed aware of his surroundings. Jared felt sick but was otherwise functioning; he'd spent enough time out of integration that he could function without it. For the moment, at least, he was in charge.

He turned to Sagan. "We need to move," he said. "Into the trees. Away from here."

"The mission—" Sagan began.

"There is no mission anymore," Jared said. "They know we're here. We're going to die if we stay."

The words seemed to help clear Sagan's head. "Someone needs to go back," she said. "Take the capture pod. Let the CDF know." She looked directly at him. "Not you."

"Not me," Jared agreed. He knew she said it because she was suspicious of him, but he didn't have time to worry about it. He couldn't go back because he was the only one who was entirely functional. "You go back," he suggested to Sagan.

"No," Sagan said. Flat. Final.

"Seaborg, then," Jared said. After Sagan, Seaborg was the next most functional; he could tell the CDF what had happened, and tell them to prepare for the worst.

"Seaborg," Sagan agreed.

"Okay," Jared said, and turned to Seaborg. "Come on, Steve. Let's get you in this thing."

Seaborg wobbled over and began removing foliage from the capture pod to get to the door, moved to open the entry and then stopped.

"What is it?" Jared said.

"How do I open this?" Seaborg said, his voice squeaky from nonuse.

"Use your . . . *fuck*," Jared said. The capture pod opened via BrainPal.

"Well, this is just fucking *perfect*," Seaborg said, and slumped angrily next to the pod.

Jared moved to Seaborg, and then stopped and cocked his head.

In the distance, something was coming closer, and whatever it was was not worried about sneaking up on them.

"What is it?" Sagan said.

"Someone's coming," Jared said. "More than one. The Obin. They've found us."

TWELVE

They managed to elude the Obin for half an hour before they were cornered.

The squad would have been better off separating, drawing the pursuing Obin in several directions and opening up the possibility of one or more of its number slipping away at the sacrifice of the others. But they stayed together, compensating for the lack of integration by staying in each other's sight. Jared led the way at first, Sagan taking up the rear to drag along Wigner. Somewhere along the way Jared and Sagan traded roles, Sagan taking them largely north, away from the Obin pursuing them.

A distant whine became louder; Jared looked up through the tree canopy and saw an Obin aircraft pacing the squad and then heading north. Ahead, Sagan skipped to the right and headed east; she'd heard the aircraft as well. A few minutes later a second aircraft appeared and paced the squad again, dropping down to about ten meters above the canopy. There was an immense rattle and branches fell and exploded around them; the Obin had opened fire. Sagan skidded to a stop as huge-caliber slugs blew up dirt directly in front of her. That was that for going east; the squad turned north.The aircraft turned and paced them, offering bullets when they lagged or when they deviated too far to the east or west. The aircraft wasn't giving chase; it was herding them efficiently toward an unknown destination.

That destination appeared ten minutes later when the squad emerged into another, smaller meadow, this one with the Obin who had been in the first aircraft waiting for them. Behind them the second aircraft was preparing to land; behind that the initial group of Obin, who had never been far behind, was now becoming visible through the trees.

Wigner, still not entirely recovered from the mental trauma of being unplugged, pushed away from Jared and raised his Empee, apparently determined not to go out without a fight. He sighted in at the group of Obin waiting for them in the meadow and yanked at the trigger. Nothing happened. To keep the Empee from being used against CDF soldiers by their enemies, the Empee required a BrainPal verification to fire. It got none. Wigner snarled in frustration, and then everything above his eyebrows disappeared as a single shot took off the top of his head. He collapsed; in the distance Jared could see an Obin soldier lowering a weapon.

Jared, Sagan, Harvey and Seaborg came together, drew their combat knives and put their backs to each other, each facing a different direction. Drawing their knives was a futile gesture of defiance; none of them pretended to imagine that the Obin needed to get within an arm's reach to kill them all. Each took some small comfort in knowing they'd die within arm's reach of each other. It wasn't integration, but it was the best they could hope for.

By this time the second aircraft had landed; from inside the craft six Obin emerged, three carrying weapons, two with other equipment, and one empty-handed. The empty-handed one swayed over to the humans in the Obin's peculiarly graceful gait, and stopped a prudent distance away, its back covered by the three weapon-wielding Obin. Its blinking multiple eyes appeared to fix on Sagan, who was closest to it.

"Surrender," it said, in sibilant but clear English.

Sagan blinked. "Excuse me?" she said. As far as she knew, the Obin never took prisoners.

"Surrender," it said again. "You will die if you do not."

"You will let us live if we surrender," Sagan said.

"Yes," the Obin said.

Jared glanced over to Sagan, who was to his right; he could see her chewing over the offer. The offer looked good to Jared; the Obin might kill them if they surrendered, but they would definitely kill them if they didn't. He didn't offer the opinion to Sagan; he knew she didn't trust him or want to hear his opinion about anything.

"Drop your weapons," Sagan said, finally. Jared dropped his knife and unslung his Empee; the others did likewise. The Obin also had them remove their packs and belts, leaving only their unitards. A couple of the Obin who had been in the original group pursuing them came over and picked up the weapons and equipment and hauled them back to the airship. When one walked in front of Harvey, Jared could feel him tense up; Jared suspected Harvey was trying very hard not to kick it.

Their weapons and equipment removed, Jared and the others were made to stand apart from each other while the two Obin bearing equipment waved said equipment over each of them, searching, Jared suspected, for hidden weapons. The two Obin scanned the other three and then came to Jared, only to cut their examination short. One of them offered up a fluty comment to the head Obin in its native language. The head Obin came over to Jared, two armed Obin trailing it.

"You come with us," it said.

Jared glanced over at Sagan, looking for clues on how she wanted him to play this and getting nothing. "Where am I going?" Jared asked.

The head Obin turned and trilled something. One of the Obin behind him raised his weapon and shot Steve Seaborg in the leg. Seaborg went down screaming.

The head Obin swiveled its attention back to Jared. "You come with us," it said again.

"Jesus fuck, Dirac!" Seaborg said. "Go with the fucking Obin!"

Jared stepped out of line and allowed himself to be escorted to the aircraft.

Sagan watched Jared step out of line and briefly considered lunging and snapping his neck, depriving the Obin and Boutin of their prize and assuring that Dirac wouldn't have the opportunity to do anything stupid. The moment passed, and besides, it would have been a long shot anyway. And then they would all almost certainly be dead. As it was now they were still alive.

The head Obin turned its attention to Sagan, whom it recognized as the squad's leader. "You will stay," it said, and gamboled off before Sagan could say anything. She stepped forward to address the retreating Obin, but as she did three Obin came forward, brandishing weapons. Sagan put her hands up and backed away, but the Obin continued forward, motioning to Sagan that she and the rest of the squad needed to move.

She turned to Seaborg, who was still on the ground. "How's your leg?" she asked.

"The unitard caught most of it," he said, referring to the uniform's ability to stiffen and absorb some of the impact of a projectile. "It's not too bad. I'll live."

"Can you walk?" Sagan asked.

"As long as I'm not required to like it," Seaborg said.

"Come on, then," Sagan said, and held out her hand to help Seaborg up. "Harvey, get Wigner." Daniel Harvey walked over to the dead soldier and picked him up in a fireman's carry.

They were being herded into a depression slightly off-center from the middle of the meadow; the small spray of trees within it suggested the bedrock below had eroded away. As they arrived at the depression, Sagan heard the whine of an airship departing and a second whine of one arriving. The arriving craft, larger than the other two had been, landed near the depression, and from its guts rolled a series of identical machines.

"What the hell are those?" Harvey asked, setting down Wigner's body. Sagan didn't answer; she watched as the machines positioned themselves around the perimeter of the bowl, eight in all. The Obin who had come with the machines scrambled to the top of the machines and retracted the metal coverings, revealing large, multibarrel fléchette guns. When all the covers had been retracted, one of the Obin activated the fléchette guns; they powered up ominously, and began to track objects.

"It's a fence," Sagan said. "They've locked us in here." Sagan took an experimental step toward one of the guns; it swung toward her and tracked her movement. She took another step forward and it emitted a painful, high-pitched squeal, which Sagan assumed was designed to serve as a proximity warning. Sagan imagined that another step toward the gun would result in her foot being shot off at the very least, but she did not bother to test the proposition. She backed away from the gun; it turned off its siren but did not stop tracking her until she had retreated several steps.

"They had those here just waiting for us," Harvey said. "Very nice. What do you think are the odds?"

Sagan stared back up at the guns. "The odds are bad," Sagan said.

"What do you mean?" Harvey said.

"These are from the science station," Sagan said, motioning to the guns. "They have to be. There's no other sort of installation anywhere close to here. These aren't the sort of things a science station would just have lying around. They've used them here before to hold people in."

"Yeah, okay," Seaborg said. "But who? And why?"

"We've had six Special Forces ships disappear," Sagan said, omitting the one the Obin attacked and destroyed. "Those crews went somewhere. Maybe they were brought here."

"That still doesn't answer why," Seaborg said.

Sagan shrugged. She hadn't figured out that part yet.

The air was filled with the sound of the airships lifting off. The noise of their engines attenuated away, leaving nothing but the ambient sounds of nature behind.

"Great," Harvey said. He chucked a stone at one of the guns; it tracked the rock but didn't fire on it. "We're out here with no food, water or shelter. What you think the odds are that the Obin are never coming back for us?"

Sagan thought those odds were very good indeed.

"So you're me," Charles Boutin said to Jared. "Funny. I thought I'd be taller."

Jared said nothing. On arrival at the science station he had been confined to a crèche, tightly secured, and wheeled through the high, bare hallways until he arrived at what he assumed was a laboratory, filled with unfamiliar machines. Jared was left there for what seemed like hours before Boutin entered and strolled right up to the crèche, examining Jared physically as if he were a large and really interesting bug. Jared hoped Boutin would come up far enough to receive a head butt. He did not.

"That was a joke," Boutin said to Jared.

"I know," Jared said. "It just wasn't funny."

"Well," Boutin said. "I'm out of practice. You may have noticed the Obin are not the sort to crack wise."

"I noticed," Jared said. During the entire trip to the science station, the Obin were utterly silent. The only words the head Obin had said to Jared were "get out" when they arrived and "get in" when they opened the portable crèche.

"You can blame the Consu for that," Boutin said. "When they made the Obin, I guess they forgot to drop in a humor module. Among the many other things they apparently forgot."

Despite himself—or because of whose memories and personality he held in his head—Jared's attention focused. "Then it's true?" he asked. "The Consu uplifted the Obin."

"If you want to call it that," Boutin said. "Although the word *uplift* by its nature implies good intentions on the part of the uplifter, which is not in evidence here. From what I can get from the Obin, the Consu one day wondered what would happen if you made some species smart. So they came to Obinur, found an omnivore in a minor ecological niche, and gave it intelligence. You know, just to see what would happen next."

"What happened next?" Jared said.

"A long and cascading series of unintended consequences, my friend," Boutin said. "That end, for now, with you and me here in this lab. It's a direct line from there to here."

"I don't understand," Jared said.

"Of course you don't," Boutin said. "You don't have all the data. I didn't have all the data before I came here, so even if you know everything I know, you wouldn't know that. How much of what I know *do* you know?"

Jared said nothing. Boutin smiled. "Enough, anyway," he said. "I can tell you have some of my same interests. I saw how you perked up when I talked about the Consu. But maybe we should start with the simple things. Like: What is your name? I find it disconcerting to talk to my sort-of clone without having something to call you."

"Jared Dirac," Jared said.

"Ah," Boutin said. "Yes, the Special Forces naming protocol. Random first name, notable scientist last name. I did some work with the Special Forces at one time—indirectly, since you people don't like non–Special Forces getting in your way. What is that name you call us?"

"Realborn," Jared said.

"Right," Boutin said. "You like keeping yourself apart from the realborn. Anyway, the naming protocol of the Special Forces always amused me. The pool of last names is actually pretty limited: A couple hundred or so, and mostly classical European scientists. Not to mention the first names! Jared. Brad. Cynthia. John. *Jane.*" The names came out as a good-natured sneer. "Hardly a non-Western name among them, and for no good reason, since Special Forces aren't recruited from Earth like the rest of the CDF. You could have been called Yusef al-Biruni and it would have been all the same to you. The set of names Special Forces uses implicitly says something about the point of view of the people who created them, and created you. Don't you think?"

"I like my name, *Charles*," Jared said.

"Touché," Boutin said. "But I got my name through family tradition, where yours was just mixed and matched. Not that there's anything wrong with 'Dirac.' Named for Paul Dirac, no doubt. Ever heard of the 'Dirac sea'?"

"No," Jared said.

"Dirac proposed that what vacuum really was, was a vast sea of negative energy," Boutin said. "And that's a lovely image. Some physicists at the time thought it was an inelegant hypothesis, and maybe it was. But it was poetic, and they didn't appreciate that aspect. But that's physicists for you. Not exactly brimming over with poetry. The Obin are excellent physicists, and not one of them has any more poetry than a chicken. They definitely wouldn't appreciate the Dirac sea. How are you feeling?"

"Constrained," Jared said. "And I need to piss."

"So piss," Boutin said. "I don't mind. The crèche is self-cleaning, of course. And I'm sure your unitard can wick away the urine."

"Not without talking to my BrainPal about it," Jared said. Without communicating with the owner's BrainPal, the nanobots in the unitard's fabric only maintained basic defensive properties, like impact stiffening, designed to keep the owner safe through loss of consciousness or BrainPal trauma. Secondary capabilities, like the ability to drain away sweat and urine, were deemed nonessential.

"Ah," Boutin said. "Well, here. Let me fix that." Boutin went to an object on one of the lab tables and pressed on it. Suddenly the thick cotton batting in Jared's skull lifted; his BrainPal functionality was back. Jared ignored his need to piss in a frantic attempt to try to contact Jane Sagan.

Boutin watched Jared with a small smile on his face. "It

won't work," he said, after a minute of watching Jared's inner exertions. "The antenna here is strong enough to cause wave interference for about ten meters. It works in the lab and that's about it. Your friends are still jammed up. You can't reach them. You can't reach anyone."

"You can't jam BrainPals," Jared said. BrainPals transmitted through a series of multiple, redundant and encrypted transmission streams, each communicating through a shifting pattern of frequencies, the pattern of which was generated through a onetime key created when one BrainPal contacted another. It was virtually impossible to block even one of these streams; blocking all would be unheard of.

Boutin walked over to the antenna and pressed it again; the cotton batting in Jared's head returned. "You were saying?" Boutin said. Jared held back the urge to scream. After a minute Boutin turned the antenna back on. "Normally, you are right," Boutin said. "I supervised the latest round of communication protocols in the BrainPal. I helped design them. And you're entirely correct. You can't jam the communication streams, not without using such a high-energy broadcasting source that you overwhelmed all possible transmissions, including your own.

"But I'm not jamming the BrainPals that way," Boutin said. "Do you know what a 'back door' is? It's an easy-access entrance that a programmer or designer leaves himself into a complex program or design, so he can get into the guts of what he's working on without jumping through hoops. I had a back door into the BrainPal that only opens with my verification signal. The back door was designed to let me monitor BrainPal function on the prototypes for this last iteration, but it also allowed me to do some tweaking of the capabilities to factor out certain functions when I saw a glitch. One of the things I can do is turn off transmission capabilities. It's not in the design, so someone who is not me wouldn't know it was there."

Boutin paused for a second and regarded Jared. "But *you* should have known about the back door," he said. "Maybe you wouldn't have thought to use it as a weapon—I didn't until I got here—but if you're me you should know this. What do you know? Really?"

"How do you know about me?" Jared asked, to derail Boutin. "You knew I was supposed to be you. How did you know?"

"That's actually an interesting story," Boutin said, taking Jared's bait. "When we decided to make the back door a weapon, I made the code for the weapon like the code for the back door, because it was the simplest thing to do. That meant that it has the ability to check the function status of the BrainPals it affected. This turned out to be useful for a lot of reasons; not the least was letting us know how many soldiers we were dealing with at one time. It also gave us snapshots of the consciousness of the individual soldiers. This also is turning out to be useful.

"You were very recently at Covell Station, were you not?" Jared said nothing. "Oh, come now," Boutin said, irritably. "I know you were there. Stop acting like you are giving away state secrets."

"Yes," Jared said. "I was at Covell."

"Thank you," Boutin said. "We know there are Colonial soldiers at Omagh and that they come into Covell Station; we've placed detection devices there that scan for the back door. But they never go off. Whatever soldiers you have there must have different BrainPal architecture." Boutin glanced over to see Jared's reaction to this; Jared gave none. Boutin continued. "However, *you* tripped our alarms because you have the BrainPal I designed. Later on I got the consciousness signature sent to me, and as you might imagine I was floored. I know the image of my own consciousness very well, since I use my own pattern for a lot of testing. I let the Obin know I was looking for you. We were collecting Special Forces soldiers anyway, so this was not difficult for them to do. In fact, they should have tried to collect you at Covell."

"They tried to kill me at Covell," Jared said.

"Sorry," Boutin said. "Even the Obin can get a little excited in the thick of things. But you can take comfort in knowing that after that point they were told to scan first, shoot second."

"Thanks," Jared said. "That meant a lot to my squad mate today, when they shot him in the head."

"Sarcasm!" Boutin said. "That's more than most of your kind can manage. You got that from me. Like I said, they can get excitable. As well as telling them to look for you, I also told the Obin they could expect an attack here, because if one of you was running around with my consciousness, it was only a matter of time before you found your way here. You probably wouldn't risk a full-scale attack, but you'd probably try something sneaky, like you did. We were listening for this sort of attack, and we were listening for you. As soon as we had you on the ground, we threw the switch to disable the Brain-Pals."

Jared thought of the members of his platoon falling from the sky and felt sick. "You could have let them all land, you son of a bitch," Jared said. "When you blocked their BrainPals, they were defenseless. You know that."

"They're *not* defenseless," Boutin countered. "They can't use their Empees, but they can use their combat knives and their fighting skills. Ripping away your Brain-

Pals causes most of you to go catatonic, but some of you still keep fighting. Look at you. Although you're probably better prepared than most. If you've got my memories, you know what it's like not to be connected all the time. Even so, six of you on the ground was more than enough. And we only needed you as it is."

"For what?" Jared asked.

"All in good time," Charles Boutin said.

"If you only need me, what are you going to do with my squad?" Jared asked.

"I could tell you, but I think you've deflected me long enough from my original question, don't you?" Boutin smiled. "I want to know what you know about me, and about *being* me, and about what you know of my plans here."

"Since I'm here, you already know we know about you," Jared said. "You're not a secret anymore."

"And let me just say that I'm very impressed about that," Boutin said. "I thought I had covered my tracks well. And I'm kicking myself for not formatting the storage device I stored that consciousness imprint on. I was in a rush to leave, you see. Even so, it's no excuse. It was stupid of me."

"I disagree," Jared said.

"I imagine you would," Boutin said. "Since without it you wouldn't be here, in many senses of the word *here*. I am impressed they were able to make a transfer back into a brain, however. Even I hadn't figured that out before I had to go. Who managed that?"

"Harry Wilson," Jared said.

"Harry!" Boutin said. "Nice guy. Didn't know he was that smart. He hid it well. Of course, I *did* do most of the work before he got to it. To get back to your point about the Colonial Union knowing I'm here, yes, it's a problem. But it's also an interesting opportunity. There are ways to make this work. Back to it, now, and let me cut short any further deflections by telling you that how you answer will help determine whether what remains of your squad lives or dies. Do you understand me?"

"I understand you," Jared said.

"Perfect," Boutin said. "Now, tell me what you know about me. How much do you know about my work?"

"Broad outlines," Jared said. "The details are difficult. I didn't have enough similar experiences to let those memories take root."

"Having similar experiences matters," Boutin said. "Interesting. And that would explain why you didn't know about the back door. How about my political views? What I felt about the Colonial Union and the CDF?"

"I'm guessing you don't like them," Jared said.

"That'd be a pretty good guess," Boutin said. "But that sounds like you don't have any first-hand knowledge of what I thought about any of that."

"No," Jared said.

"Because you don't have any experience with that sort of thing, do you?" Boutin said. "You're Special Forces, after all. They don't put questioning authority into your lesson plan. What about my personal experiences?"

"I remember most of it," Jared said. "I had enough experience for that."

"So you know about Zoë," Boutin mused.

Jared felt a flush of emotion at the child's name. "I know about her," he said, voice slightly husky.

Boutin picked up on it. "You *feel* it too," he said, coming up close to Jared. "Don't you? What I felt when they told me she was dead."

"I feel it," Jared said.

"You poor man," Boutin whispered. "To be made to feel that for a child you didn't know."

"I knew her," Jared said. "I knew her through you."

"I see that," Boutin said, and stepped away to a lab desk. "I'm sold, Jared," he said, regaining his composure and conversation. "You are sufficiently like me to officially be interesting."

"Does that mean you'll let my squad live?" Jared asked.

"For now," Boutin said. "You've been cooperative and they're fenced in by guns that will shred them into hamburger if they get within three meters of them, so there's no reason to kill them."

"And what about me?" Jared said.

"You, my friend, are going to get a complete and thorough brain scan," Boutin said, eyes to the desk, where he worked a keyboard. "In fact, I'm going to take a recording of your consciousness. I want to get a very close look at it indeed. I want to see how much like me you really are. It seems like you're missing a lot of detail, and you've got some Special Forces brainwashing to get over. But on the important things I'd guess we have a lot in common."

"We're different in one way I can think of," Jared said.

"Really," Boutin said. "Do tell."

"I wouldn't betray every human alive because my daughter died," Jared said.

Boutin looked at Jared, thoughtfully, for a minute. "You really think I'm doing this because Zoë was killed on Covell," Boutin finally said.

"I do," Jared said. "And I don't think this is the way to honor her memory."

"You don't, do you," Boutin said, and then turned back to the keyboard to jab at a button. Jared's crèche thrummed, and he felt something like a pinch in his brain.

"I'm recording your consciousness now," Boutin said. "Just relax." He left the room, closing the door behind him. Jared, feeling the pinching increase in his head, didn't relax one bit. He closed his eyes.

Several minutes later Jared heard the door open and close. He opened his eyes. Boutin had come back and was standing by the door. "How's that consciousness recording working for you?" he asked Jared.

"It hurts like hell," Jared said.

"There is that unfortunate side effect," Boutin said. "I'm not sure why it happens. I'll have to look into that."

"I'd appreciate that," Jared said, through gritted teeth.

Boutin smiled. "More sarcasm," he said. "But I've brought you something that I think will ease your pain."

"Whatever it is, give me two of them," Jared said.

"I think one will be enough," Boutin said, and opened the door to show Zoë in the doorway.

THIRTEEN

Boutin was right. Jared's pain went away.

"Sweetheart," Boutin said to Zoë, "I'd like to introduce you to a friend of mine. This is Jared. Say hello to him, please."

"Hello, Mr. Jared," said Zoë, in a small, uncertain voice.

"Hi," Jared said, hardly risking saying any more because he felt like his voice could break and shatter. He collected himself. "Hello, Zoë. It's good to see you."

"You don't remember Jared, Zoë," Boutin said. "But he remembers you. He knew you from back when we were on Phoenix."

"Does he know Mommy?" Zoë asked.

"I believe he did know Mommy," Boutin said. "As well as anyone did."

"Why is he in that box?" Zoë asked.

"He's just helping Daddy with a little experiment, that's all," Boutin said.

"Can he come over to play when he's done?" Zoë said.

"We'll see," Boutin said. "Why don't you say good-bye

to him for now, honey. He and Daddy have a lot of work to do."

Zoë turned her attention back to Jared. "Good-bye, Mr. Jared," she said, and walked out of the doorway, presumably back to where she came from. Jared strained to watch her and hear her footfalls. Then Boutin closed the door.

"You understand that you're not going to be able to come over and play," Boutin said. "It's just that Zoë gets lonely here. I got the Obin to put a little receiver satellite in orbit over one of the smaller colonies to pirate their entertainment feeds to keep her amused, so she's not missing out on the joys of Colonial Union educational programming. But there's no one here for her to play with. She has an Obin nanny, but it mostly makes sure she doesn't fall down any stairs. It's just me and her."

"Tell me," Jared said. "Tell me how she can possibly be alive. The Obin killed everyone at Covell."

"The Obin *saved* Zoë," Boutin said. "It was the Rraey who attacked Covell and Omagh, not the Obin. The Rraey did it to get back at the Colonial Union for their defeat at Coral. They didn't even actually *want* Omagh. They just picked a soft target to attack. The Obin found out about their plans and timed their arrival for just after the first phase of the attack, when the Rraey would still be weak from their fight with the humans. Once they pried the Rraey off Covell, they went through the station and found the civilians jammed into a meeting room. They were being held there. The Rraey killed all the military staff and scientists because their bodies are improved too much to make for good eating. But the colonist staff—well, they were just fine. If the Obin hadn't attacked when they did, the Rraey would have slaughtered and eaten them all."

"Where are the rest of the civilians?" Jared asked.

"Well, the Obin killed them, of course," Boutin said.

"You know the Obin don't usually take prisoners."

"But they saved Zoë, you said," Jared said.

Boutin smiled. "While they were going through the station, the Obin did a tour of the science labs to see if there were any ideas worth stealing," he said. "They're excellent scientists, but they're not very creative. They can improve on ideas and technology they find from other places, but they're not very good at originating the technology themselves. The science station is one of the main reasons they were interested in Omagh at all. They found my work on consciousness, and they were interested. They found out I wasn't on the station, but that Zoë was. So they kept her while they were looking for me."

"They used her as blackmail," Jared said.

"No," Boutin said. "More as a goodwill gesture. And I was the one who demanded things from them."

"They held Zoë, and you demanded things from *them*," Jared said.

"That's right," Boutin said.

"Like what?" Jared asked.

"Like this war," Boutin said.

Jane Sagan edged closer to the eighth and final gun emplacement. Like the others it tracked her and then warned her the closer she got to it. As near as she could tell if she got closer than about three meters, the gun would fire. Sagan picked up a rock and threw it directly at the gun; the rock struck and bounced off harmlessly, the gun's systems tracking but otherwise ignoring the projectile. The gun could differentiate between a rock and a human. *That's some fine engineering*, Sagan thought, not very charitably.

She found a larger rock, stepped up to the edge of the

safe zone, and chucked it to the right of the gun. It tracked the rock; farther to her right another gun trained on her. The guns shared targeting information; she wasn't going to get past them by distracting one of them.

The bowl they were in was shallow enough that Sagan could see over the lip; as far as she could see there weren't any Obin soldiers in the area. Either they were hiding or they were confident the humans weren't going anywhere.

"Yes!"

Sagan turned and saw Daniel Harvey coming toward her with something squirmy in his hand. "Look who's got dinner," he said.

"What is that?" Sagan asked.

"The hell if I know," Harvey said. "I saw it slithering out of the ground and caught it before it went back in. Put up a fight, though. I had to grab its head to keep it from biting me. I figure we can eat it."

By this time Seaborg had limped over to look at the creature. "I'm not eating that," he said.

"Fine," Harvey said. "You starve. The lieutenant and I will eat it."

"We can't eat it," Sagan said. "The animals here aren't compatible with our food needs. You might as well eat rocks."

Harvey looked at Sagan as if she had just taken a dump on his head. "Fine," he said, and bent down to let the thing go.

"Wait," Sagan said. "I want you to throw that."

"What?" Harvey said.

"Throw that thing at the gun," Sagan said. "I want to see what the guns will do to something living."

"That's kind of cruel," Harvey said.

"A minute ago, you were thinking about eating the

damn thing," Seaborg said, "and *now* you're worried about cruelty to animals?"

"Shut up," Harvey said. He cocked his arm back to throw the animal.

"Harvey," Sagan said. "Don't throw it directly at the gun, please."

Harvey suddenly realized that the trajectory of the projectiles would lead directly back to his body. "Sorry," he said. "Stupid of me."

"Throw it up," Sagan said. "Way up." Harvey shrugged and launched the thing high into the air, in an arc that took the thing away from the three of them. The creature writhed in midair. The gun tracked the creature as far up as it could, roughly fifty degrees up. It rotated and shot the thing apart as soon as it came back into its range, shredding it with a spray of thin needles that expanded on contact with the poor creature's flesh. In less than a second there was nothing left of the thing but mist and a few chunks falling to the ground.

"Very nice," Harvey said. "Now we know the guns really work. And I'm still hungry."

"That's very interesting," Sagan said.

"That I'm hungry?" Harvey said.

"No, Harvey," Sagan said, irritated. "I don't actually give a damn about your stomach right now. What's interesting is that the guns can only target up to a certain angle. They're ground suppression."

"So?" Harvey said. "We're on the ground."

"Trees," Seaborg said, suddenly. "Son of a bitch."

"What are you thinking, Seaborg?" Sagan asked.

"In training, Dirac and I won a war game by sneaking up on the opposing side in the trees," he said. "They were expecting us to attack from the ground. They never bothered looking up until we got right up on them. Then I almost fell out of the tree and nearly got myself killed. But the *idea* worked."

The three of them turned to look at the trees inside their perimeter. They weren't real trees, but the Aristian equivalent: large spindly plants that reached meters high into the sky.

"Tell me we're all having the same bugshit crazy thought," Harvey said. "I'd hate to think it was just me."

"Come on," Sagan said. "Let's see what we can do with this."

"That's insane," Jared said. "The Obin wouldn't start a war just because you asked them to."

"Really?" Boutin said. A sneer crept onto his face. "And you know this from your vast, personal knowledge of the Obin? Your years of study on the matter? You wrote your doctoral thesis on the Obin?"

"No species would go to war just because you asked them to," Jared said. "The Obin don't do anything for anyone else."

"And they're not now," Boutin said. "The war is a means to an end—they want what I can offer them."

"And what is that?" Jared asked.

"I can give them souls," Boutin said.

"I don't understand," Jared said.

"It's because you don't know the Obin," Boutin said. "The Obin are a created race—the Consu made them just to see what would happen. But despite rumors to the contrary, the Consu aren't perfect. They make mistakes. And they made a huge mistake when they made the Obin. They gave the Obin intelligence, but what they couldn't do—what they didn't have the capability of doing—was to give the Obin *consciousness*."

"The Obin are conscious," Jared said. "They have a society. They communicate. They remember. They *think*."

"So what?" Boutin said. "Termites have societies. Every species communicates. You don't have to be intelligent to remember—you have a computer in your head that remembers everything you ever do, and it's fundamentally no more intelligent than a rock. And as for thinking, what about thinking requires you to observe yourself doing it? Not a goddamned thing. You can create an entire starfaring race that has no more self-introspection than a protozoan, and the Obin are the living proof of that. The Obin are aware *collectively* that they exist. But not one of them *individually* has anything that you would recognize as a personality. No ego. No 'I.' "

"That doesn't make any sense," Jared said.

"Why not?" Boutin said. "What are the trappings of self-awareness? And do the Obin have it? The Obin have no *art*, Dirac. They have no music or literature or visual arts. They comprehend the concept of art intellectually but they have no way to appreciate it. The only time they communicate is to tell each other factual things: where they're going, or what's over that hill or how many people they need to kill. They *can't* lie. They have no moral inhibition against it— they don't actually have any real moral inhibitions against anything—but they can no more formulate a lie than you or I could levitate an object with our mind power. Our brains aren't wired that way; their brains aren't wired that way. Everybody lies. Everybody who is conscious, who has a self-image to maintain. But they don't. They're perfect."

"Being ignorant of your own existence is not what I'd call 'perfect,' " Jared said.

"They *are* perfect," Boutin insisted. "They don't lie. They cooperate perfectly with each other, within the structure of their society. Challenges or disagreements are dealt with in a prescribed manner. They don't backstab. They are perfectly moral because their morals are absolute—hardcoded. They have no vanity and no ambition. They don't even have sexual vanity. They're all hermaphrodites, and pass their genetic information to each other as casually as you or I would shake hands. And they have no fear."

"Every creature has fear," Jared said. "Even the non-conscious ones."

"No," Boutin said. "Every creature has a survival instinct. It looks like fear but it's not the same thing. Fear isn't the desire to avoid death or pain. Fear is rooted in the knowledge that what you recognize as yourself can cease to exist. Fear is existential. The Obin are not existential in the slightest. That's why they don't surrender. It's why they don't take prisoners. It's why the Colonial Union fears them, you know. Because they can't be made afraid. What an advantage that is! It's so much of an advantage that if I'm ever in charge of creating human soldiers again, I'm going to suggest stripping out their consciousness."

Jared shuddered. Boutin noted it. "Come now, Dirac," Boutin said. "You can't tell me that awareness has been a *happy* thing for you. Aware that you've been created for a purpose other than your own existence. Aware of memories of someone else's life. Aware that your purpose is nothing more than to kill the people and things the Colonial Union points you at. You're a gun with an ego. You'd be better off without the ego."

"Horseshit," Jared said.

Boutin smiled. "Well, fair enough," he said. "I can't say I'd want to be without self-awareness, either. And since you're supposed to be me I can't say that I'm surprised you feel the same way."

"If the Obin are perfect I don't see why they would need you," Jared said.

"Because they don't see themselves as perfect, of course," Boutin said. "They know they lack consciousness, and while individually it might not matter much to them, as a species, it matters a great deal. They saw my work on consciousness—mostly on consciousness transference but also my early notes on recording and storing consciousness entirely. They desired what they thought I could give them. Greatly."

"Have you given them consciousness?" Jared asked.

"Not yet," Boutin said. "But I'm getting close. Close enough to make them desire it even more."

"'Desire,'" Jared repeated. "A strong emotion for a species who lacks sentience."

"Do you know what *Obin* means?" Boutin asked. "What the actual word means in the Obin language, when it's not being used to refer to the Obin as a species."

"No," Jared said.

"It means *lacking*," Boutin said, and cocked his head, bemusedly. "Isn't that interesting? With most intelligent species, if you look back far enough for the etymological roots of what they call themselves, you'll come up with some variation or another of *the people*. Because every species starts off on their own little home world, convinced they are the absolute center of the universe. Not the Obin. They knew right from the beginning what they were, and the word they used to describe themselves showed they knew that they were missing something every other intelligent species had. They *lacked* consciousness. It's just about the only truly *descriptive* noun they have. Well, that and *Obinur*, which means *home of those who lack*. Everything else is just dry as dust. *Arist* means *third moon*. But *Obin* is remarkable. Imagine if every species named itself after its greatest flaw. We could name our species *arrogance*."

"Why would knowing they lack consciousness matter to them?" Jared asked.

"Why did knowing that she couldn't eat from the tree of knowledge matter to Eve?" Boutin said. "It shouldn't have mattered but it did. She was temptable—which, if you believe in an all-powerful God, means God intentionally put temptation into Eve. Which seems like a dirty trick, if you ask me. There's no reason the Obin should desire sentience. It'll do them no good. But they want it anyway. I think it's possible that the Consu, rather than screwing up and creating an intelligence without ego, intentionally created the Obin that way, and then programmed them with the desire for the one thing they could not have."

"But why?"

"Why do the Consu do anything?" Boutin said. "When you're the most advanced species around, you don't have to explain yourselves to the rock bangers, which would be us. For our purposes, they might as well be gods. And the Obin are the poor, insensate Adams and Eves."

"So this makes you the snake," Jared said.

Boutin smiled at the backhanded reference. "Maybe so," he said. "And maybe by giving the Obin what they want, I'll force them out of their egoless paradise. They can deal with that. In the meantime, I'll get what I want from this. I'll get my war, and I'll get the end of the Colonial Union."

The "tree" the three of them looked at stood about ten meters high and was about a meter in diameter. The trunk was covered with ridges; in a rainfall these could funnel water into the inner part of the tree. Every three meters, larger ridges sprouted a circular array of vines and delicate branches, decreasing in circumference as they increased in altitude. Sagan, Seaborg and Harvey watched as the tree swayed in the breeze.

"It's a pretty light breeze to make the tree sway this much," Sagan said.

"The wind's probably faster up there," Harvey said.

"Not by that much," Sagan said. "If at all. It's only ten meters up."

"Maybe it's hollow," Seaborg said. "Like the trees on Phoenix. When Dirac and I were doing our thing, we had to be careful which of the Phoenix trees we walked across. Some of the smaller ones wouldn't have supported our weight."

Sagan nodded. She approached the tree and put weight on one of the smaller ridges. It held for a reasonable amount of time before she could snap it off. She looked up at the tree again, thinking.

"Going for a climb, Lieutenant?" Harvey asked. Sagan didn't answer; she gripped the ridges on the tree and hoisted herself up, taking care to distribute her weight as evenly as possible so as not to put too much strain on any one ridge. About two-thirds of the way up, with the trunk beginning to taper, she felt the tree begin to bend. Her weight was pulling down the trunk. Three-quarters of the way up, and the tree was significantly bent. Sagan listened for the sounds of the tree snapping or cracking, but heard nothing except the rustle of the tree ridges scraping against each other. These trees were immensely flexible; Sagan suspected that they saw a lot of wind as Arist's global ocean generated immense hurricanes that lashed over the planet's relatively tiny island continents.

"Harvey," Sagan said, moving slightly back and forth to

keep the tree balanced. "Tell me if the tree looks like it's going to snap."

"The base of the trunk looks fine," Harvey said.

Sagan looked over to the nearest gun. "How far do you think it is to that gun?" she said.

Harvey figured out where she was going with that. "Not nearly far enough for you to do what you're thinking of doing, Lieutenant."

Sagan wasn't so sure about that. "Harvey," she said. "Go get Wigner."

"What?" Harvey said.

"Bring Wigner here," Sagan said. "I want to try something." Harvey gawked in disbelief for a moment, and then stomped off to get Wigner. Sagan looked down at Seaborg. "How are you holding up?" she asked.

"My leg hurts," Seaborg said. "And my head hurts. I keep feeling like I'm missing something."

"It's the integration," Sagan said. "It's hard to focus without it."

"I'm focusing fine," Seaborg said. "It's just that I'm focusing on how much I'm missing."

"You'll make it," Sagan said. Seaborg grunted.

A few minutes later Harvey appeared with Wigner's body in a fireman's carry. "Let me guess," Harvey said. "You want me to deliver him to you."

"Yes, please," Sagan said.

"Sure, hell, why not?" Harvey said. "Nothing like climbing a tree while you've got a dead body over your shoulder."

"You can do it," Seaborg said.

"As long as people don't distract me," Harvey growled. He shifted Wigner and began to climb, adding his weight and Wigner's to the tree. The tree creaked and dipped considerably, causing Harvey to inch along to keep his balance and to keep from losing Wigner. By the time he got to Sagan, the trunk was bent at nearly a ninety-degree angle.

"What now?" Harvey said.

"Can you put him between us?" Sagan said. Harvey grunted, carefully slid Wigner off his shoulder, and positioned his body so it was prone on the tree. He looked up at Sagan. "Just for the record, this is a pretty fucked-up way for him to go," Harvey said.

"He's helping us," Sagan said. "There are worse things." She carefully swung her leg over the trunk of the tree. Harvey did the same in the other direction. "Count of three," Sagan said, and when she reached *three* they both jumped out of the tree, five meters to the ground.

Relieved of the weight of two humans, the tree snapped back toward perpendicular and then beyond it, flinging Wigner's corpse off the trunk and arcing it toward the guns. It was not an entirely successful launch; Wigner slipped down the trunk just prior to launch, compromising the total energy available and positioning him off-center just before he became airborne. Wigner's arc dropped him directly in front of the closest gun, which pulverized him instantly as soon as he fell into firing range. He dropped as a pile of meat and entrails.

"Christ," Seaborg said.

Sagan turned to Seaborg. "Can you climb with that leg?" she asked.

"I *can*," Seaborg said. "But I'm not in a rush to get all shot up like that."

"You won't," Sagan said. "I'll go."

"You just saw what happened to Wigner, right?" Harvey asked.

"I saw," Sagan said. "He was a corpse and he had no

control over his flight. He also weighs more, and it was you and me in the tree. I'm lighter, I'm alive and the two of you mass more. I should be able to clear the gun."

"If you're wrong, you'll be pâté," Harvey said.

"At least it'll be quick," Sagan said.

"Yes," Harvey said. "But messy."

"Look, you'll have plenty of time to criticize me when I'm dead," Sagan said. "For now, I'd just like all of us to get up this tree."

A few minutes later Seaborg and Harvey were on either side of Sagan, who was crouched and balancing on the bent trunk.

"Any last words?" Harvey said.

"I've always thought you were a real pain in the ass, Harvey," Sagan said.

Harvey smiled. "I love you too, Lieutenant." He nodded to Seaborg. "Now," he said. They dropped.

The tree whipped up; Sagan adjusted and fought against the acceleration to keep her position. When the tree reached the apex of its swing Sagan kicked off, adding her own force to the force of the tree launch. Sagan arced impossibly high, it seemed to her, easily clearing the guns, which tracked her but could not fire. The guns followed her until she was beyond the perimeter and rapidly arcing toward the meadow beyond. She had time to think, *This is going to hurt* before she balled up and plowed into the ground. Her unitard stiffened, absorbing some of the impact, but Sagan felt at least one rib crack from the hit. The stiffened unitard caused her to roll farther than she would have otherwise. She eventually came to a stop and, lying in the tall grass, tried to remember how to breathe. It took a few more minutes than she expected.

In the distance, Sagan heard Harvey and Seaborg calling for her. She also heard a low drone from the other direction, growing higher in pitch the longer she listened. Still lying in the tall grass, she shifted her position and tried to see over it.

A pair of Obin were coming, riding a small armed craft. They were coming right toward her.

"The first thing you have to understand is that the Colonial Union is evil," Boutin said to Jared.

Jared's headache had returned with a vengeance, and he longed to see Zoë again. "I don't see it," he said.

"Well, why would you," Boutin said. "You're a couple years old at most. And all your life has been made up of doing what someone else has told you to do. You've hardly made choices of your own, now, have you."

"I've had this lecture already," Jared said, recalling Cainen.

"From someone in Special Forces?" Boutin asked, genuinely surprised.

"From a Rraey prisoner," Jared said. "Named Cainen. Says he met you once."

Boutin furrowed his brow. "The name isn't familiar," he said. "But then I've met quite a few Rraey and Eneshans recently. They all tend to blur. But it makes sense a Rraey would tell you this. They find the whole Special Forces setup morally appalling."

"Yes, I know," Jared said. "He told me I was a slave."

"You *are* a slave!" Boutin said, excitedly. "Or an indentured servant, at the very least, bound to a term of service over which you have no control. Yes, they make you feel good about it by suggesting you were born specially to save humanity, and by chaining you to your platoon mates through integration. But when it comes right down to it, those are just ways they use to control you. You're a year old, maybe two. What do you know about the universe anyway? You know what they've told you—that it's a hostile place and that we are always under attack. But what would you say if I told you that everything the Colonial Union told you was wrong?"

"It's not wrong," Jared said. "It *is* hostile. I've seen enough combat to know that."

"But all you've seen *is* combat," Boutin said. "You've never been out where you weren't killing whatever the Colonial Union tells you to. And it's certainly true that the universe is hostile to the Colonial Union. And the reason for that is, *the Colonial Union is hostile to the universe.* In all the time humanity has been out in the universe we've never not been at war with nearly every other species we've come across. There are a few here or there the Colonial Union deems useful as allies or trade partners but so few as to have their numbers be insignificant. We know of six hundred and three intelligent species inside the Colonial Union's Skip horizon, Dirac. Do you know how many the CU classifies as a threat, meaning the CDF is able to preemptively attack at will? Five hundred and seventy-seven. When you're actively hostile toward ninety-six percent of all the intelligent races you know about, that's not just stupid. It's racial suicide."

"Other species are at war with each other," Jared said. "It's not just the Colonial Union that goes to war."

"Yes," Boutin said. "Every species has other species it competes with and goes to war against. But other species don't try to fight *every other species* they come across. The Rraey and the Enesha were longtime enemies before we allied them, and who knows, maybe they will be again. But neither of those species classifies *all* the other races as a permanent threat. *Nobody* does that but the Colonial Union. Have you heard of the Conclave, Dirac?"

"No," Jared said.

"The Conclave is a great meeting between hundreds of species in this part of the galaxy," Boutin said. "It convened more than twenty years ago to try to create a workable framework of government for the entire region. It would help stop the fighting for real estate by apportioning new colonies in a systematic way, rather than having every species run for the prize and try to beat off whoever tries to take it away. It would enforce the system with a multispecies military command that would attack anyone who tried to take a colony by force. Not every species has signed on to the Conclave, but only two species have refused even to send representatives. One is the Consu, because why would they. The other is the Colonial Union."

"You expect me to take your word for that," Jared said.

"I don't expect anything from you," Boutin said. "You don't know about it. The rank-and-file CDF doesn't know about it. The colonials certainly don't know about it. The Colonial Union has all the spaceships, Skip drones and communication satellites. It handles all the trade and what little diplomacy we engage in on its space stations. The Colonial Union is the bottleneck through which all information flows, and it decides what the colonies learn and what they don't. And not just the colonies, it's Earth too. Hell, Earth is the worst."

"Why?" Jared asked.

"Because it's been kept socially retarded for two hundred years," Boutin said. "The Colonial Union *farms* people there, Dirac. Uses the rich countries there for its military. Uses the poor countries for its colonial seed stock. And it likes the arrangement so much that the Colonial Union actively suppresses the natural evolution of society there. They don't *want* it to change. That would mess up their production of soldiers and colonists. So they sealed Earth off from the rest of humanity to keep the people there from knowing just how perfectly they're being held in stasis. Manufactured a disease—they called it the Crimp—and told the people on Earth it was an alien infection. Used it as an excuse to quarantine the planet. They let it flare up every generation or two just to maintain the pretense."

"I've met people from Earth," Jared said, thinking of Lieutenant Cloud. "They're not stupid. They would know if they were being held back."

"Oh, the Colonial Union will allow an innovation or two every couple of years to make them think they're still on a growth curve, but it's never anything *useful*," Boutin said. "A new computer here. A music player there. An organ transplant technique. They're allowed the occasional land war to keep things interesting. Meanwhile, they have all the same social and political structures they had two hundred years earlier, and they think it's because they've reached a point of genuine stability. And they still die of old age at seventy-five! It's ridiculous. The Colonial Union has managed Earth so well it doesn't even *know* it's being managed. It's in the dark. All the colonies are in the dark. Nobody knows anything."

"Except you," Jared said.

"I was building the soldiers, Dirac," Boutin said. "They had to let me know what was going on. I had top-secret clearance right until the moment I shot that clone of mine. That's why I know the Conclave is out there. And that's why I know if the Colonial Union isn't killed, humanity's going to get wiped out."

"We seem to have held our own up to this point," Jared said.

"That's because the Colonial Union takes advantage of chaos," Boutin said. "When the Conclave ratifies its agreement—and it will in the next year or two—the Colonial Union won't be able to found colonies anymore. The Conclave's military force will kick them off any planet they try to take. They won't be able to take over anyone's colonies, either. We'll be bottled up, and when another race decides to take one of our worlds, who will stop them? The Conclave won't protect races that won't participate. Slowly but surely we'll be whittled back to one world again. If we're left with that."

"Unless we have a war," Jared said, not hiding his skepticism.

"That's right," Boutin said. "The problem isn't humanity. It's the Colonial Union. Get rid of the Colonial Union, replace it with a government that actually helps its people instead of farming them and keeping them ignorant for its own purposes, and join with the Conclave to get a reasonable share of new colonial worlds."

"With you in charge, I presume," Jared said.

"Until we get things organized, yes," Boutin said.

"Minus the worlds that the Rraey and the Enesha, your allies in this adventure, take for their own," Jared said.

"The Rraey and the Enesha weren't going to fight for free," Boutin said.

"And the Obin taking Earth," Jared said.

"That's for me," Boutin said. "Personal request."

"Must be nice," Jared said.

"You continue to underestimate how badly the Obin want consciousness," Boutin said.

"I liked this better when I thought you were just trying to get revenge for Zoë," Jared said.

Boutin reared back, as if he'd been slapped. Then he leaned in close. "You know what the thought of losing Zoë did to me," Boutin hissed. "You *know* it. But let me tell you something that you don't seem to know. After we took back Coral from the Rraey, the CDF Military Intelligence office predicted the Rraey would make a counterattack and listed the five most likely targets. Omagh and and Covell Station were right at the top of that list. And you know what the CDF did about it?"

"No," Jared said.

"Not a goddamn thing," Boutin spat the words. "And the reason for that was that the CDF was spread thin in the aftermath of Coral, and some general decided what he really wanted to do was try to grab a colony world from the Robu. In other words, it was more important to go after some new real estate than to defend what we already had. They *knew* the attack was coming, and they did nothing. And until the Obin contacted me, all I knew was that the reason my daughter died was because the Colonial Union didn't do what it's supposed to do: keep safe the lives of those in its protection. To keep safe my daughter. Trust me, Dirac. This has *everything* to do with Zoë."

"And what if your war doesn't go the way you want it to?" Jared asked, softly. "The Obin are still going to want their consciousness, and they'll have nothing to give you."

Boutin smiled. "You're alluding to the fact that we've actually lost the Rraey and the Eneshans as allies," he said. Jared tried to hide his surprise and failed. "Yes, of course we know about that. And I have to admit it worried me for a while. But now we have something that I think puts us back on track and will allow the Obin to take on the Colonial Union by itself."

"I don't imagine you'll tell me what that is," Jared said.

"I'll be happy to tell you," Boutin said. "It's you."

Sagan scrabbled on the ground, looking for something to fight with. Her fingers wrapped around something that seemed solid, and she pulled at it. She came up with a clod of dirt.

Aw, fuck it, she thought, and then sprang up and flung it at the hovercraft as it went past. The clod connected with the head of the second Obin, sitting behind the first. It tilted in surprise and fell off its saddle seat, tumbling to the ground.

Sagan bolted from her place in the grass and was on the Obin in an instant. The dazed creature tried to raise its weapon at Sagan; she stepped to the side, yanked it out of its hand, and clubbed the Obin with it. The Obin screeched and stayed down.

In the distance the hovercraft was wheeling around and looking to make a run at Sagan. Sagan examined the weapon in her hand, trying to see if she could make sense of the thing before the hovercraft came back her way, and decided not to bother. She grabbed the Obin, punched it in the neck to keep it subdued, and searched it for an edged weapon. She found something like a combat knife hanging from its waist. Its shape and and balance was all wrong for a human hand but there was nothing she could do about that now.

The hovercraft had now turned around completely and was bearing down on Sagan. She could see the barrel of its gun spinning up to fire. Sagan reached down, and with the knife still in hand grabbed the fallen Obin and with a grunt heaved it into the path of the hovercraft and its gun. The Obin danced as the fléchettes sliced into it. Sagan, covered by the dancing Obin, stepped to the side but as close as she dared to the craft and swung the knife as the Obin flashed by. She felt a shocking wrenching of her arm and was spun hard into the ground as the knife connected with the Obin's body. She stayed down, dazed and in pain, for several minutes.

When she finally got up she saw the hovercraft idling a hundred meters away. The Obin was still sitting on it, its dangling head held on to the neck by a flap of skin. Sagan pushed the Obin off the hovercraft and stripped it of its weapons and supplies. She then wiped the Obin's blood off the hovercraft as best she could and took a few minutes to learn how the machine worked. Then she turned the thing around and flew it toward the fence. The hovercraft crested the guns easily; Sagan set it down out of their range, in front of Harvey and Seaborg.

"You look terrible," Harvey said.

"I feel terrible," Sagan said. "Now, would you like a ride out of here, or would you like to make some more small talk?"

"That depends," Harvey said. "Where are we going?"

"We had a mission," Sagan said. "I think we should finish it."

"Sure," Harvey said. "The three of us with no weapons, taking on at least several dozen Obin soldiers and attacking a science station."

Sagan hauled up the Obin weapon and handed it to Harvey. "Now you have a weapon," she said. "All you have to do is learn to use it."

"Swell," Harvey said, taking the weapon.

"How long do you think until the Obin realize one of their hovercraft is missing?" asked Seaborg.

"No time at all," Sagan said. "Come on. It's time to get moving."

"Looks like your recording is done," Boutin said to Jared, and turned to his desk display. Jared knew it before Boutin said it because the vise-like pinching had stopped mere instants ago.

"What do you mean that I'm the thing to get you back on track against the Colonial Union?" Jared said. "I'm not going to help you."

"Why not?" Boutin said. "You're not interested in saving the human race from a slow asphyxiation?"

"Let's just say your presentation does not leave me entirely convinced," Jared said.

Boutin shrugged. "So it goes," he said. "Naturally, you being me, or some facsimile thereof, I would have hoped you'd come around to my way of thinking. But in the end, no matter how many of my memories or personal tics you may have, you're still someone else, aren't you? Or are for now, anyway."

"What does that mean?" Jared said.

"I'll get to that," Boutin said. "But let me tell you a story first. It will make some things clear. Many years ago, the Obin and a race called the Ala got into a go-around over some real estate. On the surface, the Ala and the Obin were well-matched militarily, but the Alaite army consisted of clones. This meant they were all susceptible to the same genetic weapon, a virus the Obin designed that would lie dormant for a while—long enough to be transmitted—and then dissolve the flesh of whatever poor Ala it was living in. The Alaite army was wiped out, and then so were the Ala."

"That's a lovely story," Jared said.

"Just wait, because it gets better," Boutin said. "Not too long ago, I thought about doing the same sort of thing to the Colonial Defense Forces. But doing that is more complicated than it sounds. For one thing, Colonial Defense Forces military bodies are almost entirely immune from disease—the SmartBlood simply won't tolerate pathogens. And of course neither the CDF or Special Forces bodies are actually cloned bodies, so even if we could infect them, they wouldn't all react in the same way. But then I realized there was one thing in each CDF body that was exactly the same. Something I knew my way around intimately."

"The BrainPal," Jared said.

"The BrainPal," Boutin said. "And for it, I could create a time-release virus of its own—one that would embed itself in the BrainPal, replicate every time one CDF member communicated with another, but would stay dormant until a date and time of my choosing. Then it would cause every body system regulated by the BrainPal to go haywire. Everyone with a BrainPal instantly dead, and all the human worlds open for conquest. Quick, easy, painless.

"But there was a problem. I had no way to get the virus in. My back door was for diagnostics only. I could read out and shut down certain systems, but it wasn't designed to upload code. In order to upload the code I would need someone to accept it for me and act as a carrier. So the Obin went looking for volunteers."

"The Special Forces ships," Jared said.

"We figured the Special Forces would be more vulnerable to their BrainPals locking up. All of you have never been without it, whereas regular CDF would still be able to function. And it turned out to be correct. You eventually recover, but the initial shock gave us lots of time to work with. We brought them here and tried to convince them to be carriers. First we asked, and then we insisted. Not one cracked. That's discipline."

"Where are they now?" Jared asked.

"They're dead," Boutin said. "The way the Obin insist is pretty forceful. I should amend that, though. Some of them survived and I've been using them for consciousness studies. They're alive, as much as brains in a jar can be."

Jared felt sick. "Fuck you, Boutin," he said.

"They should have volunteered," Boutin said.

"I'm glad they disappointed you," Jared said. "I'll be doing the same."

"I don't think so," Boutin said. "What makes you different, Dirac, is that none of them had my brain and my consciousness already in their heads. And *you* do."

"Even with both, I'm not you," Jared said. "You said it yourself."

"I said you're someone else for now," Boutin said. "I don't suppose you know what would happen to you if I transferred the consciousness that's in here"—Boutin tapped his temple—"and put it in your head, do you?"

Jared remembered his conversation with Cainen and Harry Wilson, when they suggested overlaying the recorded Boutin consciousness upon his own, and felt himself go cold. "It'll wipe out the consciousness that's already there."

"Yes," Boutin said.

"You'll kill me," Jared said.

"Well, yes," Boutin said. "But I did just make a recording of your consciousness, because I need to fine-tune my own transfer. It's everything you are as of five minutes ago. So you'll only be mostly dead."

"You son of a bitch," Jared said.

"And when I've uploaded my consciousness into your body, I'll serve as the carrier for the virus. It won't affect me, of course. But everyone else will get its full strength. Then I'll have your squad mates shot, and then Zoë and I will head back to Colonial Union space in that capture pod you've so thoughtfully provided. I'll tell them that Charles Boutin is dead, and the Obin will lie low until the BrainPal virus strikes. Then they'll move in and force the Colonial Union to surrender. And just like that, you and I will have saved humanity."

"Don't put this on me," Jared said. "I have nothing to do with this."

"Don't you?" Boutin said, amused. "Listen, Dirac. The Colonial Union is not going to see me as the instrument of its demise. I'll already be dead. They're going to see you, and you alone. Oh, you'll be a part of this, my friend. You don't have a choice."

FOURTEEN

"The more I think about this plan the less I like it," Harvey said to Sagan. They and Seaborg crouched at the line of the forest edging the science station.

"Try not to think so much," Sagan said.

"That should be easy for you, Harvey," Seaborg said. He was trying to lighten the mood and doing a poor job of it.

Sagan glanced down at Seaborg's leg. "Are you going to be able to do this?" she asked. "Your limp's gotten worse."

"I'll be fine," Seaborg said. "I'm not going to sit here like a turd while you two are completing the mission."

"I'm not saying that," Sagan said. "I'm saying that you and Harvey could switch roles."

"I'm fine," Seaborg repeated. "And anyway, Harvey would kill me if I took his gig."

"Goddamn right," Harvey said. "This shit is what I'm good at."

"My leg hurts, but I can walk on it and run on it,"

Seaborg said. "I'll be fine. But let's not just sit here and talk about this anymore. My leg's going to tighten up."

Sagan nodded and turned her gaze back to the science station, which was a rather modest collection of buildings. On the north end of the compound were the Obin barracks, which were surprisingly compact; the Obin either did not want or need anything approaching privacy. Like humans the Obin collected together at mealtimes; many of them would be in the mess hall adjacent to the barracks. Harvey's job was to create a distraction there and draw attention to himself, leading the Obin in other parts of the station toward him.

On the south end of the compound was the energy generator/regulator, housed in a large, shed-like building. The Obin used what were essentially huge batteries, which were constantly charged by windmills placed at a distance from the station. Seaborg's job was to cut the power, somehow. He'd have to work with what he found there to make it happen.

Between the two was the science station proper. After the power dropped, Sagan would enter, find Boutin and extract him, pounding him unconscious if need be to get him to the capture pod. If she came across Dirac, she would need to make a quick determination whether he was useful or if he had gone traitor like his progenitor. If it was the latter, she would have to kill him, clean and quick.

Sagan suspected she was going to have to kill Dirac no matter what; she didn't really think she would have enough time to decide whether he was trustworthy or not, and she didn't have her BrainPal upgrade to read his thoughts on the matter. Sagan allowed herself a moment of mirthless amusement at the fact that her mind-reading ability, so secret and classified, was also completely useless to her when she really needed it. Sagan didn't want to have to kill Dirac, but she didn't see that she had a whole lot of options in the matter. *Maybe he's already dead,* Sagan thought. *That would save me the trouble.*

Sagan shook the thought out of her head. She didn't like what that particular line of thought was saying about her. She would worry about Dirac when and if Dirac showed up. In the meantime, the three of them had other things to worry about. In the end, what really mattered was getting Boutin to that capture pod.

We do have one advantage, Sagan thought. *None of us really expects we're going to survive. That gives us options.*

"Are we ready?" Sagan asked.

"We're ready," Seaborg said.

"Fuck, yes," Harvey said.

"Let's do it then," Sagan said. "Harvey, you're on."

Jared woke from a brief nap to find Zoë staring up at him. He smiled. "Hello, Zoë," he said.

"Hello," Zoë said, and frowned. "I forgot your name," she said.

"I'm Jared," he said.

"Oh, yeah," Zoë said. "Hello, Mr. Jared."

"Hello, sweetie," Jared said, and once again he found it hard to keep his voice even. He glanced down at the stuffed animal Zoë carried. "Is that Celeste the elephant?" he asked.

Zoë nodded, and held it up for him to see. "Uh-huh," she said. "I used to have a Babar, but I lost it. Do you know Babar?"

"I do," Jared said. "I remember seeing your Babar too."

"I miss my Babar," Zoë said in a little voice, but then perked up. "But then Daddy got me Celeste, after he came back."

"How long was he away?" Jared asked.

Zoë shrugged. "A long time," she said. "He said he had things he had to do first. But he said he sent the Obin to protect me and watch out for me."

"And did they?" Jared asked.

"I guess so," she said. She shrugged and said in a low voice, "I don't like the Obin. They're boring."

"I can see that," Jared said. "I'm sorry you and your dad were kept apart for so long, Zoë. I know he loves you very much."

"I know," Zoë said. "I love him too. I love Daddy and Mommy and all the grandparents I never met and my friends from Covell too. I miss them. Do you think they miss me?"

"I'm sure they do," Jared said, and willfully avoided thinking about what happened to her friends. He looked back at Zoë and saw her being pouty. "What's wrong, sweetheart?" he asked.

"Daddy says that I have to go back to Phoenix with you," Zoë said. "He says that you're going to stay with me so he can finish up some work here."

"Your daddy and I talked about that," Jared said, carefully. "Do you not want to go back?"

"I want to go back with Daddy," she said, plaintively. "I don't want him to stay."

"He won't be gone very long," Jared said. "It's just the ship that we brought here to take you home is really small, and there's only going to be room in it for you and me."

"*You* could stay," Zoë said.

Jared laughed. "I wish I could, honey. But we'll have fun while we wait for your daddy, I promise. Is there anything you'd like to do when we get to Phoenix Station?"

"I want to buy some *candy*," Zoë said. "They don't have

any here. Daddy says the Obin don't make any. He tried to make me some once, though."

"How was it?" Jared asked.

"It was really *bad*," Zoë said. "I want jawbreakers and butterscotch and lollipops and jellybeans. I like the black ones."

"I remember that," Jared said. "The first time I saw you, you were eating black jellybeans."

"When was that?" Zoë asked.

"It was a long time ago, sweetie," Jared said. "But I remember it like it was yesterday. And when we go back, you can have any candy you want."

"But not too much," Zoë said. "Because then my stomach will hurt."

"Exactly right," Jared said. "And we really couldn't have that. A stomachache just wouldn't do."

Zoë smiled up at Jared and broke his heart. "You're silly, Mr. Jared," she said.

"Well," Jared said, smiling back. "I try."

"Okay, I'm going to go," Zoë said. "Daddy's taking a nap. He doesn't know I'm here. I'm going to go wake him up because I'm hungry."

"You go do that, Zoë," Jared said. "Thank you for visiting, Zoë. I'm really glad you came by."

"Okay," Zoë said, turned around, and waved back to him as she went. "Bye, Mr. Jared! See you later."

"See you later," Jared said, knowing he wouldn't.

"Love you!" Zoë said, in that casual way that kids do.

"Love you too," Jared whispered, as a parent. He waited until he heard a door close down the adjoining hall before he let himself release the ragged, tearing breath he had been holding in.

Jared looked at the lab, his eyes flitting over the console

Boutin had brought in to manage the consciousness transfer, and lingering on the second crèche Boutin had brought in, the one in which he would place himself before sending over his consciousness to Jared's body, wiping out Jared's existence as if he were simply a placeholder, something put there to mark time until the body's true owner could take possession.

But then, Jared thought, wasn't that actually the case? It *was* Boutin who was intended to be in this body. That was why it was created. Jared was allowed to exist only because Boutin's consciousness refused at first to take up residence. It had to be coaxed in to share the mindspace Jared had created as caretaker. And now, irony of ironies, Boutin wanted it all, wanted to push Jared aside entirely. *Damn it,* Jared thought crazily. *I just got this brain set up the way I like it!* He laughed, and the laugh sounded shaky and weird to his ears. He tried to calm himself, bringing himself into a more rational state breath by breath.

Jared heard Boutin in his head, describing the wrongs of the Colonial Union, and heard the voice of Cainen, whom he trusted more to be honest about these things, echoing the sentiments. He looked into his own past as a member of the Special Forces, and the things they had done in the name of making the universe "safe for humanity." The Colonial Union *did* straddle every line of communication, directed every course of action, kept every aspect of humanity under tight control, and fought nearly every other race they knew of with persistent ferocity.

If the universe *was* as hostile as the Colonial Union said, perhaps this level of control was justified, for the overarching racial imperative of holding ground and making a place for humans in the universe. But if it *wasn't*—if what was fueling the Colonial Union's constant wars was not competition from the outside but paranoia and xenophobia from the inside—then Jared knew that he and everyone he'd known inside the Special Forces and out of it could have, in one way or another, led to the slow death of humanity that Boutin assured him was out there. He would have chosen to refuse to fight.

But, Jared thought, *Boutin isn't reliable*. Boutin labeled the Colonial Union as evil, but Boutin also chose to do evil things. He caused three separate races—two with longstanding issues—to come together to attack the Colonial Union, exposing billions of humans and billions of other intelligent creatures to the threat of war. He had experimented upon and killed Special Forces soldiers. He was planning to kill every single member of Special Forces and every other CDF soldier with his BrainPal virus, something akin to a genocide, considering the numbers and the unique makeup of the Colonial Defense Forces. And in killing the Colonial Defense Forces, Boutin would leave the colonies and Earth defenseless against any race who chose to claim one of the colonies as its own. The Obin couldn't stop the land rush from these other races—and probably wouldn't even if they could. The reward for the Obin was not land but consciousness.

The unprotected colonists would be doomed, Jared realized. Their colonies would be destroyed and there would be nowhere for them to go. It wasn't in the nature of the races in this part of the galaxy to share their worlds. Earth with its billions might survive; it would be hard to displace billions of humans without a fight. The more sparsely populated and less ecologically burdened colony planets would be far more attractive. But if someone decided to attack Earth, and the Earth had indeed been held back by the Colonial Union for its own purposes, it wouldn't be able to fully defend itself. It would survive, but the damage would be immense.

Doesn't Boutin see this? Jared asked himself. Perhaps he did, but chose to believe that it wouldn't happen that way. But maybe he simply never considered the consequences of his actions. When the Obin contacted him, perhaps all Boutin saw was a people so desperate for the thing he could give them that they would do anything to get it. Maybe Boutin asked for the moon and didn't give a thought to what he would do with the moon once he had it. Maybe Boutin didn't really think the Obin would really, truly give him the war he asked for.

Interlaced within all of this, Jared felt a sick-making worry for Zoë: What would happen to her if Boutin failed or was killed; what would happen to her if he succeeded? Jared felt guilty for worrying about what would happen to one small child when billions of lives would be altered or ended, but he couldn't help himself. As much as anything, he was looking for a way where Zoë lived through all of it.

Jared felt overwhelmed by the choices he needed to make, and underwhelmed by the information he had to make them with, and utterly bereft at how little he would be able to do about any of it. He felt like he was probably the last person in the world who should be wrestling with all of this. But there was nothing to be done about it now. He closed his eyes and considered his options.

An hour later Jared opened his eyes as Boutin came through the door, trailed by an Obin. "You're awake," Boutin said.

"I am," Jared said.

"It's time for me to make the transfer," Boutin said. "I've programmed in the process and run the simulations; it looks like it's going to run perfectly. There's no point in putting it off anymore."

"Far be it from me to stop you from killing me," Jared said, casually.

Boutin paused; Jared saw that coming right out and mentioning his incipient murder disturbed Boutin. *Good*, Jared thought.

"About that," Boutin said. "Before we do the transfer, I can run a directive that will put you to sleep, if you want. You wouldn't feel a thing. I'm offering that to you. If you want."

"You don't seem to want it," Jared said.

"It makes the transfer more difficult, from what I can see from the simulations," Boutin said. "The transfer will take more securely if you're conscious as well."

"Well then, by all means I'll stay awake," Jared said. "I wouldn't want to make this more difficult for you."

"Listen, Dirac," Boutin said. "This isn't something personal. You have to understand that you offer a way to make this all happen quickly and cleanly, with the least amount of bloodshed on all sides. I'm sorry you have to die, but the alternative is far more death."

"Murdering every Colonial Defense Forces soldier with your virus doesn't strike me as the least amount of bloodshed," Jared said.

Boutin turned and told the Obin to start the preparations; the Obin went to the console and went to work.

"Tell me," Jared said. "After you've killed all the Colonial Defense Forces, who is going to protect the human colonies? They won't have defenders anymore. You'll have killed them all."

"The Obin will protect them in the short run," Boutin said. "Until we can create a new defense force."

"Are you sure about that?" Jared said. "Once you give them consciousness, why would they need to do anything for you anymore? Or do you plan to withhold consciousness until after they give you your *next* demand?"

Boutin gave a quick glance back at the Obin in the room, and then faced Jared. "I'm not *withholding* anything," he said. "They'll do it because they've agreed to it."

"Are you willing to bet the life of Zoë on it?" Jared asked. "Because that's what you're doing."

"Don't lecture me on *my* daughter," Boutin spat at Jared, and turned away. Jared gave a sad shudder, thinking of the choices he was making.

The Obin nodded over at Boutin; it was time. Boutin looked over to Jared one more time. "Anything else you want to say before we get started?" he asked Jared.

"I think I'll save it for later," Jared said.

Boutin opened his mouth to ask what that meant, but before he could, a noise erupted from outside the station. It sounded like a very large gun going off very rapidly.

Harvey lived for this sort of shit.

His chief worry as they approached the science station was that Lieutenant Sagan would do one of her patented thoughtful, methodical approaches; something sneaky that would require him to tiptoe around like a goddamn spy or something. He hated that crap. Harvey knew what he was and what he was best at: He was a noisy son of a bitch and he was good at making things fall down and go boom. In his few introspective moments, Harvey wondered if his progie, the guy he was mostly made from, hadn't been something really antisocial, like a pyromaniac or a professional wrestler, or maybe had done time for assault. Whoever or whatever he was, Harvey would have been happy to give him a nice big smack on the lips. Harvey was absolutely at peace with his inner nature, in the sort of way that Zen Buddhist monks could only dream about. And so when Sagan told him his job was to draw attention to himself so she and Seaborg could do their jobs, Harvey did a little dance on the inside. He could definitely draw attention to himself.

The question was how.

Harvey was not especially introspective, but this didn't mean he was stupid. He was moral, within his lights; he understood the value of subtlety even if he wasn't much for it himself, and one of the reasons he could get away with being loud and obnoxious was that he was a fair stick at strategy and logistics. Give him a job and he'd do it, usually in the most entropy-producing way possible, yes, but also in a way that achieved exactly the aim it was supposed to. One of Harvey's guiding lights in terms of strategies was simplicity; all things being equal, Harvey preferred the course of action that let him get into the middle of things and then just buckle down. When asked about it, Harvey called it his Occam's razor theory of combat: The simplest way of kicking someone's ass was usually the correct one.

It was this philosophy that had Harvey taking the hovercraft Sagan had stolen, mounting it, and, after a few moments to glean the fundamentals of navigating it, rocketing on it toward the door of the Obin mess hall. As Harvey approached, the door to the mess hall opened inward; some Obin heading to duty after dinner. Harvey grinned a mad grin, gunned the hovercraft, and then braked it just enough (he hoped) to jam that fucking alien right back into the room.

It worked perfectly. The Obin had enough time for a surprised squawk before the hovercraft's gun struck it square in the chest, punching backward like it was a toy on a string, hurling down nearly the entire length of the hall. The other Obin in the room looked up while Harvey's victim pinwheeled to the ground, then turned their multiple eyes toward the doorway, Harvey, and the hovercraft with its big gun poking right into the room.

"Hello, boys!" Harvey said in a big, booming voice. "The 2nd Platoon sends its regards!" And with that, he jammed down the "fire" button on the gun and set to work.

Things got messy real fast after that. It was just fucking beautiful.

Harvey loved his job.

From the other side of the compound, Seaborg heard Harvey start in on his happy work, and had just a little bit of an involuntary shudder. It's not that Seaborg disliked Harvey, but after a couple of combat drops with the 2nd Platoon one got the sense that if you didn't like things to explode unnecessarily around you, you would want to stay well clear of Daniel Harvey.

The crash and bang did exactly what it was supposed to—the Obin soldiers at the generator abandoned their posts to help out those of their number who were being cheerfully massacred on the other side of the compound. Seaborg did a modified sprint to the generators, wincing as he did so, and surprised what he guessed were some Obin scientists as he came through the door. Seaborg shot one with one of those weird Obin weapons, and then snapped the other one's neck. That was more disturbing than Seaborg would have expected; he felt the bones or whatever they were give way as he struck. Unlike Harvey, Seaborg was never a natural with violence; he wasn't much of a natural in anything. This was something he sensed early and hid with overcompensation, which is why so many of his training squad members thought he was an asshole. He got over it—someone is going to push you off a cliff if you don't—but what he never got over was the idea that when it came right down to it, Special Forces was not a good fit for him.

Seaborg went into the next room, which took up the majority of the shed and which housed the two massive forms Seaborg assumed were the batteries he had to destroy. Harvey's distraction was going to work only so long as Harvey managed to keep himself alive, which Seaborg doubted would be very long at all. Seaborg looked in the room for controls or panels that could help him or at least give some indication how he could shut down the power. He saw nothing; all the panels and controls were back in the room he left the two dead Obin in. Seaborg briefly wondered if he should have left one of them alive and tried to convince it to shut down the power station, but he doubted he would have been very successful at all.

"Fuck," Seaborg said out loud in frustration, and for lack of anything better coming to mind, raised the Obin weapon and shot at one of the batteries. The projectile embedded in the metal skin of the huge battery, momentarily raising sparks, and then Seaborg heard a high-pitched whine, like air whistling out of a very small hole. He looked up at where he shot—a high-pressure stream of some green gas was spurting out. Seaborg looked at it.

What the hell, Seaborg thought, raising his weapon and aiming at the hole from which the stream was emanating. *Let's see if that shit's flammable.*

It was.

The power generator blast knocked Jane Sagan right on her ass and blinded her for a good three seconds; she recovered sight just in time to see large chunks of the power generator's room hurling through the sky in her general direction. Sagan backtracked enough to avoid the debris and instinctually checked her integration to see if by some miracle Seaborg had managed to survive. There was nothing there, of course. You don't survive a blast like that. She could feel Harvey, though, shocked for a moment out of his orgy of violence. Sagan turned her attention to the science station itself, its windows shattered and parts on fire, and it took her several seconds of formulating a plan before she realized that she *had* integration once more. Knocking out the power somehow brought back her BrainPal.

Sagan took an entirely inappropriate two seconds to revel in the return of her integration and BrainPal before she wondered if she were still integrated with someone else.

The blast knocked both Boutin and the Obin to the floor; Jared felt his crèche shake violently. It managed to stay upright, as did the second crèche. The lights went out, to be replaced a second later by the soft green glow of lights running on emergency power. The Obin got up and went to the wall to activate the lab's backup generator. Boutin picked himself up, cried for Zoë and ran out of the room. Jared watched him go, his own heart in his mouth.

::Dirac,:: Jane Sagan said. ::Answer me.:: Integration flowed over Jared like golden light.

::I'm here,:: Jared said.

::Is Boutin still alive?:: Sagan asked.

::Yes,:: Jared said. ::But he's no longer the target for the mission.::

::I don't understand you,:: Sagan said.

::Jane,:: Jared said, using Sagan's first name for the first time either could remember. ::Zoë's alive. Zoë's here. His daughter. You need to find her. You need to get her away as fast as you can.::

There was an infinitesimal hesitation from Sagan. ::You need to tell me everything, now,:: Sagan said. ::And you'd better hurry.::

As quickly as he could, Jared dumped everything he learned from Boutin to Sagan, including the recordings of the conversations he'd begun to create as soon as Boutin restored his BrainPal capacity, hoping against hope that some of his squad might have survived and would have found a way in to him. Sagan wouldn't have time to go through all the conversations, but they were there, for the record.

::We should still take Boutin back,:: Sagan said, after Jared finished.

::NO,:: Jared sent the word as strongly as possible. ::As long as he's alive the Obin will come for him. He's their key to the thing they want the most. If they were going to go to war because he asked them to, they would go to war to get him back.::

::Then I'll kill him,:: Sagan said.

::Get Zoë,:: Jared said. ::I'll take care of Boutin.::

::How?:: Sagan said.

::Trust me,:: Jared said.

::Dirac,:: Sagan began.

::I know you *don't* trust me,:: Jared said. ::And I know why you don't trust me. But I also remember what you once told me, Lieutenant. You told me, no matter what, to remember that I was Jared Dirac. I'm telling you now, Lieutenant. I know who I am. I am Jared Dirac of the Colonial Union Special Forces, and my job is to save humanity. I am asking you to trust me to do my job.::

An infinitely long pause. From the hallway, Jared heard Boutin heading back to the lab.

::Do your job, Private,:: Sagan said.

::I will,:: Jared said. ::Thank you.::

::I'll find Zoë,:: Sagan said.

::Tell her you're a friend of Mr. Jared, and that he and Daddy both said it was okay to go with you,:: Jared said. ::And don't forget her stuffed elephant.:: Jared sent information on where he thought Zoë would be, just down the hall from the lab.

::I won't,:: Sagan said.

::I need to break integration with you now,:: Jared said. ::Good-bye, Lieutenant. Thank you. Thank you for it all.::

::Good-bye, Jared,:: Sagan said, and before she broke integration sent him a wave of something that resembled reassurance. And then she was gone.

Jared was alone.

Boutin reentered the lab and yelled at the Obin, who snapped some switches. The lights came back up in the lab.

"Let's get going," Boutin said to the Obin. "We're under attack. We need to get this done now." Boutin looked over to Jared briefly. Jared just smiled and closed his eyes and listened to the sounds of the Obin tapping on the panel, Boutin opening and entering his crèche, and the low thrum of Jared's own crèche powering up for the consciousness transfer.

Jared's primary regret at the end of his life was that there had been so little of it. Just a year. But that year, so many people and experiences. Jared walked with them in his mind and felt their presence a final time: Jane Sagan, Harry Wilson, Cainen. General Mattson and Colonel Robbins. The 2nd Platoon, and the closeness they shared in integration. The strangeness of Captain Martin and the Gamerans. The jokes he shared with Lieutenant Cloud. Sarah Pauling, best beloved. And Zoë. Zoë who would live, if only Sagan could find her. And she would.

No, Jared thought. *No regrets. Not one. Not for anything.*

Jared heard the soft tap as the Obin initiated the transfer

sequence. He held on to himself as long as he could. Then he let go.

Zoë screamed when there was a big roar that shook her room so hard she fell right off her bed and her TV came off the wall. Nanny came over to see if she was okay, but Zoë pushed it away. She didn't want Nanny, she wanted Daddy, and sure enough in just a minute he came through the door, sweeping her up in his arms and reassuring her and telling her that everything was going to be all right. Then he set her down and said to her that in just a few minutes Mr. Jared would be coming for her and she had to do what Mr. Jared said, but for now to stay in her room and with Nanny, because she would be safe there.

Zoë cried again for a minute and told Daddy that she didn't want him to leave, and he said that he would never leave her again. It didn't make sense because Mr. Jared was coming to get her in just a minute to take her away, but it made her feel better anyway. Then Daddy spoke to Nanny and left. Nanny went into the living room and came back holding one of those guns the Obin used. This was weird because as far as Zoë knew Nanny never used a weapon before. There were no more explosions but every once in a while Zoë could hear gunfire, going *pop pop pop* somewhere outside. Zoë got back on her bed, clutched Celeste and waited for Mr. Jared.

Nanny gave out a shriek and raised the weapon at something Zoë couldn't see and then ran out from the doorway. Zoë screamed and hid under the bed, crying, remembering what it was like at Covell and wondering if those chicken things were going to come get her again like they did there. She heard some thumping in the next room and then a scream. Zoë covered her ears and closed her eyes.

When she opened them again there were a pair of feet in the room, coming over to the bed. Zoë put a hand over her mouth to be quiet, but couldn't help a whimper or two. Then the feet became knees and hands and arms, and then a sideways head appeared and said something. Zoë squealed and tried to back out from underneath the bed, clutching Celeste, but as soon as she popped out the woman grabbed her and held her. Zoë kicked and screamed, and it was only after a while that Zoë realized that the woman was saying her name over and over again.

"It's all right, Zoë," the woman was saying. "It's all right. Shhhh. Shhhh. It's all right."

Zoë eventually stopped trying to get away and turned her head around. "Where's my daddy?" she said. "Where's Mr. Jared?"

"They're both really busy right now," the woman said, still holding Zoë. "They told me to come get you and make sure you were all right. I'm Miss Jane."

"Daddy said I had to wait here until Mr. Jared came to get me," Zoë said.

"I know he did," Miss Jane said. "But right now they both have things they have to do. There's a lot going on right now, and it's keeping both of them from coming to find you. That's why they sent me, to keep you safe."

"Nanny keeps me safe," Zoë said.

"Nanny was called away," Miss Jane said. "It's really busy here right now."

"I heard something really loud," Zoë offered.

"Well, that's one of the things keeping everybody busy," Miss Jane said.

"Okay," Zoë said, doubtfully.

"Now, Zoë," Miss Jane said. "What I want you to do is

put your arms around my shoulders, and your legs around my waist, hold on to me *real* tight, and keep your eyes closed until I tell you to open them. Can you do that?"

"Uh-huh," Zoë said. "But how will I hold Celeste?"

"Well, let's put her in between you and me right here," Miss Jane said, and put Celeste between her tummy and Zoë's.

"She'll get squished," Zoë said.

"I know," Miss Jane said. "But it'll be all right. Are you ready?"

"I'm ready," Zoë said.

"Then close your eyes and hold on real tight," Miss Jane said, and Zoë did, even though when they walked out of her bedroom Zoë's eyes hadn't closed yet and as they came into the living room Zoë saw what looked like Nanny sleeping on the floor. Then Zoë closed her eyes all the way and waited for Miss Jane to tell her to open them again.

The Obin Sagan had encountered in the science building largely avoided her, leading her to believe they were mostly specialized as scientists, but every now and again one of them would try to engage her with a weapon or try attacking her physically. The quarters were too close to wield the awkward Obin rifle with any sort of accuracy; Sagan stuck with the knife and being quick. This approach failed her when the Obin babysitting Zoë nearly took off her head; Sagan threw the knife at the Obin to distract it and then launched herself at it, fighting it out hand to hand. Sagan knew she was lucky that while they were rolling on the floor the Obin got a leg caught up in the furniture; it gave her just enough time to squirm out of its grip, get on top of it and strangle the thing to death. With

Zoë collected and held in the crook of her arm, it was time to get out.

::Harvey,:: Sagan said.

::Kind of busy right now,:: Harvey said. Through her integration Sagan could see him fighting his way toward a new hovercraft; he crashed his previous one into an airship that was trying to get off the ground and kill him from above.

::I've got the target and I need support. And a ride.::

::Five minutes and you'll have both,:: Harvey said. ::Just don't rush me.::

::I'm rushing you,:: Sagan said, and then stopped the conversation. The hallway in front of Boutin's apartment led north, past Boutin's lab, and east, into other parts of the building. The lab hallway would connect her quicker to where Harvey could pick them up, but Sagan didn't want to risk Zoë seeing either her father or Jared as they went by. Sagan sighed, went back into the apartment, and retrieved the Obin weapon, felt it balance awkwardly in her grip. It was a two-handed weapon, and the hands were meant to be Obin, not human. Sagan hoped that everyone had abandoned the building or would be busy going after Harvey, and that she wouldn't have to use it.

She had to use it three times, the third time using it to batter an Obin when the ammunition ran out. The Obin screamed. So did Zoë, each time Sagan had to use the weapon. But she kept her eyes shut, like she promised.

Sagan reached the place where she came into the building, a blown-out window on the first floor of a stairwell. ::Where are you?:: she said to Harvey.

::Believe it or not, the Obin aren't keen to give me their equipment,:: Harvey sent. ::Stop bugging me. I'll be there soon.::

"Are we safe yet?" Zoë asked, her voice muffled from her head being buried in Sagan's neck.

"Not yet," Sagan said. "Soon, Zoë."

"I want my daddy," Zoë said.

"I know, Zoë," Sagan said. "Shhh."

From the floors above Sagan heard movement.

Come on, Harvey, Sagan thought. *Get moving.*

The Obin were really beginning to piss Harvey off. Mowing down a couple dozen of them in the mess hall had been a uniquely satisfying experience, to be sure—cathartic, particularly in light of how the Obin bastards killed off most of the 2nd Platoon. And ramming the little hovercraft into that airship had held its own special pleasures. But once Harvey was on foot, he began to realize just how many of those damn Obin there were, and how much more difficult it was to manage them when one was hoofing it. And then here was Sagan—integrated again, and that was a good thing—but telling him she needed a *ride*. As if he weren't *busy*.

She's the boss, Harvey said. Getting one of the parked hovercraft was proving to be difficult; the Obin had them in a yard with only one way in. But there were at least two of them out and around, looking for him.

And look, Harvey said, as one zoomed into view, *here comes one now.* Harvey had been crouched down and trying to be inconspicuous, but now he stepped out where he could be seen and waved his hands broadly. "Hey!" Harvey yelled. "Asshole! Come get me, you creepy fuck!"

Whether by hearing him or seeing him move, the Obin operating the hovercraft turned toward Harvey. *Okay,* Harvey thought. *Now what the fuck do I do?*

The first order of business, it turned out, was jumping

clear of the stream of fléchettes that blasted out of the hovercraft's gun. Harvey rolled, came out of the roll prone and lined up his Obin weapon to shoot at the now-receding Obin. Harvey's first shot wasn't even close; the second took off the back of the Obin's head.

That's why you wear a helmet, jackass, Harvey thought, and went to retrieve his prize and then retrieve Sagan. Along the way a number of Obin on foot tried to do to Harvey what he had done to the Obin previously driving the hovercraft. Harvey preferred to run them down rather than shoot them, but he wasn't picky.

::Ride's here,:: Harvey said to Sagan, and then was more than a little surprised to see what Sagan was carrying. ::That's a kid,:: he said.

::I know that,:: Sagan said, positioning Zoë securely on the hovercraft. ::Get to the capture pod as fast as you can.:: Harvey accelerated to full speed and fled straight. There didn't seem to be any immediate chase.

::I thought we were supposed to bring back Boutin,:: Harvey said.

::Change of plans,:: Sagan said.

::Where's Boutin?:: Harvey asked.

::Dirac's taking care of him,:: Sagan said.

::Dirac,:: Harvey said, surprised again. ::I figured he was dead.::

::I'm pretty sure he is,:: Sagan said.

::Then how is he going to take care of Boutin?:: Harvey said.

::I have no idea,:: Sagan said. ::I just know he will.::

Boutin opened his eyes in a brand-new body.

Well, not brand-new, he corrected. *Gently used.*

His Obin assistant opened his crèche and helped him out of it; Boutin took a few tentative steps and then a few non-tentative ones. Boutin looked around the lab and was fascinated to see how much more vibrant and engaging it was; it was if his senses had been at low volume all his life and then were suddenly cranked up to full. Even a science lab looked good.

Boutin looked over to his old body, which was brain-dead but still breathing; it would die of its own accord in a few hours or a day at most. Boutin would use this new body's capabilities to record its death and then take the evidence with him to the capture pod, along with his daughter. *If the pod's still there,* he quickly amended; it was clear that the Special Forces squad they had captured had somehow escaped. One of them might have taken it back. *Well,* Boutin thought, *that's fine.* He was already spinning an alternative story in his head, one in which he—as Dirac—killed Boutin. The Obin, denied their prize of consciousness, would stop the war and give Dirac permission to leave with Boutin's body and Zoë.

Hmmmm, that's not quite *believable,* Boutin thought. He'd have to work out the details. Whatever story he thought of, however—

Boutin suddenly became aware of a small image flitting across his field of vision. It was a picture of an envelope.

You have a message from Jared Dirac, read a block of text that appeared in the bottom of his field of view. To open it, say "open."

"Open," Boutin said out loud. This was curious.

The envelope opened and then faded. Rather than a text message, it was a voice message.

"Hello, Boutin," it said, in a simulated voice that sounded just like Dirac—sounded just like *him* now, actually, Boutin corrected. "I see that you have gone ahead and taken this body. But before I go, I thought I'd just leave you some final thoughts.

"A wise creature once told me that it was important to make choices," the voice continued. "Through much of my short life I made no choices at all, or at least no choices of consequence. But now at the end of my life, I am faced with a choice. I can't choose whether to live or die—you have made that choice for me. But when you told me that I had no choice but to help you with your plans, you made a mistake. I do have a choice, and I've made it.

"My choice is not to help you. I can't judge whether the Colonial Union is the best government for humanity; I didn't have the time to learn everything I should have learned about it. But I choose not to risk the deaths of millions or even billions by helping you engineer its overthrow. It may be that this will ultimately be the wrong decision to have made. But it is my decision, the one I think that best allows me to do what I was born to do. To keep humanity safe.

"There is some irony here, Boutin, in that you and I share so many of the same thoughts, share a common consciousness, and perhaps share the same goal of doing the best for our people—and yet with all we have in common, we have reached opposite conclusions on how to do that. I wish we had had more time between us, that I had been able to meet you as a friend and a brother instead of what I became to you, a vessel to pour yourself into. It's too late for that now. Too late for me, and although you don't realize it, too late for you also.

"Be that as it may, I want to thank you. For better or for worse, I was alive because of you, and for a brief time, I was able to experience the joys and sorrows this life has to offer. And I was able to meet and love Zoë, who I pray now will find a way to be safe. I owe you my life, Charles, just as I owe you my death.

"Now, allow me a digression, which I promise will come around to a compelling point. As you may or may not know, one of the interesting properties SmartBlood has is the ability to instantly oxidize—to combust. I can't help but think someone encoded that property into SmartBlood as something of a cruel joke, because I first saw it being used to kill insects that were trying to suck SmartBlood out of a Special Forces soldier. But it turned out to be useful too—it once saved my life in combat.

"Charles, you have engineered a virus that you plan to use to conquer the Colonial Union. Since you know about viruses as they relate to computers, maybe you've heard of the term *Trojan horse* as well. This message, my friend and brother, is a Trojan horse. When you opened the letter, you also executed a small program I created. The program instructs every nanobot in my SmartBlood to combust simultaneously on my command. I estimate it's taken exactly this long for the program to propagate through all of my SmartBlood.

"Let's find out."

Sagan received a message as she was placing Zoë into the capture pod. It was from Jared Dirac.

::If you're reading this, Charles Boutin is dead,:: it said. ::I had this message scheduled to be sent right after my former BrainPal executed a program to combust my Smart-Blood. If the combustion doesn't kill him—and it will—he'll be dead of asphyxiation in just a few minutes. Either way, he's gone and so am I. I don't know if you'll get it but I hope you do, and that you are safe and well. Good-bye, Lieutenant Sagan. I'm glad to have known you. And if you see Cainen again, tell him I listened to him and made my choice.::

Sagan shared the message with Harvey. ::Very nice,:: Harvey said. ::He was Special Forces through and through.::

::Yes, he was,:: Sagan said, and motioned Harvey toward the capture pod. ::Get in, Harvey::

::You're joking,:: Harvey said.

::Someone needs to go back with Zoë,:: Sagan said. ::I'm commanding officer. I stay behind.::

::Lieutenant,:: Harvey said. ::That kid doesn't know me. You're the one who pulled her out of there. You're the one who needs to go back with her. And besides, I don't want to go back yet. I'm having too much *fun*. I'm guessing that between now and the time the Colonial Union drops a rock on this place I can clean it out. And when I'm done with that maybe I'll go in and see if there's anything worth salvaging. So you go ahead, Sagan. Have them send a capture pod for me in a couple of days. I'll be fine, or I'll be dead. Either way I'll enjoy myself.::

::All right,:: Sagan said. ::If you do go into the compound again, try to get the storage devices from the transfer module in Boutin's lab. Make it a priority.::

::What's on them?:: Harvey said.

::It's not what,:: Sagan said. ::It's who.::

There was a hum in the distance. ::They're on to us,:: Harvey said. ::Get in, Lieutenant::

"Are we safe now?" Zoë asked, a few minutes after launch.

"Yes, Zoë," Sagan said. "I think we are."

"When is Daddy coming to see me?" Zoë said.

"I don't know, Zoë," Sagan said, and stroked Zoë's hair. "I don't know."

In the cramped confines of the capture pod, Zoë put her arms up to be held. Sagan held her.

FIFTEEN

"Well, Szi, you were right," General Mattson said. "Jared Dirac came in handy after all."

Mattson, General Szilard and Colonel Robbins were in the general's mess, eating lunch. All of them, this time: General Mattson had been the one to formally break the tradition of not letting subordinates eat by ordering Robbins a huge plate of spaghetti Bolognese, and responding to another outraged general's reaction by saying, clearly and loudly, "Shut the fuck up, you dried-up turd. This man deserves some goddamned pasta." Since then, other generals had begun to bring in their staffs as well.

"Thank you, General," Szilard said. "Now, if you don't mind, what I want to know is what you're doing to fix these problems with our BrainPals. I lost seven ships because your people left a back door wide open."

"Robbins has the details," Mattson said. They both turned to Robbins, who had a mouthful of beef Wellington. Robbins swallowed carefully.

"In the short run, we pulled out that back door, obviously," Robbins said. "We've propagated the fix on a priority upgrade to the BrainPals. That's fixed. In the slightly longer run, we're going through all the BrainPal programming looking for legacy code, back doors and other code that could represent a security issue. And we're also instituting virus checks for messages and information sent between BrainPals. Boutin's virus transmission wouldn't work now."

"It shouldn't have worked at all," Szilard said. "There have been virus blockers since right near the dawn of computing and you didn't implement it for BrainPals. You could have killed us all because you forgot to program in basic computer hygiene."

"It was never programmed in because there was never a need for it," Mattson said. "BrainPals are a closed system, totally secure from outside attacks. Even Boutin's attack ultimately didn't work."

"But it came damn close," Szilard said.

"Yes, well, it came damn close because someone at the table wanted to create a body we could stuff Charles Boutin's consciousness in," Mattson said. "Not that I'm going to name names."

"Hmmmm," Szilard said.

"The current series of BrainPals are coming to a close anyway," Robbins said. "Our next generation of BrainPals have been tested by the Gamerans and they're ready to be implemented across the CDF population. It's a completely different architecture, fully organic, and the code is optimized, without the legacy issues of earlier BrainPal code. The window is closing on this sort of attack, General."

"At least by anyone who worked on the previous generation," Szilard said. "But what about those who are working on the current generation? You need to find out whether any of them are going to go off the ranch."

"We'll look into it," Robbins said.

"See that you do," Szilard said.

"Speaking of off the ranch," Mattson said. "What are you going to do about Lieutenant Sagan?"

"What do you mean?" Szilard said.

"Not to put too fine a point on it, she knows too much," Mattson said. "Through Boutin and Dirac, she knows about the Conclave and she knows how tightly we're keeping that information bottled up. She doesn't have clearance for that information, Szi. That's dangerous stuff."

"I don't see why it's dangerous," Szilard said. "If for no other reason than it's the truth. The Conclave is out there. And if it ever gets its act together, we're going to find ourselves up the proverbial creek."

"It's dangerous because it's not the whole truth, and you *know* that, Szi," Mattson said. "Boutin didn't know anything about the Counter-Conclave and how deeply we're involved with *that*, and how we've been playing one side against the other. Things are moving fast. We're getting to the point where alliances have to be formed and choices will have to be made. We won't be able to formally stay neutral anymore. We don't need Sagan out there telling people half the story and starting rumors."

"Then tell her the whole damn story," Szilard said. "She's an intelligence officer, for God's sake. She can handle the truth."

"It's not up to me," Mattson said. Szilard opened his mouth; Mattson put up both hands. "It's *not* up to *me*, Szi. If the Counter-Conclave formally breaks with the Conclave, you know what that's going to mean. The entire goddamn galaxy is going to be at war. We won't just be able to rely on our recruits from Earth anymore. We're going to have to ask the colonies to pony up as well. We may even have to start conscription. And you know what *that's* going to mean. The colonies will riot. We'll be lucky if we avoid a civil war. We're keeping the information from the colonies not because we want to keep them ignorant but because we don't want the whole fucking Union to fly apart."

"The longer we wait, the worse it's going to get," Szilard said. "We're never going to find a good way to break it to the colonies. And when they do find out, they're going to wonder what the hell the CU was doing keeping it from them for so long."

"It's not up to me," Mattson said.

"Yes, yes," Szilard said, testily. "Fortunately for you there's a way out. Sagan is close to the end of her term of service. She has a few months left, I think. Maybe a year. Close enough that we can retire her. From what I understand she was planning to leave the service when her time was up anyway. We'll put her on a brand-new colony and there she can stay, and if she talks to the neighbors about some Conclave, who the hell cares. They'll be too busy trying to get a crop in."

"Do you think you'll get her to do it?" Mattson said.

"We can entice her," Szilard said. "A couple of years ago, Sagan became quite attached to a CDF soldier named John Perry. Perry's a few years behind her in his term of service, but if we needed to we could spring him early. And it seems like she's become quite attached to Zoë Boutin, who is an orphan and who needs to be placed. You see where I'm going here."

"I can," Mattson said. "You should make it happen."

"I'll see what I can do," Szilard said. "And speaking of secrets, how are your negotiations with the Obin going?"

Both Mattson and Robbins looked at Szilard warily. "There are no negotiations with the Obin," Robbins said.

"Of course not," Szilard said. "You're not negotiating with the Obin to continue Boutin's consciousness program for them. And the Obin are not negotiating with us to knock down whichever of the Rraey or Eneshans is still left standing after their upcoming little war. No one's negotiating with anyone about anything. And how are these non-negotiations not going?"

Robbins looked at Mattson, who nodded. "They're not going surprisingly well," Robbins said. "We probably won't reach an agreement in the next couple of days."

"How not wonderful," Szilard said.

"I want to get back to Sagan," Mattson said. "When do you think you'll be able to get an answer from her?"

"I'll put it to her today," Szilard said. "And I'll tell her to be ready in a week. That should give her time to take care of things that need to be done."

"Like what?" Mattson said.

"Good-byes and closure, of course," Szilard said. "And a few other decisions I am going to ask her to make."

Jane Sagan peered into what looked like a miniature light show. "What is this?" she asked.

"It's Jared Dirac's soul," Cainen said.

Sagan glanced over to him. "I remember you once told me that Special Forces soldiers didn't have souls," she said.

"That was another place, and another time," Cainen said. "And I am not so very foolish now. But very well, it's his consciousness, then," Cainen said. "Retrieved by one of your soldiers, I believe, and from what I understand recorded by Charles Boutin. And I understand it is your job to decide what to do with it."

Sagan nodded. Szilard had come to her, offering her discharge, the discharge of John Perry and the custodianship of Zoë Boutin, on the condition that she keep her mouth shut about the Conclave and that she make a decision about what to do with Jared Dirac's consciousness.

::I understand about the Conclave,:: Sagan said. ::But I don't understand about Dirac.::

::I'm just curious what you'll do,:: Szilard said, and refused to explain it any further than that.

"What will you do with it?" Cainen asked.

"What do you think I should do?" Sagan asked.

"I know precisely what you should do with it," Cainen said. "But I am not you and I will not tell you what I would do with it until I hear what you would do with it first."

Sagan looked over at Harry Wilson, who was watching with interest. "And what would you do, Harry?"

"Sorry, Jane," Wilson said, and smiled. "I plead the Fifth as well. This is your call."

"You could bring him back," Sagan said to Cainen.

"It's possible," Cainen said. "We know more about it now than we did before. It's possible we could condition the brain better than they conditioned Dirac's brain to accept Boutin's personality. There's some risk of the transfer not taking, and then you'd have a situation like what happened with Dirac, where another personality would grow instead, and the other personality would slowly impinge. But I think it's less of a risk now, and in time, it won't be a serious risk at all. I think we could bring him back, if that's what you wanted."

"But it's not what Jared wanted, is it?" Sagan said. "He knew his consciousness had been recorded. He could have asked me to try to save it. He didn't."

"No, he didn't," Cainen agreed.

"Jared made his choice," Sagan said. "And it was his choice to make. Erase the recording, please, Cainen."

"And now you see why I know you have a soul," Cainen said. "Please accept my apology that I ever doubted it."

"Apology unneeded," Sagan said. "But apology accepted."

"Thank you," Cainen said. "And now, Lieutenant Sagan, I was wondering if I could ask a favor of you. Or perhaps it's not so much of a favor as calling due a debt between us."

"What is it?" Sagan asked.

Cainen looked past Sagan to Wilson, who looked suddenly very uncomfortable. "You don't have to stay for this, my friend," Cainen said to Wilson.

"Of course I'll stay," Wilson said. "But let me reiterate: You're a damn fool."

"Noted," Cainen said. "And I appreciate the thought."

Wilson crossed his arms and looked vexed.

"Tell me," Sagan said.

"I wish to die, Lieutenant," Cainen said. "Over the last several months, I have begun to feel the effects of the antidote you provide lessen. Every day I am in increasing pain."

"We can give you more," Sagan said.

"Yes, and perhaps that would work," Cainen said. "But I am in pain, beyond the mere physical aspect. I am far away from my people and my home, and far from the things that bring me joy. I cherish the friendships I have with Harry Wilson and with you—you! of all people—but every day I feel the part of myself that is Rraey, the part that is *truly* me, grow colder and smaller. Not too long from now there will be nothing left of it and I will be alone, absolutely alone. I will be alive, but I'll be dead inside."

"I can talk to General Szilard about releasing you," Sagan said.

"That's what I told him," Wilson said.

"You know they'll never release me," Cainen said. "I've done too much work for you now. I know far too much. And even if you did release me, do you think the Rraey would welcome me back? No, Lieutenant. I am far from home, and I know that I can never go back to it."

"I'm sorry I did this to you, Cainen," Sagan said. "If I could change this for you I would."

"Why would you?" Cainen said. "You've saved your people from war, Lieutenant. I am merely part of the cost."

"I am still sorry," Sagan said.

"Then repay that debt to me," Cainen said. "Help me die."

"How would I do that?" Sagan said.

"In my studies of human culture I've learned about seppuku," Cainen said. "Do you know it?" Sagan shook her head. "Ritual suicide, from your Japanese people. The ritual includes a *Kaishakunin*, a second—someone who eases the pain of the person committing seppuku by killing them at the moment of their greatest agony. I would choose to die from the disease you inflicted on me, Lieutenant Sagan, but I fear that when the agony is greatest I would cry for mercy, as I did the very first time, shaming myself and setting myself in motion on the path that led us here. A second would keep me from that shame. I ask you to be my second, Lieutenant Sagan."

"I don't think the Colonial Defense Forces will allow me to kill you," Sagan said. "Outside of combat."

"Yes, and I find that ironic beyond belief," Cainen said. "However, in this case they will. I've already asked General Mattson for permission, and he has granted it. I've also asked General Szilard for permission for you to be my second. He has granted it."

"What will you do if I refuse?" Sagan asked.

"You know what I will do," Cainen said. "When we first met you told me that you believed that I wanted to live, and you were right. But as I said earlier, that was a different place and a different time. In this time and place, I want to be released. If it means I do it alone, than I will be alone. But I hope that will not be the case."

"It won't," Sagan said. "I accept, Cainen. I will be your second."

"From the depths of my soul I thank you, Lieutenant Sagan, my friend." Cainen looked to Wilson, who was crying. "And you, Harry? I asked you to attend me before and you refused. I ask you again."

Wilson nodded, violently. "Yes," he said. "I'll do it, you lousy son of a bitch. I'll be there when you die."

"Thank you, Harry," Cainen said, and once again turned to Sagan. "I need two days to bring things to a close here. Will you come to visit me on the third day, in the evening?"

"I'll be there," Sagan said.

"Your combat knife, I think, should be sufficient," Cainen said.

"If that's what you want," Sagan said. "Is there anything else you would have me do for you?"

"Only one other thing," Cainen said. "And I'll understand if you can't do it."

"Name it," Sagan said.

"I was born on the colony of Fala," Cainen said. "I grew up there. When I die, if I can, I'd like to return there. I know it will be a difficult thing to manage."

"I'll manage it," Sagan said. "Even if I have to take you there myself. I promise it, Cainen. I promise that you'll go home."

* * *

A month after Zoë and Sagan returned to Phoenix Station, Sagan took Zoë on a shuttle to visit the gravestone of her parents.

The shuttle pilot was Lieutenant Cloud, who asked after Jared. Sagan told him that he had passed on. Lieutenant Cloud was quiet for a moment and then began telling Sagan the jokes that Jared had told him. Sagan laughed.

At the gravestone, Sagan stood while Zoë knelt and read the names of her parents, clearly and calmly. Over the month, Sagan had seen Zoë change from the tentative girl she'd first met, seemingly younger than she really was, asking plaintively for her father, to someone happier and more talkative and closer to the age she was. Which was, as it happened, only a little younger than Sagan.

"My name is here," Zoë said, tracing the name with her finger.

"For a while, when you were first taken, your father thought you were dead," Sagan said.

"Well, I'm *not* dead," Zoë said, defiantly.

"No," Sagan said, and smiled. "No, you definitely are not."

Zoë put her hand on her father's name. "He's not really here, is he?" Zoë asked. "Here under me."

"No," Sagan said. "He died on Arist. That was where you were before we came here."

"I know," Zoë said, and looked over to Sagan. "Mr. Jared died there too, didn't he?"

"He did," Sagan said.

"He said he knew me, but I didn't really remember him," Zoë said.

"He did know you, but it's hard to explain," Sagan said. "I'll explain it to you when you're older."

Zoë looked at the tombstone again. "All the people who knew me have gone away," she said, in a small, singsong voice. "All my people are gone."

Sagan got down on her knees behind Zoë and gave her a small but fierce hug. "I'm so sorry, Zoë."

"I know," Zoë said. "I'm sorry too. I miss Daddy and Mommy and I even miss Mr. Jared a little, even though I didn't know him very much."

"I know they miss you too," Sagan said. She came around to face Zoë. "Listen, Zoë, soon I'm going to be going to a colony, where I'm going to live. If you want, you can come with me."

"Will it just be you and me?" Zoë said.

"Well, you and me and a man I love very much," Sagan said.

"Will I like him?" Zoë asked.

"I think so," Sagan said. "I like him, and I like you, so it stands to reason you would like each other. You, me, and him."

"Like a family," Zoë said.

"Yes, like a family," Sagan said. "Very much like one."

"But I already have a daddy and a mommy," Zoë said.

"I know, Zoë," said Sagan. "I would never want you to forget them, ever. John and I would just be the two grown-ups who will be very lucky to get to live with you."

"John," Zoë said. "John and Jane. John and Jane and Zoë."

"John and Jane and Zoë," Sagan repeated.

"John and Jane and Zoë," Zoë said, standing up and moving to the rhythms of the names. "John and Jane and Zoë. John and Jane and Zoë! I like that," Zoë said.

"I like it too," Sagan said.

"Well, okay then," Zoë said. "And now I'm hungry."

Sagan laughed. "Well then, let's get you something to eat."

"Okay," Zoë said. "Let me say bye-bye to Mommy and Daddy." She ran to the headstone and planted a kiss on it. "I love you," she said, and then raced back to Sagan, and took her hand. "I'm ready. Let's eat."

"Okay," Sagan said. "What would you like?"

"What do we have?" Zoë said.

"There are lots of choices," Sagan said. "Pick one."

"All right," Zoë said. "I'm *very* good at making choices, you know."

"Well," Sagan said, hugging the girl close. "I'm so very glad to hear it."

ACKNOWLEDGMENTS

First off, to everyone who thinks writing a sequel should be easy because you've already created the universe: Bwa ha ha ha ha ha ha! Heh. No.

With that in mind, allow me to first acknowledge my editor, Patrick Nielsen Hayden, for occasionally dropping me a casual e-mail to let me know how much he was looking forward to reading the next chapter, rather than strangling me dead, which he probably should have done and *may* yet do, because now he's gotten the entire manuscript and there's no penalty in doing so (unless he wants another book).

Other absolutely magnificent Tor people who deserve love and/or chocolates: Teresa Nielsen Hayden, Liz Gorinsky, Irene Gallo, the dearly departed Fiona Lee (she's alive, just in China), Dot Lin and Tom Doherty. However, as a general rule, everyone who works at Tor deserves love and/or chocolates, and I'm not just saying that because I've made them suffer by blowing deadlines. Well, maybe a bit. But it doesn't make it any less *true*. Thanks also to Rich Klin, for truly heroic copyediting.

Admit it: You think the cover rocks. Well, it's true, it does, and we all have John Harris to thank for that.

Thanks as ever to Ethan Ellenberg, my agent, whose judicious wrangling of contracts is a sight to behold.

One of the reasons that *The Ghost Brigades* exists is that the first book in the series, *Old Man's War*, was fortunate enough to have been praised online by folks whose taste in books is trusted by their readers. I thank all of them and add special thanks to Glenn Reynolds, Cory Doctorow, Stephen Green, Stephen Bainbridge and Eugene Volokh. If you ever wondered if online word of mouth worked, by the way: Oh, my, *yes*.

If you're wondering why particular things in the book seem so good, the short answer is because I've seen them work in other books and said, "What an excellent thing. I think I'll steal that." Writers from whom I've consciously stolen include Nick Sagan (his consciousness transference idea, used to excellent effect in *Edenborn*), Scott Westerfeld (whose awesome space battles in *The Risen Empire* and *The Killing of Worlds* will make you weep with joy) and David Brin, whose concept of "Uplift" (see: *The Uplift War*) gets a quick ping. Thanks also to the various SF/F authors I namecheck throughout the book.

As ever, Regan Avery served indispensably as my reader of first resort. Every writer should have a Regan. But you can't have Regan Avery. She's *mine*. Grrrrrrrrrrr.

Chad Brink mailed me a copy of one of my books to sign, and it took me several months to return it to him. In fact, I may still have it here. I figure putting him in the acknowledgments of this book makes up for being a bad book-mailer-backer. Also, clearly, you should not mail your books to me to sign. It's not you, it's me.

Deven Desai, Natasha Kordus, Kevin Stampfl, Mykal Burns, Daniel Mainz, Justine Larbalestier, Lauren McLaughlin, Andrew Woffinden, Charlie Stross, Bill Schafer, Karen Meisner, Anne KG Murphy, Cian Chang, Kristy Gaitten, John Anderson, Stephen Bennett, Erin Barbee, Joe Rybicki, and many others whom I can't remember because it's 4:30 in the morning but you know who you are, I love you all and wish to have your babies. Twins, even.

Lastly and not leastly, a moment to thank Kristine and Athena Scalzi for being as patient with me as they could possibly be in the writing of this book. The writing of this book was particularly trying for Athena, who at one point turned to her mother and declared, "Daddy's become *boring*." Well, sweetheart, I promise to be less boring from now on, starting right this very instant.

Turn the page for a preview of

John Scalzi's

THE
LAST
COLONY

(0-7653-1697-8)

Available in hardcover from
Tor Books

Let me tell you of the worlds I've left behind.

Earth you know; everyone knows it. It's the birth-
place of humanity, although at this point not many consider it our "home" planet—Phoenix has had that job since
the Colonial Union was created and became the guiding
force for expanding and protecting our race in the universe. But you never forget where you come from.

Being from Earth in this universe is like being a small-
town kid who gets on the bus, goes to the big city and
spends his entire afternoon gawking at all the tall buildings. Then he gets mugged for the crime of marveling at
this strange new world, which has such things in it, because the things in it don't have much time or sympathy
for the new kid in town, and they're happy to kill him for
what he's got in his suitcase. The small-town kid learns
this fast, because he can't go home again.

I spent seventy-five years on Earth, living mostly in the
same small Ohio town and sharing most of that life with

the same woman. She died and stayed behind. I lived and I left.

The next world is metaphorical. The Colonial Defense Forces took me off Earth and kept the parts of me it wanted: my consciousness, and some small part of my DNA. From the latter they built me a new body, which was young and quick and strong and beautiful and only partially human. It stuffed my consciousness inside of it, and gave me not nearly enough time to glory in my second youth. Then it took this beautiful body that was now me and spent the next several years actively trying to get it killed by throwing me at every hostile alien race it could.

There were a lot of those. The universe is vast, but the number of worlds suitable for human life is surprisingly small, and as it happens space is filled with numerous other intelligent species who want the same worlds we do. Very few of these species, it seems, are into the concept of sharing; we're certainly not. We all fight, and the worlds we can inhabit swap back and forth between us until one or another of us gets a grip on it so tight we can't be pried off. Over a couple of centuries, we humans have managed this trick on several dozen worlds, and failed this trick on dozens more. None of this has made us very many friends.

I spent six years in this world. I fought and I nearly died, more than once. I had friends, most of whom died but some of whom I saved. I met a woman who was achingly like the one I shared my life with on Earth, but who was nevertheless entirely her own person. I defended the Colonial Union, and in doing so I believed I was keeping humanity alive in the universe.

At the end of it the Colonial Defense Forces took the part of me that had always been me and stuffed it into a third and final body. This body was young, but not nearly as quick and strong. It was, after all, only human. But this body would not be asked to fight and die. I missed being as strong as a cartoon superhero. I didn't miss every alien creature I met trying very hard to kill me. It was a fair trade.

The next world is likely unknown to you. Stand again on Earth, our old home, where billions still live and dream of the stars. Look up in the sky, at the constellation Lynx, hard by Ursa Major. There's a star there, yellow like our sun, with six major planets. The third one, appropriately enough, is a counterfeit of Earth: ninety-six percent of its circumference, but with a slightly larger iron core, so it has 101 percent of its mass (you don't notice that one percent much). Two moons: one two-thirds the size of Earth's moon, but closer than Luna, so in the sky it takes up the same amount of real estate. The second moon, a captured asteroid, is much smaller and closer in. It's in an unstable orbit; eventually it will tumble and fall into the planet below. Best estimate is this will happen in about a quarter of a million years. The natives are not terribly concerned at the moment.

This world was found by humans nearly seventy-five years ago; the Ealan had a colony there but the Colonial Defense Forces corrected that. Then the Ealan, shall we say, checked the math on that equation and it was another couple of years before it was all sorted out. When it was, the Colonial Union opened the world to colonists from Earth, mostly from India. They arrived in waves; the first one after the planet was secured from the Ealan, and the second shortly after the Subcontinental War on Earth, when the Occupation-backed probationary government offered the most notable supporters of the Chowdhury regime the choice of colonization or imprisonment. Most went into exile, taking their families with them. These people didn't so much dream of the stars as had them forced upon them.

Given the people who live on the planet, you would think it would have a name that reflects their heritage. You would be wrong. The planet is called Huckleberry, named no doubt by some Twain-loving apparatchik of the Colonial Union. Huckleberry's large moon is Sawyer; the small one is Becky. Its three major continents are Samuel, Langhorne and Clemens; from Clemens there is a long, curling string of volcanic islands known as the Livy Archipelago, set in the Calaveras Ocean. Most of the prominent features were dubbed in various aspects Twainania before the first settlers arrived; they seem to have accepted this with good grace.

Stand on this planet with me now. Look up in the sky, in the direction of the constellation Lotus. In it there is a star, yellow like the one this planet circles, around which I was born, two other lives ago. From here it is so far away as to be invisible to the eye, which is often how I feel about the life I lived there.

My name is John Perry. I am eighty-eight years old. I have lived on this planet for nearly eight years now. It is my home, which I share with my wife and my adopted daughter. Welcome to Huckleberry. In this story, it's the next world I leave behind. But not the final one.

The story of how I left Huckleberry begins—as do all worthy stories—with a goat.

Savitri Guntupalli, my assistant, didn't even look up from her book as I came back from lunch. "There's a goat in your office," she said.

"Hmmmm," I said. "I thought we'd sprayed for those."

This got an upward glance, which counted as a victory as these things go. "It brought the Chengelpet brothers with it," she said.

"Crap," I said. The last pair of brothers who fought as

much as the Chengelpet brothers were named Cain and Abel, and at least one of them finally took some direct action. "I thought I told you not to let those two in my office when I wasn't around."

"You said no such thing," Savitri said.

"Let's make it standing order," I said.

"And even if you had," Savitri continued, setting down her book, "this assumes that either Chengelpet would listen to me, which neither would. Aftab stomped through first with the goat and Nissim followed right after. Neither of them so much as looked in my direction."

"I don't want to have to deal with the Chengelpets," I said. "I just ate."

Savitri reached over to the side of the desk, grabbed her wastebasket and placed it on top of her desk. "By all means, vomit first," she said.

I had met Savitri several years before while I was touring the colonies as a representative of the Colonial Defense Forces, talking it up to the various colonies I was sent to. At the stop at the village of New Goa in the Huckleberry colony, Savitri stood up and called me a tool of the imperial and totalitarian regime of the Colonial Union. I liked her immediately. When I mustered out of the CDF, I decided to settle in New Goa. I was offered the position of village ombudsman, which I took, and was surprised on the first day of work to find Savitri there, telling me that she was going to be my assistant whether I liked it or not.

"Remind me again why you took this job," I said to Savitri, over the wastebasket.

"Sheer perversity," Savitri said. "Are you going to vomit or not?"

"I think I'll keep it in," I said. She grabbed the wastebasket and set it in its former position, and then picked up her book to resume reading.

I had an idea. "Hey, Savitri," I said. "Want my job?"

"Sure," she said, opening her book. "I'll start right after you finish with the Chengelpets."

"Thanks," I said.

Savitri grunted. She had returned to her literary adventures. I steeled myself and walked through the door of my office.

The goat in the middle of the floor was cute. The Chengelpets, sitting in the chairs in front of my desk, were less so.

"Aftab," I said, nodding to the older brother. "Nissim," I said, nodding to the younger. "And friend," I said, nodding to the goat. I took a seat. "What I can do for you this afternoon?"

"You can give me permission to shoot my brother, Ombudsman Perry," Nissim said.

"I'm not sure that's in my job description," I said. "And anyway, it seems a little drastic. Why don't you tell me what's going on."

Nissim pointed to his brother. "This bastard has stolen my seed," he said.

"Pardon?" I said.

"My seed," Nissim said. "Ask him. He cannot deny it."

I blinked and turned toward Aftab. "Stealing your brother's seed, then, is it, Aftab?"

"You must forgive my brother," Aftab said. "He is prone to hysteria, as you know. What he means to say is that one of his goats wandered from his pasture into mine and impregnated this nanny here, and now he claims that I have stolen his goat's sperm."

"It wasn't just any goat," Nissim said. "It was Prabhat, my prizewinner. I stud him out for a very good price, and Aftab didn't want to pay the price. So he stole my seed."

"It's Prabhat's seed, you idiot," Aftab said. "And it's not

my fault you take such poor care of your fence that your goat was able to get onto my land."

"Oh, that's rich," Nissim said. "Ombudsman Perry, I'll have you know that fence wire was cut. Prabhat was tempted onto his land."

"You're delusional," Aftab said. "And even if it were true, which it is not, so what? You have your precious Prabhat back."

"But now you have this pregnant goat," Nissim said. "A pregnancy that you did not pay for, and which I did not give permission for. It's theft, pure and simple. And more than that, you're trying to ruin me."

"What are you talking about?" Aftab said.

"You're trying to breed a new stud," Nissim said to me, and pointed at the goat, which was nibbling the back of Aftab's chair. "Don't deny it. This is your best nanny. By breeding it with Prabhat you'll have a buck you can stud out. You're trying to undercut my business. Ask him, Ombudsman Perry. Ask him what his goat is carrying."

I looked back to Aftab. "What is your goat carrying, Aftab?"

"By sheer coincidence, one of the fetuses is male," Aftab said.

"I want it aborted," Nissim said.

"It's not your goat," Aftab said.

"Then I'll take the kid when it's born," Nissim said. "As payment for the seed you stole."

"This again," Aftab said, and looked over to me. "You see what I am dealing with, Ombudsman Perry. He lets his goats run rampant across the countryside, impregnating at will, and then he demands payment for his own shoddy animal husbandry."

Nissim bellowed in outrage and began yelling and gesticulating wildly at his brother; Aftab followed suit. The goat came around the desk and eyed me curiously. I reached into my desk and fed the goat a candy I found there. "You and I don't actually need to be here for this," I said to the goat. The goat didn't respond, but I could tell she agreed with me.

As originally planned, the village ombudsman's job was supposed to be simple: Whenever the New Goa villagers had a problem with the local or district government, they would come to me, and I could help them run through the red tape and get things done. It was, in fact, just the sort of job you give a war hero who is otherwise useless to the daily life of a largely rural colony; he's got just enough notoriety with the higher-ups that when he shows up on the doorstep, they have to pay attention to him.

The thing was that after a couple of months of this, the New Goa villagers started coming to me with their other problems. "Oh, we don't want to bother with the officials," I was told by one of the villagers, after I questioned why I was suddenly the go-to guy for everything from farm equipment advice to frontline marriage counseling. "It's easier and quicker to come to you." Rohit Kulkarni, New Goa's administrator, was delighted with this state of affairs, since I was now handling the problems that used to come to him first. It gave him more time to fish and play dominoes at the tea shop.

Most of the time this new and expanded definition of my ombudsman's duties was perfectly fine. It was nice to help people, and it was also nice that people listened to my advice. On the other hand any public servant is likely to tell you that just a few annoying people in their community will take up the vast majority of their time. In New Goa, those roles were occupied by the Chengelpet brothers.

No one knew why they hated each other so much. I

thought it might be something with their parents, but Bhajan and Niral were lovely people who were just as mystified about it as anyone. Some people just don't get along with some other people, and unfortunately, these two people who did not get along happened to be brothers.

It wouldn't have been so bad if in fact they hadn't built farms right next to each other and thus were in each other's faces and business most of the time. At one point early in my tenure I suggested to Aftab, whom I regarded as the slightly more rational Chengelpet, that he might consider checking out a new plot of land that had just been cleared out on the other side of the village, because living away from Nissim might solve the majority of his problems with him. "Oh, he'd like that," Aftab said, in a perfectly reasonable tone of voice. After that I abandoned any hope of rational discourse on the matter and accepted that my karma required me to suffer through the occasional visit from the Outraged Chengelpet Brothers.

"All right," I said, quieting the brothers down from their fratriphobic rantings. "Here's what I think. I don't think it really matters how our lady friend the goat got knocked up, so let's not focus on that. But you both agree that it was Nissim's buck that did the deed."

Both the Chengelpets nodded; the goat stayed modestly quiet. "Fine. Then the two of you are in business together," I said. "Aftab, you can keep the kid after it's born and stud it out if you like. But the first six times you do, Nissim gets the full stud fee, and after that half of your stud fee goes to your brother."

"He'll just stud it out for free the first six times," Nissim said.

"Then let's make the minimum stud fee after those first six times the average of those first six," I said. "So if he tries to screw you he'll end up screwing himself, too. And this is a small village, Nissim. People here won't stud with Aftab if they think the only reason he's hiring out his goat is to mess with your livelihood. There's a fine line between value and being a bad neighbor."

"And what if I don't want to be in business with him?" Aftab said.

"Then you can sell the kid to Nissim," I said. Nissim opened his mouth to protest. "Yes, sell," I said, before he could complain. "Take the kid to Murali and get an appraisal. That'll be the price. Murali doesn't like either of you very much so you'll get a fair estimate. Okay?"

The Chengelpets thought it over, which is to say they racked their brains to see if there was any way either one of them was more unhappy with this state of affairs than the other. Eventually they both seemed to come to the conclusion that they were equally displeased, which in this situation was the optimal result. They both nodded their assent.

"Good," I said. "Now get out of here before there's a mess on my rug."

"My goat wouldn't do that," Aftab said.

"It's not the goat I'm worried about," I said, shooing them out. They left; Savitri appeared in the door.

"You're in my seat," she said, nodding to my chair.

"Screw you," I said, propping up my feet on the desk. "If you're not going to handle the annoying cases, you're not ready for the big chair."

"In that case I will return to my humble role as your assistant and let you know that while you were entertaining the Chengelpets, the constable called," Savitri said.

"What about?" I asked.

"Didn't say," Savitri said. "Hung up. You know the constable. Very abrupt."

"Tough but fair, that's the motto," I said. "If it was really important there'd be a message, so I'll worry about that later. In the meantime I'll catch up with my paperwork."

"You don't have paperwork," Savitri said. "You give it all to me."

"Is it done?" I asked.

"As far as you know, yes," Savitri said.

"Then I think I'll relax and bask in my superior management skills," I said.

"I'm glad you didn't use the wastebasket to vomit earlier," Savitri said. "Because now there's a place for mine to go." She retreated back to her desk before I could think up a good retort.

We'd been like this since after the first month we'd worked together. It took her that first month to get used to the fact that even though I was former military I wasn't actually a colonialist tool, or at the very least if I was, I was one with common sense and a reasonable sense of humor. Having established I wasn't there to spread my hegemony over her village, she relaxed enough to start mocking me. It's been our relationship for seven years, and it's a good one.

With all the paperwork done and all the problems of the village solved, I did what anyone in my position would do: I took a nap. Welcome to the rough and tumble world of colonial village ombudsmanning. It's possible it's done differently elsewhere, but if it is, I don't want to know.

I woke up in time to see Savitiri closing up the office for the day. I waved good-bye to her and after a few more minutes of immobility hauled my own ass out of the chair and through the door, on the way home. Along the way I happened to see the constable coming toward me on the other side of the road. I crossed the road, walked up to constable and kissed my local law enforcement official full on the lips.

"You know I don't like it when you do that," Jane said, after I was done.

"You don't like it when I kiss you?" I asked.

"Not when I'm on the job," Jane said. "It erodes my authority."

I smiled at the thought of some malfeasant thinking Jane, a former Special Forces soldier, was soft because she kissed her husband. The ass-kicking that would ensue would be terrible in its magnitude. However, I didn't say that. "Sorry," I said. "I'll try not to erode your authority anymore."

"Thank you," Jane said. "I was coming to see you, anyway, since you didn't return my call."

"I was incredibly busy today," I said.

"Savitri briefed me on just how busy you were when I called back," Jane said.

"Oops," I said.

"Oops," Jane agreed. We started walking in the the direction of our home. "What I was going to tell you is that you could expect Gopal Boparai to come by tomorrow to find out what his community service would be. He was drunk and disorderly again. He was yelling at a cow."

"Bad karma," I said.

"The cow thought so, too," Jane said. "It butted him in the chest and sent him through a shop window."

"Is Go okay?" I asked.

"Scratches," Jane said. "The pane popped out. Plastic. Didn't break."

"This is the third time this year," I said. "He should be up in front of the actual magistrate, not me."

"That's what I told him, too," Jane said. "But he'd be up for a mandatory forty days in the district gaol and Shashi is due in a couple of weeks. She needs him around more than he needs gaol."

"All right," I said. "I'll figure out something for him."

"How was your day?" Jane asked. "Besides the nap, I mean."

"I had a Chengelpet day," I said. "This time with a goat."

Jane and I chatted about our day on our walk home, like we do every day on our walk home, to the small farm we keep just outside the village proper. As we turned onto our road we ran into our daughter Zoë, walking Barbar the mutt, who was typically deliriously happy to see us.

"He knew you were coming," Zoë said, slightly out of breath. "Took off halfway down the road. Had to run to keep up."

"Nice to know we were missed," I said. Jane petted Barbar, who wagged up a storm. I gave Zoë a peck on the cheek.

"You two have a visitor," Zoë said. "He showed up at the house about an hour ago. In a floater."

No one in town had a floater; they were ostentatious and impractical for a farming community. I glanced over to Jane, who shrugged, as if to say, *I'm not expecting anyone.* "Who did he say he was?" I asked.

"He didn't," Zoë said. "All he said was that he was an old friend of yours, John. I told him I could call you and he said he was happy to wait."

"Well, what does he look like, at least?" I asked.

"Young," Zoë said. "Kinda cute."

"I don't think I know any cute guys," I said. "That's more your department, teenage daughter."

Zoë crossed her eyes and gave a mock sneer. "Thanks, ninety-year-old dad. If you had let me finish speaking, you would have heard the clue that tells me you might actually know him. Which is that he's also *green*."

This got another shared glance between me and Jane.

CDF members had green skin, a result of modified chlorophyll that gave them extra energy for combat. Both Jane and I had had green skin once; I was back to my original hue and Jane was allowed to choose a more standard skin tone when she changed bodies.

"He didn't say what he wanted?" Jane asked Zoë.

"Nope," Zoë said. "And I didn't ask. I just figured I'd come find you and give you advance warning. I left him on the front porch."

"Probably sneaking around the house by now," I said.

"Doubtful," Zoë said. "I left Hickory and Dickory to watch him."

I grinned. "That should keep him in one place," I said.

"My thought exactly," Zoë said.

"You are wise beyond your years, teenage daughter," I said.

"Makes up for you, ninety-year-old dad," she said. She jogged back to the house, Barbar padding behind.

"Such attitude," I said to Jane. "She gets it from your side."

"She's adopted," Jane said. "And I'm not the smart-ass in the family."

"These are details," I said, and took her hand. "Come on. I want to see just how scared shitless our guest is."

We found our guest on the porch swing, watched intently and silently by our two Obin. I recognized him immediately.

"General Rybicki," I said. "This is a surprise."

"Hello, Major," Rybicki said, referring to my former rank. He pointed to the Obin. "You've made some interesting friends since the last time I saw you."

"Hickory and Dickory," I said. "They're my daughter's companions. Perfectly nice, unless they think you're a threat to her."

"And then what happens?" Rybicki asked.

"It varies," I said. "But it's usually quick."

"Wonderful," Rybicki said. I excused the Obin; they went off to find Zoë.

"Thank you," Rybicki said. "Obin make me nervous."

"That's the point," Jane said.

"I realize that," Rybicki said. "If you don't mind me asking, why does your daughter have Obin bodyguards?"

"They're not bodyguards, they're companions," Jane said. "Zoë is our adopted daughter. Her biological father is Charles Boutin." This got a raised eyebrow from Rybicki; he was of sufficiently advanced rank to know about Boutin. "The Obin revere Boutin, but he's dead. They have a desire to know his daughter, so they sent these two to be with her."

"And this doesn't bother her," Rybicki said.

"She grew up with Obin as nannies and protectors," Jane said. "She's comfortable with them."

"And it doesn't bother *you*," Rybicki said.

"They watch and protect Zoë," I said. "They help out around here. And their presence with us is a part of the treaty the Colonial Union has with the Obin. Having them here seems like a small price to pay for having them on our side."

"That's true enough," Rybicki said, and stood up. "Listen, Major. I have a proposition for you." He nodded to Jane. "For both of you, actually."

"What is it?" I asked.

Rybicki motioned with his head toward the house, in the direction Hickory and Dickory just went. "I'd rather not talk about it where those two might hear, if it's all the same. Is there some place we can talk privately?"

I glanced over at Jane. She smiled thinly. "I know a place," she said.

* * *

"We're stopping here?" General Rybicki asked, as I pulled up short, halfway across the field.

"You asked if we had someplace where we could talk privately," I said. "You've now got at least five acres of grain between us and the next set of ears, human or Obin. Welcome to privacy, colonial style."

"What kind of grain is this?" General Rybicki asked, pulling at a stalk.

"It's sorghum," Jane said, standing next to me. Barbar sat next to Jane and scratched his ear.

"It sounds familiar," Rybicki said, "but I don't think I've ever actually seen it before."

"It's a staple crop here," I said. "It's a good crop because it's heat and drought tolerant, and it can get pretty hot around here in our summer months. People here use it for a bread called *bhakri* and for other things."

"Bhakri," Rybicki said, and motioned toward town. "These folks are mostly from India, then."

"Some of them," I said. "Most of them were born here. This particular village is sixty years old. Most of the active colonization here on Huckleberry is on the Clemens continent now. They opened it up around the same time we arrived."

"So there's no tension about the Subcontinental War," Rybicki said. "With you being American and them being Indian."

"It doesn't come up," I said. "People here are like immigrants everywhere. They think of themselves as Huckleberries first and Indians second. In another generation none of it will matter. And Jane's not American, anyway. If we're seen as anything, we're seen as former soldiers. We were a curiosity when we arrived, but now we're just John and Jane, with the farm down the road."

Rybicki looked at the field again. "I'm surprised you farm at all," he said. "The two of you have real jobs."

"Farming is a real job," Jane said. "Most of our neighbors do it. It's good for us to do it too, so we can understand them and what they need from us."

"I meant no offense," Rybicki said.

"None taken," I said, interjecting myself back into the conversation. I motioned to the field. "We've got about forty acres here. It's not a lot—and not enough to take money away from the other farmers—but it's enough to make the point that the concerns of New Goa are our concerns, too. We've worked hard to become New Goans and Huckleberries ourselves."

General Rybicki nodded and looked at his sorghum stalk. As Zoë had noted, he was green, good-looking and young. Or at least gave the appearance of youth, thanks to the CDF body he still had. He'd look twenty-three years old for as long as he had it, even though his real age was some number over hundred by now. He looked younger than me, and I was his junior by fifteen years or more. But then, when I left the service, I traded my CDF body for a new, unmodified body based on my original DNA. I looked at least thirty by now. I could live with that.

At the time I had left the CDF, Rybicki had been my superior officer, but he and I went back before that. I met him on my first day of combat, back when he was a lieutenant colonel and I had been a private. He'd offhandedly called me *son*, as a reference to my youth. I was seventy-five at the time.

This was one of the problems with the Colonial Defense Forces: all that body engineering they do really messes with your age sense. I was in my nineties; Jane, born an adult as part of the CDF Special Forces, was sixteen or so. It can hurt your head if you think about it.

"It's time you tell us why you're here, General," Jane said. Seven years of living with naturally-occuring humans had not blunted her Special Forces-bred way of ramming through social courtesies and getting right to the point.

Rybicki grinned wryly, and tossed his sorghum to the ground. "All right," he said. "After you left the service, Perry, I got a promotion and a transfer. I'm with the Department of Colonization now; the folks who have the job of seeding and supporting new colonies."

"You're still CDF," I said. "It's the green skin that gives you away. I thought the Colonial Union kept its civilian and military wings separate."

"I'm the liaison," Rybicki said. "I get to keep things coordinated between the both of them. This is about as fun as you might think it is."

"You have my sympathy," I said.

"Thank you, Major," Rybicki said. It'd been years since anyone referred to me by my rank. "I do appreciate it. The reason I'm here is because I was wondering if you—the two of you—would do a job for me."

"What kind of job?" Jane asked.

Rybicki looked over to Jane. "Lead a new colony," he said.

Jane glanced over to me. I could tell she didn't like this idea already. "Isn't that what the Department of Colonization is for?" I asked. "It should be filled with all sorts of people whose job it is to lead colonies."

"Not this time," Rybicki said. "This colony is different."

"How?" Jane said.

"The Colonial Union gets colonists from Earth," Rybicki said. "But over the last few years the colonies—the *established* colonies, like Phoenix and Elysium and Hokkaido—have been pushing the CU to let their people form new colonies. Folks from those places have made the attempt before with wildcat colonies, but you know how those go."

I nodded. Wildcat colonies were illegal and unauthorized. The CU turned a blind eye to wildcatters; the rationale was that the people who were in them would otherwise be causing trouble at home, so it was just as well to let them go. But a wildcat colony was well and truly on its own; unless one of your colonists was the kid of someone high up in the government, the CDF wouldn't be coming when you called for help. The survival statistics for wildcat colonies were impressively grim. Most didn't last six months. Other colonizing species generally did them in. It wasn't a forgiving universe.

Rybicki caught my acknowledgment and went on. "The CU would prefer the colonies keep to their own knitting, but it's become a political issue and the CU can't brush it off anymore. So the DoC suggested that we open up one planet for second-generation colonists. You can guess what happened then."

"The colonies started clawing each other's eyes out to be the one whose people got to colonize," I said.

"Give the man a cigar," Rybicki said. "So the DoC tried to play Solomon by saying that each of the agitants could contribute a limited number of colonists to the first wave colony. So now we have a seed colony of about twenty-five hundred people, with two hundred and fifty from ten different colonies. But now we don't have anyone to lead them. None of the colonies want the other colonies' people in charge."

"There are more than ten colonies," I said. "You could recruit your colony leaders from one of those."

"Theoretically that would work," Rybicki said. "In the real universe, however, the other colonies are pissed off that they didn't get *their* people on the colony roster. We've promised that if this colony works out we'll entertain the idea of opening other worlds. But for now it's a mess and no one else is inclined to play along."

"Who was the idiot who suggested this plan in the first place?" Jane asked.

"As it happens, that idiot was me," Rybicki said.

"Well done," Jane said. I reflected on the fact it was good thing she wasn't still in the military.

"Thank you, Constable Sagan," General Rybicki said. "I appreciate the candor. Clearly there were aspects of this plan I didn't expect. But then, that's why I'm here."

"The flaw with this plan of yours—aside from the fact that neither Jane nor I have the slightest idea how to run a seed colony—is that we're colonists now, too," I said. "We've been here for seven years."

"But you said it yourself: you're former soldiers," Rybicki said. "Former soldiers are a category all their own. You're not really from Huckleberry. You're from Earth, and she's former Special Forces, which means she's not from anywhere. No offense," he said to Jane.

"That still leaves the problem of neither of us having any experience running a seed colony," I said. "When I was doing my public relations tour of the colonies way back when, I went to a seed colony on Orton. Those people never stopped working. You don't just throw people into that situation without training."

"You *have* training," Rybicki said. "Both of you were officers. Christ, Perry, you were a major. You commanded a regiment of three thousand soldiers across a battle group. That's larger than a seed colony."

"A colony isn't a military regiment," I said.

"No it's not," Rybicki agreed. "But the same skills are required. And since you've been discharged, both of you

have worked in colony administration. You're an
ombudsman—you know how a colony government works
and how to get things done. Your wife is the constable here
and is responsible for maintaining order. Between the two
of you, you have pretty much all the skills you'll need. I
didn't just pull your names out of a hat, Major. These are
the reasons I thought of you. You're about eighty-five percent ready to go as it is, and we'll get you the rest of the
way there before the colonists head for Roanoke. That's
the name we've chosen for the colony," he added.

"We have a life here," Jane said. "We have jobs and re-
sponsibilities, and we have a daughter who has her own
life here as well. You're casually asking us to uproot ourselves to solve your little political crisis."

"Well, I apologize about the casual part," Rybicki said.
"Normally you would have gotten this request by Colonial diplomatic courier, along with a full load of documents. But as it happened, I was on Huckleberry for
entirely different reasons and thought I would kill two
birds with one stone. I honestly didn't expect I'd be pitching you this idea standing in the middle of a field of
sorghum."

"All right," Jane said.

"And as for it being a little political crisis, you're wrong
about that," Rybicki said. "It's a medium-sized political
crisis, on its way to becoming a large one. This has become
more than just another human colony. The local planetary
governments and press have built this up as the biggest
colonization event since humans first left Earth. It's not—
trust me on that—but that fact doesn't really matter at this
point. It's become a media circus and a political headache,
and it's put the DoC on the defensive. This colony is getting away from us because so many others have a vested
interest in it. We need to get on top of it again."

"So it's all about politics," I said.

"No," Rybicki said. "You misunderstand me. The DoC doesn't need to get back on top of this because we're counting political coup. We need to get back on top of this because *this is a human colony*. You both know what it's like out there. Colonies live or die—*colonists* live or die—based on how well we prepare and defend them. The DoC's job is to get the colonists as prepared as we can get them before they colonize. The CDF's job is to keep them safe until they get a foothold. If either side of that equation breaks down, that colony is screwed.

"Right now, the department's side of the equation isn't working because we haven't provided the leadership, and everyone else is trying to keep anyone else from filling the vacuum. We're running out of time to make it work. Roanoke is going to happen. The question is whether we manage to do it right. If we don't—if Roanoke dies—there's going to be hell to pay. So it's better that we do it right."

"If this is such a political hot potato, I don't see why throwing us into the mix is going to help things," I said. "There's no guarantee anyone will be happy with us."

"Like I said, I didn't just pull your names out of a hat," Rybicki said. "Over at the department we ran a slate of potential candidates that would work for us and would work for the CDF. We figured if the two of us could sign off on someone, we could make the colony governments accept them. You two were on the list."

"Where on the list?" Jane asked.

"About halfway down," Rybicki said. "Sorry. The other candidates didn't work out."

"Well, it's an honor just to be nominated," I said.

Rybicki grinned. "I never did like your sarcasm, Perry,"

he said. "I understand I'm dropping a lot on you at once. I don't expect you to give me an answer now. I have all the documents here," he tapped his temple, signifying he'd stored the information in his BrainPal, "so if you have a PDA I can send them to, you can take a look at them at your leisure. As long as your leisure is no longer than a standard week."

"You're asking us to walk away from everything here," Jane said again.

"Yes," Rybicki said. "I am. And I'm appealing to your sense of duty, too, since I know you have one. The Colonial Union needs smart, capable and experienced people to help us get this colony going. You two fit the bill. And what I'm asking of you is more important than what you're doing here. Your jobs here can be handled by others. You'll leave and someone else will come in and take your place. Maybe they won't be as good, but they'll be good enough. What I'm asking of you two for this colony isn't something that just anyone else could do."

"You said we were in the middle of your list," I said.

"It was a short list," Rybicki said to me. "And there's a steep drop-off after you two." He turned back to Jane. "Look, Sagan, I can see this is a tough sell for you. I'll make you a deal. This is going to be a seed colony. That means that the first wave gets in and spends two or three years preparing the place for the next wave. After the second wave comes in, things will probably be settled enough that if you want, you and Perry and your daughter can come back here. The DoC can make sure your house and jobs will be waiting for you. Hell, we'll even send someone to get in your crop."

"Don't patronize me, General," Jane said.

"I'm not," Rybicki said. "The offer is genuine, Sagan.

Your life here, every part it, will be waiting for you. You won't lose any of it. But I need the two of you *now*. The DoC will make it worth your while. You'll get this life back. And you'll be making sure Roanoke colony survives. Think about it. Just decide soon."